V-6

For Every Season

Amish Vines and Orchards, Book 3

For Every Season

Amish Vines and Orchards, Book 3

CINDY WOODSMALL

New York Times Best-Selling Author

WATERBROOK
PRESS

FOR EVERY SEASON
PUBLISHED BY WATERBROOK PRESS
12265 Oracle Boulevard, Suite 200
Colorado Springs, Colorado 80921

All Scripture quotations are taken from the King James Version.

The characters and events in this book are fictional, and any resemblance to actual persons or events is coincidental.

ISBN: 978-1-61129-110-0

Cover design by Kelly L. Howard

Published in the United States by WaterBrook Multnomah, an imprint of the Crown Publishing Group, a division of Random House Inc., New York.

WATERBROOK and its deer colophon are registered trademarks of Random House Inc.

Printed in the United States of America

To Alan and Carla Weatherly

Thank you for being such wonderful friends, great encouragers,
gentle yet strong spiritual teachers, and all-around remarkable people.
As a pastor and pastor's wife, you've each faced many challenges
while fulfilling your God-given roles.
The constant needs of others are as rhythmic
as the beating hearts of the many you've helped.
You are to those in need who you were to us thirty-something years ago:
a godsend who nourished and strengthened us
so we could go forward and do so for others.
But, Carla, hopefully you won't need to shelter all the others
as often as you have us of late.
Otherwise, to whom would we go when we sojourn to your area?
Much love to both of you!
I look forward to our years ahead
and a few trips to Amish auctions!

Amish Vines and Orchards series

The story so far...

In *A Season for Tending,* Rhoda Byler, a twenty-two-year-old Amish girl, struggles to suppress the God-given insights she receives. Her people don't approve of such intuitions. Because of their superstitions and fears, Rhoda spends most of her time alone in her bountiful fruit and herb garden or with her assistant, Landon, canning her produce for her business—Rhode Side Stands. Although she lives with her parents, two married brothers, and their families, Rhoda is isolated and haunted by guilt over the death of her sister two years ago.

Thirty miles away, in the Amish district of Harvest Mills, three brothers—Samuel, Jacob, and Eli King—are caretakers of their family's apple orchard. Samuel has been responsible for the success of Kings' Orchard since he was a young teen, but due to Eli's negligence, one-third of their orchard has produced apples that are only good for canning. If Samuel doesn't find a way to turn more profit on those apples, he'll have to sell part of the orchard, resulting in even smaller harvests in the future.

When Samuel and Rhoda meet, they see eye to eye on very little until she shows him her fruit garden. He soon realizes that her horticultural skills are just what he needs to restore the orchard, and her canning business could provide an established outlet for their apples—if he can convince her to partner with them. Without telling his girlfriend, Catherine, he asks Rhoda to work with Kings' Orchard.

Rhoda declines...until someone maliciously destroys her garden and her livelihood. She gives her land to her brothers and commits to partnering with Kings' Orchard. Before long she and Jacob begin courting, and Samuel severs his relationship with Catherine.

Just as they begin to harvest the apples, a tornado destroys most of the orchard and almost costs Samuel his life. In an effort to make a new start, Jacob, Samuel, Rhoda, Landon, and others decide to buy an abandoned apple orchard in Maine that they can restore. As the families commit to establishing an Amish community in Maine, Samuel realizes he's in love with Rhoda.

As *The Winnowing Season* opens, a small group is preparing to move to Maine—Rhoda Byler, her brother Steven, his family, her assistant Landon Olson, brothers Samuel and Jacob King, and their sister Leah. Their goal is to establish a new Amish community and to cultivate an abandoned apple orchard to replace the income from the orchard the tornado destroyed.

But the day before they leave, Rhoda's church leaders insist she attend a meeting, because Samuel has reported Rueben Glick for vandalizing her garden. She's upset with Samuel and dreads going, but to make matters worse, Jacob, her boyfriend, is called away at the last minute. Samuel goes with her and is outraged at the hostility and suspicion they express toward Rhoda. Although the meeting does not go well, Rhoda is given permission to move to Maine in good standing with the church.

The following day the Bylers and Kings leave, except for Jacob, who never returned. Rhoda feels alone in her new surroundings as she continues to see her late sister and begins to hear music and a new voice calling her to meet an isolated couple, Camilla and Bob Cranford. She tries to confide in Samuel, but he pushes her away for fear she'll discover he's in love with her.

When Jacob arrives, Rhoda begins to learn about his past. Their love and loyalty to each other are unshaken, and everyone at the farm soon settles in to revitalizing the orchard. Whenever Jacob's past calls him away, the others work extra to make up for his absence.

Although most of their neighbors welcome the Amish, Rhoda finds herself in legal trouble as three teenagers from powerful families accuse her of giving them drugs. That forces Jacob into hiding to protect Rhoda from negative scrutiny because of his past. As pressures mount, Samuel helps her find strength.

Months pass with Jacob gone, and Samuel continues to withhold his feelings from Rhoda. After she is finally cleared of charges, Samuel is alone with her in the barn, and the conversation turns personal. His emotions get the best of him, and he kisses her. Rhoda is swept up in the moment before pushing him away. Almost immediately Jacob arrives home and discovers what has happened. He breaks up with her and is furious with his brother. Without explanation, Samuel withdraws from her. Rhoda realizes she has lost both men, so she moves in with Bob and Camilla, hoping Jacob will eventually forgive her.

For a list of main characters in the Amish Vines and Orchards series, see the Character Chart at the end of the book.

ONE

Rhoda tiptoed across the dark kitchen. Only the blue flame under the pan on the stove and a lone candle illuminated the room. Electric lights first thing in the morning bothered her. Besides, when she got up before Bob and Camilla, she found comfort in the familiarity of a wavering flame.

She measured out freshly ground cloves, nutmeg, and cinnamon and mixed it into her apple purée and sugar mixture. The aroma of simmering apple butter filled the air. Since she couldn't start her days at the farm alongside her sister-in-law Phoebe in the kitchen, this was the second best thing—alone and trying new recipes.

Choose... A female voice sliced through the quietness.

Rhoda's heart clenched. Had she wakened Camilla? Or was Rhoda hearing her sister again? It had sounded like a real person, and something moved, maybe someone in a dress, near the doorway. She turned off the flame under the pan before easing toward the living room. She saw no one.

Choose! The shriek jolted her like an unexpected clap of thunder, and Rhoda stumbled against a table.

Something fell over, and cold water, a lot of it, splashed on her dress and bare feet. The word *choose* continued to echo in her ears.

Her heart pounded as she skimmed her hands over the tabletop, searching for what she'd knocked over. Perhaps she felt stems of some kind and what seemed like cool textured glass rolling back and forth. A vase, a large one that apparently had been filled with water. She set it upright. As her eyes adjusted to the soft glow of moonlight, she padded across the wooden floor and reached for the light switch. But she paused mere inches from it. How had it come to this—she, a devout Amish woman, taking refuge in an *Englisch* home?

She lowered her hand, leaving herself in the dark.

The easy answer was that Jacob had banished her from living on the farm. Well, more or less.

He hadn't *made* her go. But he'd invited her to leave and then had refused to talk to her. Fresh ache flooded her. Not a minute had gone by that she didn't miss him. He felt the same way. She knew he did.

Still, here she was. An outcast.

Choose...

The taunting voice was clearer now. It sounded like Emma, her late sister. Although it had been as real as if someone were in the room with her, Rhoda realized it was her own conscience blaring at her.

She had chosen, but Jacob was too wounded to listen to her. Shoving back her frustration and regret, she set her will to get through the coming day. She returned to the kitchen to get a towel. The digital clock on the microwave glared at her: 5:19.

She'd been up for hours, and thankfully it'd be daylight within the hour. Despite feeling out of place in an Englisch home, she was here, in the dark, trying a new recipe for the canning business and hoping she didn't disturb her hosts.

It wasn't a disagreeable place, but she would never feel fully at ease inside this house. Sadness tried to rob determination from her. She was no longer a part of the farm's mealtime discussions about the workday. Or part of the camaraderie, chats, or even disagreements that were vital to running the business.

What was she going to do if Jacob's anger and hurt didn't dissolve?

A tapping noise caught her attention. "Rhoda, are you okay?" Camilla's whisper seemed to come from the front of the house. She was probably outside Rhoda's bedroom door.

Poor Camilla. Rhoda had to be the most unpleasant houseguest ever, but the Cranfords were too good to ask her to leave. For that she was grateful.

She went in that direction, shielding her eyes from the bright light in the hallway. "I'm in here. So sorry to disturb you." Rhoda turned around to see long-stemmed white roses scattered and water dripping off the edge of the round mahogany table. Bob had brought home a couple of bouquets a few days ago. "I'm so sorry." Rhoda hurried back to the spot and spread the kitchen towel over as much of the puddle as she could.

Camilla joined her and picked up the flowers and put them back in the vase. "Neither the mess nor the noise matters." Her tone was difficult to define at times, usually somewhere between guarded and caring.

Rhoda knelt, and her lone braid fell over her shoulder as she began mopping up the water. "I was trying so hard not to wake you and Bob."

"We're fine. It's you we're worried about." Camilla put her hands on her hips, making her short gray ponytail sort of wave. "But it smells wonderful in here. You're working on recipes again, aren't you?"

"Ya." Did Camilla mind?

"So just how long have you been up?"

"A while."

"You need sleep more than new recipes. Is something keeping you up at night?"

Since Rhoda had arrived on her doorstep two weeks ago in need of a place to stay, Camilla had voiced concerns over why she'd left the farmhouse. She wished Camilla would stop asking, and so far Rhoda had managed to sidestep the questions. Nonetheless, of all the people she had ever known, Camilla was one of her favorites.

Rhoda continued drying the floor. It was tempting to open up…except she couldn't bear to know what Camilla would think of her once she heard. Truth was, Rhoda had no one else she could talk to right now. Even her brother and sister-in-law were disappointed in her. Since Leah was Samuel and Jacob's younger sister, Rhoda couldn't confide in her either. It'd be wrong to put Leah in the middle of this mess.

What had possessed Rhoda to think that two families—the Kings and the Bylers—could live under the same roof while trying to establish a new Amish community?

It had been naive.

Camilla wandered to the couch and picked up Rhoda's prayer *Kapp*. Rhoda had placed it there hours ago, meaning to put it on before anyone else was up. Camilla ran her fingers down the long strings of the Kapp. "I read once that Amish women wear these even in their sleep."

Was she changing the subject or aiming to start an easygoing conversation in hopes Rhoda would open the floodgates?

"Some do." Rhoda flipped the towel and pushed it across the floor. The women who wore them at night were the kind who might wake and start praying. But lately Rhoda was more the kind who woke and stewed.

She was beyond disappointed in herself over this mess. But what had Samuel been thinking? And Jacob… What kind of a man was he to cut her off the way he had?

She wasn't sure who she was the angriest with—Samuel, Jacob, or herself. But her frustration with the trio kept her in turmoil.

Camilla put the prayer Kapp back and crouched near her. "Rhoda." She touched the back of Rhoda's hands, stopping her from cleaning up the water. "I only want to help you the way I wish someone had helped me when I was your age."

Rhoda eased from Camilla's gentle touch and ran the towel in wider circles.

Camilla stood. "Bob and I don't mind being awakened. But I believe you need to talk about why you're staying with us."

"I can't." She took the wet towel through the kitchen and into the laundry room. What could she say—that she was a hypocrite, a girl who dressed and lived plainly because she wanted to honor God but had let two good men, devoted brothers no less, each kiss her?

Rhoda was desperate to talk but not to Camilla. If she could get to the one man who could restore some measure of peace to her, she would. But neither brother had any desire to talk to her. She loved Jacob, but she needed to talk to Samuel…after she yelled at him for messing up her life as well as the relationship between the three of them. He would have answers, half-baked ones most likely, but by the time they were finished, she'd at least feel some clarity, enough to start sleeping again.

When she came out of the laundry room, Camilla was in the kitchen with the lights on. "Were you making apple butter by candlelight?"

Rhoda blew out the candle. "Between it and the glow from the gas burner and all the electronic things in the room, I could see well enough."

Camilla's wry smile didn't quite override the hint of bewilderment in her eyes. "I'm sorry, but I need to say what's on my mind. I didn't ask why Jacob never accompanied you when you came to visit us or why he disappeared altogether when your legal troubles began. *And* I let you push Bob and me away during that whole mess of false accusations of drug trafficking. But aren't you ready to talk?" Camilla moved in closer. "For your sake, child."

In spite of her desire to keep Amish matters among the Amish, Rhoda's resolve began to falter. The whole situation was ridiculous. Jacob was finally home after months of being in hiding, and yet Rhoda had never felt so lonely. For her, that was really saying something. She'd spent so much of her life ostracized and alone. Then Jacob swooped in and made the pain of all those days vanish like apples from trees during the harvest.

A faint smile crossed Camilla's face. "Las Vegas has a motto: what happens in Vegas stays in Vegas. But they have nothing on the Amish or on Rhoda Byler, do they?"

Rhoda leaned against a counter, lost in her heartache. "I don't know how I got to the place of living with the Englisch. It all happened in the blink of an eye."

Actually, it'd happened in the length of a kiss.

Samuel.

She ran her cold, damp fingertips across her lips, remembering the power of those few moments. "Do you understand men?"

Camilla set a few dishes in the sink. "It took me a lot of years and many a mile traveling down a rocky path after the wrong men, but eventually...after..."

Rhoda heard the rest of Camilla's sentence as if she'd spoken it aloud—*after my poor decisions caused my son to walk out, never to return.*

Rhoda's heart turned a flip. It was the strongest confirmation she had felt that Camilla did have a son. The day Rhoda moved into the farmhouse, and even before she met Camilla and Bob, she had often sensed a man and a child trying to tell her something. It was eerie, and Rhoda wished it would go away, but since then, whenever she gently hinted about Camilla having children, Camilla denied it, retreating like a stray dog being chased off by a landowner.

Camilla picked up a kitchen towel and wiped her hands. "The important thing is I have a bit of a handle on the subject of men these days, and I've been biting my tongue since you arrived. But here goes… Are you here because of an abusive man?"

Was that what Camilla thought—that Jacob, with all his hidden, mysterious ways, was violent? "No."

"You're sure? I told Bob last week that I was suspicious of why you needed to get away from that house." She shrugged. "He said I should mind my own business. But, well, did your boyfriend hurt you? Are you afraid of him? Or was it that man who came here looking for you one night? What was his name?"

"Samuel. He's Jacob's brother."

She hadn't told Camilla the truth of why she was here because she'd thought it would sound sordid and ugly, but her thinking Jacob or Samuel was violent was even worse.

"Both men are the reason I'm here. But it's not what you're thinking. And probably one good argument could clear the air between me and Samuel."

"He's the one who was angry the night he came here looking for you."

"He wasn't angry. He was worried. It was the middle of the night, the temperature was dropping, and I was missing." How could Camilla not put that together even without knowing Samuel? "They're good men, truly."

Camilla pursed her lips. "You're welcome to live here for months if you need to, so don't misunderstand me. But if you get on so well with them, why do you need a place to stay?"

Rhoda hesitated. How much should she tell her? She turned on the heat under her batch of apple butter, hoping she hadn't altered the quality by turning it off in the middle of the cooking time.

Camilla picked up the wooden spoon and stirred the concoction. "Perhaps I've been wrong about why you moved out. It's possible I'm seeing things that aren't there." She tapped the spoon against the pan before setting it aside. "See, I was married for seventeen years to an abusive man."

Rhoda wasn't sure what to say. She knew a little bit about Camilla's past because she'd had an intuition about Bob and Camilla, and when they both denied having children, she'd asked Landon to run a Google search on them. She still didn't have any proof about a child, but she had learned there were police reports on a man Camilla was once married to. Even so, hearing the pain in Camilla's voice was quite different from Landon reading random facts on a computer screen. Rhoda's knees felt shakier than when she'd heard the voice earlier. "I'm sorry."

"I refused to talk about it, just as you're doing. When forced to discuss it, I made excuses for his behavior. Year after year and injury after injury. To say I have a suspicious nature toward men is an understatement. I know how they can lie and manipulate us. Nowadays I can't make myself sit by if any woman I know is caught in that." She lifted her head, her eyes searching Rhoda's. "You most of all. Can you understand that?"

It never ceased to amaze Rhoda how the most unexpected people carried invisible and unbearable weight while looking as whole and happy as the next person. Rhoda still carried the grief of losing her sister, but, fortunately, Jacob had helped her let go of her guilt.

She nodded. Camilla's concerns made more sense in light of what she'd been through. Rhoda had felt drawn to Camilla from the day she met her, when Rhoda followed the sound of an unfamiliar instrument through the woods to find Camilla, on the patio, playing what she said was a cello. She and Bob had been warm and friendly, so it surprised Rhoda to learn later that they were known for being reclusive.

"I get your desire to protect me, and I appreciate it, but you have to believe me. Neither Jacob nor Samuel would ever hurt a woman." Samuel would raise his voice and snap his answers. Apparently Jacob would walk off and refuse to talk. But both would die before using their strength against a woman.

Camilla studied her and slowly slid her hands into the pockets of her thick terry cloth housecoat. "Okay, if you're sure, because—" Her expression changed and apparently so did the subject on her mind. "Oh, yeah." She pulled out a folded envelope. "Saturday morning Bob brought in a letter for you, but you'd already left to go work at the farm, so I slid it into my pocket without thinking. I forgot all about it until now. I hadn't worn this housecoat since—until I heard the crash a few minutes ago."

It was a business-size envelope, and excitement skittered through Rhoda. "From Jacob?"

Camilla shook her head.

Disappointment erased Rhoda's hope, but she took the letter. The return address had a government seal from Orchard Bend, Maine, on it. She had a response from them already? Maybe it wasn't going to take as long as she thought to get licenses for her canning business.

She opened the envelope and pulled out the papers.

"Good news, I hope."

"I…I'm not sure." She flipped through the pages of forms.

Clearly she had a lot to fill out. She was still paying the price for some teenagers' accusations that she supplied them with marijuana, and it still angered her. While her life was in limbo due to her legal troubles, she hadn't had the time or the presence of mind to pursue the licenses she needed to set up her canning business and be fully functional by harvest—a mere four and a half to five months away. But she'd expected that once she was cleared of the accusations, Samuel and Jacob would help her make up for lost time.

Since that wasn't happening, she'd come up with Plan B: pretend her heart wasn't broken, act like a woman with a brain, and do what she could without their help. If she intended to sell canned goods throughout the Northeast and parts of the Midwest, she didn't have time to wait until the King men were ready to talk to her again. She had to keep moving toward her goal, including creating new recipes for her label.

Looking at the cover letter again, she began to understand the situation better. "It's an explanation of what type of kitchen facility will and won't be approved."

Ach, there was so much she needed to discuss with Samuel and Jacob. Instead, she was forced to make all the tough decisions on her own.

"And?" Camilla peered over the top of the papers.

Rhoda's mind and heart felt as if they were mired in quicksand. "For the type of license I need, the facility can't be an in-home kitchen that is also used concurrently for family purposes."

"You didn't check the licensing laws before moving?"

"Sure, but most of our plans were undermined because of my legal issues—like the two families who backed out of coming. They were supposed to lift some of the workload of restoring the orchard while we put our energies into solving the kitchen issue. And because those families aren't here, Phoebe and Steven haven't had time to find a home of their own. We had been sure we could find a house with either a second kitchen or the space and plumbing to add one. My legal mess is one reason Jacob was gone so much and hasn't had time to add a canning kitchen onto the farmhouse. I had to help do Jacob's work while he was gone, so I wasn't able to deal with any of this before now."

"But he has time now, right?"

"Time, maybe." Although their workload in the orchard was increasing as rapidly as the spring temperature. "But no desire." Rhoda folded the letter and shoved it back into the envelope.

"So now what?"

"I don't know. Jacob is the one who comes up with ideas out of thin air. Samuel is the one who has the know-how to change thin air into reality."

"But?"

Rhoda shrugged. Camilla knew enough to draw her own conclusions. Neither man was talking to her. Actually, she knew Samuel would talk to her if she could get him alone. But if she was going to restore Jacob's faith in their relationship, she had to avoid being seen with Samuel.

She went to the kitchen window and pulled back the thick, insulated drapes. Dawn had begun to chase away the darkness, and soon sunlight would shimmer off the patches of remaining snow. It was already the second week of April, but the ground was cold and wet, and mounds of snow still dotted some places, especially in the woods. She needed to dress warmly and head to the farm for another day of partnering with Landon—while being avoided by both Jacob and Samuel.

Had they moved all this way and gone through so much only to face defeat because she'd kissed—or been kissed by—one brother while the other was away?

TWO

Leah opened the back door to go outside. The blue heelers, Ziggy and Zara, charged from the kitchen and nearly knocked the basket out of her hands as they darted past her and raced for the greenhouses. They ran straight to the third one and started barking.

Well, at least Leah knew where to find Rhoda this morning. Those dogs made a beeline for her when allowed. Ziggy and Zara rounded the corner heading to the front of the greenhouse, and Rhoda apparently let them in, because they hushed.

Streams of early morning light cast a heavenly glow as Leah carried the basket of food to Rhoda. But the gorgeous scenery didn't change the fact that today was another ordinary workday, nothing special. She'd already washed and hung out two loads of laundry and then helped cook breakfast and clean up afterward. And it wasn't even nine o'clock! But those parts of the day were easy compared to what the next few minutes would be like.

She went into the greenhouse and found Rhoda kneeling, patting the dogs. A row of saplings filled one of the worktables.

Rhoda looked up. "*Guder Marye*, Leah."

Leah felt queasy. Why did the air itself have to be so thick between her and Rhoda? "Morning." Leah set the basket on a table. "Here you go." She wanted to say so much more to Rhoda than a flippant "Morning" or "Here's some food."

Two weeks ago Leah had lured her brothers into the barn, hoping to get them talking, but her plan had backfired. Within seconds her brothers were embroiled in an argument—one that frightened her. Leah had thought that, despite their upbringing, they were going to have a fistfight. Or worse.

When Jacob yelled, accusing Samuel of trying to ride off with Rhoda, Leah could only guess what he meant.

The ill will between her brothers made her sick. But she'd learned her lesson that day: stay out of their quarrel. And that meant leaving well enough alone with Rhoda too.

Besides, Rhoda wasn't going to open up, so this is what life had become—a few minutes of speaking, passing Rhoda a lunch made for her by Phoebe, and then leaving. It stunk, and it made her heart heavy.

"Denki." Rhoda rubbed the dogs' bellies one last time before standing. "How are you this morning?"

"Gut. Un du?"

"Gut."

Leah didn't believe her. Rhoda wasn't good, but Leah admired her strength.

"Leah,"—Rhoda set another tree on the worktable—"would you mind terribly if I asked you to fill in for me as Landon's work partner today? I'd like to get these trees planted." Rhoda cradled the thin branches. "I think it's late enough in the season, but if I'm wrong, I'll know soon enough."

"I'd be glad to do that, but if you're unsure, why not wait?"

Rhoda pursed her lips as if trying to contain a torrent of sadness. "While walking here today, I thought that if I'm in the field by myself, Jacob might be more willing to approach me and talk." She forced a smile. "It's worth a try. Now go on, and keep what I said to yourself."

So Rhoda was still willing to try to work things out with Jacob. That was good. Leah set Rhoda's lunch on the table, picked up the basket, and went to the barn.

The Kings' Orchard in Harvest Mills, Pennsylvania, began generations ago. But after a tornado devastated the orchard last summer, Samuel, Jacob, Rhoda, and others pooled their money, took out a loan for the rest, and bought this foreclosed farm in Maine. Because of the damage in Harvest Mills, this orchard's success was the only way to keep the Kings' Orchard brand solvent.

If Rhoda still wanted to patch things up with Jacob, surely it could be done.

Leah went into the barn. Landon stood in the back of the buckboard as Samuel passed him tanks of oil for spraying the trees. Landon looked up. "Ah, the daily ration of food for me and Rhoda to take to the orchard."

"Wrong. Can't you non-Amish folks get anything right?" Leah grinned at him.

Samuel paused, clearly waiting for her to explain Rhoda's plans for the day.

"Rhoda said she'll work the field by herself today, planting some of the greenhouse stock."

Landon tugged at his gloves. "And just when did this change of plans take place?"

"About five minutes ago."

Samuel nodded and hoisted another tank into the back of the wagon.

"Landon,"—Leah went to the front of the wagon—"Rhoda said it's me and you on the back forty, so to speak."

"My kind of day." Landon smiled. "And we're having a picnic."

"In your dreams." Leah set the basket below the bench seat. "This ain't no picnic. It's only a way to keep us from starving while we work until sunset. Have I taught you nothing?" Leah tried to keep a straight face.

Landon straightened, working the kinks out of his back while Samuel turned to get another tank. Leah's eyes met Landon's, and he winked. It was a bold move for him, but the longer she knew him, the more she liked his willingness to flirt. He mocked a scowl. "How come I don't mind this plan and you do?"

Leah's heart pounded. Could an Amish girl break away from the fold and live happily ever after in an Englisch home?

A ring from the phone in the barn office jolted her. Samuel gestured that way. "Could you grab that while we finish loading?"

"Sure." When Leah stepped into the office, she was surprised at the messiness of Samuel's desk. There were several foot-high stacks of paper.

She grabbed the receiver. "*Hallo.*"

"*Ya. Des iss* Iva Lambright."

The girl's voice trembled, but she'd said her name as if Leah should recognize it. Leah suppressed a desire to give a sassy reply: *This is Leah King. Big deal.* She chose to respond as Rhoda would have. "Hello, Iva. Is there something I can do for you?"

"*Ya. Duh Du will helfe?*"

Did she want help? For the most part Leah wanted help all the time, but what did that have to do with anything? "I'm not following you."

"I sent you a letter last week."

"To me?"

"Well, actually"—the girl took a deep breath—"I read about you in the newspaper, and it sounded as though you could use some help with your orchard and settlement now that your trouble with those girls is cleared up. I thought maybe you might hire me. Am I speaking to Rhoda Byler?"

"Oh." The conversation was starting to make a little sense. Rhoda had talked about hiring more help, and she'd even written a want ad to put in *The Budget,* looking for someone Amish, but that was before the blowup with Samuel and Jacob. "No. This is Leah King." Leah flipped through stacks of envelopes, searching for the one from Iva Lambright. Most were addressed to Rhoda, and none had been opened. How could they be? Rhoda didn't visit Samuel's office anymore.

"Leah, hallo. Sorry for the confusion, but do you know what Rhoda's answer was to my query?"

"Maybe." If she had the letter and knew what the exact question was, she would have some idea what to tell her. It'd be easier to tell Iva to call back later, but if she took a few minutes with her now, it'd keep Samuel from having to deal with it later. "Can you hang on while I locate your letter?"

"Sure. And denki."

The girl sounded as hopeful as she did nervous. Leah dug through the piles of stuff and uncovered a new work schedule Samuel had made out. Clearly he intended for them to hire more help, because the schedule had everyone's name on it, plus several question marks for a new worker or two. But that was something her brother needed to discuss with Rhoda before any plans could be put into place. Just one more item in limbo. But did it have to be that way?

What were Samuel, Rhoda, and Jacob waiting on anyway, the office to crumble under their feet?

Ah! Here was Iva's letter. It wasn't even opened. Of course not. It was addressed to Rhoda, and Samuel's hands were tied about such matters until he and Rhoda were working together again. Jacob had never made decisions concerning the orchard. He'd always said that when it came to the orchard, he was there only to offer ideas and support.

Leah opened the letter and scanned it. Iva wanted to work for Kings' Orchard, at least until fall. Hmm.

But the return address was Indiana. That was quite a ways from Maine.

Still, maybe the answer to keeping the office afloat and Leah from having to do laundry and dishes before starting the rest of the day's work was staring her in the face. Since the others weren't making these decisions, maybe she should.

Then again, maybe she should leave everything alone. But how could she do nothing while the family business staggered because no one was making any decisions?

What this new settlement needed, if indeed they were going to be a settlement and not become a lost tribe, was a few more workers—preferably women to help with the meals and laundry. Besides, it couldn't hurt to have a single woman or two sashaying around to remind her brothers there were other fish in the sea. Maybe that reminder would be all that was needed for them to stop feuding over the same woman.

Leah's eyes widened at the thought. Was it possible? Could the issue between Rhoda, Samuel, and Jacob be that she was the only available Amish woman in this new settlement?

"Iva?"

"Ya?"

Leah's mouth went dry. She could get in serious trouble for what she was about to do, but if it had even a chance of helping to ease the stress around here, it'd be worth living in the doghouse for a year.

"How soon can you get here?"

Three kerosene lanterns, hanging on rusty nails inside the dark barn, cast a glow as Jacob wired new lights for a carriage. The radiance from the lamps flickered against the weathered walls of the old building, barely illuminating his work. It was still dark outside.

Last night when he went by Leah's bedroom to tell her good night, she said that Rhoda had worked by herself that day, and Leah asked if he'd seen her. He hadn't. It had been his goal *not* to see her, and it was easy to miss someone on an eighty-acre farm, sixty acres of which were filled with apple trees. The difficulty came in finding someone when you were searching for them. But he knew Leah's question held hope.

When things went wrong, as they had with Rhoda, all his words got lost inside him. If words burrowed deep, it didn't matter what he wanted to say or how much he wanted to speak up, he was mute.

But it wasn't his inability to deal with what had happened between Samuel and Rhoda that kept him silent while she moved out. It was that he wanted Rhoda as far from Samuel as possible.

He'd begun repairing and refurnishing this rig within a few days of her leaving, and now it was done.

Finally.

It made no sense for her to traipse almost a mile through the woods each way to get to the orchard from the Cranford's house. Besides, it was past time he showed up there and asked Rhoda to go for a buggy ride. Whether he felt ready or not to hear what she had to say, they needed to talk.

He tested the turn signals. They worked now. Everyone had avoided using a horse and buggy since they'd arrived in Maine almost seven months ago. The carriages had been damaged in the move, making them difficult to steer. They also needed new shocks and better lights. With the heavy snow, rain, and fog, he felt as if Rhoda would be taking her life into her hands to drive these narrow roads in a buggy, especially since the people around here weren't accustomed to having a horse and carriage on the road. Regardless of what Samuel thought,

Rhoda was far safer walking through the woods until Jacob had the rig in good order.

His musings stopped cold when he heard a door slam. No one left the house until dawn, and it was still dark outside. He grabbed the buggy by the whiffletree and pushed the rig into its stall. The rigs had to be fixed, regardless of Rhoda's situation, but he didn't want Samuel to know what he was doing, and Jacob was sure that's who was prowling around at this time of the morning. He quickly put away his tools and extinguished one of the lanterns.

Jacob went to the bale of hay he'd tossed down from the loft earlier. Samuel stepped into the barn, glanced at Jacob, and went to the office. This was their relationship now. Acting as if they didn't see each other. Not speaking for concern of what would be said…or done. Eating at different times because they couldn't tolerate sitting at the table together.

It couldn't go on this way.

Jacob grabbed some hay and began feeding the horses.

Samuel came out of the office and walked toward him holding two rolls of flagging. "The fog is as thick as pea soup. Even when the sun comes up, I doubt it'll burn off before lunchtime." Samuel set the flagging on a beam near him and returned to the office.

Jacob gritted his teeth. He couldn't decide if he wanted to cram the rolls down Samuel's throat or go on about his business.

Hadn't he dealt with enough betrayal? He'd spent months away from home, away from Rhoda, trying to help Sandra, a woman he'd considered a friend. But right before Jacob came home, his lawyer had told him that he believed Sandra had spent the last few years lying to him, using him, and maybe even setting him up to take the fall for her illegal activities.

Jacob sighed. He wasn't sure what to call Sandra anymore—although a few names came to mind. He once called her a friend. He then called her his mission work, someone from his days among the Englisch who deserved better than life had dished out. She needed his support. But how had he allowed his life to get so intertwined with hers years ago that he had to move back home and hide among the Amish to keep them both out of court?

He tried to be invisible. But invisibility was a double-edged sword. He'd spent years working to be exactly that. But in his worst imaginings of what life might throw at him, he never dreamed that he would become invisible to Rhoda while trying to hide from the judicial system.

He had come home emotionally beaten and bruised, drowning in anger and the humiliation of having been duped. What he had needed was hope and the companionship of the woman he loved.

Then he'd stepped into this barn to discover his brother was after his girl—and apparently had kissed her. Was Rhoda in love with Samuel? Could Jacob win her back? If he could, how much of her heart would still belong to Samuel...and for how long?

He yanked up the rolls of flagging. Samuel had asked him to mark the path between Camilla's and the barn time and again since Rhoda had moved out. But Jacob had a different plan. A better one. He glanced out the door. Fog rolled across the yard. He should have gotten the rig to Rhoda before today, but when it was a respectable time of the morning *and* when Samuel went into the orchard, Jacob would drive the rig to Camilla's. He couldn't stand the idea of his brother knowing anything about his life or plans. He had no clue what would come of finally talking with Rhoda, but for better or worse, it was time he did so.

He walked into Samuel's office and set the rolls of flagging on his desk. "When it comes to Rhoda, you need to mind your own business."

Samuel studied Jacob for a moment before lowering his eyes to the mounds of work on his desk, looking repentant. He picked up a pen and reached for a stack of papers. "That'd be my preference."

Jacob grabbed the rolls and tossed them at Samuel. "You can get these out of sight. I'm not going to mark the trail."

"Fine." Samuel shoved them into his pocket before he pushed the flashing red button on the phone that indicated messages had been left.

"Jacob...please...I'm sorry...I know I was wrong...but we need to talk." Sandra's sobs rang through the tinny machine. "Ache-up..."—three-year-old Casey called to him—"I miss you. You there?"

Jacob's head began to throb. He'd gladly boot Sandra out of his life, but he could never turn his back on Casey. His reason was the same today as it had been the night Casey was born: without Jacob, Sandra wasn't strong enough to give Casey what she needed. Sandra came by her baggage honestly enough, and he doubted that anyone who'd survived all she had could cope any better. She'd had a difficult childhood, and he knew her bipolar issues often led to lies and poor decisions. He cringed at the thought of the word *bipolar*. But after years of knowing her, he had realized she wasn't that different from others. Everyone lived with conflicting natures. And despite her disorder, she had far more value than even she knew.

Still, he wasn't ready to talk to her.

The phone beeped, going to a second message. "This is Craig Ryer with the law office of Epps and McCarthy. I'm calling for Jacob King. Please have him call me as soon as possible."

As soon as possible? Jacob didn't like the sound of that.

Concern flickered through Samuel's eyes as he punched the button to reveal the caller's phone number. "The battery's dead. His number doesn't show up, and he didn't leave one."

"I know how to reach him."

"Then I'll leave you to it." Samuel stood.

"It's not like the lawyer's office is open this time of day." Jacob wasn't sure why he was telling Samuel anything except to rattle him enough to get the truth about Rhoda out of him.

Samuel nodded. "When you talk to him, I hope he has good news for you."

"Do you?" Jacob knew he was being condescending, and he waited for Samuel to snap back at him. But Samuel just stood there, clearly thinking hundreds of things he would not say aloud.

Jacob had left Rhoda time and again over the last six months, either to make sure he was flying below the radar so he didn't bring any trouble onto his own head or to keep from bringing more speculations and accusations down on Rhoda during her recent legal troubles. Each time he left, Samuel pushed Jacob to see a lawyer to get free of what dogged him so he could build a life with Rhoda.

Unfortunately, what Jacob found out didn't give him any type of freedom, and his staying away until he could see the lawyer only afforded Samuel more time alone with Rhoda. But in all Jacob's struggles, he never once thought his brother and his girl would fall into each other's arms.

Samuel had no idea what he'd done.

None.

Samuel drew a deep breath. "This thing with the lawyer or Sandra, is there anything I can do?"

"No. And before you do anything else to *help*, let me know so I can just walk off a cliff or something." Jacob was going to keep jabbing at Samuel until his brother exploded. It was his only chance of figuring out what had happened—and what still existed—between Samuel and Rhoda.

Samuel's face tightened, a sign he was fighting with his temper. "I'm trying to be patient."

"Well, that's real good of you since *you* are in the wrong."

Sandra and her little girl had been so sick at Christmastime that Jacob had abandoned Rhoda again to help them. If he'd been able to stay home, he'd planned to ask Rhoda to marry him.

Would she have said yes?

He used to think their relationship was a gift from God. Now he didn't know what to think—other than he was a fool not to realize that Samuel would betray him for a chance with the most beautiful, amazing woman Jacob had ever known.

"Look, I know you don't want to hear anything I have to say, but you can't leave things as they are with Rhoda. Talk to her. She—"

Jacob held up his hand. "Spare me your assurances of her love for me." He wanted to talk to her, and yet he dreaded finding out the truth. What if she wanted Samuel instead of him? Then what?

Samuel grimaced. "We can't keep going like this." He gestured to the paperwork on his desk. "Neither the business nor the settlement can survive what's happening with the three of us. I regret my actions completely, but are you going to destroy Kings' Orchard over them?"

"I don't care what happens to your precious family business. It means as much to you as Rhoda does to me, and it'd serve you right to lose it."

"Is that attitude supposed to shock me?" Samuel yanked off his felt hat. "Since you were fourteen and left the farm to apprentice as a carpenter, you've been busy escaping from the family business—until you had nowhere else to run."

"At least I wasn't running into the arms of someone else's love."

Samuel turned red. "I *know* what I did. You can stop browbeating me with it. Put your energy into talking to Rhoda. Whether you want to admit it or not, if you ruin your relationship with her because you're angry with me, you'll have no one to blame but yourself."

"Are you giving me advice or a warning?"

"Jacob,"—Samuel's voice was calm, but his taut, flushed face didn't hide his volatile emotions—"this incident is crippling all communication and planning. We're getting too little done, and apparently Rhoda isn't going to talk to me about the business unless you're okay with it. Our family and our community back home are supporting this venture with prayer and money. So is Rhoda's family. They believe in us, and they believe this settlement is the start of something that will benefit Amish families for hundreds of years. But if we don't work this out soon, our business won't survive. If that's what you want— to ruin this new venture because I deserve that—it's fully within your power to do it." Samuel headed for the door of the office and then paused. "If that's how it's going to be, could you let me know as soon as possible? The best time to sell a property is in the spring, and since the trees will bud soon, spring would be the ideal time to catch a buyer's eye."

With that, Samuel walked out.

Disbelief shrouded Jacob like fog, hampering his ability to see more than a few feet in front of him. It seemed no matter what he did to figure out the bond that existed between Samuel and Rhoda, he only made the situation worse. He went to a window and watched as his brother disappeared into the dark, misty night, walking toward the orchard.

He'd only been sure of one thing in his life—through thick and thin, Samuel had always been on his side.

Until now.

THREE

Tell them.

The whisper echoed through the dark guest room. Rhoda stood in front of the full-length mirror, bathed in the soft glow of a night-light, a long braid dangling down her back while she tied her black apron. Sleep continued to elude her.

A reflection of shadows behind her shimmied against the wooden floor as if a window were open and a breeze were blowing them around. An eerie sensation crept up her spine. She was picking up on something just outside the physical realm. God was all around His people, trying to woo and warn and encourage. Was this also Him? She remained in place, tempted to give in to the odd feeling. What would happen if she yielded? Would she discover it was nonsense, or would her mind be opened to whatever she had *almost* perceived since the first night she arrived in Maine?

She closed her eyes.

Tell them I exist. A little girl's voice pleaded with her. *I need their...*

Chills ran up Rhoda's spine and fear gripped her as her father's kind, authoritative voice reminded her: *"Remember the slave girl from the Bible, Rhoda. This 'gift' may well be a temptation to sin. Pray hard against it, child."*

But what if her *Daed* was wrong?

She used to find comfort in her Daed's belief that if he was wrong to try to stop her intuitions, God would hold him responsible, not her. Was that still true even though she was twenty-three and no longer living under her Daed's roof?

Tell...

Fear stole her breath—whether of the unknown or of angering God, she wasn't sure. She forced air into her lungs. "Stop." Rhoda's loud whisper echoed through the room.

She grabbed her hairpins and prayer Kapp off the nightstand and scurried out of the room. The house was dark except for the odd blue and red glows coming from a few electronic gadgets.

Once in Camilla's dining room, Rhoda went to the hutch and found an emergency candle and matches. She missed the warmth of the farm's kitchen with its large, open fireplace. No matter how early the day started, she enjoyed the lively conversations that took place around the table—even the heated discussions between her and Samuel. At least then he'd been willing to face her and stand his ground.

Refusing to think about Samuel, she put the candle in a holder and lit it. She removed from the hutch the stacks of new recipes she'd been working on and set them next to the copies she'd made of her great-great-grandmother's apple canning recipes.

Long before Rhoda was born, her *Mammi* Byler had ten or so apple trees she tended on the same property where Rhoda had grown up. The trees were gone, but when Rhoda met Samuel, she'd been excited by the idea of sharing these recipes with him. Rhoda's one-acre fruit garden had all types of berries—strawberries, raspberries, blueberries, blackberries—but she hadn't canned apple products.

She soon discovered she couldn't find her grandmother's recipe book. So her sisters-in-law began hunting for the recipes. By then her stormy relationship with Samuel and Kings' Orchard had reached the point where she needed to decide whether she would partner with them. When, after some difficulty, her sisters-in-law found the recipes, Rhoda believed it was a sign to partner with the Kings. Samuel and Jacob remodeled an old summer kitchen on their property and turned it into a canning kitchen. But they had little more than a week of harvesting and canning before the tornado came through.

Maybe she wasn't supposed to partner with Kings' Orchard after all.

Or maybe, as her community had believed since she was a young child, she was simply bad luck.

"Good morning, Rhoda." Camilla tied the sash to her housecoat, but her gray shoulder-length hair looked freshly washed and dried.

Rhoda pulled from her thoughts, realizing the candle was giving off a black, smoky light. "Oh, what am I thinking? It's daytime."

"Not really. Just threatening to be in a bit."

"Still, I should get my shoes on and hair pinned and—"

Camilla moved next to her and put her arm around Rhoda's shoulders. "Would you mind taking some time to share a cup of hot chocolate with me before going to the farm? Bob won't be up for hours. We don't have to talk about uncomfortable subjects."

Rhoda didn't walk through the woods in the dark, not since she'd gotten lost, but it'd be daylight soon. Some days she stayed here until later in the morning, working on new recipes. Did she really need to hurry to get to the orchard on any day? She couldn't go to the office for fear Jacob would think she was sneaking time alone with Samuel. She couldn't step inside the house to speak until Samuel and Jacob had gone to the orchard—in opposite directions—or it'd start a fresh argument or deepen the angry silence between the two men.

No one looked forward to her arrival.

Camilla squeezed her shoulder. "Rhoda?"

"I'd like that."

"Good, because I've been pulling recipes from lots of places. What do you think about apple salsa?"

Before long they had steaming cups of hot chocolate in hand and recipes scattered across the table. Even though dawn had arrived, Rhoda remained put. She had no desire to trade a good conversation here for being ignored at the farm.

"This one looks like a pretty good recipe for apple salsa." Rhoda placed the card on the table and scratched out the word *dried* in front of *cilantro.* "I tried this kind of salsa once before." She picked up the card. "Not so sure its failure had anything to do with the recipe."

"It didn't sell well?"

Tell her.

The child's voice was so clear…and yet imaginary. It felt as if someone had thrown cold water on Rhoda. The words had urgency, and she had to say something to try to relieve the internal commotion the voice caused. "Do you ever sense something that you have no proof of?"

"Sure." Camilla pushed a torn page from a magazine toward her. "I sense this apple salsa recipe will be a big hit in this home even if no place else."

Rhoda lifted it. "I'll make enough to last you all next year if…"

"Deal." Camilla tapped the table with the palms of her hands. "So what do you want?"

"To talk to you about something without angering or upsetting you."

Camilla smiled. "That's what I've been wanting. You can tell me anything, and I won't get angry."

"Not about me."

"What then?"

"I'm not sure, but I think…your son."

Camilla arched an eyebrow, and her face changed. She looked nothing like the woman Rhoda had come to know. She seemed suddenly cold and unfeeling. "Pick a different topic, Rhoda. Now."

If Rhoda dared to push for answers, would Camilla ask her to leave too?

Samuel made his way through the woods, trudging on dried leaves and occasional patches of snow as he flagged the trees. In his twenty-five years of life, he'd never understood how it must feel for people to dislike themselves.

But now he was making up for lost time.

He *hated* the trouble he'd caused. It dogged him day and night. He had little doubt that Rhoda hated him too. Regardless of what she felt toward him, though, he wasn't waiting one more day for Jacob to mark the path for her.

When Samuel went into the field each morning to work, he kept the dogs near him so they'd alert him when their beloved Rhoda approached the property. But some days she didn't arrive until nine or so. He didn't know why. Maybe she'd gotten turned around, or maybe she'd left Camilla's late for some reason, but at least he knew when she arrived. However, when she left at night, he had no way of knowing if she would arrive safely back at Camilla's.

He hadn't wanted to interfere or to act as if Rhoda was his to protect, but no one besides him and Jacob knew the way through the woods to Camilla's, and Jacob left him no choice. Well, Rhoda knew the trail, but she'd also been lost in these woods before.

Fog surrounded him, making the woods look like something from a dream.

But if he were asleep, Rhoda would appear in the distance, a shrouded vision that would make his heart go wild as she slowly moved toward him. When he could see her clearly, she'd look him in the eye, and he'd see the same respect and love he had for her. Then she'd take his hand, and they'd walk and talk.

Dreams were for fools. In reality, he'd fallen for a woman who belonged to his brother. What had he been thinking to pull her into his arms the way he had? He'd ruined two of his most important relationships—probably, at least to some degree, for the rest of his life.

He loved Jacob. And his brother was a better man than he in many, many ways, but…

Samuel tugged at the elastic flagging until he tore off another piece. He wasn't going to think about what Jacob lacked. Samuel had his own shortcomings to look at if he wished to evaluate such things.

He wrapped another strip of flagging around a tree. Thankfully, Jacob spoke to him today. That was a good sign.

Some might think Jacob's silent treatment of Rhoda and him was a character flaw or weakness. Maybe it was to some extent. But mostly it was Jacob's deep sense of gentleness that caused extreme disappointment or hurt to mute his vocal cords. At least he wasn't like Samuel when upset—yell now, think later. Jacob's calmer, more thoughtful disposition seemed to draw women. The call from Sandra, with her daughter in the background asking for "Ache-up," was a clear reminder of that. But Jacob was a one-woman man. No one doubted that.

Samuel had been doing a little better about not losing his temper since starting each day with the Scriptures and prayer. He'd become diligent in seeking God shortly after moving here *because* he was so drawn to Rhoda. Despite his effort to wrestle temptation into submission, he'd kissed her. And now his Bible, the one she gave him for Christmas, lay closed beside his bed. He'd managed to read it for a few minutes here and there, but the words were no longer encouraging. They were a weight he couldn't carry. Even if he spent all day reading the Word, he'd never have an easy-going, laid-back personality.

But he'd never meant to charge into territory that wasn't his and try to take over. Never. He longed to apologize for making Rhoda's life harder. No one needed that, especially not Rhoda. He'd like to ask what he could do to make up for the trouble he'd caused.

At the same time, he was livid with her. Why didn't she blurt out the truth to Jacob and get it over with—that Samuel was fully to blame for kissing her?

A thousand emotions gnawed at him. He was far more angry with himself than anyone else, but if Jacob truly cared about what was best for Rhoda, he would find a way to look her in the eye and deal with what had happened. And if Rhoda would simply throw Samuel to the wolves and be done with it, Jacob would be back to himself by this time tomorrow, and she would save the settlement and the business.

He was weary of thinking about it, of being so in love he couldn't stand it. But regardless of all that, it was time to focus on the one thing he could perhaps do—save the orchard from failure and keep the small settlement from having to sell and move back home. But with Jacob threatening to leave, and probably taking Rhoda with him, how much chance did he really have?

FOUR

Rhoda sat across from Camilla, fidgeting with papers as she explained about the time she'd sensed that a neighbor in Pennsylvania was in trouble and she broke into her home to get to her. The elderly woman had fallen days before and broken her hip. Once the woman was in the hospital, her doctor said she would've died if she had stayed in the house a few more hours. "But my family discouraged me from speaking to the woman if I saw her outside, let alone entering her house uninvited."

"Or breaking her window. But why wouldn't she want to talk to you?"

"I've had things come to me since I was quite young, but a lot of people think *knowing* the things I do is akin to witchcraft."

"People feel that way just because of an inkling? That seems a bit over the top, don't you think?"

"I'm hoping you keep thinking like that." Rhoda stacked and restacked the papers as if her movements had a purpose. "I found your home because I was drawn to it."

Camilla shrugged. "My playing the cello outdoors drew you, right?"

"That too. But…"—her heart raced—"I know you have a son."

The lines on Camilla's face grew taut as she stared at the table. "Had." She took a sip of her drink. "The thing about intuitions is they're based on what a person picks up that is not obvious to others—body language, pictures, whispers between people. You probably subconsciously noticed that your neighbor hadn't been around for a while. When you walked past her home on the way to a store, every piece of subconscious information came together in your conscious mind—only it felt like a forewarning rather than a gathering of half-hidden pieces of information. As for my son, if I'd realized you have a keen sense for noticing the unobvious, I might not have opened my doors to you quite so quickly."

She'd been told Camilla and Bob were reclusive, yet they'd willingly opened their house to her as soon as she met them. Were they more open to her because she was Amish? Or perhaps God had warmed their hearts to feel that way, to prepare them to hear about her shadowy intuitions concerning Camilla's grandchild. Rhoda wavered between hoping she'd never find out the full meaning of *tell them* and hoping she'd know all of it so she could be free.

"Your son's name is Zachary," Rhoda offered, hoping Camilla would believe her about her *knowing.*

She nodded. "Zachary," she whispered reverently. "It's been six years, and I still have bad days when I can't contain my grief."

It was a relief that Camilla remained calm at Rhoda's gentle prodding. She seemed to have dismissed where Rhoda claimed she got her information. But there was so much more she wanted to say, like, *Do you know you have a grandchild? Somewhere. Maybe.* It'd be cruel to say such a thing, especially since it might not be true. Perhaps questions were best. "What happened?"

Camilla shook her head. "You know enough. Trust me. And that's far more than anyone else around here knows." She reached across the table and clutched Rhoda's hand. "He would be about your age now." *But unlike you, he wanted nothing to do with me.*

The hairs on Rhoda's arms and the back of her neck stood on end as she heard what Camilla hadn't said. So her son was Rhoda's age, but he had died six years ago, at or near seventeen years old. The girl's voice Rhoda heard was around six or seven years old, wasn't she? Would Camilla's son have fathered a child as a teen?

Rhoda's Daed came to mind. *"Remember the slave soothsayer from God's Word, Rhoda, and mind your ways."*

She squeezed Camilla's hand, willing to let go of this conversation. "I'm glad we met. We both grieve what can't be undone—me with my little sister and you with your son."

"Seems so." Camilla wiped at a stray tear. "I'm glad you know. It helps. But there's really nothing else on that topic to talk about." She cleared her throat. "I do, however, have something we need to explore, and I'd like for you to hear me out."

Maybe it was best to keep approaching the subject of Zachary slowly. But a memory hit hard. The first day she met Camilla, she heard—or maybe imagined—that the little girl said, *Tell them while I still have a home.* Perhaps time wasn't on her side. It had been more than five months since then.

Rhoda shook free of those thoughts and focused on Camilla. "Okay."

Camilla pointed out the window. It was daylight. "It could take a little while."

"I've decided I'm in no rush this morning."

"Good." Camilla took a sip of her drink, looking reluctant to speak her mind. "I'm concerned you're not fully grasping why you felt the need to move out."

"I thought we'd covered this already. I give you my word that no one in that home is violent."

"And I believe you, but your needing to move in here is a red flag. Do you know how many women get down the road in a relationship and then say, 'I should've seen the warning signals long before now'?"

"I don't understand."

"I think you need a way to keep your canning kitchen business separate from Kings' Orchard. Surely having to move out has opened your eyes that you have too little control in the relationship."

"I...I'm hoping the separation will end soon. Surely it will." It had to. Rhoda couldn't imagine life any other way.

"I believe you need to reexamine where you're headed, because as soon as the chips were down, you were put out on your, uh, keister."

Rhoda couldn't take her eyes off Camilla. Even knowing that Samuel and Jacob weren't violent, Camilla still had serious concerns about the situation between Rhoda and them. "They didn't throw me out. I chose to leave. Sort of."

"Take it from a woman who put all her eggs in one basket: you should maintain your rights and power so that if Kings' Orchard chooses to send you packing, you, at the very least, leave with what you had when you joined them."

"I love the business we've started, and no one's interested in booting me out."

Camilla ran her fingers through her silvery hair. "And yet here you are."

Rhoda couldn't keep going round and round with Camilla. "Because I'm seeing Jacob, but I've caught Samuel's eye...I guess." How did Samuel really feel about her? She rubbed her forehead. Why would she even ask herself that question? It didn't matter, and besides that, she knew the answer. He'd had a moment of insanity.

"Oh." Camilla folded her hands, studying them. "That eases some of my concerns." She placed her hands flat on the table and leaned in. "But it adds new ones. Before I share those, is it safe to assume one those two holds your heart?"

She nodded. "Jacob."

"Is he the one you mentioned that you could get things straight with if you could talk to him?"

Rhoda fidgeted with her thumbs. What would Camilla make of her response? "No. He's hurt, and he's harder to reach. You know?"

"Afraid I don't."

Rhoda tapped her temple. "He keeps so much of himself inside his head and heart, and I'm not sure how to clear the air with him. Samuel does too, I suppose, but at least he'll stand his ground and argue. And if I could get a few minutes alone with him, I'd give him something to contend with."

Camilla chuckled. "Well, I guess that clears up all fears of either of them being aggressive with you. So Jacob, the one you're dating, doesn't want you anywhere near Samuel, who is the one you'd like to talk to."

"The one I'd like to yell at is more like it, but yes."

Camilla angled her head. "You care for both of them. You realize that, right?"

"Of course I like them both but not the way you're thinking. They're as different as fall and spring."

"I always thought of those seasons as being similar."

"Spring is the start of growing season, and for apple farmers fall is the main harvest."

"So which man is the end of the wintry, barren season, bringing all its newness, and which one is the harvest with all its abundance?"

Rhoda's offhanded remark to compare them with seasons hadn't been well thought out. "I…I didn't mean it that way. For me, Jacob is both. He was my first love. My first courtship. My first kiss. My first hope of having a family of my own someday. But we haven't been together long enough to reach any kind of harvest yet."

"Just remember this, and I'll drop the topic: follow your heart. Don't stay in a relationship because you think you should or because you believe you owe it to Jacob or even because you loved him first. I once heard it put this way: If you're torn between two men, choose the second. If you had truly loved the first, there wouldn't have been a second."

"There is no second love, Camilla. There's only Jacob."

"Okay." Camilla patted Rhoda's hand. "I believe you, but even so, don't give any one person too much of your power, Rhoda—not over your business or your personal life. A truly good man can handle you maintaining some control, whether that means earning your own money or keeping your canning business separate from Kings' Orchard."

Camilla held feminist views, and that wasn't the Amish way. Most Amish women married young, and if they had a job or income, they gave it up before their wedding day. But Rhoda's situation was consistent with the rest of her life as an Amish woman—an oddity.

Camilla's cautioning words did make Rhoda realize one thing, however. If she was going to restore Jacob's faith in their relationship, she needed a place to live and work that would keep her and Samuel from crossing paths a gazillion times each day and night.

"Even if I liked your idea of acquiring and keeping a canning kitchen separate from Kings' Orchard, there is no money for such a plan."

"But you're open to the idea?"

"Actually"—Rhoda fidgeted with her braid—"I think I am."

"Good. That's where we start." Camilla grabbed a pen. "How large does the kitchen need to be?"

Did Rhoda hear a horse and buggy on the road? A desire to look outside drew her, and without really thinking about it, she went to a window facing the road. She couldn't see the road for the fog, but that didn't stop her from going to the window on the other side of the room. She peered at the woods.

She saw movement through the gray mist. Slowly someone moved in closer.

Samuel.

He was several yards from the house. Emotions as strong and raw as a nor'easter pushed and prodded her. Anger was the strongest, but hope was a close second. Did he have news for her that Jacob was willing to see her? Maybe he knew what she could do to set things right with Jacob.

Samuel attached something to a tree.

"What's he doing?"

Camilla came to the window. "Flagging the trees, best I can tell. I'd say he doesn't intend for you to get lost again."

"Why wait to do that until I've been here for two weeks?"

"No idea."

Samuel turned and retreated toward the farm. Was he not coming to Camilla's door? Would he travel the long distance through the woods and then leave without speaking to her? Anger swelled. "I ought to ignore him." But she had to talk to him while there was no chance of Jacob seeing her. "I'll be back in a minute." Rhoda dashed out of the room. She grabbed her coat off the rack and opened the back door.

"You have nothing on your feet."

Rhoda paused. "What?"

"Your feet."

Rhoda looked down. "Oh."

"There's a pair of galoshes." Camilla pointed to a corner.

Rhoda quickly slipped her feet in them and slammed the door on her way out, cringing that in her rush she was being careless. Hopefully she hadn't just awakened Bob.

"Samuel!" He didn't stop but continued walking toward the farm. She cupped her hands around her mouth and yelled with all her might. "Samuel King!"

He turned, looking surprised—and maybe apologetic—as he hurried toward her. "What are you doing out here dressed like that?"

She realized her hair was down and her head was uncovered. "You haven't said a word to me in two weeks, and that's all you've got on your mind? Why would you come so close to the house without at least trying to speak with me?"

"Is that what you want? To talk? To *me*?" His brown eyes bore into her. "*Kumm* on, Rhoda. You brushed me off without even a pause of doubt."

A shadowy figure seemed to step out from behind him, and Rhoda thought of her late sister. It only caused more frustration. Sometimes she'd like to banish all thoughts of both of them.

"I had no idea you felt anything for me other than friendship and partnership. Then you pulled me into your arms. *And* without asking permission, I might add. How could you turn around and tell Jacob what had happened? I begged you not to. But you did it anyway, and then you sauntered off with Nicole?"

"Oh, for Pete's sake! What does Nicole have to do with anything?"

"It's insulting! Amish women have no choice but to all dress alike, in layers of pleated clothes, with our hair pulled back. And then Nicole shows up in jeans with her shiny hair hanging down her back, and you go after her. Intertwining your life with Nicole's isn't like Leah seeing an outsider. She hasn't joined the faith. You have. And if you're not careful, you'll destroy the reputation of this settlement and take the business with you."

"I'm sick of your issues with Nicole. I needed her skill in order to install solar panels. But you want her off the property? It's done." He snapped his fingers. "But I'm not the one who holds the power to ruin the business. Jacob has that—and apparently every woman he comes into contact with—in the palm of his hand. Why didn't you tell him the incident was all me? It was! We both know it. I owned up to it, but you wavered. Why not tell him the truth?"

Rhoda shook all over, trembling like a woman freezing to death. But it was his question, not the temperature, that rattled her. "I can't believe this. You of all people are blaming me? Do you have any idea how frustrating it is that you messed up my life, and then you go on with yours as if nothing happened? And to add insult to injury, you avoid me as if I have the plague."

"Try joining the real world, the one where you understand why I'm avoiding you."

And suddenly she did know. He was avoiding her for the same reason she was avoiding him—to keep Jacob from having any reason to be more upset with them.

Despite the flagging and Camilla's explanation of what he was doing, she wanted Samuel's answer. "Then why are you here?"

He motioned at the flagging around the tree. "You're arriving late some mornings, and—"

"I'm what?" She looked through the woods, seeing flagging every ten or so feet until the forest became a blur of trees. "How would you know? You're as absent lately as Jacob was when he was away."

But she could see it in Samuel's eyes. He wasn't absent. Somehow he knew when she arrived and when she left. Her heart pounded. She'd been confident that he had pulled her into his arms as a momentary temptation brought on through loneliness more than any real feelings.

Was that not accurate?

He tightened his hat onto his head. "Has Jacob said anything to you since that day?"

"No. Not yet. When I saw you, I'd hoped you were bringing word that he wanted to talk."

"Even if he were ready, he wouldn't tell me. He's got nothing for me but anger. I know some of his hostility is because he's mortified. Even after realizing I'd kissed you, he confessed that you mean the world to him in front of both of us."

Samuel's brown eyes told her much more than he ever would. Jacob wasn't the only one mortified. It was as if the earth trembled under her feet at everything Samuel felt.

Anger drained as so many things about this man—things that hadn't added up since the day they came to Maine to view the property—began to unfold. She used to complain, "I don't understand you." And time after time he assured her she didn't need to. In her quiet time with God, He seemed to confirm that Samuel had a right to remain a mystery. Samuel had been backpedaling from her for quite a while, hiding so much of his true self. He was considerate but closed off. Giving yet hiding his actions. A constant support but emotionally distant. He made sense now, and she couldn't help but admire him for what he'd tried to do—fill in for Jacob while keeping her at arm's length.

All his efforts were dishonored in one heated moment.

Should one mistake between friends or brothers define forever who they were to each other?

She reached for Samuel's hand. "Samuel—"

A snapping noise made her turn.

Jacob stood only twenty feet away, staring at her.

FIVE

With the light from a lone candle guiding her, Iva quietly got on her knees and reached into the crawlspace behind the wall of her closet. She tugged on the straps of the carrying case that held her camera, easing it from its hiding place. Most who lived under this roof were asleep.

She came out of the closet on her hands and knees, candle clasped between her thumb and index finger.

"I can't believe you still have your camera." Her sister Minnie took the candle and set it on a nightstand.

Iva stood, dusting dirt off her dress. She could hardly breathe for the discomfort filling the space between them. Her sister had disagreed with her buying it in the first place, and Iva had dared to hide it while their father sold piece after piece of their household to buy food. But she'd earned the money for it back when jobs weren't so scarce, and she'd rather go without food than her camera. "Do you think it's already daylight in Maine?" Time to get her sister focused on something else.

"Probably." Minnie rolled up a pair of black stockings and tucked them into Iva's hand-me-down suitcase.

Iva dusted off the top of the camera case. "I read that they're about seven hundred miles farther east than we are. Same time zone, though."

Minnie slid a stack of underwear into the bag. "I've…I've been thinking. Maybe me and *Mamm* are wrong, and this is a foolish plan."

Iva ignored the icy fingers of fear. What could be worse than staying here?

"Piffle." She looked inside the camera case just to make sure it was all still there—the camera and lenses and all the paraphernalia she'd spent years buying. She zipped it again, double-checking each compartment on the bag.

Minnie blinked, looking curious and a bit hurt. "What?"

Their quiet voices were only for each other as the rest of the household slept.

"You heard me. Would you prefer a different word? How about *horseshoes, malarkey, hooey, baloney,* or *hogwash*?"

"I know what you said, but why?"

"Because you're saying you've changed your mind *while* you're packing my bag." As if it mattered what Minnie or Iva wanted. Mamm had come to Iva privately, shimmying with fear like a pond during a windstorm. She needed Iva to do this. The family was desperate. Iva had been a disappointment in more ways than she could bear to think of but not this time. Not again.

Minnie jerked an armful of clothes out of the bag and threw them onto the bed. They had ironed and folded everything before dinner. But Iva understood her sister's feelings were every bit as raw and torn as her own.

Iva moved closer and placed a hand on her sister's protruding belly, talking to the unborn one. "Your Mamm is a bit wishy-washy these days. All plans. No backbone to carry them out. She didn't used to be like this." Minnie was as nervous as a long-tail cat in a room full of rocking chairs, but years ago she would have gone into that room anyway.

Now the changes within the Indiana Amish community had all of them wavering on what to do and clamoring for answers.

Minnie placed her hand over Iva's. "What if you travel all that way and they don't want you there?"

"I don't know."

It was all too much. The economy. The toll on the men's self-esteem. The fear that after getting through the worst of the downturn by her siblings selling their homes and moving in together, her family still might lose the house she'd grown up in. The house now shared by four families.

According to her Daed, it was fixable by what he called "a godsend of a man." His real name was Leon Schwartz, and he was a kind and good widower with young children who needed a Mamm. But Iva couldn't imagine having to hold hands with him, let alone what her Daed had in mind—marrying him and having his children.

Iva looked into her sister's eyes. "Mamm's been putting back a little from the food money for almost two years, the whole time hoping God would show her the best thing to do with it. She thinks this is it, and I'm going." Iva got the last items out of the drawer and tossed them and the rest of her messy clothes into the suitcase.

"Daed will be furious when he realizes you're gone, and I doubt Mamm will be able to hide what she's done."

"He'll only be upset because of how it will look to others. Inwardly he'll be glad to have one less mouth to feed. Your husband will be secretly glad I've taken the lead to do what he can't—go see if the Maine settlement is a good place to take your family."

"It's not your responsibility to have to go to another part of the country to look for work."

"That's not Mamm's only reason for getting me out of here, and you know it."

"You're sure that going that far and into the unknown by yourself is necessary?"

"Ya." Iva looked out the window. "My ride's here."

A car sat idling at the end of the lane, hazard lights flashing to let her know she needed to scamper down the driveway.

"You'll call as soon as you're there and safe, ya?"

"I'll do my best. But don't worry." Iva slid the strap of her camera bag over her shoulder before she grabbed her tripod with one hand and the suitcase with the other.

Minnie eased open the door. Then she took the tripod and walked down the stairs with her, not saying a word until they were on the gravel lane.

Iva looked back at the house. Mamm stood at her bedroom window, quietly bidding Iva a final good-bye. Iva blew her a kiss and waved.

Minnie sighed. "You have her believing you like this plan."

"What would you have me do? Heap guilt on top of her fears?"

They finished walking in silence.

If only the hard times would disappear, she could stay here where life felt safe and familiar. But that was childish thinking. Adults were equipped to think in terms of attainable goals. Her goal was to find a place with jobs for her family, preferably where the employers would be more likely to hire Amish rather than others. If nothing else, she had to work there long enough to get sufficient money to come home. The girl she talked to on the phone, Leah, didn't sound extremely confident about Iva being hired, but she did give permission for her to come. Once there, Iva would do her best to make herself indispensable. Maybe they'd let her sleep on the couch or something.

"If you'd marry…" Minnie dropped her sentence.

"What, Minnie? What would happen if I married Leon as Daed wants me to? Leon would save us from our financial troubles, and it would cost no one anything, except me. And Leon. We both deserve better."

"He loves you."

Her insides knotted. "Maybe. He's a good man." That's all she had to say on the matter, but love wasn't the same as need, and Leon was so lonely. She understood, and he would have given all he had, which was a lot, to help her family if she would marry him.

What was love anyway? Was it as simple as one person meeting the other's needs in a way that made them feel better about themselves and life? If so, that wasn't good enough.

But it wasn't her refusal to marry Leon that had moved Mamm to ask her to go to Maine. No one else was open to the idea of venturing into any new territory, so Mamm was circumventing the men's objections by quietly sending Iva. Should she admire Mamm for her courage or pity her for feeling so desperate she'd go behind the men's backs?

When they arrived at the car, she put her stuff in the backseat and closed the door. "Minnie, I'll be fine. Stop worrying." But Iva's insides were quaking enough for both of them. "I don't think God puts us on this huge earth so we can be afraid of stepping into the unknown. Isn't tomorrow an unknown even if we all stay right here where tradition is kept and every piece of ground is familiar?"

"And if you and Mamm are wrong?"

"Then I will ask God to forgive me."

Minnie hugged her. "Do be careful."

"I promise." Iva got into the car and waved as the driver pulled off.

Jacob had barely stepped out of the rig when he'd heard Rhoda's voice, yelling for Samuel. So he'd eased around the side of the house, and by the time Samuel had finished tromping back to where Rhoda stood, Jacob could hear everything they said and not be seen. Maybe he was a jerk to eavesdrop, but he had to know where Rhoda's heart was. He would never play the fool for another woman, not even for one he loved with his whole heart.

"Interesting, isn't it? We're in another state, and months have passed, but we've been in this situation many times—where I find you two because of the yelling."

He wasn't sure if his goal was to add a little humor or simply have an opening line. Either way, Rhoda didn't move toward him or say anything.

He couldn't take his eyes off her. He'd never seen a more beautiful woman. He also had never seen her without her hair pinned up and under a prayer Kapp.

Lately, Jacob didn't know what to think of her. Or himself. Or Samuel.

Her eyes searched his, and as if realizing where his attention was, she ran her fingers across her head. She gasped and pulled a white knit scarf out of her coat pocket, but it fluttered to the ground. He grabbed it and held it out to her.

"Denki," she whispered, her hands trembling as she took it and put it on. For a brief moment he didn't care what had kept them apart since he'd returned. He wanted only one thing: Rhoda. Even if she cared nothing for Samuel, could he and Rhoda ever have what they once had—new, fresh, innocent love?

He gestured toward the driveway at the front of the house. "I brought a rig for you. I thought maybe we'd go for a ride and talk."

A faint smile curved her lips. "I'd like that."

But he needed to know something first. "Samuel asked a question you didn't answer."

Her brows tightened. "When?"

Jacob pointed to the side of the house, where he'd been standing. "I got here about the same time as Samuel."

She nodded, and he imagined she was trying to remember all that had been said. "And?"

"If *it* was all Samuel's doing, why didn't you just say that when I asked?"

Rhoda slid her hands into her coat pockets. "All three of us have to take responsibility for what happened. I grew careless, willing to get physically close without thinking what Samuel might be feeling. And we *are* close, Jacob. That's the responsibility you need to take. You weren't here when I needed you the most. You didn't call or write. I had no way to reach you, and I spent months needing to share my burdens with someone. Then elation came when the drug investigation was over and the allegations were dropped. From the moment I got the news, you didn't have to hide for my sake, not for one hour longer, but I still didn't hear from you for a week. And that hurt. It really hurt."

Jacob drew a deep breath. He needed a few moments to gain perspective before speaking. Her soft-spoken complaints stung.

When she was cleared, Jacob *had* written to her. Maybe he should've called. In their earlier phone conversations, like when he had to leave over Christmastime to help Sandra, Rhoda had sounded sad and lonely, *and* a call would have stolen their thunder of celebrating in person. But she never got his letter, and when he mentioned sending it, she'd thrown a bitter doubt in his lap. She probably didn't remember half of what she'd said to him the day he came home and unearthed that she and Samuel had kissed. But the only thing that mattered at this point was how she felt now. If the last two weeks of living away from the farm had done nothing else, it should have given clarity to her mind and heart.

Jacob cleared his throat. "Is it just me? Am I hearing you wrong? Everything you've said since I realized what happened sounds as if you're defending Samuel."

Anger flashed through her eyes. "I'm not defending him!"

Until their clash over what had happened with Samuel, she'd never raised her voice to him. Had she lost all sense of who they were together?

She shifted. "Samuel is one-third wrong, and you just overheard my anger at him. But you have no idea what all I had to deal with while the senator's wife used her skill and money to try to frame me. If you want to hate your brother for those five seconds, I won't help you do it. But I'm asking you not to throw away all that the three of us are to each other, because we were caught in a situation none of us could prevent. Don't toss us away because Samuel and I mishandled a few seconds. If we hadn't become close, you would have had no need to hide for my sake, because I probably wouldn't be alive."

His heart jolted. "What?"

"There's so much you don't know."

He continually learned more about what had taken place while he was gone, and it haunted him like a stalker he couldn't escape. "Tell me what you meant by 'wouldn't be alive.'"

"One night I got lost in these stupid woods. I kept circling these acres, wishing you were here to find me." Her eyes brimmed with tears. That wasn't like her, and the chip on Jacob's shoulder began to quake. "All I wanted was *you*. Here. For me. I didn't think I had a chance of anyone else noticing I was missing. When I was too exhausted and too lost to know how to get back to the farm, I sat in the snow, and the temperature continued to drop. Your brother should've thought I was in my room asleep. But he knew I wasn't"—she tapped the center of her chest—"like I sometimes know things. And he knew it because we'd grown close as I went through the worst time I could imagine. He came through the woods on horseback, calling for me." She smiled at Samuel. "He woke me. Brought me light to see and strength to lean on so I could get home. Of course, he complained like I was a disobedient child." She tossed a whispery laugh in Samuel's direction.

Jacob was unbelievably grateful she'd been found, but that didn't keep possessiveness from burning inside him. He didn't want to be *that* guy. One of the beautiful things about his relationship with Rhoda was he'd felt secure in who they were. They'd had an easy, fun connection.

She looked into his eyes, and even though he still had concerns about her feelings for Samuel, she was right. He had to accept some of the responsibility for what had taken place.

Disappointment pressed in on him. He glanced at Samuel, seeing a man caught in a storm he wasn't prepared for. Still, something about Samuel's rash behavior nagged at him, but he couldn't quite grasp what it was. "Okay. I'll carry my share of the blame. But you seem so confident in your loyalty to Samuel. Where am I in all this?"

Her gentle smile gave him hope. He'd let his disillusion with Sandra change what he knew to be true about Rhoda. She wouldn't hide the truth from him. That was encouraging.

Then another realization hit. What if she was unaware of her real feelings for Samuel?

She moved closer and caressed Jacob's face. "Friends enrich our lives. Business partners add to who we are. But you are the foundation I want to build my life on."

Her words dropped understanding into his consciousness: people make mistakes and need grace for their relationships to continue to grow. The chip on his shoulder fell, and the weight that was lifted surprised him. He slid her hand from his cheek to his lips and kissed her palm, taking a welcome sigh of relief.

Besides, he knew Samuel drove her nuts by being hardheaded. Her gratefulness for all Samuel had done could not erase the reality that the two of them were oil and water. Some days they were dynamite and matches. She and Jacob were like sunshine and vacation. Some days they were the ocean and scuba diving—a favorite pastime of his, discovered during his time with the Englisch.

And like him and the ocean, he and Rhoda were a perfect combination that had been separated too often and for too long.

Regardless of what his lawyer had to say to him, Jacob wouldn't do one more thing that would hinder building a life with Rhoda.

He turned to Samuel but couldn't bring himself to offer his hand. Despite whatever peace Rhoda would fight to gain between Samuel and him, could he risk the three of them remaining on the same farm? He didn't think so.

But that was trouble for another day. For now he wanted to forget about Samuel and have some time alone with Rhoda.

"How about that buggy ride?"

SIX

Rhoda hurried, putting on her stockings and shoes. Jacob had wanted to wait for her in the buggy, but Camilla stepped onto the porch and insisted he at least step inside for these few minutes. As Rhoda pinned up her hair and secured her prayer Kapp, she could hear that they were still standing in the foyer. Jacob had probably politely refused to come in and take a seat in the living room. She imagined Camilla had far more questions for Jacob than he'd ever answer.

She stepped out of her bedroom and into the foyer.

Jacob looked her way. "You ready?"

She suddenly remembered she wasn't. "The dishes and apple butter... I need to clean up the kitchen."

Camilla hugged her. "You go. I'll clean up. It'll be payment for that year's worth of salsa you're going to make for us."

"Deal." She put on her coat again.

As she walked toward the rig, she went through the Cranfords' yard just ahead of Jacob. The disquiet between them was as uncomfortable as when her sister had hidden her shoes on a church day and Rhoda had to wear a pair entirely too small.

Jacob stepped ahead of her and opened the carriage door. When she stood mere inches from him, staring into his green eyes, she wanted to put her hands on his face and pull his lips to hers. But she didn't feel he would welcome that. Was it her imagination? As she climbed in on the passenger's side, she could no longer deny that everything between her and Jacob had changed.

How long would it take to get back what they'd once had?

There was no way to know, but she was a nurturer at heart. It's why she loved tending herbs and fruits. All she needed to do was understand what nutrients and natural elements—like sun and water—were missing and instill those daily in the right amounts. With time and effort she could regrow and replenish almost anything that harsh conditions had caused to wither.

"You ready?" He flipped on the new headlights and tapped the reins against the horse's back.

"Absolutely." She smiled, using one of his favorite sayings.

He pulled onto the road, and she searched for something to talk about. "The buggy looks great. Lights, mirrors."

He pushed a fleece blanket her way.

"Denki."

"I've been fixing it up for you so you'd have a better way to get back and forth between here and the farm."

Several emotions churned, mixing into one that was relatively new and yet entirely too old. Knowing he'd been thinking of her and doing something kind during the two weeks of silence was like a balm on her heart. But disappointment fought against that. He still didn't want her to move back to the farm? Heartache and optimism swirled into what could best be described as hopeful torment. Was that to be her new relationship with Jacob?

"I would need a paddock for the horse."

"I've been thinking about that. There's one not too far from the Cranfords' house. It just needs some fixing up, a little fence mending, and I'd be glad to do it. Or I could come get you each morning and…take you home each evening. It'd be more like us having a real courtship."

He didn't look at her. Was he afraid she'd turn him down? What had *his* life been like during those long months they were apart?

"It'd be really nice to have some time alone with you before and after the workday."

He reached across the seat, and she thought he was going to hold her hand, but their fingers barely touched before he withdrew his hand. The warmth of his touch made her long to slide in closer, but she didn't dare. They rode in silence. Was Jacob doing the same thing she was—biting his tongue in fear of saying the wrong thing? Did he have accusations against her? She still had a few grievances she wanted to air, but morally speaking, she was in the wrong, not him. Still, they would have to talk honestly with each other if they wanted to heal.

"How are Sandra and Casey?"

He grimaced. "I haven't talked to Sandra." When he spoke, his voice was heavy. "I need to…for Casey's sake. Sandra gets along better when I stay in contact, but I can't seem to pick up the phone."

Insight dropped into her heart: despite his sense of humor and gentleness, Jacob wasn't good at facing the harder side of any relationship. "Can I do anything?"

He shook his head.

She slid her hands under the blanket. "Maybe I could call her for—"

"That's not a good idea, even though I'd like to have some answers without having to talk to her. But you wouldn't know any more afterward than you know now. That's the way it is with Sandra."

"Oh."

Had she become useless to Jacob? That was a silly thought, rooted in insecurity. Sandra was just a part of his life that wasn't open to her. Or anyone. He'd just shared more than usual. But what could they safely discuss?

"Jacob, I'm lost here. Everything I want to talk about, I'm afraid to bring up, afraid it could break us. I have no experience with relationships. You know that. Please, I…I need your help."

He looked thoughtful. "Confusing, isn't it?" He sounded sympathetic. A few minutes later he pulled off the road onto a graveled area. After staring ahead for several long moments, he turned to face her. His presence drew her as it had the day she first kissed him. She'd known then that he had secrets, but she hadn't realized that meant he was so skilled at holding back his thoughts and feelings from her too.

He squeezed the reins. "I'm not sure what to tell you, Rhodes."

She placed her hand over her aching chest. He'd used her nickname and done so with tenderness. Emotions pressed against her like water against a dam.

His attention moved to her lips before he lowered his eyes. Was he thinking of Samuel kissing her? He took a deep breath. "The awkwardness between us can't be resolved with a single decision or a brief conversation. It'll have to fade on its own, little by little. Until it does, we have to act as normal as we know how. We need to spend time together until we stop thinking about that day."

She wanted him to kiss her. She longed to forget about Samuel's lips against hers. "I'm glad you came to me." Her voice cracked.

"Me too. It helps…some." He clicked his tongue, urging the horse back onto the road.

What they needed was a little laughter. That's what had drawn them together. Jacob had taught her to laugh. Something she'd long forgotten, even before her sister's death.

She inched closer. "What did the girl octopus say to the boy octopus?"

A hint of a smile crossed his lips. "I'm a gurgle, gurgle, gurgle?"

"No." She freed her hands from the blanket and held them out. "May I hold your hand, hand, hand, hand, hand, hand, hand, hand?"

He put his arm around her shoulders and pulled her close. "Is that the best you have?"

"No. The *best* I have is you."

He splayed his fingers, and she intertwined hers with his.

He gazed into her eyes, a smile slowly spreading across his face. "Did it hurt when you fell from heaven?"

She grinned. "Are you hinting that I'm an angel or Lucifer?"

He laughed. "Rhodes." His correcting tone was pure jest, and hope filled her that he'd find his way through the darkness and to their future.

***

The barn loft smelled of hay, and every movement caused a hollow, sandpaper-like echo against the old wood. Leah stood near Steven and Landon, searching through boxes they'd brought from Pennsylvania and trying to ignore Landon's incessant whistling. They were hunting for the containers to make snares for codling moths. The contraptions weren't needed right away, but Samuel wanted to know what supplies they had so he'd know what to order. After all, combating apple-eating pests throughout each season was nonstop work.

Her hands ached. Her back hurt. She was hungry, tired, and cold. But she couldn't stand to hear any more of her own griping, even the silent kind. "It was good to see Rhoda and Jacob arriving together."

"Ya." Steven opened a box. "That was a welcome sight."

Rhoda's brother didn't sound as relieved as Leah thought he should be. It sort of confirmed some of her worries. Jacob and Rhoda were stiff throughout the day, and even though Rhoda had stayed for dinner the last two nights and Jacob had driven her home, they were more like strangers trying to get to know each other than a couple who'd had a spat.

Leah decided to change the subject. "We've checked the attic and here. Landon, have you stored any boxes somewhere else?"

"Nope." He shifted more boxes, whistling as he went.

"Hey, Landon."

He stopped. "Yeah?"

She raised her eyebrows. "You're doing it again."

"What? This?" He started whistling again.

She pointed at him, and he grinned. Landon was breathing a sigh of relief now that Jacob and Rhoda were talking again. If only the same could be said for Samuel and Jacob. On Rhoda's first night to rejoin the family for dinner, Samuel had made an appearance after everyone else had eaten. He spoke and was friendly as he fixed himself a dinner plate. But about a minute after Samuel's arrival, Jacob said he needed to get Rhoda back to the Cranfords'.

The room went silent as it dawned on everyone that Rhoda would continue living with the couple.

Suddenly a walkie-talkie popped and crackled. "Steven?" Phoebe's voice filled the loft.

Steven yanked the radio out of his pocket. "Ya?"

"Did you take my kitchen ladder?"

Steven made a face. "Ya. Sorry. And then I forgot to bring it back." He paused before pushing the button on the walkie-talkie again. "Don't climb a chair. Do you need it right now?"

"Sort of. I can wait a bit, but I'll need it to heat up supper."

All Phoebe was going to do was throw leftovers in a pot? They'd had cold cereal for breakfast and sandwiches for lunch. Leah's stomach was already growling, and it was only two-thirty.

"Coming." Steven turned. "You two let me know if you find the box."

"Sure thing." Landon gave a half wave. When the top of Steven's head disappeared from the haymow, Landon turned to Leah. "I've known him for years while working with Rhoda, and I've never heard him get frustrated with Phoebe."

Leah arched an eyebrow. "I hope you're taking notes." She rubbed her back, sighing.

Landon strode to a bale of hay and grabbed it. He set it in front of the loft window, grabbed an old blanket out of a box, and tossed it over the bale. "Sit. Take a load off."

"It's about time someone made such an offer."

He smiled, pulling a couple of granola bars from his pocket and passing one to her. "You seem distracted."

She unwrapped the bar and took a bite. "Just grumpy and trying not to share it with everyone around me, so hush up and eat."

"I'm not *everyone*. If something's on your mind, I want to know about it."

"It's just that I woke up realizing I keep waiting for things to get easier, and they don't."

"What things? Relationships or work?"

"All of it. We seem to wander from one storm to the next. I'm trying to have a good attitude, because I really don't want to spend the next five years hating my life."

"Five years?" Landon stared at her for several moments. He drew a breath before he sat next to the window and leaned against the barn wall. "I didn't realize you were planning on staying that long."

"Me either, but let's face it. I've been dreaming. I came to Maine under false pretenses, thinking I was only staying long enough to help my family recover from the tornado and then I was going out on my own. The harvest may start in five months, but there's always another storm on the horizon. It feels as if my brothers and the business are going to need me forever. Maybe it's God letting me know I'm meant to remain Amish."

"If you want to stay, you should do so, no matter what anyone else wants." He stared at the ceiling as if thinking before speaking. "Even though it'll take me a while to get over it."

She wanted to smile and cry at the same time. That summed up most of what she felt about Landon—joy and sadness. "You say the nicest things."

He scoffed. "What I just said wasn't *nice*. Actually, it sounded like a lot of heartache for both of us."

"Really?" Did he care for her more than she realized?

"Fine." He shrugged. "Apparently just one of us. Me."

"I didn't mean it that way. I'm surprised *you* feel that way. We haven't even had a real date yet."

His eyes grew large, and he stared at her. "We've been going somewhere a night every week and attending church on Sunday evenings and on your between Sundays. What exactly constitutes a bona fide date for the Amish?"

"You never asked me out on a date. I thought that's how you Englisch boys did things."

He shook his head. "I'm confused."

"I thought we'd agreed to just be friends."

"We did, but then…" He sighed. "When I heard other guys complain that women are hard to understand, I thought they were exaggerating. I guess that's something else I've been wrong about."

"And mostly when we go out, we get pizza and go to your grandmother's to watch movies. Besides, you've never even tried to hold my hand."

"And I never will. I'm not a hand holder."

"Or tried to kiss me."

"When I asked if you'd like to go for a ride one time, you went ballistic, accusing me of only wanting someone who was easy."

Leah almost burst out laughing. He was really cute. "True." She swallowed the last bite of her granola bar. "So what I thought was us just hanging out has been us dating?"

"I guess it's been whatever you tell me."

She pursed her lips, trying to hide a grin. "Hmm. I think it's been a marriage proposal."

"What?" He laughed.

She threw the empty wrapper at him. "Yep, that's what I think."

He grabbed two handfuls of hay from the bale. She jumped up, and in a flash she was going down the ladder.

Even though he had to peel himself off the floor, he soon stood above her, holding the handfuls out. "How's shimmying down that ladder going to help?" He released the hay onto her head.

"Hey." She knocked the stuff off her hair and prayer Kapp.

"That's right. It is indeed *hay.*"

Laughing, she missed the next rung with her foot and lost her grip as well. She landed on the dirt floor with a thud.

"Leah!" Landon all but jumped from the loft. "You okay?"

"I think I've been rendered unconscious."

He knelt. "Finally." He waved his hands in mock exaggeration. "You quoted a line from a movie. Of course it's a girly, kid movie."

"You be nice. I love *Anne of Green Gables.*"

He helped her sit up. "Does anything hurt?"

"Are you daft? I just fell off a ladder." She leaned into him as she stood.

His eyes met hers. "Be serious."

"I'm fine." She brushed off her dress. "Unless saying otherwise would get us a day off."

He chuckled. "Don't think it works that way. Nice try, though."

"Ya, you're right. Around here it'd mean getting patched up, given an herbal remedy for pain, and then having to make up any lost work time due to the mishap." She rolled her eyes. "Ah, the joys of living Amish."

Landon gave a half smile and shrugged. "It's not permanent unless you want it to be."

She went to the barn door and looked out. "Leaving used to sound so easy. Jacob always made it look that way." She leaned against the doorframe. "I thought everything about him was so cool, and I thought Samuel was an old stick-in-the-mud. But now..." She played with the strings to her prayer Kapp.

She'd watched these long months as Rhoda had yearned for Jacob to free himself of his past and come home. Watched as Samuel had helped her get through the trials only to be tossed aside as soon as Jacob returned. Was that also who Leah was? Someone who could waltz in and out of her family's life when it suited her? She hated the amount of work it took to keep the Old Ways, but was that a good enough reason to sever all ties with her family and the Amish? "Funny how we see things so differently after catching a glimpse of someone else's experience."

"Meaning you're seeing Jacob through Samuel's eyes?"

"And Rhoda's. All of us are paying for Jacob's years of freedom."

"Your thoughts are everywhere today. Why?"

"Because I came here so sure of what I wanted—to help until the business was stable and then leave. Now I don't know what I want. Waiting for the right time is one thing. Staggering around like a newborn calf is another."

The desire to get free of the Amish life was almost unbearable, and yet as she watched and felt the heartache of the difficulties between Rhoda and her brothers, Leah couldn't stand to think how many hearts would shatter if she left. Among the Englisch, young adults were expected to leave the nest and land wherever they chose. But her leaving would break her family's hearts—even if they chose to act as if it didn't.

Was she strong enough to do that to them?

The phone rang, and she went into the office. "Hello?"

"Hallo. This is Iva Lambright. I'm at the train station in Bangor. I was told I'll need a ride from here. Any suggestions who to call?"

Leah's heart moved to her throat. What had she done? In her desire to get some extra help on the farm, she'd gone around her brothers and Rhoda, not to mention the upheaval she'd caused in Iva's life.

"Hold on." She put the phone on mute. "Landon?"

He ambled into the office. "You rang?"

"Do you know where Bangor is?"

"Sure. It's about forty minutes north of here."

"There's a young Amish woman at the train station who needs a ride."

"Why?"

"She called looking for a job, and I, uh, sort of told her she should come this way."

"Leah King!" He shook his head, clearly more amused than annoyed. "I'll pick her up, but I'm not getting between you and Rhoda on this."

Leah unmuted the phone. "Iva?"

"Ya."

"Our friend Landon will pick you up in his truck in about an hour. He'll be able to spot you by your head covering, right?"

"Ya."

After Leah described Landon's truck for Iva to watch for, Iva thanked her, and they ended the call.

Landon pulled out his keys. "You coming?"

She wanted to, but doing so would only pack Iva's first hours on the farm with even more tension. "I need to tell the others about Iva coming, and maybe the worst of the storm will be over by the time you get back."

"Okay."

As he walked out of the office, Leah's stomach clenched. What if this girl was beautiful and charming and she had just put her and Landon alone in a truck for an hour to get to know each other?

"Landon." She hurried out of the office.

He turned.

"You're in a relationship. Don't forget that."

He ambled back to her, a smile showing his straight white teeth. "Decided that, did you? Then I already like this Iva girl being here."

"Yeah, your appreciation of her is my concern."

All hints of humor fell from his face. "Leah King, if you think that I'm so shallow or that you're so easily replaced, you've got a lot to learn."

Her heart palpitated to the familiar beat of confusion. "Lately I seem to waver on everything."

"Sure you do. You're eighteen years old. But I'm not going anywhere, and your family isn't going anywhere."

"My fear is *I'm* not going anywhere either."

"Oh good grief. If you want to go, go. If you want to stay, stay. If you don't know, stop fretting. Is it too much to simply let life rock along until you're positive about what you want?"

She finally knew why she felt like one of dogs' rope toys being chewed and tossed and tugged—fear that if she didn't choose soon, Landon would move on to some other girl, one who was older and more sure about what she wanted from life. "I can't expect you to hang around while I rock along not knowing what I want."

"Let's play the *if* game. *If* you left the Amish today, and *if* we were so in love we wanted to marry, I'm not ready for a wife, not yet, and you're not ready for a husband." He straightened his ball cap. "I get that some days you want to leave the Amish and on other days you want to stay Amish." He shrugged. "That's a gamble I'm willing to take, but as far as you're concerned, *I'm* a sure bet. Okay?"

An overwhelming desire to kiss him rushed through her. "It seems dangerous to give our feelings room to grow if I'm going to stay Amish."

"That ship has already sailed, Leah. We like each other." He shrugged. "I wouldn't change that for whatever the future holds."

"What if you don't want to hang around long enough for me to decide?"

"You have too many insecurities. You know that?"

"Indulge me. I want an answer."

He rolled his eyes. "Fine. To paraphrase the words of Simon Peter that we heard in church a few Sundays back—to whom would I go?"

She couldn't move. Worse, she couldn't think of a cheeky retort. "I... uh..."

He smirked. "I believe I just rendered you speechless."

She nodded.

"I'd better go." He walked away, and she followed him.

He opened the door to his truck and turned. "But I hate to leave now, because I'm sure this serene quietness from you will be long gone by the time I get back." He laughed.

Was Landon as good as he seemed? If he was, she feared that alone would sway her about leaving the Amish. But should a man be the deciding factor?

She'd asked herself that question before, and the answer was still the same—she didn't think so.

As Landon pulled onto the road, Leah took a cleansing breath, feeling all her earlier anxiety release its grip. She didn't have to fret over making the right decision. She could simply live and know that her heart would eventually reveal where she needed to land.

With that bit of anxiety dispelled, she had to move on to the next bit of drama—calling a meeting. She pulled out a walkie-talkie. "Samuel? Rhoda? Jacob?"

"Ya?" Each answered, one after the other.

Leah braced herself. "I know you're busy, but how soon could you come to the barn for a meeting? We need to talk."

"About?" Samuel asked.

"It'll wait until you get here." She figured it wouldn't take more than half an hour for them to find a stopping point on whatever they were doing and get to the barn. "See you in thirty minutes." She flicked off the walkie-talkie.

No point getting into it any sooner than necessary.

SEVEN

Samuel walked into the office and found Jacob sitting by himself behind the desk, fiddling with a pen. He barely glanced up. Samuel couldn't ask where Rhoda was or anything about her coming to the office without angering Jacob.

"Where's Leah?" Samuel sat, hoping Jacob would answer him.

Jacob picked up a note. "Went to get some snacks."

"Something to appease us. That doesn't sound too good."

Jacob shook his head, letting the note fall to the desk. He wasn't himself yet, but at least they were talking without arguing.

The whole situation was foreign to them, but nothing was stranger than how Rhoda was dealing with it. She'd avoided Samuel, perhaps for Jacob's sake, yet when Jacob had challenged her, she had refused to throw Samuel onto the compost heap as Jacob had. She hadn't wavered in her friendship for Samuel. At the same time, by moving out of the farmhouse, she'd let Jacob know she was willing to do whatever he wanted of her. Despite Samuel's humiliation over the last few weeks, he found her method of dealing with the situation interesting. Admirable, really.

He was desperate to put his energies into making the orchard a success, but his future was in Jacob's hands. He shifted in his chair. "Did you call the lawyer?"

"I did." Jacob bumped one end of the pen and then the other end against the desk in slow, easy movements that belied the simmering distrust in his eyes. "Come hell or high water, I'm not leaving Rhoda again. I don't care what he wants."

Samuel nodded. The last thing he wanted was for Jacob to go away again!

But Samuel felt he could now cope better with his feelings for Rhoda regardless of whether Jacob was here or not. His emotions and desires were no longer a pent-up force to be reckoned with. He loved Rhoda. But the fact that she and Jacob knew his feelings had released some of the reckless intensity. That was his silver lining, and he hoped Rhoda had one too.

Ziggy wandered into the office, wagging his tail and nudging Samuel for attention. The dogs had gone out earlier with Rhoda, and they usually stayed pretty close to her wherever she walked, so she wasn't far from the office now.

Jacob opened a drawer and tossed the pen into it. "Since the moment I came home, something's been nagging at me, and I couldn't put my finger on it. Even a couple of days ago, when Rhoda explained some things that happened while I was gone and said she wanted me to be the foundation she built her life on, I still couldn't let go of my anger toward you. But I couldn't figure out why until just now."

Samuel rubbed his hands together, warming them. "I hope that the understanding helps you forgive me and that we can move on once and for all."

"Hardly. The conclusion I reached isn't helpful. You wouldn't have tried to take her from me unless you believed you're the better man for her." Resentment shadowed Jacob's features as he squared his shoulders.

Samuel shifted, feeling the challenge being hurtled at him. Although Jacob had shown little of his gentle nature since the incident, Samuel never doubted his brother was a good man with a kind and caring heart. The problem was he had a past that chased him. It kept him away from Rhoda time after time, and, ya, Samuel *did* think he was a better fit for Rhoda. But if he said what he really thought, how long would it be before Jacob left for good, taking Rhoda—and all chances for this orchard's success—with him?

It wasn't up to Samuel to decide who was best for Rhoda, and he'd never meant to let anyone know how he felt, including Rhoda. Just as he'd never meant to pull her into his arms.

Zara sauntered into the doorway, so where was Rhoda?

Jacob stood. "Deny that you think you're better for her than I am, and I'll chalk this whole mess up to the momentary mistake Rhoda wants me to believe it was."

Samuel wasn't going to add lying to his ever-growing list of sins, and he couldn't think of anything helpful to say.

Rhoda walked into the office, saving him from having to answer Jacob's challenge. She skirted Zara, studying several envelopes in her hands. "I went by the mailbox. Along with all the business stuff, we have some letters from our families." She glanced at the desk, and her eyes widened as she studied the piles. "Oh my. Don't either of you ever work?" She grinned at Jacob. "Need a hand, hand, hand, hand, hand, hand, hand, hand?"

This was Rhoda—upbeat and clever. How did she manage to respond as if they weren't in the midst of a raging river of emotions threatening to drown them?

"Always." Jacob winked.

"I think you need the arms of an octopus to clean up this mess." As she grabbed a pile of letters, one fell from her hand and landed under Samuel's chair. "Don't get up." She made a shooing motion. "Just get out of the way."

Samuel rocked back on two legs of his chair, giving her what she'd asked for—to stay seated while moving out of the way.

She pushed Ziggy to the side, but just as she picked up the envelope, she lost her balance, scattering the letters in her hand. The dog nudged her as Rhoda grabbed a spindle on the back of Samuel's chair, knocking him off balance.

Samuel fell backward as she tumbled forward. Jacob dove for her, squatting to catch her by the arm. He fell too. Both dogs fled the office, yelping. A moment later, when all was silent, Samuel realized that he couldn't see, but he could tell their legs and arms were a tangled mess. Rhoda's apron lay across his face, and he was pinned between the filing cabinet and Rhoda, waiting for her to get up. So he dared not move.

Someone lifted the fabric from his face, and he stared up at Jacob.

His brother clenched his jaw, and Samuel raised both hands in surrender. "Can I please be banned from entering this office altogether?"

Hardness drained from Jacob's face. "After Rhoda fell, I slipped on the letters and tripped over a dog." He helped Rhoda up before holding out a hand to Samuel.

Samuel took it. Jacob pulled him to his feet, their eyes met, and a hint of a smile on Jacob's face let Samuel know his brother's heart was softening.

Leah came to the doorway, carrying a tray with cups of coffee and slices of cake. When she saw the letters strewn around the floor and the fallen chair, fear crept into her eyes, and Samuel knew she thought they'd been fighting.

"Kumm." Samuel took the tray from her. "Don't worry about the mess. My story is the dogs did it."

Rhoda huffed, straightening her dress as she focused on Jacob. "Exactly who is he calling a dog?"

Jacob didn't respond, but it was clear that she was going to act as normal as possible until all three of them felt that way again. It was a worthy goal, and Samuel could only pray they'd reach it.

Rhoda bent and picked up a few letters.

"Ach, no." Jacob gently tugged on her arm. "Let's not have a repeat performance, especially with hot drinks in the room. Why don't you sit down, and I'll get the letters."

"Fine. Be that way. One little mishap, and everyone thinks I'm a complete klutz." She glanced at Samuel, and he caught a hint of a glimmer he hadn't seen in a while. Had she tripped on purpose?

Rhoda cleared off a spot on the desk, and Samuel set down the tray. Since there was no more room on the desk, she stacked the papers in a corner of the floor.

Leah whistled. "Mamm always said Jacob kept the messiest room in the house."

"I do. But this is a barn, decorated mostly by the lovely Rhoda Byler." Jacob set the stuff he'd collected on top of the filing cabinet.

Rhoda curtseyed to him, and Jacob's half smile was undeniable.

He pointed at the walkie-talkie on Leah's apron. "You've got what you wanted—all of us here without balking. You can turn that on again."

Leah's cheeks tinged with pink, but she did as he said before passing them each a plate with a slice of cake.

Samuel took a bite. "What's this about?"

"Well." Leah handed him a napkin. "Look around. Think about our daily work list. There's just too much for us to keep up with. Can anyone in this room deny that?"

"I will." Rhoda lifted her fork. "We *can* do it. We just haven't done so lately."

Leah cleared her throat. "I think we need to hire someone."

"Sure we do." Jacob took a sip of coffee. "When we can afford it and have time to interview people. Late summer. Maybe early fall."

Leah grimaced. "We don't have that long."

"What do you mean?" Samuel asked.

"I've hired someone. She'll be here in just a bit."

"You what?" Samuel plunked his plate on the tray. "What are you talking about?"

Leah explained everything.

Rhoda's fork clanked against her plate as she pushed it away from her. "That was inappropriate. We know nothing about this girl. We don't have any money to pay her. And you may have just invited trouble, as if we haven't had more than our fair share lately."

Leah turned to Jacob. "Every one of us knows we need help. Rhoda was going to run an ad in *The Budget*."

"Whoa." Rhoda motioned for Leah to hush. "That was going to be for a specific type of help when the harvest began. Months from now. We'll have a product to sell and some cash flow to hire one really good worker by then."

"But we need someone now. See all the stuff stacking up in this office?" Leah looked to each of them.

"No one can tend to this except one of us three." Rhoda gestured at Samuel and Jacob.

Samuel was sure she was being diplomatic. Except for the occasional quick job of accounting, Jacob had never been one for paperwork, and after being gone so much, he wouldn't know where to start. How many of Rhoda's responses had been carefully weighed since Jacob returned as she aimed to create peace?

Leah focused on Jacob, her steady ally when she wanted her way. "Phoebe needs more help with meals and laundry than I can give her, unless you don't want me to work in the field."

Jacob nodded. "Leah's right about us needing help."

"And I'm not?" Rhoda took Jacob's empty plate. "There isn't money to hire anyone else, and we know absolutely nothing about this girl." She placed it on the tray with a clang. "What are the chances of this woman being the right person?"

Leah fidgeted with her apron. "You didn't interview me, and I've worked out pretty well. Why wouldn't Iva?"

"You're selling yourself short to think just anyone can do what you do. You're a perfect fit inside a hot canning kitchen day after day." Rhoda brushed crumbs into the trash can. "And I most certainly did interview you, starting the first day we met. It's just that none of us realized it at the time."

Leah seemed surprised by Rhoda's confidence in her. In the distance a car door slammed. "Landon's back already?"

Jacob went to the window. "Ya. And he's got the girl with him. She doesn't look old enough to legally leave home."

Rhoda sighed. "Leah, what have you done?"

EIGHT

Iva got out of the truck, clutching the front of her coat. Her research had said the April temperatures in Maine and Indiana were similar, but it felt a lot colder here. She grabbed her suitcase and followed Landon.

She had recharged her camera battery and taken lots of pictures during a four-hour layover at Union Station in Washington. While waiting in Bangor for Landon to pick her up, she had walked around and snapped a few more. But when he arrived, he seemed shocked that she had a camera, so she shoved it and the tripod into her suitcase. If he reacted that way as an Englisch man, she wasn't about to let these Amish see it. She needed to make a good first impression, but now her ancient carrying bag was quite heavy and bulging.

Landon pulled out his walkie-talkie. "Leah?"

"We're in the office."

"Okay." Landon motioned for Iva to follow him. "They're in the barn. You need some help with that?"

"No, I'm good. Thanks." But her arms ached as she carried the bag.

Between her exhaustion and nerves, Iva's whole body trembled, making even walking a challenge. She had left home more than forty-eight hours ago, changed trains three times, and would have slept until morning if she could've curled up in a corner at the station.

The peeling red paint of the barn caused a thrill to run through her. She'd seen such barns before, but this one would make a gorgeous photo. She turned a full circle while walking, seeing the old farmhouse and a wagon hitched to a horse and a few apple trees in the distance.

She itched to get shots of the new scenery. Although the buildings were in need of paint and repair, to her the place was absolutely gorgeous. Actually, the more scarred and worn the subject, the more fascinating she found it. Character, that's what made an image endearing. Still-life subjects were fascinating, although animals made for interesting pictures too. She rarely took a snapshot of people, partly because the Amish frowned on such things and partly because inanimate objects awakened her appreciation of the world too few seemed to notice.

Once in the barn she spotted an old shoe nailed to a wall, and she couldn't take her eyes off it. Landon went through a narrow door, and she followed him, studying which angle would give her the best light to capture the shoe on the wall.

When her suitcase bumped hard against the doorframe, she was jolted out of her thoughts. "My camera!" As soon as the words left her mouth, she gasped.

Landon took her suitcase. "I'm sure it's fine. I'll put this somewhere in a moment." He motioned as he spoke. "This is Leah King, her brothers Samuel and Jacob. And this is Rhoda Byler."

Iva looked from one man to the other before her eyes locked with one of them. "There's no denying you're brothers."

Leah frowned. "They don't look that much alike. Do they?"

No one answered. Except for Leah, they all seemed speechless.

Iva searched for something to say to break the ice. "I saw all of you, except him"—she pointed to the man standing next to Rhoda, unsure which one was Samuel and which was Jacob—"on television when you got the news that Rhoda had been cleared of the lies those girls told, right?"

Leah glanced to Landon before returning her focus to Iva. "Indiana Amish watch TV?"

"Oh no, but I used to clean house for an Englisch woman before she got laid off, and she recorded the news and showed it to me one day."

Jacob extended his hand. "You didn't see me. I'm Jacob."

Iva shook his hand. "Ah, the one who wasn't questioned by the bishop for being seen on television, right?"

"Actually"—Rhoda pressed her fingertips against the desk—"we don't have a bishop or a preacher. Not yet."

"Really? No wonder I liked the idea of coming here."

When Rhoda's eyes widened and her startled face turned to Samuel, Iva realized how her statement sounded. What must they be thinking about her now? "Beneath everyone's love and respect for the church leaders is a desire not to have to answer to them on occasion." She stared into blank faces. "I guess that could just be me. It seems I've managed to put both feet in my mouth."

Jacob glanced at Rhoda and chuckled. "She fits right in. A bit clumsy, colors outside the Amish lines by owning a camera, and is drawn to avoid church leaders at least once in a while."

"Is that who we are?" Rhoda's brows furrowed as she studied Jacob.

He nodded. "Afraid so. Don't you think?"

Rhoda pursed her lips. "Ya, I suppose it is. But it's not our intention or our goal." She took a seat behind the desk. "Iva, it was good of you to come all this way. Would you care to sit?" She gestured to a chair.

Iva sat, feeling very much on the hot seat. "I thought I was going to be traveling by train for just a day, but I read the tickets wrong. I've been traveling for more than two days straight. The view and the layovers were nice, though. Interesting."

"Did you get some good shots?" Jacob asked.

She tried to suppress her enthusiasm. It'd been a wonderful couple of days of capturing on her digital camera things she'd never seen before. But now that she didn't have access to her Englisch neighbor, she wasn't sure how she'd upload images or recharge the batteries. "I think so."

Rhoda looked to Samuel. Was she waiting for him to speak up?

When he said nothing, Rhoda cleared her throat. "Iva, how old are you?"

"Twenty-one."

Surprise flickered across Rhoda's face. Iva was used to that. Most people thought she looked seventeen at the most. "I have proof if you—"

"Nee." Rhoda shook her head. "I believe you."

Iva was relieved, because her proof was a driver's license, which probably wouldn't endear her to them.

Rhoda tapped her fingers on the desk, seemingly reluctant to speak her mind. "I'm sure you need some rest, and dinner will be ready soon, but there's been a mistake. We simply aren't in a position to hire."

"Please. I just arrived. My Mamm spent all she had to get me here."

"Why would she…" Rhoda's countenance radiated disbelief. "I'm sorry. That's none of my business. But—"

"But," Jacob interrupted, "we can talk about the job aspect a little later." He picked up the tray and handed it to Leah. "Why don't you show Iva to the empty bedroom."

"Empty?" Rhoda shifted, looking up at Jacob.

Iva sensed his words bothered her. "If it's being used, I'm willing to sleep anywhere, even in the barn." She lifted the tray from Leah. "I know I've not said the right things, and I've probably made a bad impression, but if you'll give me a chance, you'll find I'm a hard worker."

"I'm sure you are." Rhoda's gentle smile added to the sympathy mirrored on her face.

Jacob picked up a stack of mail and eased it in front of Rhoda. "Maybe we need to be more ready to hire someone than we are."

"Maybe." Rhoda nodded. "But there isn't any money right now."

What? If they didn't have money to pay her, why had she come? How would she ever get home? Her Mamm couldn't send any money. Besides, Iva would rather earn the right to stay than have them figure out a way to send her back home. If she went back, her Daed would start pressuring her again to marry Leon. If barely liking him wasn't enough reason to remain single, she also wasn't interested in marrying a man mired in grief.

"I don't mind the money." Iva shifted the tray. "At least not for now. If I have a place to stay and food, I'm better off than most."

Rhoda nodded. "That's a very kind offer, but…" She turned to Landon. "Would you take her luggage to the *empty* bedroom? Leah, see that she meets Phoebe and gets fresh towels and something to eat."

Iva thanked them for letting her stay and left the office, trying not to cry.

What if, come tomorrow, they told her to go home?

Rhoda turned to Jacob, tempted to share her disappointment. He was ready to hire the girl full-time *and* give her Rhoda's bedroom. Was he never going to invite her back home? "So now what?"

Jacob closed the door. "I think she should stay."

Rhoda already knew that much. Needing something to do other than stare at Jacob, she began looking through the pile of mail. "You think that because you have a good heart. I appreciate that about you, but we can't afford her." Not daring to look at Samuel, she sorted letters to her into one pile. "Samuel?"

"There's no way we'd consider hiring someone we know this little about if she hadn't just shown up. We have far more questions than answers. I don't like it. Leah let herself get talked into something, and I say Iva stays for a day or two to get some rest, and then we send her home."

"And use what to purchase her ticket? Our good looks?" Jacob asked.

Rhoda held up a few envelopes. "We're still getting money from folks who want to help because of all the legal trouble. We haven't used any of it yet."

"There's no reason to use it to send Iva home."

Jacob had more compassion than wisdom, but this was hard to believe. Rhoda straightened a stack of envelopes. "Look at what came from three girls who used our greenhouses to party. It turned into a nightmare. Why would this girl's mother send her to beg off strangers unless Iva isn't as eager to please as she'd have us believe?"

Jacob put his hand on the mail in front of her. "You're both being skittish because of all Rhoda's been through."

Rhoda stared at him. "Don't you find the whole thing strange?"

"Sure. But the way we connected with you was odd too."

"I consider how we came together to have been a God thing."

"And it's too early to say this isn't one too."

Rhoda rose, gazing into Jacob's eyes. "Why are you so much in favor of her staying?"

"I think we should talk alone."

Samuel got up.

"Samuel, wait." She turned. "Jacob, he should be a part of this discussion." That was putting it mildly. Samuel *was* Kings' Orchard long before she joined them and during the years Jacob was absent, working for his uncle and then traveling on his own.

She couldn't believe Jacob wanted Samuel to leave what was clearly a business meeting. "I know that Samuel and I have lost most of our power business-wise and, in many ways, relationshipwise. We can't even breathe for fear of angering you. But you can't possibly make a decision about Iva without Samuel being in the room."

"Is that what you think? That *you're* powerless?"

She saw it in his eyes. Her words described how he felt. "You just gave away my bedroom. The farmhouse is my home. You haven't even mentioned me returning. And then you offer my room to a perfect stranger."

"She needed a place to stay."

"And what about what *I* need, Jacob? Do you even have a clue what that is?"

Samuel went to the door. "This is becoming personal, so I'll go. But I'd like to remind both of you of something. Jacob, Rhoda did nothing wrong." He turned the handle. "Rhoda, Jacob did nothing wrong. I don't know what else to say." He closed the door behind him.

Silence hung in the air, and yet Rhoda heard condemnation loud and clear. If Samuel thought she was faultless, he was fooling himself. She remembered every second of being in his arms, and the feelings of those few moments haunted her.

Jacob owned her heart, so why couldn't she get her flesh free of that memory with Samuel? Without a confidant the mess might stay a confusing jumble inside her brain. Would it ever fade? Would it become one more grief she had to learn to live with?

Jacob went to the file cabinet and began gathering items from it. "You don't trust my opinion anymore?"

She could ask him the same thing. Instead, she flipped through the mail.

"Kumm on, Rhodes. *We* need Iva here."

"What do you mean?"

"I overheard some of what you said to Samuel about Nicole. And it sounded to me as if you're jealous of her."

"What?" Her raised voice made hurt flicker through his eyes. She took a breath, determined to measure her tone as well as her words. "Even if that were true, and it's not, I don't see what that has to do with Iva."

"Then look again. If I try hard enough, I can make myself believe that your attitude about Nicole comes from your fear that an Englisch woman has an eye for a lonely Amish man. But what am I supposed to think now that you want to keep Iva away from him just as much?"

"You're supposed to realize I'm being practical. We know nothing about Iva. We can't afford her. And her mother paid good money to send her to a community that doesn't know her and may be desperate enough for help to let her stay. Your forte is math. Add up those facts, and tell me we should open up our lives to that."

"There are other things that need to be factored in." He moved to the office door. "She came in facing this direction. You and I were directly in front of her. Leah was to her left, and Samuel was on the far side of Leah. Yet the only person Iva saw when she came in was Samuel. Their attention seemed glued for a bit, and maybe I'm seeing what I need to, but I think there were sparks."

She didn't see any of that, but it was possible Iva was caught off guard by Samuel's presence. Rhoda was when she first met him. Of course she was also frustrated and annoyed by him. "He doesn't want her here either. You heard him."

Jacob strode back to her. "Of course not. He's looking at it strictly from a business perspective."

"That's the only one that matters where Iva is concerned."

He sat on the corner of the desk, facing her. "I don't like that you're so against her staying."

She put down the mail and leaned back in her chair. "You gave her my room, not just for a night or two, but in hopes she'll stay. How do you expect me to react?"

He angled his head, studying her. "Your feelings are hurt."

She swallowed hard, embarrassment creeping up her neck. "I'd hoped you'd invite me to move back home."

He drew a deep breath. "I know it's been only a couple of days, but I like picking you up in the mornings and taking you home in the evenings. It's the closest thing to a courtship we've ever had. And..."

"And what?"

He shook his head. "Never mind."

"Don't do that. Finish your thought."

"I don't want you and Samuel under the same roof, where by the time anyone else in the house is up, you two have shared half a pot of coffee and an hour of conversation. I don't want to wake during the night wondering if you've bumped into him while getting a glass of water. It's not a good situation for now."

"Jacob." She stood and cradled his face. She wanted to kiss him. It'd be their first since before he'd left to go into hiding in mid-January.

"It's how I feel." The sadness in his eyes made her ache.

Would things between them ever be as they once were? "If you need me to stay at Camilla's, then that's what I'll do." She smiled. "I have to admit, your coming to pick me up is fun. I woke last night looking forward to it. But hiring Iva and letting her stay—"

"Until other Amish move here, we're a tiny settlement. Your brother has Phoebe and their children. Leah has all of us, including Landon. You and I are starting to really talk again, and Samuel has no one he can open up to."

Rhoda sighed. "Unless Iva stays."

"Exactly."

She was tired of the unrest between her and Jacob. With the months of silence when he'd been absent and the weeks of stilted conversation because of what had happened with Samuel, their relationship had been prickly for too long. Still, she wasn't ready to just surrender. "I'll agree on one condition. I want to be free to work with Samuel again."

Jacob's green eyes bore into her, his gentle nature so evident. "It's hard to believe you'd even bring up such a thing. It's more than business. It's a friendship. Isn't my friendship enough?"

"Is mine?"

"Absolutely."

"You say that, but in all the time I've known you, I'm not the one you share everything with. But it doesn't diminish what we have between us or how much you love me. Does it?"

He played with her fingers, running his hand across her calluses as he mulled over an idea he clearly didn't like. "Rhodes..."

"Samuel and I must be able to work together, to talk and yell and maybe even laugh. It makes me feel sick to have to avoid him or to have only a brief, stiff conversation where nothing is accomplished."

Jacob stared into her eyes, and she could see how much he loved her. "Okay." It came out as a whisper, and he looked more resigned than accepting. "I can understand that."

Joy stirred inside her for the first time since Jacob had come back. Was it possible there would be healing for the three of them?

"I love you, Jacob."

He gazed into her eyes, a tender smile curving his lips. "You've never said that before."

She hadn't, mostly because his past kept raising its ugly head and causing her to move slowly and carefully. But she did love him. "I should have."

He eased his face closer to hers. When his lips were mere inches from hers, she couldn't see anything but Samuel. In this very room, so close she could hear his heart thumping, sense the strength of his feelings for her.

She wanted to pull away from Jacob so the memory would stop, but if she did, it might ruin all the work they'd done to get to this point.

Her thoughts were broken by the dogs' barking and a horn blasting.

Jacob took a breath, his warm hands still cradling her face. "We need a vacation."

She chuckled. "Think so?"

He moved to the window.

"Who is it?"

"Sandra."

"Here?" Rhoda peered out the window. She wanted a good look at this mystery woman, but she could only see flowing dark hair. The dogs circled the car, barking.

"It's my fault. I should've returned her calls."

"What does she want?"

"Forgiveness." He sighed. "I need to talk to her alone first."

"You do what you need to. Isn't she going to get out?"

"Not with the dogs right there. She has a phobia of them."

Rhoda rested her hand on his chest. "Are you getting your past sorted out?"

"I'm working on it. Even hired a lawyer, but he wants things of me I'm not sure I'm willing to give."

"You have to. For us."

He stared into her eyes, and she saw determination replace reluctance. "You're right." He wrapped her hand with his. "We'll talk about what's going on with her later, okay?"

"I'll always be here, waiting for you."

An endearing boyish grin lit his face. He pulled the walkie-talkie out of his pocket. "Samuel."

"Ya."

"Rhoda needs to see you in the office after dinner. There is a ton of mail to discuss and work plans to go over." By using the two-way, he had let everyone know that he approved of Samuel and Rhoda working side by side again. He slid the radio into his pocket.

"Denki."

He kissed her on the forehead. "We're gonna get to where we were before I left here, and when we do, we'll keep right on going until our grandchildren are awed to see what real love is." He smiled. "Now go eat, and then get busy before we drown in letters and paperwork."

Disappointment and relief warred within her as he left the office. She'd wanted a real kiss, and yet she'd been unable to lean into his embrace. It had to be guilt from when she'd been in this same room in Samuel's arms. Rhoda closed her eyes. That had to be it.

She couldn't even stand to think about what else it might be.

NINE

Samuel finished climbing the stairs to the second floor of the farmhouse, clasping the walkie-talkie. What Jacob had said on the two-way wasn't the end result he'd expected when he'd left the office. But the proclamation had sent relief and happiness bouncing around inside him. Maybe he and his brother would weather this storm.

He went to Rhoda's old room and tapped on the door. What agreement had Jacob and Rhoda come to?

"Kumm," Iva said.

Samuel eased open the door. She stood at the dresser folding some items before putting them in a drawer. Her head covering was oval rather than heart shaped, and her apron, which didn't have a bib, matched her dress. Other than that, it seemed the Indiana Old Order Amish were similar to the Pennsylvania Amish...or rather what was now the Maine Old Order Amish.

She shook out a pair of stockings and began neatly rolling them. "Did you find any hangers?" She glanced up and gasped, almost dropping the stockings. "I...I thought you were Leah."

It was really nice for someone in this house to look at him without a hint of suspicion. "I can't say I usually have that effect on people."

"I'm sure you don't." She shoved her stockings into the drawer and slammed it shut. "Your hands are too hairy."

He laughed, looking at his hands. They weren't very hairy. "That's the only difference?"

She shrugged, making a face. "Speaking of hands, did you come with news of my future in yours?"

He held them out. "No news." He glanced at them. "Just dirt." He rubbed at the stains, but they didn't come off. "I want to apologize for your coming all this way only to learn the job isn't a done deal."

"There was no misunderstanding. Not really. I knew there was only a chance of employment."

"That's good." What were her circumstances that she'd travel for days on just the possibility of getting a job? "Phoebe sent me to tell you that supper will be ready in about fifteen minutes. We're hoping you'll join us, but if you're too weary, we understand. Someone will bring you a tray."

She froze. "I'd love to join everyone at dinner." She choked up a bit. "Sorry. You're all just so kind."

Samuel didn't feel they'd been particularly welcoming, but maybe they'd exceeded her expectations. "We try to be very well mannered—at least until someone's second day."

She ducked her head, perhaps trying to hide a smile. "Is that an invitation for me to be gone before daylight?"

"No, of course not." Samuel determined to keep a straight face. "It becomes the next day at midnight. Why would you wait until dawn?"

After a quick laugh she reeled in all hints of finding him humorous. "May I at least eat first?"

"That's why I tapped on your door."

"I'd like to go on down now. Maybe Phoebe could use a hand."

"It's not necessary, but if that would make you feel better…" Samuel gestured for her to leave the room.

When they stepped onto the landing, Rhoda was coming their way. His heart thudded. If she were in a relationship with anyone except his brother, Samuel would pursue her without ceasing.

The three of them halted.

Rhoda offered a warmer smile than when Iva had first arrived. "Will your accommodations suit you if you stay?"

"Ya." Iva's eyes lit up. "I could be perfectly happy with that room."

Rhoda nodded, and Samuel studied her. If only he could catch a few minutes alone with her to see what was up. He was pretty sure that's what she wanted too.

He stepped toward the wall of the long, narrow landing. "Iva, we'll see you downstairs."

"Sure." She scurried away.

Rhoda put her back toward the banister. "If you don't mind, we'd like for her to stay."

We? Samuel didn't believe Rhoda had changed her mind. Who would want anyone hired in the manner Iva had been? "If you can live with it, I can."

"Gut. Denki. Jacob thinks it's a wise decision."

"And what do you think?"

"It worked out as it needed to while I got to a really good place with Jacob."

"Meaning?"

"He's agreed that you and I can talk and work together."

"But you're not moving back in?"

"No. That and Iva are my part of the bargain."

"I should be the one to move out. The only reason I haven't mentioned it before is because I didn't want to stir Jacob's suspicion about the nature of our relationship."

"You were wise to keep those thoughts to yourself. Besides, where would you go that wouldn't cost money we don't have? Landon's? I can't see that being sensible. You and Landon aren't made for sharing close quarters. He's on his computer so much, surfing the Net, as he calls it, sometimes with music going while watching television. And an owner of a business shouldn't need to beg a room from an employee. We have enough strange things going on with employees as it is." She smiled, looking a little less burdened. "The upside is I really like Camilla and Bob."

"And Iva?"

"I'm sure she's a lovely person, but it's too early to tell how she'll do."

"Jacob wants Iva here because he's hoping I'll like her, isn't he?"

She nodded. "Or that she'll be a distraction or just a friend to talk to. If I have to hire a hundred single girls that we can't afford in order to help Jacob overcome what we put him through, it's a small price to pay."

Now he understood her reasoning. "I agree."

Her eyes met his for just a moment before she looked the other way. She seemed lost for a moment before the dogs started barking, catching her attention. She went down the landing toward the alcove that had a window overlooking the driveway.

He followed her. She peered out before stepping to the side so Samuel could look.

Jacob was behind the steering wheel and pulling out of the driveway.

"That's Sandra." She studied the car. "Casey is in a car seat in the back. I met them briefly before coming inside. He said they needed to talk."

It seemed odd that Jacob hadn't invited them in to at least get a drink of water and use the bathroom. But Samuel wouldn't point that out. Driving a car wasn't the Amish way, but since Jacob had yet to be baptized into the church, and because he was trying to get his life straight so he could join the faith, Steven would say little if anything to him.

Samuel glanced at Rhoda. "Steven will become an official preacher soon with all the authority that comes with it. Jacob isn't doing himself any favors by driving off with an Englisch woman."

"My brother won't have to be patient much longer. Jacob all but promised he'd confess his wrongs and begin instruction as soon as his legal troubles were squared away."

That must have been quite a bartering session between you two, Samuel thought, and he wondered how Rhoda really felt about all the concessions she'd had to make. "I never wanted to do anything that would undermine you and Jacob."

"I know. I think somewhere inside, Jacob does too." She watched the car disappear. "No more guilt about it. Jacob and I will be stronger in the long run." She stepped away from the window. "May I be completely honest?"

"If you think it will help."

"I want and need both of you in my life." She paused. "I'll marry Jacob, but I don't want to be without your friendship."

How could he feel such relief for her and Jacob while struggling with so much heartache at the same time? "I understand."

"And you'll need to forgive my bossiness,"—she smoothed her apron— "but I have to speak my mind."

"I can take it. Dish it out."

"Don't ever again leave me in the lurch because you're busy walking on eggshells with Jacob."

"I haven't done that."

"You most certainly have. I was the only one telling Leah she shouldn't have had Iva come here expecting to get a job, and I was the only one standing against Jacob—for all the good it did me. But you didn't say a word until I asked for your opinion."

"Damage control with Jacob is more important than having a say in business matters."

"Figure out how to do both." Her tone and the seriousness on her face indicated she wasn't kidding.

Clearly his milder, gentler approach concerning the orchard annoyed her. Despite the recent issues between Jacob and him, she wanted him to lead as needed, but he didn't like her tone. "Should I salute now? Or bow?"

"Spare me any smart-alecky responses." Her half smile ignited another round of sparks in him. "And you need to talk to Leah. She can't pull anything like this again. It was all I could do to remain polite about it."

"I'll talk to her."

Did Rhoda know that Jacob had wavered in his support of the farm, that if he didn't have a change of heart, he might prefer for Samuel to sell the place?

He wouldn't hint at what Jacob had said. His brother could've been blowing off steam. But Samuel didn't want her shocked if he did have to sell it. "There's a lot stacked against us—financially."

"Of course there is." She ran her apron over the windowsill, removing some dust. "We knew before we arrived here that no one except Landon would draw a salary until the harvest. But we're still receiving gifts of money from our families, your district, and even strangers. That, along with our savings, is enough to keep the mortgage paid and food on the table, right?"

When he didn't answer immediately, she looked stunned. Since coming to Maine, she had been absorbed in nurturing the orchard, surviving the turmoil of the drug allegations, and adjusting to the ever-changing circumstances of Jacob's past. When she had run her own business, she and Landon had taken care of everything: product, marketing, and finances. But when she'd joined the much larger Kings' Orchard, she had focused on her strengths: horticulture and canning.

"Samuel?"

His eyes rested on the little handprints on the wall behind her, probably from the children playing in this nook. "We've gone through all our savings. Yours, mine, and Jacob's."

"What? How's that possible?"

"There wasn't a lot left after I closed on this place, and since our arrival here, everything that could go wrong has gone wrong."

She angled her head, staring at him in disbelief. "Jacob's the accountant in all this. He knew we'd be without an income until the first harvest."

Samuel slid his hands into his pockets. "He'd factored in that we'd all do something to bring in a little income, only one day a week or less, but it would've added up. He thought he could pick up a few remodeling jobs nearby, assuming Landon could be his driver. Since Steven is a handyman by trade, we thought he could do that around town a few times a week. Phoebe had planned on baking pies and cakes with Leah and selling them to local stores. Leah could've made children's clothes and sold them at a consignment shop. I could've given horseback riding lessons. You could have sold herbs or herbal teas, but the police confiscated everything from the greenhouses. Nothing has worked out in our favor. Because no other Amish families moved in to help with the farm work and because Jacob was gone, we've only had time for one thing: restoring the apple orchard."

He'd hoped his long explanation would give Rhoda a little perspective, but she massaged her temples. "We haven't even tackled the canning kitchen issue yet. I received a letter from the state saying I can't get a business license to sell goods that are canned in a kitchen where daily meals are prepared for a family."

Samuel gazed out the window. Should they just give up? If they sold everything, the place might bring a profit. At the least they might break even. Jacob and Steven had made repairs to the house and outbuilding. Samuel and Rhoda had the orchard in better shape than they'd expected.

She snapped her fingers. "Hello?"

He pulled from his thoughts and looked at her.

"There's a solution, right? There has to be. We need a canning kitchen and the means to make ends meet until we can earn some money off the harvest."

As she stared at him, her eyes beseeching him for answers, he realized what he could do. Why hadn't he thought of it before unloading the stress of the situation on her? He could sell some of the farm acreage in Pennsylvania. He'd need to talk to his Daed, but Samuel knew he would easily agree if that's what it would take to get them through the first harvest. In all Samuel's days of tending Kings' Orchard in Pennsylvania, he'd never once been willing to sell an acre of it. Before leaving Pennsylvania, they'd done what they could to begin the restoration from the tornado damage. His youngest brother, Eli, was there, tending it and helping their Daed with the small dairy farm. In about five years that orchard should be producing well again.

Still, he hated the thought of selling even one blade of grass. But he'd do it. There was a neighbor who'd said he'd buy a few acres that connected their properties. His Daed wouldn't like it. If the orchard side of the farm had acreage to spare, his Daed would want to use it for the cows.

"Ya." Samuel nodded. "Now that you've needled me, I think there is a way. Are you sure you want to make a go of it here? After the stress I've caused between—"

"Am I sure? A better question is, have you lost your mind? How can you even ask that?"

His heart leaped with enthusiasm. This was the motivation he needed. If Rhoda was still fully committed to this orchard, so was he. He'd let guilt lie to him. Holding on to this farm wasn't in Jacob's hands.

He smiled. "I know what needs to be done."

Her love of this orchard was contagious. Surely she would infect Jacob with those same desires.

"Gut." Relief changed her countenance. "Whew. You had me worried."

The walkie-talkie crackled. "To all who can hear me, we're ready to eat," Phoebe announced.

Rhoda rubbed her belly and moved toward the stairs. "It may take me a few minutes to get my appetite back."

"Rhoda…"

"Ya?" She paused.

He wanted to thank her for sticking by him, for sacrificially bartering with Jacob, for fighting to keep their friendship. He wanted to thank her for making him believe in himself and Kings' Orchard Maine again. But those thoughts also made him want to challenge her to take another look at who they could be together.

"You mentioned possibly hiring a hundred single girls. I think I like that idea."

She glanced his way, looking as if he were full of nonsense.

"What?" He shrugged. "Can't you work on that right away?"

She chuckled.

Samuel smiled. They were in about as good a place friendshipwise as they could be.

Now if his affection for her would fade into nothingness, he could return to being the man he once was—focused on the practical side of life and making this settlement a success.

TEN

Jacob clutched the wheel. He needed to be alone with Sandra to talk about the lies she'd spent years telling him. Leaving the farm would help some, but what he had to say shouldn't be said in front of Casey either.

"Ache-up." Casey sang his name. "Did you miss me?"

Jacob looked in the rearview mirror at the little raven-headed angel. He'd gotten her out of the car for a few minutes, hugging her and gazing into her eyes while she clapped her hands and laughed. Then he'd buckled her in again and climbed behind the wheel. She was so excited to see him. Right now, she had only the best parts of her mother. Jacob hoped to be there for her, keeping Sandra buoyed enough to cope with her bipolar disorder in a way that was healthy for Casey.

Neither of Sandra's parents had been even a half-decent person. By the time she was a teen, her dad had kicked her out of the house. Jacob didn't doubt Sandra was a handful even then, but her parents hadn't realized she needed help and support, not a boot in the backside. He doubted they were the kind of people who could've helped her even if they'd known. Could dysfunctional alcoholics see anything beyond their own stupor?

He reached across the seat and touched Casey's cheek. "I missed you every minute of every day." It was their pat answer, a game of sorts. His desire to see that she made it to adulthood safely was strong, but it had to come second to getting his life straight with the law. Rhoda needed that from him, and he wouldn't let her down.

She'd only grown close to Samuel because he had been absent. He'd only been absent because of the mistakes he'd made years ago and because Sandra had lied to him. Right before returning to the farm, Jacob had met with a lawyer, Craig Ryer. Jacob had taken what little bit of paperwork he had to back up his story, and he'd told Craig every stinking bit of the whole mess.

It had been embarrassing, but Craig had listened without flinching. He took notes, did some research, had his assistant make some calls, and then explained his theory—that Jacob wasn't as legally culpable as he'd thought. And Craig said he'd stake his reputation on the fact that Sandra had been lying to him.

When Jacob had returned his lawyer's call a couple of days ago, Craig had said there was a civil suit in Virginia about the deck collapse, but it hadn't gone to court yet because of numerous delays. Skeet Jones, the owner of the construction company Jacob had worked for, had already gone to trial. He'd been found guilty and sentenced, but Jones was appealing the verdict.

Craig had said the district attorney would likely give Jacob immunity in exchange for his testimony. He was going to check into that and let Jacob know. Craig also volunteered to find him a lawyer in Virginia who could represent him. Jacob wasn't seen as negligent for his part in the collapsed decks, but Craig added, "If I were you, I'd want to know why Sandra's been lying all this time because, depending on her answer, you could be aiding and abetting a criminal."

Jacob shook his head. *Who could ever know if she's telling the truth?*

The lawyer had said, "With what I now understand of this case, if I could question her directly, I think I could get to the bottom of it. I'd at least have a good hunch concerning her involvement."

Jacob pulled his thoughts back to the present, turning on an iPod that was attached to the car radio. Winnie-the-Pooh songs filled the car. He didn't need to ask Sandra why she'd come to the farm or what she wanted from him. He knew her answer. After adjusting the speakers so the sound was fully in the back, he turned to Sandra. "How could you lie to me all this time?"

"What exactly did that lawyer say?"

"That you've been lying to me. He thinks if everything went wrong that could go wrong concerning the legal and civil cases involved, I'd get a year of probation at the most. But he's aiming to get me immunity in exchange for my testimony."

"He's wrong."

"So this is how it's going to play out? I'm loyal to you for years, support you financially, and you're going to continue to lie to me?"

"This is Blaine's fault. He's the one who lied to you."

Jacob knew that was true, but Sandra could have set the record straight before Jacob left the Englisch, convinced he had to return to his people to hide from the law.

"Baine bad. Hate him. Kick. Kick. Kick." Casey smiled, swinging her foot in the air.

Jacob sighed. "You shouldn't tell her those things. There's no reason for her to say she hates him."

"She doesn't know Baine, as she calls him, is her d-a-d."

"You'll have to tell her one day, and your hatred of her father will taint every good memory she'll have of your love. Is that what you want for her?"

"Your Amish roots are showing, Jacob. Children everywhere are able to separate what their parents feel for them from what the parents feel toward each other." She shook her head. "Besides, I'm careful. I was talking to her sitter, and Casey overheard me. She only says *kick* because she thinks that is the most horrible thing one person can do to another." She slouched against the car seat. "Boy, does she have a lot to learn."

Jacob glanced at Sandra.

She huffed. "I know. I get it. A parent's job is to protect a child's innocence for as long as possible." She shrugged. "I'll do better. I just need you in my life to be the best me I can be."

Jacob knew that. He'd known it since before she conceived Casey, and he'd seen to it she went to every doctor's visit throughout her pregnancy. He was never sure why it meant so much to him. But beneath his disdain for Sandra were certain things he admired about her. With all she'd been through, it amazed him she was sane and still standing. But she was more than that. Her priority was Casey, and he was awed by Sandra's dedication, even if they didn't share the same parenting values.

Sandra had adored Blaine—until he betrayed her and left her to pay for his misdeeds. Jacob would have sworn that Blaine loved her, but he hadn't taken into account that Blaine was addicted to gambling.

"You convinced me that Blaine set me up to take the fall for his crimes."

"If you hadn't thought that, you would've gone straight to the law." She cut a look at him. "Right before you left me and Casey behind forever."

"I wouldn't have abandoned you."

She stared out the window. "You already did. I had to come to you."

"Look at what your lies have done! I needed time, but I was going to call you. And years ago you threw *me* out. But I kept calling and sending money. You've got no right to whine about how I've handled the last few weeks. You've spent years turning my life upside down, Sandra."

"How? In what way is your life worse off because of a few lies? You returned home and were invisible to the law. You healed. You met Rhoda. And now you'll live happily ever after."

He didn't know if she really believed her lies had done good things or if she was just saying it to feel better. "I want you to talk to my lawyer."

"No way!"

He glanced in the rearview mirror.

Casey stopped playing with her hands. "What's wrong, Mama?"

"Nothing." She rolled her eyes. "Just your Ache-up wanting me to walk into a lion's den."

"He gives legal advice. He won't do anything I don't want him to."

"That *you* don't want him to?"

Jacob drew a slow breath at the suspicion in her tone. "I've earned more of your trust than that."

She studied him, and he knew a war was raging inside her.

He wouldn't push for an immediate answer. It was best to let her volunteer it.

She tapped her fingers against the door handle. "It's hard to trust someone who leaves, either physically or by giving the silent treatment, when he learns something upsetting."

If Jacob could change one thing about himself, he'd stand firm when trouble struck and deal with the bitter disappointment right then—not weeks, months, or years later. "Harder than forgiving someone who lies for years to get her way?"

"Maybe."

The woman beside him was as hardened as they came and yet as fragile as Casey. At least she had come to the house rather than give up on him.

He pulled into a parking spot near a café advertising pizza and sandwiches. "Hungry?"

Sandra's dark eyes pierced him. "If I see this lawyer of yours, after you hear what I have to say, you'll want to walk away and never come back."

"I've felt that way plenty of times since this whole mess began years ago. And rightly so. And yet here I am." He turned off the car. "But I have to know the truth from here on out, and that begins with you going with me to see my lawyer."

"He won't believe me."

It seemed a bit strange she wasn't focusing on whether it was a setup to send her to jail.

She stared, blank faced. "You'll side with him."

"Probably, but then we'll figure out the next step together."

"Maybe you want me to go to jail or be killed. Then you can look after Casey the easy way."

"I don't mean to be blunt, but are you taking your medication regularly?"

She glared at him, looking as insulted as she was angry, but then she nodded. "Yes."

"Have I ever asked you to give up Casey?"

"I do love her, you know."

"I know that, and she needs you. No one can take your place. No one."

She kept her eyes focused outside her window. "I think I do pretty good staying strong and steady for her, as you call it, with you only coming in and out as needed."

"Absolutely."

"A counselor once said the best way to stay strong is to understand yourself and your limitations." She licked her lips, seeming to struggle a bit with what she needed to say. "I know this about me: I can't stay determined to manage my bipolar issues unless you're there for me and Casey."

Her statement was actually a question. He ran his hand over the steering wheel, knowing he had to say the answer he could live with, not the one he'd like to give. There had to be ways to be there for Sandra while building a life with Rhoda. Otherwise, Casey would pay for his negligence. Why was Casey so important to him? "I won't abandon you."

She sobbed a quick wail of relief before taking a deep breath and regaining control. "Okay. I'll go."

He got out of the car and opened the back passenger door.

"Ache-up!" Casey clapped her hands and waved her arms for him to un-buckle her.

"Hi again, Casey." He got her out. "We're going to have to find that miss-ing *J* for Jacob again, aren't we?" He had worked with her before, and she could do it. She could do a lot of things with a little effort poured into her.

She stared at him with a haunting look—one that made him absolutely positive she had worlds to conquer as an adult, worlds that would help others in ways he couldn't wrap his mind around. But it could only happen if some-one made sure she got there in one piece. She hugged his neck, squeezing him with all her tiny power.

Jacob held her tight.

Sandra came around to the side of the car. "I'm really sorry, Jacob. You deserved better than what you got."

He closed the passenger door. "You did too."

She said nothing, but she had to know what he meant. Someone should have gotten help for her when she was a teen, not sent her packing. Someone should have loved her the way the two of them loved Casey.

"How about some food?"

Wiping at a tear, she went ahead of him and held open the door. "You're the best."

Her words hadn't come easily. He knew that. "Just remember thinking that when it's time to face the lawyer, okay?"

He hoped the man could get him immunity. If he could, Jacob would finally be free. If he couldn't, Jacob would have to continue to hide as much as possible.

ELEVEN

Leah opened Erlene's dryer and began removing another load of clothes. She glanced at Landon. "How is it that when I do laundry for your grandmother, I end up washing more of your clothes than hers?"

Landon opened the washing machine. "Just lucky, I guess."

She carried the dry clothes into the living room and dropped them onto the couch. More than a week had passed since Iva's arrival, and she seemed to be working out pretty well. Thank goodness. Other than Samuel telling Leah she could never make a decision like that on her own again, no one else had complained. She imagined that when Jacob and Sandra met with the lawyer next week, Samuel and Rhoda would get a feel for whether Iva was any real help or not. If she couldn't help take up for the slack caused by Jacob's absence, they'd know it pretty quickly.

Landon came into the room. "After the next load dries, we're done."

"Only with laundry. We're supposed to make a plate of cookies to take to Unity Hill tomorrow night."

"We? You're the one who added your name when they passed around the volunteer sign-up sheet."

She smacked him with a shirt. "It's a church event, and *you're* helping." She folded the shirt. "You go through too many clothes in a week. How do you manage to mess up four shirts a day?"

"Uh, messy eater?"

Erlene walked into the room with some hangers. "Because anything he's tried on ends up on the floor."

Leah's face froze. "Tried on? Is it that hard to decide what to wear when you're coming to work?"

Erlene set the hangers next to the clothes on the couch. "Ayeah." Erlene's Maine brogue came through thick this time. "He must've tried on eight shirts before picking you up tonight."

She gnawed on her lower lip, refusing to speak or smile. "Hmm."

"Well,"—Landon shrugged—"you didn't think I was perfect, did you?"

"I did. But I stand corrected."

Landon tried to pull the shirt out of her hand. "I'll do them myself."

She tugged back, and he let go, making her fall back on the couch.

"Seems to me you aren't standing at all." Landon grabbed another shirt from the pile. "And what is one of your faults I'm not aware of, Leah King?"

"I have none." She actually had a lot, but who confessed their flaws? Her biggest mistake was Michael Yoder, a lousy excuse for a man and an even worse boyfriend. She stood and snapped wrinkles out of the shirt. "Have you dated much?"

"Not really. I was an awkward teen, too shy around girls to ask anyone out. That whole fear of rejection thing ruled my life for a while."

"It's hard to believe you felt tongue-tied."

"Why, because I can't shut up?"

"Something like that, ya."

He dangled his keys in front of her. "It's a long walk home from here, Leah."

She eyed them, timing the moment before she snatched them.

"Whoa." He stared at her. "What are you, some kind of Houdini?"

The phrase sounded familiar, and she had no doubt he was quoting a line from television. It seemed to be his talent, and she wasn't very good at it. "I've never driven before." She clutched them tight, grabbed her coat, and headed for the front door. "I hope you have plenty of insurance."

"Me too." He turned toward the kitchen. "Hey, Gran, we're going out for a bit."

"Drive careful, honey."

"I'd like to be the one driving," he mumbled.

Leah hid her laughter and swooshed out the front door. She tossed the keys into the air while walking, but Landon plucked them in midair. "Hey."

"No, Leah. This isn't *hay*. These are *keys*, and if you don't know the difference, you shouldn't be driving."

"Give them back."

"Not happening."

She pushed him. "Now!" She held out her hand.

He dangled them high, and when she tried to grab them, she couldn't reach them. Their laughter echoed against the still night, and she couldn't imagine not being with Landon forever. She'd never known anyone more real.

"You win. This time." She went to his truck and leaned against it, staring into the vastness of the night sky. "But shouldn't I learn to drive?"

"If that's what you want. The laws are pretty specific, but it's just a matter of going through the steps. You'll need your birth certificate and Social Security number."

"I don't have either."

"Everybody has a birth certificate, don't they?"

"I was born at home."

"But the midwife should've registered the birth with the state. I'm pretty sure it's the law. Ask your brothers about it. Samuel had to have both to take out a mortgage. If they don't know about your birth certificate, ask your mom."

"It might cause her to ask a hundred questions."

"So?"

She shrugged. "And then she's likely to turn me down. Besides, I'm not used to being straightforward with my parents. Being sneaky or keeping my mouth shut is more my style with them."

"It sounds like maybe you don't really want a license."

"Are you giving up before we even try?"

"You're the one who doesn't want to answer a few probing, uncomfortable questions from your mom." He leaned into her shoulder. "Decide whether you're willing to pursue and pay the price for what you want. It seems to be what life is all about." He straightened. "I don't want to be the one talking you into or out of anything. You know?"

She was beginning to, and she liked the sense of trust he had in her. It was her life, her decisions, and he was there for moral support only. "You make it sound like talking to Mamm will be easy. But she'll believe I'm entering into sin to want a license. The thought of it will break her heart."

"Sounds like her idea of what constitutes sin is off the mark."

"How can you be so sure?"

"I'm not. Back in the day when my granny was a young woman, good manners and skilled social behavior were equal to godliness, and the lack of it was considered a sin. In her mother's day, using one's imagination was looked down on. To daydream was considered a sin. Does God really judge someone based on table manners or an inventive mind? *Or* for wanting to get a driver's license?"

Her heart suddenly felt as light as a helium balloon bouncing toward the sky as someone held tight to the tether. But she still didn't want to upset her Mamm. Just the thought of hurting her made Leah cringe. "Is there another way to get a birth certificate?"

"Maybe. Each state has centralized offices where a copy can be ordered, but that's only going to work if the midwife recorded your birth with the state."

"Let's check that out first." She shrugged. "That would make it easier to sidestep Mamm knowing what I'm really like."

His eyes fixed on her until he bent and picked up a rock. "You don't believe she likes you."

How had he nailed the way she felt so squarely? "It's my fault. I was born into a home with lots and lots of rules, and I didn't keep them. My parents love me, but their ability to like me is thin at best."

He didn't move for several moments. "If that's true, it's really sad. And it's their loss." He threw the rock across the road. "Is that how they feel about Jacob? He's a rule breaker too."

"It's different for guys. Parents expect them to be rowdy, and if they're a little less unruly than they could be, parents are pleased. Samuel stepped into my grandfather's shoes, loving the orchard from the time he was young, and they couldn't be more proud of who he is. Jacob loved carpentry, and although his leaving home to move to our uncle's bothered them, they were always pleased with his ability to build homes. My specialty was sarcastic wit and hiding in the hayloft to read novels. Mamm and Daed never really liked anything about me."

"Sarcastic wit is an art, best used on anyone except yours truly. And it seems to me most parents would be thrilled for their children to love reading. Mine were. As a kid, I could pick up *TV Guide,* and they'd get all twitterpated."

She laughed. "Get what?"

"I'm not telling, but the next movie on our list is *Bambi.*" He picked up a rock and held it out to her. "It helps to lob a rock as far as you can. Try it."

Her insides quaked from talking about her parents. Did Landon know that? "I may not do anything about getting a license for a while yet." She took the stone from him. "If I cause a fuss with my parents, it could alter what I can and can't do here in Maine. It's nice to have no one balking at me coming here or slipping away on Sunday nights."

"There's no pressure from me. If you want a license, I'll help you. If you never want a license, I'm sure my truck will be the safer for it." His chuckle warmed her insides.

He was too good to be true. She threw the rock as far as she could, and it barely made it to the edge of the road. But he was right; it did make her feel better. She grabbed another one and tossed it. It landed a few feet from the truck.

Landon chortled. "What was that?"

She tugged on his coat sleeve. "Our cue that it's time to make those cookies for tomorrow night."

"You do remember that it's also a church Sunday for you. The Amish church day will barely be over by the time you need to slip out the back door to go to Unity Hill."

"It's their special music night. I'm not missing that if I have to walk there."

He grinned. "You love that part most of all, don't you?"

"Does a horse have a tail?" She headed for the front door.

He followed her. "What does that have to do with anything?"

"A team of wild horses could not drag that answer out of me."

"What?"

"You heard it straight from the horse's mouth."

"If I'd let you drive my truck, could I have been spared all these horse sayings?"

"We'll never know, will we?"

Growing up Amish had limited Leah's choices in everything from hairstyles to clothing to education and beyond. But if she wanted it, Landon was willing to open the world to her.

Maybe she should jump at the chance to get a license, but right now she was content just knowing the door to her future was unlocked.

TWELVE

Night fell, and the horse's hoofs beat a steady, endearing pace in Rhoda's ear as the buggy jostled them down the empty road. Jacob held the reins loosely as he drove the rig. They'd had a wonderful Sunday evening thus far, and the awkwardness between them continued to melt. She had to admit, buggy rides with her beau were precious. "I thought Steven did a good job preaching the sermon today."

"Ya."

They'd had a perfect date night—board games and a walk in the orchard. Then they'd begun this carriage outing a couple of hours ago. He'd told dozens of jokes throughout their time together. But now he was really quiet. Had she done or said something that had offended or hurt him? "Did you have a favorite part of the sermon?"

"Not really. Seems like he could add a little humor." He slowed the rig as they came to a stop sign. "While he was talking about Adam and Eve, I thought of a joke I heard once. Adam was lonely, so God said He'd give him a companion, one who would cook and agree with every decision he made and bear children. Adam asked what the woman would cost, and God said an arm and a leg. So Adam asked what he could get for a rib."

She chuckled, but her mind was busy trying to piece together more of the puzzle that was Jacob King. "Maybe you could give him some pointers on how to lace his sermons with some laughter."

"I doubt he needs *me* offering tips about preaching." Jacob clicked his tongue, and the horse went through the intersection.

Despite the joke, his countenance seemed heavy. She slid across the seat, closing the space between them. "Jacob?" She caressed his jaw line. "Talk to me." She kissed his cheek. "Please."

He put his arm around her shoulders and squeezed. "Sorry. Sometimes the subject of God is an uncomfortable one." Lines in his handsome face constricted. "Most of the time, I guess."

"Why?"

"Ever heard this one? A father was at the beach with his children when his four-year-old son grabbed his hand and led him to the shore where a sea gull lay dead in the sand. 'Daddy, what happened to him?' the boy asked. The dad replied, 'He died and went to heaven.' The boy thought for a moment and then said, 'Did God throw him back down?'"

She couldn't help but laugh even though the joke didn't seem to be in line with their conversation.

Jacob turned onto another road, making his way toward the Cranfords'. "I haven't been able to really pray in years. I've felt as if God would throw me back down, breaking my bones and killing me in the process."

"Oh…" Her heart broke for him. "He wouldn't. You know that, right?"

He nodded. But that was a brush-off. How many times did he brush her off without her realizing it? Getting him to open up was never easy, but when he did talk candidly, it strengthened them.

She rested her head on his shoulder. "I need you to talk to me."

He drew a deep breath. "I've been a fool, Rhodes. An idiot. No one is saying it, and it hurts to admit it aloud, but you and everyone else at the farm know it's true."

"Nobody says that, because nobody is thinking that. You made some bad decisions as a teenager, and then Sandra lied for years in order to manipulate you."

He pulled into the Cranfords' driveway and drew the rig to a stop. "I appreciate you saying that. It helps. But I walked into that mess wanting to be a hero. Blaine needed supplies to finish building a few homes so they could go to closing and not breach any of the contracts. I figured out a solution, and even after I learned what I was doing wasn't legal, I kept on doing it. I tuned out every warning, and when I feared I would go to jail, I used my Amish roots to hide behind."

"You cared about your friends and tried to help. If that's wanting to be a hero, then we're all guilty of it."

"But they weren't friends, were they? Blaine was using me and my ignorance to cheat and steal from the construction company. As it turned out, the owner of the company and even Sandra were in on it. I keep asking myself over and over, why am I letting her stay in my life?"

"You must have at least one reason."

He closed his eyes. "Casey. The night she was born, when Sandra put her in my arms, I felt so sure she had a wonderful destiny, a good, productive future that others will draw from—if only she could reach adulthood strong enough to carry it out. Sandra loves her, but she struggles with bipolar issues and needs some kind of stabilizing force. For better or worse, that's what I am to her."

Rhoda snuggled against him. He hadn't told her that Sandra was bipolar. "That's plenty to know. And you're right. Casey needs you to be involved in her life."

He shifted, gazing into her face. "Do you really believe that?"

"You mean like when I knew your home was going to be destroyed by that tornado? No, not like that. I know it because you know it, and I trust you."

His blank stare eased into a grin. "Knowing all you know now, you still trust my judgment?"

"Absolutely. Although some of your corny jokes do make me wonder about you."

He tilted her chin and stared into her eyes. "You are the best thing that's ever happened to me, and I want to be that for you too."

"You are."

He smiled before kissing her lips. It was more like a peck, really, but it was genuine, and she was grateful for it.

She tugged on his coat. "It's only around eight. Why don't you come inside for a bit? Camilla's said you're welcome any time."

"Not tonight. I'd like to spend a little time alone with God."

Joy had her heart thudding. Oh, how she longed for him to be whole, with no blockades of guilt between him and God—and no dark secrets between him and her.

He set the brake. "Maybe *He* will appreciate my jokes."

"I think He's heard them already." She kissed his cheek. "I'll see you tomorrow morning." Once out of the rig and at the Cranfords' front door, she waved to Jacob as he drove away.

She tiptoed inside, expecting Bob and Camilla to be retired to their bedroom, either sleeping or watching television, but she noticed the living room lights were on. She passed her bedroom and went to speak to whoever was still up.

Camilla was in a wingback chair, smiling and talking. Bob was near her, and both were engaged in a conversation with someone Rhoda couldn't see. Bob was laughing and talking at the same time, relaying a story of some kind. She'd never heard him like this before. Maybe she should go on to bed since they had company.

Camilla spotted her. "Rhoda, dear." She gestured. "We were waiting for you."

"We?"

She stepped into the room, and fear shot through her. *Samuel!* She glanced behind her, making sure Jacob hadn't changed his mind about coming in. He wouldn't like his brother walking to the Cranfords' to see her. "What are you doing here?" She hoped she sounded polite enough since Bob and Camilla were in the room.

He rose. "We need to talk."

There was a cup and saucer on the end table beside him. He'd been here long enough to share at least one cup of coffee with the Cranfords. "Something that couldn't wait until tomorrow?"

"Maybe. I wasn't sure."

Camilla got up. "We'll give you two a few minutes, unless that's not enough and we should say good night now."

Rhoda's nerves were on edge. She didn't want to be alone with Samuel for one moment longer than necessary in case Jacob did return. "No, I'm sure we only need a few minutes."

Bob grinned. "Good. Samuel and I have been discussing the many ways one can fish in Maine."

While Bob and Camilla disappeared into the kitchen, Rhoda removed her coat. "I can't believe you did this."

"If Jacob finds out I'm here, he'll blame me, not you."

She hung her jacket on the coatrack. "That's no consolation. Is it supposed to be?" She was doing her best not to come between the brothers. They had been every bit as close as she and Emma. When she turned back toward Samuel, she saw Emma behind him.

Samuel looked over his shoulder. Apparently he'd read her face. Did he have any idea what she saw time and again? Would he think she was crazy? She shook off the vision.

"What's going on, Samuel?"

He gestured toward the couch, and Rhoda sat down.

Samuel leaned forward in the wingback chair next to her. "Your Daed called about ninety minutes ago."

"What's wrong?" She hadn't spoken to him in weeks, but she'd written. Letters kept her from slipping up and revealing more than she intended and also kept her Daed from hearing any uncomfortable tone or stress in her voice. He'd written to her too.

"Your Uncle James is in the hospital. He had a heart attack Saturday afternoon. When your Daed was called yesterday, they thought he might not make it—"

Her heart raced. "How is he?"

"There's only good news."

Relief eased through her, and she was glad Samuel had chosen to come to the house rather than call. It wasn't his words that brought her comfort as much as seeing in his eyes that he believed what he said.

Samuel sat back in his chair. "He's doing a lot better today than yesterday, so your Daed was glad about that. The doctors are going to do some kind of procedure and put him on medications. Both will help prevent him from having another heart attack, and he's expected to make a full recovery."

"Gut. I'm happy to hear it. My Daed and Uncle James are very close."

"As were you and your Daed. When you and I met, you were as close to him as any daughter I've ever seen. Don't you need to regain that?"

She wanted to. It just wasn't that simple. Since the day she'd left Pennsylvania, she'd had Jacob's secrets to hide. But she didn't appreciate Samuel questioning her about it, especially on the heels of the news he'd brought. "Is that why you came here? To correct me?"

Disbelief and frustration registered on his face. "I'm going to spare us an argument by ignoring that." He intertwined his fingers and let out a slow sigh. "There's one more thing. Your Daed phoned last night while you were out with Jacob, and he knows you're living here. He sounded hurt that you hadn't told him."

"What? How?"

"Iva didn't know it was a secret."

Rhoda was sick of the word *secret*. "Iva didn't need to know. We told her not to answer the phone. So why did she?"

"I asked her that, only more gently. She said she was in the office yesterday, and the phone kept ringing. He was ending his calls before the answering machine could pick up, and then he would call back. She thought it was an emergency."

"And clearly it was, but then she forgot to tell anyone?"

"He didn't mention your uncle to her. Your Daed simply told her to have you call him. She left a message on the desk, and she intended to tell Jacob when he arrived home, but he came in late, and she was asleep. Then today, with it being a church Sunday, no one went to the office, and Iva didn't think to relay it. When your Daed didn't hear from you, he tried again. This time I was in the barn feeding the livestock, so I picked up."

"I'll call my Daed before going to bed."

Samuel propped his chin on his fist. "When you started working with us in Harvest Mills, you called him every day and had Landon take you home every Saturday afternoon. Since we moved here, you rarely call him, you refuse to let him come because he'd find out that Jacob went into hiding, and now he learns you've moved out. Have you talked to Jacob about how his situation is affecting your relationship with your Daed?"

"No, and you won't either. He's dealing with all he can, and he's doing what's needed to get his problems straight. What more do you want from—"

Camilla returned to the living room with a pot of coffee in one hand and an empty cup and saucer in the other. "It's decaf." She held up the pot. Samuel lifted his cup from the side table and moved to Camilla.

"Thank you." He went to the couch and sat beside Rhoda. Why had he done that?

Camilla poured coffee into the empty cup. "I put a bit of sugar and cream in it for you."

Rhoda eased it from Camilla's hand. "Thank you." She picked up the spoon that lay on the saucer.

Camilla removed the dishcloth from her shoulder and laid it on the coffee table before setting the carafe on it. "I'd just pulled a cake out of the oven when Samuel arrived. It's cool enough now to frost. If you'll give us a few minutes to make the frosting and put the layers together, I'd love to share it with you."

Rhoda stirred her coffee. "That's really nice of you, but none for me. I'm not far from turning in for the night."

Bob sat in the wingback chair and started talking to Samuel.

While the aroma of cake swirled in the air, an insight swept through Rhoda, and she saw Camilla making a cake for her son on his ninth birthday. But then snapshot after snapshot flashed in her mind as the boy grew into a young man. Emotions pounded like a force she imagined was reserved for the likes of Niagara Falls. Images continued to come at her. "Stop," Rhoda hissed under her breath.

All eyes turned to her.

Mortified, Rhoda wasn't sure what to say.

Samuel set his coffee on the saucer. "I brought her some sobering news about her uncle's health and how her Daed is feeling since he's close to his brother. I'm sure her emotions are a bit unsettled. That's all."

Bob cleared his throat, smiling. "We all deal with difficult news differently… So, Samuel, have you ever fished for salmon?"

The conversation picked up again. Even Camilla joined in with the men. But the longer Rhoda sat there, the stronger she sensed she needed to do something. But what?

She turned to Samuel. "It's like the moments before the tornado came through."

Samuel studied her. "What is it about?"

"Camilla."

Camilla set her cup and saucer on the coffee table. "Is everything okay?"

Samuel nodded. "Sure. Except maybe we should have a slice of that cake after all. If you don't mind."

"Cake it is." The words leaving Camilla's mouth and the look of doubt in her eyes didn't match. "It'll take us a few minutes." She seemed unable to take her eyes off Rhoda as she and Bob left the room.

Rhoda buried her head in her hands. "She thinks I'm a cracked pot."

"You came on really strong, talking to yourself, whispering to me when they could hear at least some of what you were saying."

She lived with these people. If she freaked them out like she did herself, where could she go?

Samuel leaned in. "What's happening?"

Despite his excuse to Bob and Camilla that the news about her uncle was the reason for her behavior, he knew better.

"She has a grandchild. I know she does, and she must wonder about it too, because she's been searching the Internet for her deceased son's girlfriend. She's looking for someone named Jojo."

"And you just *know* this?"

She nodded.

His eyes were wide. "No wonder you have times of struggling with who you are. Of all the gifts God gives, this one is scary, and it feels dark."

Only Emma had viewed the gift as he did, and his words brought comfort. "Exactly. It scares me too."

"Sure it does."

"My Daed and the church leaders hate it."

"Are any of us comfortable with it? But God didn't ask your Daed or the bishop or Jacob or me or even you what we thought about you having such a gift. I understand the concerns we feel. Scammers and profiteers often abuse such things."

"And the soothsayer slave girl in the Bible had a demon cast out of her."

"You shouldn't worry about that part."

What? He'd said that so matter-of-factly. She wanted to yank him by his shirt collar and yell, *Do you know what you're saying?* Instead, she measured her tone. "Why?"

"We can't disqualify what's real because counterfeiters exist. If that were the case, there wouldn't have been disciples or teachers of God's Word."

"Why haven't you told me before now that this is how you feel?"

He shrugged. "We're muddling through this while we're talking, and I'm realizing some of this as we go. Look, you shouldn't keep putting up roadblocks to receiving things. Haven't you wondered why you didn't pick up on what those girls were doing in the greenhouses before they lied, saying you laced your herbal teas with marijuana?"

"Ya, sure. I still don't know the answer."

"I'd like to take a stab. Is it because you suppress your gift to the point you won't even read body language?" He paused, and when she didn't answer, he continued. "God knows all and sees all. If He chooses to let you in on something, I think you need to relax and let yourself hear what He's trying to tell you."

She'd spent her life trying to outrun the premonitions. Sometimes she succeeded. Other times she didn't. Her heart pounded as his words echoed inside her. She would like to at least read body language. Then she'd understand Jacob better. "I keep seeing Emma."

"Related to the premonitions?"

"No."

"You're sure?"

"Completely. I have no doubts about that, and I know it's not really her I'm seeing. The dead don't return from heaven. But it's been three years since she was murdered. Why can't I get past whatever part of my grief makes me see her?"

Compassion radiated from him. "I wish I knew, but if she's not connected to your premonitions, why are you bringing it up now?"

She shrugged. "Hoping you'd have an answer, I guess."

"Sorry. I'm clueless."

She fidgeted with one of the strings to her prayer Kapp. "I hate when something like this Jojo issue comes to me."

"You try so hard *not* to hear. Why not try *hearing*?"

As if brought to life by Samuel's encouragement, the word *Dumont* shouted inside her.

Even after all Samuel had said, her gut reaction was to resist. She closed her eyes. "Because it's terrifying, Samuel. And because I'd rather not know anything than give in to this and share what I think when I could be wrong."

"You have a gift for horticulture, and you don't get all out of sorts when you're wrong about some plant idea or you spend months trying to cultivate something that doesn't work. You chalk it up to learning and keep going."

"This is completely different, and you know it."

"I doubt it's as different as you think. You work with your plants and herbs, not against them. Try that with your sense of knowing. And trust that whatever else your gift is, it's not evil."

Despite the avalanche of skepticism inside her against his reasoning, Samuel's words rang with truth. She'd known that, and yet because her church leaders and family believed it was wrong, she only trusted herself to act on her premonitions when they overwhelmed her. Maybe now, armed with this new perspective, she could trust them more.

Fresh caution waved its flag. Wasn't it odd, maybe even inappropriate, for Samuel and her to be this close, not just physically, but emotionally and spiritually, after what had happened a few weeks back? She had needed answers, and he was good at helping her find them, but they should part now.

"Denki, Samuel." She tried to find her smile. "But you should eat the cake and go."

He gave a nod, as if he'd been thinking the same thing.

Camilla walked in carrying two plates, each with cake and a fork. Bob was behind her carrying two plates also.

Would they accept what she needed to say to them? Or would they consider her mentally unstable and ask her to move out?

Rhoda stood. "Camilla, I need to tell you something." She took the plates from her and set them on the coffee table.

Camilla glanced at Samuel, a hint of suspicion flickering through her eyes. "Okay."

Rhoda drew a deep breath. "Since we talked about you having a son named Zachary, I think you've been looking for the girlfriend he had when he died."

"Have you been checking the browsing history on my computer?"

"No, I wouldn't do that and don't even know how." Nervous sweat trickled down her back. "Did you only know her as Jojo?"

Bob set the plates in his hands on the table with the other ones. "What is she talking about, Camilla?"

Her face turned ashen. "I...need some water, Bob. Would you mind?"

He left the room, and Camilla eased onto the couch, staring up at Rhoda. "What you say is true. But I didn't want Bob to know I'm trying to find Jojo."

"Maybe only your son called her that. It's short for Joella, Joella Dumont, and I...I think you have a granddaughter."

Pain etched Camilla's face. "No, Rhoda. Zachary was too young to marry without a parent's consent. And there is no chance I might have a grandchild." Tears welled. "Trust me. You're wrong on both accounts."

Bob returned with a glass of water. "Is everything okay?"

Camilla nodded. "We're fine. Rhoda was mistaken. That's all."

Rhoda trusted that Camilla fully believed there was no chance her son had married or that she had a grandchild, but she felt more convinced than ever that Camilla was the one who was mistaken.

Rhoda wished her gift had told her more—something concrete she could share with Camilla to confirm she was right and to encourage Camilla to look for Jojo and her daughter.

But for now Rhoda had pushed as hard as she dared. Any more pressure on Camilla, and Rhoda might put a wedge between herself and the Cranfords. It seemed the best thing she could do now was wait and hope she received more insight into the little girl.

Rhoda picked up the two plates from the coffee table and passed one to Samuel. "This looks delicious."

THIRTEEN

Jacob sat in the lawyer's office, squeezing his fists. His hands shook as he tried to contain his anger while Sandra answered Craig Ryer's questions. She'd driven to the farm to get him early that morning, and yet even knowing they were coming here, she hadn't said a word about any of this. The calendar on Craig's desk said it was April 24. Jacob should be helping Rhoda in the orchard. Instead, he was gritting his teeth as Sandra tried to justify her actions to Craig.

Just the other night, after he had dropped off Rhoda at the Cranfords', he'd found an isolated place to park the rig, and he'd stayed there a long, long time, thinking and crying out to God to help him find his way.

When he had chosen to help the company in its unethical and illegal activities, he had done more than disregard his conscience. He had decided he could handle life on his own terms. Later, when he realized his error in judgment and realized he needed God, dishonor kept Jacob from turning to Him. Shame and guilt were wicked taskmasters, filling his mind with lies. His ego and fear of being seen in a poor light by others had kept him chained. When Jacob had prayed Sunday night, he shook as the walls around him fell.

Now he sat here, determined to give to Sandra what God had given to him—true and complete forgiveness without walking away.

"So,"—Craig tapped his pen on the notepad—"when you worked as a secretary for Jones' Construction, did your responsibilities include placing orders?"

Sandra answered, explaining her duties and how she performed them. It'd taken a while for Craig to get her to open up.

Why hadn't she told him all this when Blaine disappeared? Some part of this didn't add up. But what?

Sandra chewed on a thumbnail. "What happens when you know the whole story?"

Craig had stacks of papers on his desk that he'd flip through occasionally and pull out something to talk to her about, but for the most part he only took notes while she talked. He'd done a lot of research since Jacob's last visit, and a lawyer in Virginia had sent PDF files and faxed a number of documents to him.

"We look at all the options." Craig took a sip from the mug on his desk. "This mess is like a pile of spaghetti, but I'm determined to get to the bottom of it. Do you have any copies of order forms signed by you or your husband?"

Sandra turned toward Jacob, trembling.

He nodded. "It's okay. I trust him."

She had no confidence in this man, but she was doing as Jacob asked. She removed a folded, tattered manila envelope from her purse and passed it to Craig. The lawyer opened it and reviewed the contents.

He picked up the papers Jacob and Sandra had signed earlier and stood up. "I need to consult a colleague for a few minutes."

"Sure."

Sandra tucked some hair behind one ear. "He could be notifying the police right now."

Well, at least she hadn't been lying to him all these years about thinking a lawyer would turn them in. She honestly believed that's how lawyers operated. He found that a bit comforting.

Jacob stood.

"Where are you going?" Her voice wavered as she grabbed his arm. There was no convincing her that he wouldn't abandon her, but the temptation right now to do just that and not look back was almost irresistible. He wasn't sure how he could stand by her.

"To get my bottle of water." He pointed to a table behind them.

She released his arm. Her insecurities wearied him, and yet, even though his family had always been there for him, always cherished him, he understood that kind of anxiety all too well. Didn't every human? Each one was so frail and needy, so dependent on others.

He picked up his water and moved to a window. The parking lot was directly below. A little farther out was a busy intersection, roads and traffic lights, and a multitude of people with goals and destinations. Were any of them as off-center with their lives as he'd been?

His thoughts moved to Rhoda. They were never far from her. If it weren't for her, he might still be running. But if she learned the full truth about him, would she walk away? He didn't think so. It might cause a few rough weeks, but she wasn't one to give up easily on a struggling plant. He loved that about her.

Actually, he loved everything about her.

His behavior after he'd learned Samuel had kissed her and she'd tried to cover for him was ridiculous. If that hadn't destroyed them, surely finding out the rest of his secret wouldn't undo them.

Craig returned, a magnifying glass in his hand. "Ms. McAlister, were you aware that the signatures on the order forms don't match Jacob's?"

She fidgeted with her hair and ran her fingers over her lips. "I could use a cigarette."

Jacob recalled his first meeting with Craig Ryer in this office. After Jacob had told his story, Craig speculated that Sandra had been lying to him, tricking him from the beginning. Now they had proof. But Jacob *had* signed those order forms, hadn't he? He sat down and fought to keep his voice even. "Answer the question, Sandra."

"How could they be his? He only signed for an order twice, and even then he didn't have the authority to do so."

The lawyer turned to another paper. "Are you aware that your name on these papers doesn't match *your* signature?"

"What?" She held out her hand, and he gave them to her.

"But I worked as the secretary at times. I did sign them." She pulled the papers closer. "Well," she said a moment later, "clearly I didn't sign these. But I signed some just like them."

"Your husband gave you those copies just before he disappeared, saying they matched the ones on record in the office, right?"

"Yes."

"But you never looked at them?"

"I glanced at them before I filed them away for safekeeping and started treading water to cope with what was happening. A few days later Jacob helped me pack up and move. I haven't looked at them since then. Our whole world was coming down around us. Who would've signed them?"

"I don't know. I suspect someone who didn't intend for you to pay for his crimes. It appears that whatever you did sign was never used to order goods through other companies."

She gaped at the man, unable to move. "Blaine? He...he tried to protect me?" Sandra was shaking from her hands to her feet.

"These are forgeries of your handwriting. Did you purchase subpar materials and sign for them?"

"I...I did as Blaine told me to. I signed whatever he said. I'm confused. Does this mean I didn't break the law?"

"There are three trials coming up. Two are civil suits in the wrongful deaths of the two women who died when the deck collapsed. Since neither of you signed these forms, neither of you have any legal liability in the cause of those women's deaths—"

Jacob dropped his water bottle, sending the clear liquid across the tiled floor. "None?"

"In their deaths, no."

Stunned, Jacob couldn't budge. Despite needing to clean up the spill, he watched as drips of water fell from the mouth of the bottle into the puddle on the tile floor. It looked just like his life: drained and pouring out the last drops for no apparent purpose. He grabbed some napkins off the serving table and mopped up the mess. When he sat down again, Craig looked up from his notes.

"As you know, I've been in contact with a Virginia lawyer who's been involved in this case. As I said when we spoke by phone two weeks ago, the owner of the construction company is in prison."

Jacob cleared his throat. "I don't understand why I never saw it in the paper. I've been looking for any news about Skeet Jones and the company since the incident with the deck."

"You probably didn't see anything about it because there were so many other criminal cases taking up space in all the papers when the housing bubble burst. Small business misconduct made only the local news."

"But why is Skeet in prison? I'm the one who devised the borrowing scheme before I realized it was illegal."

"Your pirating from one job site to give to the next was not the real problem for several reasons. Your very detailed plan, which, by the way, was remarkable, was meant to give the homebuyers what they'd paid for, right?"

"Ya, but no matter how meticulous I was with the math and supplies, we kept getting more and more behind."

"Skeet and Blaine were embezzling from the company. This is where your liability comes in, Jacob. When you realized Blaine was using funds to gamble, you should've taken the situation to the authorities. By trying to cover for Blaine, even though your aim was to dig the company out of the hole he'd dug, you became an accomplice."

"But you just said—"

"That you have no liability in the deaths of the women, and you don't. However, your liability regarding the embezzlement of funds from the construction company isn't as clear-cut. But I believe we can make a deal."

Jacob drummed his palms against the ends of the armrests. "What does that mean?"

"Even though Skeet is in prison now, within the next year he's going to trial again, on an appeal. The district attorney wants your testimonies. Jones defrauded a lot of people and made huge profits. He was found guilty of involuntary manslaughter, fraud, and racketeering, among other things." Craig tapped his pen on a stack of papers. "Do you know where your husband is, Sandra?"

"My guess is he's on a beach in Mexico. When the two women died, he said an investigation into why the deck fell would uncover all the shenanigans inside Jones' Construction, so Blaine disappeared that day. I've not seen or heard from him since."

"He was right about what the investigation into the deaths brought to light." Craig leaned back in his chair. "Jacob, I did as we discussed and contacted the district attorney. After I told him your side of the events and sent him

all the information I'd gathered, he feels you're a witness to more than you realize. And if you'll testify, he'll give you immunity, which means that whether
you've broken any laws or not, you can never be held accountable for those
actions."

Jacob leaned forward. "He simply agreed to it over the phone?"

Craig pulled out a book. "There are no set rules concerning how a district
attorney handles a situation like this. It's a judgment call the DA is free to
make. He could have insisted on meeting you face to face before deciding, but
he didn't. If you'll agree to testify, you have immunity."

Relief washed over Jacob. *Immunity.* What a beautiful word. But even as
he rejoiced over the news, he wondered how long he would be gone from the
farm while testifying.

Craig laid the book on his desk. "He didn't ask about Sandra, and I didn't
bring her into the conversation, but I'm sure I can get the same deal for her if
she's willing for me to talk to the DA about her." He flipped through the book.
"This is a deposition. It's the typed testimony where a lawyer asks questions
and the witness answers. It's what you'll need to give in the privacy of an office.
You'll take an oath, and it's paramount you tell the complete truth. I don't have
a license to practice in Virginia, but if you want to have a lawyer present, I can
find one for both of you."

"No." Sandra bolted to her feet. "I can't go back to Virginia." She turned
to Jacob. "Please, I can't. That would be too dangerous for me."

Craig gestured for her to sit. "There's some missing information here that
keeps me from understanding why you're so skittish and why you've been lying
to Jacob all this time. Are you going to tell us what it is? Why you feel you can't
go back?"

She grabbed the wooden armrests of her chair with a death grip. "You
won't believe me."

Craig pulled a file out of his desk. "I have a lot of information we haven't
discussed. If your story lines up with the facts, I might believe you."

Sandra chewed on her thumbnail for several long moments. "Even before
that deck fell, Blaine was gathering his money, getting his affairs in order. I
didn't know why at the time, and when I asked, he always had some lame ex-

cuse. I thought he was planning to leave me. It was clear I'd need money for Casey and me. The housing market was crashing, and construction had come to a halt. Even Jacob couldn't find work. So I went to see a loan shark that Blaine and I had gotten money from before."

Jacob moaned, too disgusted to want to hear the rest. "I told you I'd take care of you. I still had plenty of money to help with the bills."

"Yeah, just what I wanted, to live in poverty while Blaine disappeared to Mexico with enough cash to live like a king."

Jacob bristled at her definition. "You lived on a budget in older, small apartments. That's not poverty."

"So what happened with the loan shark?" Craig asked.

Sandra hesitated, and Jacob put his hand over hers. "I'm not leaving you, no matter what, but you need to tell us what you did and why you feel your life will be in danger if you return to Virginia to testify."

She nodded and recounted the frightening events.

Craig took notes, underlining the loan shark's name. Something she said seemed to catch the usually stone-faced lawyer off guard. Craig's eyes moved to Jacob's, and the steely coolness faded.

"Sandra, where is your daughter right now?"

"My sitter couldn't keep her today, so she's at Jacob's farm."

"Does anyone know where he lives—friends or relatives in Virginia that you're in contact with?"

"No. We ran away without leaving a trace."

Craig gestured to Jacob. "I never would have believed it before today, but, Jacob, you did the right thing in helping her hide." Craig rubbed his jaw as if needing some time to take it all in. "Go on."

FOURTEEN

Rhoda drove the wagon of saplings along the upper west ridge with Landon beside her and Zara in the back with the trees. While Jacob and Sandra were at the lawyer's office, she and Landon had been planting sprigs. Field work on a glorious day like this one was quite welcome. Golden rays of sunlight warmed her face as a light breeze played with the strings of her prayer Kapp. The temperature had to be almost fifty today, but after being outside for a while, it still felt nippy. Her fingertips were cold because her gloves left them exposed.

But her heart was filled with contentment and warmth. Jacob continued to make strides toward freedom, and it seemed a perfect day to take a deep breath.

She'd yet to stop pondering Samuel's visit to the Cranfords' the day before yesterday. He'd freed her somehow. Pieces of what he'd said kept circling inside her: *God didn't ask what we thought about you having such a gift... It's not evil... We can't disqualify what's real because counterfeiters exist.*

Since talking with Samuel, she was working to simply unwind within herself, to stop fearing her intuitions. It was...refreshing.

Camilla and Bob didn't seem to hold anything against her from the other night. Was Camilla right? Was there no grandchild? Rhoda wasn't sure. Despite not being believers, they were wonderful, loving people.

Rhoda had since called her Daed. She then did something she'd never done before—snuggled into bed and talked on the phone for a really long time. It'd been the best conversation she'd had with him since she'd moved to Maine.

As she rode past several Duchess apple trees, she thought she saw a hint of buds on the branches. In April? In Maine? It grabbed her full attention. She tugged on the horse's reins, drawing the rig closer.

Her heart stuck in her throat. "Some of the trees are starting to bud."

Landon grabbed a branch, staring at it, but he remained silent. Was he struck by fear too?

She'd never been a part of an apple orchard during this time of year. The trees on the east side of the orchard weren't this far along. She'd only come to this ridge in search of the best area for planting the young Honeygold apple trees.

The sight of healthy trees spread out before her was gorgeous. Mesmerizing, really. They were whole and thriving, just as everyone had hoped by this point, even though it would take two to four years for the orchard to be fully restored after having been abandoned for a few years. But what had her heart barely beating were the signs that the trees were on the verge of blossoming.

Apple trees could bear up under harsh winter conditions and thrive. Even the saplings in the back of the wagon needed only the ground to be thawed from winter; they'd thrive once they were planted. But Samuel had said that frost on a budding tree could destroy most of the crop, and they could still get freezing temperatures.

A dog barked in the distance, and she searched for Ziggy. In the dip below the ridge, she spotted him running toward her. Behind the dog was a wagon driven by Steven. Rhoda dropped off Landon and several saplings as Ziggy barreled toward her, barking and demanding attention. She motioned for him to jump up next to her, and then she patted him and let him hop into the back of the wagon with Zara. As she drove the rig toward her brother, she saw two little girls in coats and scarves dancing in the back of the wagon. Why were Arie and Casey with him? As she drew closer, she heard them singing.

Samuel came around the back of Steven's wagon, a soil test kit in hand. Five-year-old Isaac was right behind him, carrying a spade. Samuel glanced up, and a brief smile greeted her.

Despite her concerns about the buds, she couldn't manage to dampen her smile while going toward them. Soon she pulled the rig to a stop. "The soil-testing project is a family affair, I see."

The dogs jumped down and began hopping about and scuffling with each other.

"Phoebe's not feeling well," Steven volunteered. "And Leah continues to search for the containers to make coddling moth traps. I didn't expect to see you until supper."

"Landon and I are planting trees, and Ziggy's barking gave you away."

Steven nodded.

"Samuel," Arie called, *"mich kumm raus."* She waved her little arms, adding to her plea for Samuel to free her from the confines of the wagon.

"Ya, you can come out." He turned his back and leaned against the wagon. Arie looped her arms around his neck from behind, and he twirled her around once before stooping until her feet touched the ground. She clapped her hands. *"Singe. Singe."*

Casey held up her Winnie-the-Pooh book, pressing a button on it that made a tune ring out. She bobbed her little head up and down. Apparently she knew exactly what Arie was saying.

Samuel looked a bit sheepish. *"Alleweil?"* he said to Arie, clearly uncomfortable that they wished him to sing. "Now?" he repeated in English to Casey.

The girls squealed loudly, each begging in her own language for him to sing.

He glanced at Rhoda, shaking his head. "I have a fan club."

"I see that." How many times had he sung this song to them today?

He drew a breath and sang the song about the chubby little cubby being stuffed with fluff.

Arie danced around, singing it in English as best she could. Casey remained silent, watching Samuel with cautious delight.

Rhoda had to turn her back for a few moments to keep from laughing out loud.

"Kumm." Arie motioned for Casey. The two girls seemed to have no problem playing together even though neither spoke the other's language.

Casey eyed Samuel as she eased to the side of the wagon. He smiled, acting like he had nothing better to do than help children enjoy their day. Casey put her fingers on his face.

"Yes." Samuel remained still while the little girl ran her hand over his forehead. "I favor Jacob. Not enough to pass for him but enough to confuse you." He touched the end of her nose. "Want down?"

She looked at the horse before she backed up, shaking her head.

"Just as well." Steven motioned to his daughter. "Arie, kumm."

Arie held her arms up to Samuel. He lifted her and received a hug and kiss before he deposited her into the safety of the wagon. The scene stirred Rhoda. Children were such a gift, and to see them in this orchard, embracing the day alongside family and loved ones, made her yearn for years and years of it. For the first time in what seemed like forever, a desire for children and a future took hold of her.

"Du gut?" Samuel asked. Arie nodded. "There you go." Samuel helped the girls get situated so the bumpiness of the wagon wouldn't tussle them about. He then covered their legs with a blanket. It appeared that he'd had practice doing this today.

Steven released the brake. "We need to ride up a piece and get more soil samples. We'll be back in a few." He turned to Isaac. *"Witt geh?"*

Isaac clutched Samuel's hand. *"Nee."* Surely Steven knew that Isaac preferred to be Samuel's shadow when allowed.

"I'll watch him," Samuel offered. Rhoda expected Jacob to return home anytime now, and because of that, she was glad everyone wasn't dispersing. Hopefully, Steven would return as quickly as he'd indicated. She'd rather not be seen in a field alone with Samuel, but she needed to talk to him.

Arie's face clouded, and Samuel propped his arms on the sides of the wagon, telling her she should stay with her friend, that she could come with him another day. She grinned and nodded.

Rhoda's niece blew kisses to her as they rode away. Casey giggled and followed suit.

He chuckled. "They're quite sweet, but they behave like three-year-olds. Excited about life one minute while crying over a piece of graham cracker falling out of the wagon the next."

"At least they have an excuse." Rhoda blew them a final kiss. "They're acting their age."

"True. But when Casey was finally willing to get close, she did that face-poking thing a dozen times without ever letting me lift her out of the wagon. She's a thinker. Arie seems to be one to dive in first and reconsider later. It's interesting. I wonder if it's their lifelong personalities already peeking through."

"Got me. We'll just have to find out as time goes on. So where's Iva?"

"In the office organizing the personal and business mail into folders so she and I can go through as much as possible as quickly as possible later on. She's also making you a folder so you and I can go through that at some point. Since she's not fond of the outdoors, I'm not sure how great she'll be in the orchard, but she seems remarkable at handling paperwork."

"Maybe she'll be remarkable in helping with the canning this fall."

"I hope so. Otherwise she's really not needed, is she?"

If that's how he felt after Iva had been here for almost two weeks, Rhoda wasn't sure Jacob's hopes would come to fruition. An unwelcome question tumbled through her. How long had he and Rhoda worked together before he felt attracted to her?

"Don't you dare go there," she whispered.

He studied her.

"Sorry. I was talking to myself that time." She shuddered. "When will you have the soil test results?"

"I'm not sure. I have to mail them in, and I hope to hear back within a couple of weeks." He pulled a fallen branch from the tree. "We might need to add some specific nutrients when we get the results." He tossed it to the ground. "How have things been with Camilla and Bob since I left the other night?"

It was nice of him to ask, but why did it feel so...wrong? "Gut. They seem to accept that I made a mistake and have dropped the subject."

"And you?"

She wanted to tell him how much difference their talk had made for her and ask a few questions, but it seemed inappropriate. Isaac grabbed the stick Samuel had tossed to the ground and whipped it through the air. The dogs danced around the end of it, trying to catch it.

Samuel touched the top of the boy's black felt hat. "Whoa." He gestured farther out, and Isaac took numerous giant steps away from them, counting aloud as he went.

"I'm much better. I talked to Daed for a long time, and I invited him to visit. He's too busy right now, and I'm hoping he doesn't come until everything is settled with Jacob." She cradled a budding branch. "It's too early for this, isn't it?"

"Ya."

As soon as he answered, anxiety rippled through her.

"Ziggy!" He clapped his hands once, and the dog calmed its frenzied play before knocking Isaac down. "According to what I read in the paper yesterday, the apple trees in Maine almost never bud this early. We could be in for a fight if it frosts in the next few weeks."

"Fight?" The word eased some of her tension. "How?"

"We build fires in containers using wood, coal, and oil. Smoke, air matter, carbon dioxide, and water vapor mix to hold a smog-like barrier that'll keep the heat we create hovering around the trees. As long as the temperature is at thirty-two degrees or below, we'll have to man the fires around the clock."

"What are our chances of winning?"

"Anytime there's a freeze after budding, we lose a percentage. I can't say how large a percentage—maybe as little as ten or as much as ninety. The outcome depends on too many factors." His even-toned voice projected peace.

She stared at him. "You say that as if it's no big deal."

"It's a huge deal. Possibly the life or death of Kings' Orchard Maine. We'll fight until we win...or lose. But all we can do is our best. I don't know what else to tell you." He gazed up at the sky and pointed. A hawk soared across the powder blue expanse. "I hope he and all his relatives nest nearby. He would be a good help against rodents."

She wasn't interested in where the hawk lived, and she put the back of her fingers on her forehead. "Check yourself for a fever. You're way too calm."

"No need." He removed his hat. "I'm not calm. I'm determined. But what would you have me do?"

"I guess I expected to see anger or fear in your eyes."

"I think I'm drained of it for now. We worked so hard, and then the tornado came through. Another huge blow was when Jacob…" He shook his head.

She could imagine several things Jacob had said or done that had exhausted him.

"Anyway." Samuel removed his gloves and put them in his pocket. "I walked these fields last night, absorbing the serene beauty while thinking and praying, and I saw the need to keep it all in perspective. If we lose this year's crop, I try again."

"We."

A hint of something flickered across his face. Maybe doubt?

"We."

But she wasn't sure he believed that.

A smile tugged at his lips. "Where would Kings' Orchard be if you hadn't entered our lives? No orchard or crop would mean anything if death had stolen my family or"—he stared at the buds on a nearby branch, clearly struggling to speak his mind—"you."

Her heart raced as he shared his deepest, most hidden thoughts. Jacob must have told him that she'd sent Jacob to get everyone out of the house and into the cellar while she searched for Samuel in the orchard.

He pulled a bud off a tree. "This is important,"—he held it toward her—"and we'll fight with all we have to protect the orchard from every enemy it has, whether it's pests, frost, or something else. But it's just an orchard. It's not family."

She would have loved being out here with him last night as he got peace and perspective in a way she never had.

He walked toward Isaac and let the boy lead while meandering from rock to stick to tree.

She stopped, unable to quit staring at Samuel while he walked. This was the same man she had met last July, who so fully felt the stress of keeping Kings' Orchard solvent that he was like a pressure cooker? He'd argued with her at every turn, angry that she dared to challenge his patriarchal mind-set when it came to almost anything, including herself, Leah, and business in general.

The dogs barked while running toward them. Steven's wagon topped the hill with the girls yelling the Pooh Bear song. Apparently Steven had picked up Landon while running the soil tests. When her brother's wagon was near hers, the one she'd deserted before walking with Samuel, Landon hopped down and got into it. The dogs came to a brisk halt, turned, and ran in a different direction, howling as they went. But she saw no one.

She cupped her hands and blew into them. "Am I the only one whose nerves are grated by the dogs barking so easily when they're outside?"

Samuel pulled his wool gloves out of his coat pocket. "Every time you hear it, just remember they're sounding the warning to all deer who wish to eat from the trees." He held the gloves out to her.

"No, I can't work in those. I have to settle for these without fingertips."

The wagon moaned as Steven brought it to a stop. "The girls aren't far from having all the outdoor fun they can take, and it'll be time for supper soon."

Landon parked the other rig a few feet from them and got out.

Steven hopped down. "We'll get a soil sample from this low-lying area, and then I'm taking the girls in. Anyone else want a ride?"

Rhoda chuckled at the busy zaniness of family and friends rolling love and work into one. Her eyes met Samuel's, and she knew he was enjoying it too.

When Ziggy and Zara finally stopped barking, Rhoda looked in that direction and saw Jacob topping a hill, petting the dogs as he walked.

This is what she wanted her life to be. Where the beauty of the day, talk of faithfulness and love, the exuberance of children, and work all collided into an array of blissful fulfillment. Even as joy skittered through her, she prayed she'd have the privilege of tens of thousands of days just like this one. Her heart palpitated at the thought.

Jacob's stride indicated he'd regained some of his former confidence. But how did he find them on this eighty-acre farm? He hadn't used the two-way to ask where they were. He waved, his endearing smile evident even at a distance. She hoped he'd received the best, most freeing news possible while at the lawyer's office.

Someone clapped several times, and she turned to see her brother. "I said, how many more trees will need to be planted tomorrow?" He sighed. "Once Jacob shows up, do you see or hear anything else going on around you?"

Her eyes met Samuel's for a moment, and a torrent of feelings stole her thoughts and threatened to snatch her breath. She swallowed and looked to her brother. "About ten." Without waiting on him to respond, she strode toward her wagon. "Whoever doesn't ride back to the house with Steven will be on their own. My only passenger is not in this little group." She gestured at the rest of them. "Oh—" She turned back, and her voice faltered. Emma was there, standing amid the group of men.

Rather than shutting out the why of it, she pondered it. Emma was simply Rhoda's heart trying to tell her something. "Uh..." She tried to focus. "Tell Phoebe we'll be in soon but not to hold supper for us." She had hundreds of questions for Jacob, and she yearned for substantive answers.

She urged the horse to move faster. By the time she reached Jacob, her face was pulled tight from the grin she couldn't control. "Where is your coat?"

He hopped onto the bench seat and embraced her. "Who needs a coat if they have thoughts of you to keep them warm?"

With her arms around him, she peered over his shoulder into the sky, hoping he had good news for her, for them. "So how do you manage to find me so easily on this farm?"

He chuckled and settled into his seat. "Listen."

They sat in silence, and she heard the soft, distinctive noise of the group she'd just left. It was heartwarming. "But it's an eighty-acre farm."

"All I do is go in the direction of where I think you'll be, get to a high point, and simply listen. That's even more true since Samuel got the dogs."

"Why not just use the walkie-talkies?"

"I do sometimes. But they're like using a net to scoop up fish in a bucket."

She hadn't realized this part of him. "You're a hunter at heart."

"More of a fisherman. I liked fishing for what was right for me when my Daed just wanted me to be a farmer. When I left the Amish, I loved fishing for the right construction jobs in the right places near oceans. And my greatest love was the real kind of fishing, the deep-sea kind. That was as much fun as being on the ocean itself."

It had been quite a while since he'd had true joy in his voice, but did he just say he didn't like being a farmer? "How'd it go at the lawyer's office?"

He placed one hand on the backrest behind her. "Overall, I'd say it was great, so much so I'm not sure where to begin."

She tapped the reins against the horse's back. "Tell me the most surprising news first." That seemed a safe thing to ask.

"Craig is extremely cautious with his words, but while Sandra was explaining the real reason behind her years of lying to me, he looked straight at me with a horrified expression and said I'd done the right thing to help hide her."

"Really?" Rhoda looked into his green eyes, pleased and relieved for him that he hadn't played the fool as much as he'd thought.

He rubbed her back through her wool coat. "It gets better. The lawyer did extensive checking into every aspect, and not only are Sandra and I not as legally accountable as I'd thought, but he also got immunity for me from the DA in Virginia. That means I have no threat of jail time or even probation, in exchange for my testimony."

If Rhoda were any happier, she might bounce straight out of the rig and land in the tops of the trees. "That's wonderful. So what's the worst news?"

Jacob shifted away from her, a frown furrowing his brows as he stared at her. "That's it? I've been under this thing for years, and all you have to say is it's wonderful?"

She pulled on the reins, halting the wagon. She stood and cupped her hands around her mouth. "Amazing! Remarkable! Extraordinary! Astonishing!" She turned back to Jacob. "Is that better?"

He smiled. "Getting there."

"The next words that come to mind are *bewildering, shocking, weird,* and *bizarre,* but I can continue cheering if you like."

"Nee. Let's stop while I'm ahead."

She sat. "I really am very pleased for you. A little confused for me, because I only understand some of what took place. But being a little lost in what all happened seems to be a part of it. So are you free in every way now—bloggers can blog, photographers can post your image and name? You know, all those things the Amish never do, but I seem to draw the Englisch who want to do them about us."

"I'm not quite that free, but I will be. First, I need to find Sandra a new place to hide...somehow."

"But Sandra is innocent, right?"

"Innocent would be the wrong word when talking about Sandra." He intertwined his fingers. "Or me."

"Or any of us."

Golden light seemed to cover the fields and trees like a dusting from heaven. A light breeze played with the tree branches. She would never forget the beauty of when Jacob returned home with such great news.

He eased his arm through hers as she held on to the reins. "I love you, Rhodes."

She pulled the rig to a stop and tapped her lips with her index finger. He smiled as he leaned in and put his warm lips over hers. After the best kiss she'd had since coming to Maine, she sat up straight, smiling. "Denki."

He laughed. "You're welcome."

She tapped the reins against the horse's back, and they started on their way again. "So finish telling me about Sandra."

"She's done plenty of unethical stuff, but she's done nothing against the law, so she doesn't need to hide for those reasons."

"I thought her husband betrayed you and her, making both of you look guilty even where you had no guilt."

"So did we—until today. Now we're not so sure. Anyway, the problem is, while she was borrowing money from a loan shark, another deal was going down, and apparently someone with power and a love of violence thinks she saw a murder."

Sometimes the land of the free felt like the land of the violent. After her sister was murdered, Rhoda had read that the country had one of the worst homicide rates in the world. Was that really true? Even if it wasn't, there were times when it felt like it.

She detested this topic, but she aimed to reel in her emotions. "You're the one who said she lies all the time. How can you be sure she didn't actually see it?"

"Craig questioned her a dozen ways, changing subjects and going back to it, drawing diagrams, using statistical information of what's physically possible, and not only did her story never shift, but it worked out in every way he could check it."

"So what's next?"

"This is where it gets sticky."

She didn't like the sound of that. "What does that mean?"

"I'm not sure. But it seems it'd be best if Sandra broke away from me and disappeared before I'm under oath. If the law can reach her through me, they may want to question her about her husband. But if it becomes known she's back in Virginia, she'll draw the attention of those who want to kill her."

In some ways, having Sandra move without their knowing how to find her sounded sort of nice, but Rhoda understood and respected Jacob's need to stay connected to her and Casey. A lot of what he'd said sounded like those dark shoot-'em-up movies she'd heard about. She'd never wanted to watch one, but now she felt as if she were living in one through Jacob.

"So she needs to move again?"

"Yeah, it seems so."

"Then what's the solution?"

"I have no idea. I asked Sandra to stay through supper, and I thought maybe if the three of us talked, we could think of something. There have to be answers, don't there?"

She understood how he felt. His past seemed to have tentacles that kept reaching out to strangle all life from his future. But she wasn't accepting that for the long run, just for the here and now. They *would* sever those monstrous tentacles and walk free.

"I have a better idea." She leaned into his shoulder. "Let's see who else would be willing to brainstorm this with us."

Skepticism filled his face. "No one but you wants to help dig me out of this pit."

Is that what he thought? "Jacob, that's not even a little bit true."

He shrugged. "I think you would find out otherwise pretty quick."

"Then we'll find out together."

He nudged her elbow. "I have a question for you. When I go to Virginia to answer questions, the first thing will be a deposition. Would you go with me?"

Excitement skittered through her. It was an idea that never would've occurred to her, but considering that not long ago he couldn't look her in the eyes for feeling betrayed, she was more than happy to say yes.

FIFTEEN

Samuel sat across the table from Iva, noticing her when he should have his head bowed in prayer. She seemed very nice. He thought she was a helper at heart rather than a leader, and there was something to be said for that. She was attractive, with light brown hair and brown eyes. She had a patch of faded freckles that ran across her cheeks and nose. He thought the freckles were cute. Given time, he wondered if he'd conjure an interest in her.

Maybe he needed to push himself a bit—spend some time with her, at least try to free himself of Rhoda's death grip on his heart.

Casey whined and smacked her highchair, interrupting his thoughts. Samuel glanced down the table and saw Sandra watching the others. The tautness of her face indicated discomfort and nervousness. She glanced toward Samuel and smiled. Was he being a bad witness? His failure to join in the mealtime praying might make him look uncaring toward God, but that's not where his heart was.

It was so easy to give the wrong impression. Did he have the wrong idea about Sandra too? Maybe she wasn't the cord of restlessness that had tugged Jacob away from the farm so many times. Hadn't Jacob been a wanderer long before he met her?

The prayer ended, and Iva raised her head and stared straight at him.

"How'd your day go?" Samuel asked as he passed her the bowl of mashed potatoes.

Landon had stayed for supper too, and he passed the green beans to Samuel.

Casey's wails grew louder when Sandra tried to console her. She put some food on the little girl's plate, but Casey hurled the plate onto the floor. Phoebe started to get up, but Sandra told her to keep her seat and began cleaning up the mess.

Isaac asked in Pennsylvania Dutch why Casey was acting up at the table. His Daed assured him that he and his sister had done the same when they were little.

Samuel tried not to frown. What would Sandra think of the parents and children conversing in a language she didn't understand? Did she know that Amish children only knew Pennsylvania Dutch until they were school age? Isaac was starting to learn English, but he couldn't converse well in this new tongue.

Iva seemed unperturbed by the racket as she picked up the plate of oven-fried chicken. "There is a desk underneath all that paperwork, Samuel. That's the good thing to remember. But I don't know what to do with most of the piles I've made until we talk about them."

"How about after supper?"

"Perfect." After getting a piece of chicken, she passed the plate back to him. "I'm writing a thank-you note to each person who's sent money to help with Rhoda's legal troubles. Most of the checks are made out to her, but she seems to have even less time than you. Did you want to read those and sign the notes, or should I wait on her?"

Steven took a bite of bread. "I wouldn't say she has less time. She uses her hours differently, sort of like why she's not here now."

Iva wiped her mouth. "I didn't mean anything negative."

"It was a good question." Samuel hoped to assure her. "I'll take a glance at the notes and decide then."

Sandra lifted Casey out of her highchair, and the little girl arched her back, kicking and crying. Exhaustion had gotten the better of her. Those around the table tried to talk despite Casey's grumpiness.

When the meal was almost over, Samuel heard the front door swoosh open. Moments later Jacob and Rhoda walked into the kitchen. Without any hesitation Jacob took the fussy child from Sandra.

In an instant all was silent. Welcome, beautiful silence.

Jacob set the little girl in his lap and took a seat next to Rhoda. Sandra sat back in her chair, her tense expression easing for the first time since she'd come to the table. Casey visibly relaxed.

"It was good of everyone to help watch Casey today. Thank you." Sandra picked up her fork.

Jacob brushed some stray hair from Casey's face. "If she can't sleep tonight, perhaps Samuel would sing her a few verses of 'Winnie-the-Pooh.'"

The others—Phoebe, Steven, Leah, Landon, and Iva—laughed.

Rhoda looked apologetic. "Sorry, Samuel. I was just telling Jacob about Casey's day, and that sort of slipped out."

"Sure it did." Samuel elongated the words for effect, but he didn't mind. It was time Jacob began teasing him again. He took a drink of water and sang a line of the song. Arie clapped and Casey smiled. The others laughed.

"What's so funny?" Samuel asked.

Rhoda put food on her plate. "You can't see it? A broad-shouldered, outdoorsy man singing a children's song?"

Jacob tore pieces of chicken into tiny bits and set them on his plate. Casey grabbed them and gobbled them. After years of knowing that Jacob had called and mailed letters to someone each week, Samuel found it odd to actually see him interacting with Sandra and Casey at the table. The little girl slumped against him as if she hadn't thrown a tantrum only moments ago.

Jacob took a long sip of water. "I told Rhoda this already, but you all need to know too. Things went well at the lawyer's office." He gave a reassuring nod to Sandra. "But I'll need to go to Virginia in the next week or two for a deposition."

"What's a deposition?" Phoebe asked.

"I'll meet with some lawyers, take an oath that I'll speak the truth, and answer their questions about a deck that collapsed—one that I worked on when I was employed by Jones' Construction."

"Just you or you and Sandra?" Steven asked.

A hint of something Samuel didn't understand shadowed his brother's face.

"Just me. I should only be gone three days. Four at the most. It takes twelve or thirteen hours to get there by train, so half the time will be spent traveling." He focused on Steven. "I'd like to take Rhoda with me."

Steven's fork clanged against his plate. "Are you serious?"

"I know it's asking a lot."

Steven stared at him, his mouth a hard line. "You shouldn't ask such a thing. I know you spend a lot of time among the Englisch, but surely you haven't forgotten that single Amish women don't travel with men unless they're a family member or with chaperones."

"Phoebe and the children could go."

"Until Samuel sells the land in Pennsylvania, there is no money."

"Sells what land?" Rhoda's eyes opened wide. "That's how you're getting the money? That's not a good plan. We can't buy it back. Can't we—"

Samuel held up his hand. "Let it go. If there were another way, I would've done it. The decision is made, and it's not up for debate."

She pursed her lips. "Jacob, did you know about this?"

"No." His brother glanced his way. "But we've not talked about much lately." He wiped Casey's hands with a napkin. "I still have a little money left from my construction work this past winter. I used most of it to pay the lawyer, but I think I have enough for Phoebe and the children to go with us."

Steven bristled. "I understand that Phoebe is out of sight because she doesn't work in the field or tend to the livestock, but what she gets done each day in keeping everyone fed is directly related to the energy and success we have in the orchard." He shifted. "I'm sorry, but we can't spare anyone right now. Maybe this could wait until after the harvest."

"It can't." Jacob put his water glass to Casey's lips. "Later this week the lawyer's office will call with a day and time that I have to be there. It's moving fast because the trials already had court dates. They dragged on for two years, but now it's all on a tight schedule."

Jacob looked to Rhoda, disappointment evident in his expression. But surely Rhoda had known what Steven's response would be.

Jacob scowled at Samuel. "I have no choice about going, not if I want to be rid of this problem."

Samuel felt his brother's familiar challenge of late, but he refused to react to it. So he leaned in. "And we want that for you too, Jacob. All of us. Isn't that right, Steven?"

Steven hesitated, as if realizing how abrupt he'd sounded. "Ya, of course. If we can help from here, just tell us what you need, but my sister cannot go with you. You'll be done in a day?"

"The deposition should take only a day, but the district attorney has been looking for Blaine. He's Sandra's husband and was my immediate boss at the construction job. He was neck high in illegal and unethical behavior, and by trying to help, I crossed into some of that same kind of activity—illegal and unethical. He disappeared just before everything fell apart. I may also have to go back in a few months to testify. I don't fully understand the process, so I'm taking my lawyer's word for how things will go. He says this is a good deal for me, and if I follow through, my name should be cleared."

"If they want to know about Blaine, why isn't Sandra going?" Leah asked.

A look passed between Sandra and Jacob.

Rhoda put her hand over Jacob's. "There are some serious safety issues for Sandra and Casey if they go to Virginia." She focused on Samuel. "We need to talk about possible solutions."

Samuel knew she wanted his help, and he wanted to give it. He placed his napkin next to his plate. "Then let's brainstorm."

"Denki." Rhoda smiled a kind of smile that spoke of truly appreciating him.

She'd barely touched her food, but she pushed back the plate. "The topics may not be comfortable for everyone. This plan will be completely legal, but it'll also be a little sneaky, sort of like the believers lowering Paul in a basket during the night so the violent ones couldn't get hold of him."

"Who's Paul?" Sandra asked.

"She's referring to something in the Bible." Jacob looked at Casey. "Are you full?" She nodded, and Jacob carried her to the sink and rinsed her hands and mouth. Then he turned her around to face him, and she laid her head on his shoulder.

Steven rose. "I think we should get the children ready for bed."

"Sure," Rhoda answered. "We'll clean up the kitchen."

Sandra watched Steven and Phoebe leave.

Rhoda fixed a fresh glass of water. "Don't worry about him. He's just not comfortable with us talking about anything sneaky." She set the drink in front of Jacob and removed the one Casey had been sipping from.

Iva stood and began scraping the dishes clean and stacking them. "There are plenty of references in the New Testament to people being sneaky if it was to protect someone. In one place it even sounds as if Jesus became invisible in order to walk through a crowd who wanted to stone Him."

While the women made short work of cleaning up the kitchen and Samuel went to his room to get paper and pencils, Jacob patted Casey's back until she was sound asleep. Soon Rhoda, Jacob, Iva, Leah, Landon, and Samuel were at the table, ready to help a woman and child only Jacob really knew.

Iva made one last swipe with the dishrag over the table. "I should probably go."

Samuel liked having Iva around. It sort of evened out the boy-girl ratio, and it seemed to lessen some of Jacob's tension. "You sure?"

"This is a family meeting."

"More than half of us aren't related," Landon said. "Samuel, Jacob, and Leah are. With Steven and Phoebe gone, Rhoda isn't related to anyone. Neither is Sandra nor me."

Jacob tapped the table. "If you're fine with the word *sneaky* and can be discreet, we'd welcome you to stay."

Iva sat and propped her elbows on the table. "I'm ready."

Jacob took a sip of water. "So here's the problem."

As Jacob expounded on the issues concerning Sandra, Samuel began to understand a little better why his brother felt so protective of her, and it made sense to him why Jacob had sacrificed so much to help her and Casey. He never doubted that Jacob's heart was in the right place concerning Sandra, but he hoped for Rhoda's sake that Jacob didn't continue to have people or problems that came ahead of her.

SIXTEEN

Iva listened intently as Jacob explained the problems facing Sandra in detail for everyone at the table. She'd never known a man to go this far out of his way to help any woman, wife or girlfriend, let alone an Englisch woman. It seemed to her that was akin to offering a hand to a leper in the time of the Bible. But the little girl asleep on Jacob's shoulder was *so* precious. Perhaps she was a terror when exhausted, but that came with being three years old, didn't it?

When Jacob finished telling of Sandra's predicament, everyone remained silent, clearly processing all he'd said and trying to think of a solution.

Landon asked about sending Sandra and Casey to live with Rhoda's parents, but that was soon discounted. Samuel suggested Sandra change back to her maiden name, and Rhoda tossed out the idea of Sandra locating her dad and moving in with him. They found weaknesses in every suggestion.

Silence fell, and the clock struck the hour as they pondered without speaking.

Iva had an idea, but what if she hadn't understood everything? Would the others think her stupid?

Jacob looked around the table. "Anything else? Anyone?"

Iva meekly raised her hand. "Sort of… Maybe."

"By all means." Jacob's smile was welcoming. "Don't be afraid. You just heard a long list of my mistakes while I tried to help Sandra, and you see where they got us. Sandra's too. You heard other people's not-so-bright ideas, and I can tell you even less brilliant plans Samuel's had over the years…and Leah… and—"

"Enough." Leah dipped her fingers into Jacob's water and flicked the drops at him. "She's got the idea."

Jacob wiped his face, amused at the unexpected sprinkling. "I feel particularly compelled to recall numerous brilliant schemes of Leah's."

His sister grabbed the glass and threatened to toss the whole thing on him.

Jacob cradled Casey's head and pointed a finger at Leah. "If you wake her, you deal with her." His grin reflected triumph even before she set the glass on the table and took her seat.

Iva liked this family. There was a respect for women unlike what she'd experienced in her own community.

Samuel tapped his paper with a pencil. "What's your idea, Iva?"

"I think Sandra needs to move away from here…and if she's to be somewhere Jacob doesn't know about, then he shouldn't be at the table while we talk about it."

Jacob rocked back in his chair, considering her. He got up and pointed at Samuel. "She's a smart one."

Samuel seemed less confident of Jacob's proclamation, but he nodded.

"I'll be in the rocker in the living room."

After he was gone, Samuel motioned for everyone to shift closer, filling in the empty chairs between them. Suddenly Iva felt very self-conscious. "We need to move Sandra to some place new, right?"

They all nodded.

"The problem is it must be done without involving relatives or leaving a paper trail, so she can't hire anyone to help her. I saw all of you on television, which means a lot of people did too. So none of you can do it. If whoever wants to harm Sandra happens to come looking for her, and a neighbor says she left with one of you, they'd know where to start searching for her. That might be a ridiculous long shot, but the goal is to be so careful that whatever new place she's set up in, she never has a shadow of any concern about being found, right?"

Samuel set the pencil down. "Jacob sold you short. You're more than just smart, and you're covering angles I never would've thought of."

"When you're Amish and you love photography, you learn to cover your tracks so no one confiscates your camera."

The group nodded, almost chuckling. All, that is, except Sandra. "Amish can't have cameras?"

"They're frowned on," Iva volunteered. "But I bought one anyway."

"Good for you," Sandra said. "I admire you Amish, but what you do without to hold on to your beliefs and culture staggers the mind." She tucked her dark hair behind her ear. "It must be worth it to be surrounded with this kind of good people."

"It has its upsides, no doubt." Iva picked up her glass, but it was empty.

Samuel rose. "Hang on. I'll get you some water."

That was so out of character for the Amish men Iva knew. Her heart had almost soared when Steven spoke of all Phoebe did for everyone. He talked as if she were a partner of the orchard even though she was mostly the cook who never even went into the field. Unlike her father, Steven didn't hint that his wife was an underling who was doing a poor job of earning her keep. She'd like to marry a man who thought as highly of her as Steven did Phoebe.

Samuel set the drink in front of her. "You said what wouldn't work. Any ideas about what will?"

Iva took a sip. "No one would recognize me."

Rhoda studied her. "We'll need two drivers. One for her car, and one for a pickup to move her things. Can you drive?"

Iva tried not to smile, but it didn't work. "I can. I even have a driver's license."

"Landon?" Rhoda glanced at him.

"Yeah, I could loan her my truck."

"What?" Leah yelped, laughing. "I'll get you for that, Englisch boy."

Landon's smile indicated he was up for Leah's challenge. He popped his knuckles. "She has a license." He leaned in. "You know, read the manual, knows the laws, has experience. The kind of thing that's important before letting someone get behind the wheel of your vehicle."

Leah arched an eyebrow. "Nevertheless, you *will* pay."

He rolled his eyes playfully. "Of course I will."

"So"—Sandra ran her fingers through her hair—"where am I going?"

Sandra's voice was loud, and Iva covered her lips with her index finger. "*You* should get an idea of what state, but tell no one." Iva deadeyed her. "No one. We'll figure out the rest as we go. That way if an attorney asks Jacob if he knows anyone who knows where you are, he can honestly say no. I'll show up one day, and we'll get you moved." Iva played with the condensation on her glass. "But wherever you go, they'll require deposits and such. Is there money for that?"

Rhoda's eyes moved to Samuel's. Without so much as a whisper between them, he seemed to understand what she was thinking. He nodded, and her smile reflected approval. Sometimes, like now, Iva had a hard time distinguishing who Rhoda favored—Jacob or Samuel.

Samuel stood. "Ya, we can get the money to do this. Is this the plan?"

All eyes turned to Rhoda, so Iva looked to her too.

Rhoda took a deep breath. "This is a good plan, Iva, and it warms my heart that you'd be willing to take such a risk just to help us." She nibbled on her bottom lip. "But this is a huge, intimidating task. Why would you want to do this?"

"So far I've been of no real help around here, other than giving Phoebe a hand with some chores and going through the mail. The office work will be caught up soon, so this is my chance to show you I'm valuable in all sorts of ways. I hope it will make you want to keep me around for months yet. If you do, I'll have even more time to prove my value. On top of that, what you see as intimidating, I see as great opportunities to photograph so much more than my community in Indiana and around here."

"Good answers." Rhoda nodded. "Really, they are, but I think all of us, including you, should take a few days to think this over before we commit to it."

Everyone nodded, apparently seeing it as reasonable, but Iva was a little disappointed that Rhoda didn't support the idea then and there. It was a good, solid one.

Did Rhoda not trust her?

Rain poured off the end of Jacob's winter hat as he stooped to grab the morning paper from the cracked concrete driveway. Samuel usually had it snagged by this time. Where was his brother anyway?

Suspicion tried to lay hold of him. Jacob wasn't very good at refusing distrust the power to turn him into a paranoid suitor. Still, he and Rhoda were doing very well, and he and Samuel were trying to mend the gash between them.

He removed the plastic cover from the newspaper and shoved it into his pocket. One glance at the headline—"The Frost Man Cometh"—roiled frustration within him.

It was the last day of April, and they were facing a frost in May!

This is why he hated farming. They could work around the clock for eleven months, and a few nights of freezing temperatures could undermine everything in a matter of hours. As could powerful winds, a warm winter, rain during pollinating season, and a number of other acts of nature.

According to the paper, when the rains moved out, freezing temperatures would swoop through the Pine Tree State. Freezing weather in Orchard Bend wasn't uncommon this time of year. Budding trees were.

He headed for the office. If Samuel wasn't there, he would leave the paper on his desk. Samuel would go there before he went to supper.

Jacob dreaded sharing this news. This kind of weather was why his first love was construction work, even with its seasonal ups and downs. His pleasure in carpentry had been taken from him through the jumble of misdeeds and poor management by Jones' Construction. But after he'd known Rhoda for only a few weeks, she had begun helping him fight the battle against his truckload of guilt. She had helped him work through his reservations and slowly learn to love having a hammer in his hand again. The fact that she made it possible for him to heal, albeit without knowing about the two fatalities that resulted from the collapse of a deck he had built, gave a picture of who they were together—strong but silent on a lot of subjects.

Building houses, hotels, apartments, stores, offices, and whatever had its own set of challenges, but a carpenter's work had a definite final outcome. Really bad weather could put a crew behind. But a few nights of freezing temperatures at an odd time of year meant very little, and it certainly didn't wreck months and months of hard work. Even if something as disruptive and destructive as a tornado came through, the workers were paid for every hour they'd worked.

When he stepped into the barn, he heard soft voices talking and laughing. He jerked open the office door.

Iva and Samuel looked up.

"You startled me." Iva pressed a hand to her throat.

But the look on Samuel's face said he knew why Jacob had purposely burst into the room.

"Sorry." Jacob relaxed his fists. "Why was the door shut?"

"Oh,"—Iva went to the file cabinet—"Ziggy and Zara smell like dogs tend to when they're wet, and I shooed them out and closed it. I'm surprised they're not trying to follow you in."

"They probably went looking for Rhoda"—Samuel punched several numbers on a calculator—"who's sure to be in one of the greenhouses." He grabbed an opened envelope from the desk. "I sold two acres, with Daed's approval, and this is the agreement with the buyer. We'll get the check as soon as it's surveyed and I write up a bill of sale."

"I know that was hard to do." Jacob doubted anyone knew it more than he did. Before Rhoda, Samuel saved without spending, and no matter how tight money got, he'd never been willing to sell an inch of property, let alone two acres. Was he going to do so now because of the feelings he had for her or because of the businesses they were trying to launch with her?

Samuel looked at the envelope. "He'd love to buy more land later on, if I'll sell it, but two acres is all I can stand to part with and all he can afford right now. The economy's taken a toll on him too. But the money from those acres should give us enough to pay the bills, rent a house with a kitchen you can update, plus cover the supplies and the pickers."

"There may not be money for *all* that." Jacob unfolded the newspaper and set it in front of Samuel. "The fight begins."

Samuel pulled the paper closer. "I knew a week ago this was a possibility. Since then close to seventy-five percent of the orchard has blossomed. You're right, Jacob. The battle will start within twelve hours of the rain moving out."

Iva pulled a folder from the cabinet. "All hands on deck. All prayers appreciated." She gave Jacob an apologetic shrug. "It's something my mother used to say at times like this."

Samuel didn't look up from the paper, but Jacob was sure he wasn't feeling well. After numerous times of being tempted to sell an acre or two over the years, Samuel had finally done it, only to be faced with needing more money for far more than debts and the cost of remodeling a canning kitchen.

Samuel took a deep breath. "We can do this." He tapped the desk in front of him, fingers splayed. Iva put a pen directly in his path. He grabbed it and circled several pieces of information. Jacob liked how well Iva and Samuel were getting along.

He took a seat. "You two seem to work together efficiently."

Iva tapped her chest. "I work. He plays."

Jacob propped his feet on the desk. "Sounds about right to me." He missed those times when his attraction to Rhoda was free of disappointment and heartache. Those first few months were so blissful, even after the tornado in Pennsylvania. They didn't hit a rough patch until Sandra needed him on the same night Rhoda had to face her church leaders. Samuel went in his stead. That was the beginning of Jacob's past slowly and painfully revealing itself to her. The beginning of not being who she needed him to be and trying to make it up to her.

Samuel frowned, never lifting his eyes from the paper. "Maine's weather pattern this year has been so unpredictable—mild when it should've been howling snow, warm when it should've been freezing, and now several frosty nights predicted for the first week of May."

Iva grabbed a notepad and laid it beside Samuel. "What's the plan?"

Samuel tapped the paper with his pen. "If we all work together, and if the temperature doesn't drop below twenty-nine, which is what they're predicting, we may lose only ten to fifteen percent of the crop. We have ten smudge pots in the hayloft."

Iva frowned. "We have what?"

"It's an oil-burning device. The fuel is in the bottom, and there's a long chimney neck where the fire burns. It creates a type of smog. The ones in the loft belonged to our grandfather. They're about four feet high. We'll use them, but that's not nearly enough for an orchard this size. Despite my best efforts over the last week, we still don't have enough fifty-five-gallon drums. So getting more of those, along with plenty of wood, is our first—"

The phone rang, and Samuel paused to pick up the receiver. "Kings' Orchard Maine." He listened for a moment, and soon his eyes reflected angst. "Hang on, please." He held the phone out to Jacob. "It's your lawyer's secretary. She has a deposition date for you."

Jacob moaned. *Not now!* Surely he could help battle the frost before having to leave for Virginia. But then an issue even more pressing came to the forefront—getting Sandra somewhere without him knowing where.

He pushed mute. "Has Rhoda indicated what she thinks of the plan?" Not that he actually knew what the plan was, only that Rhoda had asked for some time to think it over.

"Not that I know of." Samuel gestured toward Iva. "You?"

She shook her head. "I told her I was comfortable moving forward, and she thanked me, but she was still unsure."

"Everyone else is on board with the plan?"

Samuel nodded. "Appears so."

Jacob had been patient and supportive these last six days, trying to free Rhoda's mind and heart so she could figure out what needed to be done. Apparently that hadn't helped. Did Rhoda not understand how important it was that Sandra have someone to support her as she was uprooted again? That little bit of emotional encouragement of not having to do this on her own could mean the difference between her coping and her spiraling into a complete depression. Sandra could disappear for a long time, but he didn't doubt she'd show up again. But when? And with how much damage inflicted on Casey's soul in the process?

Jacob fidgeted with the phone, ready to get back to the call. "I've been trying to nudge Rhoda to figure out how she feels about Iva's plan, but it hasn't worked."

Iva moved to a chair. "Since she needs to keep the plan from you, maybe you're the wrong person to get her to decide."

"Maybe so. I hadn't thought of that. Her mood's been reflective and unsure. If she gets emotionally charged, like when the tornado came through, she's completely positive about what needs to be done."

Samuel closed the newspaper. "I don't think her instincts work like that."

"It's worth a try. I can't go to Virginia knowing where Sandra is going to be, and letting her strike out on her own would be a huge mistake."

"Try what?" Samuel asked.

Jacob pointed to the paper. "While she's absorbing the bad news about the weather, ask her about Iva's plan."

Samuel looked at her. "He just doesn't want to be the one to tell his girlfriend the frost man cometh."

She smiled at Samuel, an intimate smile, Jacob thought.

"Ya. Okay, but I doubt I use that weather report like you're thinking." Samuel gestured impatiently. "Answer the phone already."

He unmuted the phone. "This is Jacob…"

SEVENTEEN

Rhoda sat on the floor of the playroom, reading to Arie while Isaac trotted about the room astride a stick horse. Rain pattered against the windows, and Phoebe was in the next room, lying down with a wet washcloth pressed to her lips. The farm itself felt welcoming of her—apple trees as far as the eye could see, a barn with livestock, a kitchen with a fire to knock the edge off the chill and plenty of food for all, the laughter of children, and squabbles inside an old house that had been home to at least a half-dozen generations.

These past few hours of enjoying the homey side of living had warmed Rhoda's heart like adding wood to banked embers. This was what she wanted from life—to enjoy the beauty and power of being alive. She'd spent too much of her life trying to pacify others while having to sneak around to follow her intuitions.

Samuel was right—God hadn't asked any of them whether He should give Rhoda a gift of insight. He'd simply done it to a girl living inside one of the most conservative Christian groups on the planet. And now she finally felt as if she could accept the oddity of it and stop questioning her motives.

"Rhodes?" Jacob called through the walkie-talkie.

It surprised her when his voice made a sort of loneliness wash over her. She missed him even when they were together, and she imagined he would say the same of her.

By now they should've shaken off all the distant feelings of being apart throughout the winter. Did the kiss still stand between them?

Thoughts of those few seconds made her heart thump a little harder.

She shifted Arie and fumbled with her apron, trying to dig into the hidden pocket.

What had happened between her and Samuel? Obviously the kiss, but what *really* led up to it?

She pressed the button on the two-way. "Ya?"

"Are you in one of the greenhouses?"

"Nee. Phoebe's not feeling well, so I'm in the playroom helping with the children."

"Okay, denki."

Rhoda read about the hundred-acre wood from the book Casey had given Arie. Her niece played the lively theme song of Winnie-the-Pooh over and over again. Thankfully, sound didn't easily travel through the solid-wood doors that separated the playroom from where Phoebe was resting.

While on the last page of the book, Rhoda was interrupted by a knock on the door. "Kumm."

Samuel stepped into the room, and her skin prickled at the surprise.

"Hi." He had a newspaper tucked under his arm.

Isaac hurried to him, scooping up two plastic horses as he went. He held up one to Samuel.

"You're not the King I expected to come through that door."

"I know." Samuel took the toy. "Jacob sent me. We need to talk."

She didn't want to discuss business right now, especially not if Jacob wanted her to have answers on a decision she didn't want to make. "I'm in the middle." She jiggled the book a bit, giving him a hint. "And if I continue, Arie will likely fall asleep."

"Then finish reading. I'll wait." He sat on the floor with the toy, and Isaac prattled to him excitedly.

While Samuel talked and played horses, Rhoda finished reading to Arie. But the words could have been about anything. All she could hear was Samuel's soft murmuring to Isaac. It made this cozy rainy day and her contentment with life seem even more complete.

When Rhoda closed the book, Arie didn't budge from her lap.

Isaac ran to the toy shelf and picked up a red barn.

Samuel leaned his back against a chair and stretched his long legs. "Phoebe's not feeling well again?"

"Too nauseated to be on her feet."

A half smile tugged at his lips. "A good kind of nauseated, I hope."

She covered her mouth with an index finger. "Ya. It's as you're thinking, but she's struggling this time, needing to stay off her feet, so they won't share the news for a while yet."

Arie turned, snuggling against her as her eyelids became heavier. She finally closed them, drawing the deep breaths of sleep.

When Rhoda looked up, Samuel's gaze unnerved her.

She lowered her eyes, studying Arie's innocent face. "So what's going on?"

"Jacob wants your blessing on Iva's plan. He feels that while you've been with him you've been too passive to be in the right mood to know what you think about it."

"So basically you're here to rattle my cage."

His eyes met hers, a hint of an apology reflected in them. "It's a given that we have no problem annoying each other, and that often helps us decide on a good course of action." He returned his attention to the horse and galloped it across the floor as far as his arm could reach. "In his defense you are the one who hates 'I don't know' responses, and that's all you've given him for days."

One night last fall she'd dragged Samuel into an argument she was having with Jacob. Sitting here now, she realized her disagreements with Samuel were nothing like the ones with Jacob. She and Samuel were harsher, but when they were done, the air felt like springtime after a rain. She and Jacob held back. He said very little, because it's who he was, and he needed her to be soft-spoken and careful with her words. But when they were done, she felt as if they weren't done.

They needed to work on that.

"Why is it important I have an answer now?"

It was several moments before he cleared his throat. "The lawyer's office called, so Sandra needs to move soon. Jacob wants your decision."

"The whole plan makes me anxious." It defied good sense to give Iva almost three thousand dollars in cash to help Sandra get settled somewhere. They didn't know Iva that well, but Rhoda couldn't see a good reason for doubting her, especially after Jacob challenged Rhoda's attitude about Nicole.

From his spot on the floor, Samuel gazed out the window. "May I remind you that you're the one who wanted everyone to brainstorm? Now you're the one who's wavering."

"If you're that clear about it, why don't you give Jacob the answer he wants?"

He looked at her, one eyebrow raised slightly. "It wouldn't help. If something backfires or we run short of money for the business because it was spent on this, Jacob needs to know *you* supported the plan."

"Do you agree with it?"

"I think when Jacob feels strongly about something pertaining to you or Sandra, he's probably right." He ran his hand over the braided area rug. "I wish I could go in Iva's stead. That would make the most sense."

"You? It'd be against your role as a church member."

"I've broken the rules a few times, and I haven't perished yet. Most would say partnering with you and allowing you to take on such a leadership role in the business is breaking the *Ordnung*."

She was glad he went against the grain on that, but she couldn't say it without sounding inappropriate. It seemed to her she couldn't think half of her thoughts or questions about Samuel without them being inappropriate.

She steadied her heart and focused on why he'd come to speak with her. This situation with Sandra was representative of Jacob and her—one of them having a need the other couldn't fill. That wasn't uncommon for couples. No one person could fulfill all the other's needs. The least she could do was give him peace about what needed to be done. "Iva should follow through on her plan. The checks are cashed, and the money is in the safe."

Samuel picked up the newspaper and unfolded it. "You won't have time to miss Jacob while he's in Virginia."

She read the headline, her heart pounding. "When will the temperature drop?"

"In two or three days." He sounded so calm. "If Jacob could postpone the deposition, I know he would. But he said it's lined up with the attorneys and a court reporter."

Several times Jacob had accused her of defending Samuel, but it seemed more like Samuel was the one who found ways to defend his brother. Should she tell him he didn't need to? Since the night before moving to Maine, she'd realized Jacob had obligations that came ahead of her.

Cradling Arie, she smiled down at her. Phoebe was at the beginning of another long journey of bringing a child into this world.

Love was worth all it took to yield a harvest.

Wisps of Arie's baby-fine hair had broken free from its confines, and Rhoda brushed it off the little girl's face. Before Jacob left, she needed to be perfectly clear to Samuel.

"In a way I suppose Jacob and I might be similar to the orchard and the approaching storm, but I won't let an untimely frost ruin the crop between us."

When Samuel said nothing, she looked up.

He stood. "I want that for both of you."

But as he walked out and closed the door behind him, she realized she had lost her earlier sense of contentment.

EIGHTEEN

Iva sat in a booth of a diner with Sandra and Casey. Every muscle in her body ached as she looked through the ads in the local newspaper. There were no shortages of small houses for rent around here, but the prices seemed high. Then again, how would she know? It wasn't as if she had experience in buying or renting homes in Indiana, let alone here. Is this where Jacob would want his friends, in a small town in New Hampshire? Or should she take them elsewhere?

Casey picked up a clump of spaghetti with both hands, ate the middle section, and put the rest on her head.

"Eat. Don't play with your food." Sandra removed the spaghetti from the little girl's hair. "Iva, are you full already?"

Iva looked at her half-eaten burger. "Ya." She moaned while stretching. "You like it here?"

"Better than where we were." Sandra reached into her purse and pulled out a bottle of ibuprofen. "Jacob will be pleased, if that's your concern."

Iva hoped Sandra was right. It was awkward being in a position to lead and make decisions. She hadn't realized how much she'd hate the responsibility until she'd driven Landon's truck to Sandra's apartment that morning. There she faced the reality that Sandra and Casey would have to live with every choice she made for the next forty-eight hours—at least for now. But she believed Jacob was the reason she'd been invited to stay at the farm, and she wanted to return the favor by helping him out of this jam. And Samuel had been so very kind to her.

She also needed to prove to Rhoda that she was a good employee. So everything she was doing was worth it. If she had to move Sandra around every month in order to stay out of Indiana, it'd be worth it.

She circled an advertisement for a small home in a nearby town. "I didn't realize people could pull up stakes and move so easily."

"I wouldn't call it easy. But that's what you did by moving to Maine, isn't it?"

"I didn't have any furniture to move or need to find a place to live or have a little one to protect."

Sandra took two ibuprofen tablets. "You Amish sure seem to have a thing about protecting children."

"I imagine, as a whole, Christians across the world feel the same way. It's part of the teaching and culture of Christ. Besides, look at her."

Casey had marinara sauce over most of her face.

Sandra held out two tablets to Iva. "Jacob used to talk of his faith...before I dragged him down to a place where God didn't exist."

"That's not possible. Wherever a person is, God is there."

Sandra had told her a lot today about her relationship with Jacob. The peek inside his life among the Englisch captivated and confused her.

Iva picked up her water and swallowed the tablets. "It sounds as if he'll feel much better once he testifies." How nervous did he feel about now, the night before he was to give his deposition? She turned the paper around for Sandra. "See any I haven't marked that might be worth looking at?"

Sandra straightened her ball cap and skimmed them. "No."

"You barely looked."

Sandra passed her back the newspaper. "Beggars can't be choosers."

Iva laid the paper on the table. Maybe it would help Sandra to know a few things about her story. "We're all beggars at some point. I arrived at the King farm, begging them not to send me home. My Daed begged me to marry a wealthy widower, and I begged him to reconsider. When he didn't, my Mamm begged me to take her stash of money and find a place where the men in my family could earn a living." Iva took a sip of her milk shake. "Of course no one actually begged, but you get the idea."

Sandra grabbed a napkin and wiped Casey's hands. "Your dad sounds like a man who's willing to sell his daughter for what he wants."

Was that what she had conveyed? "No, not at all."

"I'm not convinced. Are you?"

"He encouraged me to marry a good man. Later he added more and more pressure, but the decision was mine."

"It was still selfish."

"He doesn't see it that way. In his eyes he's put an acceptable, godly request on the table. Leon's a fine man who's aware of what my father wants from him, and he's willing to give it."

"In exchange for you marrying him."

"Well...yes."

"That's just a nicer way of selling someone, only it'd be for a lifetime."

"My father believes I'm the one being selfish to do only what I want."

"He's rationalizing. In his mind he's figured out all the reasons he's not wrong. He can probably even put scripture to it. But Jacob once told me something I've never forgotten. If you can remove all chance of making any money or perks from a venture, does that change how you feel about it? If that man were poor and couldn't help your family, would your dad still want you to marry him?"

"I hadn't thought of it like that, but I'm sure he wouldn't."

"If your Daed's motivation was in your best interest, he wouldn't let money be the deciding factor. He's hoping to profit from it while you give up your future to a man you don't love."

"So what was Jacob's motive for breaking the law?"

"Helping me and my husband so we didn't go bankrupt. Finding solutions so Jacob's buddies on the construction site didn't lose their jobs. He wasn't going to make a penny more for his efforts. Later he tried hiding Blaine's crimes so my husband wouldn't go to jail. But too many people were lying to Jacob, including me—all of us rationalizing our actions and trying to get what we wanted. We ruined his ability to do what he wanted—to make right the wrongs we'd done."

"Go now!" Casey slapped the table. "Go *now*!"

Sandra pointed at her daughter. "Use your nice words."

Casey's eyes clouded with tears. "Go home?"

"Yes." Sandra glanced at the motel across the road. "Such as it is." She gathered her purse and the diaper bag. "I'm going back now to bathe her before she has a meltdown. You coming?"

Iva shook her head. "Jacob should be at his hotel soon. He seemed under a lot of stress this morning concerning you, Casey, and me. I thought I'd relieve as much of that as I can. He's got enough pressure with needing to testify and the frost coming." She pointed. "And there's a pay phone here."

"Oh, that's right. You can't call from the motel without a credit card."

"Even if I could use that phone, its number would show up on his caller ID. But at home when I received a call from someone at a pay phone, it never revealed the caller information."

Sandra stood and picked up Casey. "I loaned him my cell. You need that number?"

"It's in the vault." Iva tapped her forehead, rolled her eyes, and pulled up the long sleeve to her dress. "Jacob wrote it in permanent ink before boarding the train."

Sandra chuckled. "You're okay. You know that?" She shifted Casey. "You look to be about sixteen, but you've got the maturity of someone my age."

"So I look like a teen and think like a mom. Got it."

Sandra raised an eyebrow. "That was a Jacob statement if I ever heard one."

Sandra looked to be pushing forty, but Jacob said she wasn't much older than him. As Iva was driving Jacob to the train station before dawn, he'd given her a few tips for helping Sandra. He'd been right—listening and humor would lead to smooth sailing.

She waited until nine o'clock to go to the pay phone. After putting some change into the slot, she dialed the number.

"This is Jacob."

It sounded quiet where he was. "Hi. It's Iva."

"Is everything okay?"

"Ya, that's why I called—to let you know we're doing fine."

"That's nice of you. A phone number didn't come through, so I don't even have an area code. How many hours did you travel today?"

"I'm not saying. We had no mishaps along the way. So how are you?"

"Sort of relieved to be at this point but far more nervous than anything."

"I can't imagine having to take an oath and then answer every question about anything. I might pass out."

"Me too."

She laughed. "There is good news for both of us."

"I'd love to hear it."

"We are not manning the orchards all night, keeping those fires going. We'll be inside, snuggly warm."

Jacob chuckled. "I'd rather be there than here."

"Next time a frost comes through, I demand you tell the others that Sandra needs to move again."

"From here on out, I don't intend to lie for any reason, so I can't help you there. But after the orchard is established and the canning business is running smoothly, maybe a year from now, Samuel will hire some more workers, and you won't have to help in the fields. A little success for Kings' Orchard, and you'll be sleeping in a warm bed while the farmhands work around the clock."

"If that's the plan, will I still be needed?"

He didn't say anything for a moment. "That's my plan, ya."

She liked the sound of that. "Have you talked to anyone at the farm?"

"No. They have a heavy work load tonight, so calling would only slow them down."

Iva unfolded the map. "I've been looking at the map and train schedule, and I think the best depot for you to get off at when you return is Old Orchard Beach. It'll save me having to fight Boston traffic or going an hour north of the farm to get to our usual depot."

"You sure that plan will work? Last fall, when making train reservations for the move to Orchard Bend, I hoped to get a few hours at the beach along the way, but I learned the train only stops there at certain times of the year."

"I checked. Off-season is officially over, and the train began stopping there again about two weeks ago. It's never easy for me to read these train schedules, but I think that unless you can board the train in Virginia by five thirty on Friday, you'll have to catch the late one on Saturday, and I'll meet you in Orchard Bend on Sunday around noon."

"Craig said we might not be done until seven or eight tomorrow night. So let's plan on me arriving there Sunday."

"Sounds good. You'll do great tomorrow."

"Glad you think so. Then maybe I can finally have my life back."

Now that she had Sandra's version, so many questions about the position Jacob was in were zipping through Iva's mind. But they needed to hang up before she had to add any more coins to the phone box. "I'd better go. Bye, Jacob."

As she gathered her assortment of maps, train schedules, and classified ads, she felt an unfamiliar weight. Since getting her driver's license a little more than three years ago, she'd traveled to a few places close to home, either alone or with a girlfriend or two. Those road trips were just for the fun of it. It'd been exhilarating when she had money to visit places just to see them and take pictures, but Jacob trusted her to find a safe, affordable place for Sandra.

In her desire to prove her value to the budding settlement, she had forgotten to ask herself what would happen if she proved the opposite.

NINETEEN

The skies were a gorgeous red and orange as the sun dipped below the horizon. Leah bundled her coat around her as she trudged through the orchard, her toes and fingertips stinging with the early night's frosty bite. This would be their first night to maintain the fires.

As she approached one of the steel drums, she noticed it needed more wood. She took two logs from a nearby pile and tossed them into the oversize can. Ashes and embers flew out. The logs popped and sizzled away the bits of frost that had accumulated on them.

"Hallo?" Samuel's voice crackled through her two-way. "Has anyone checked on barrels thirty-one through thirty-six in the last couple of hours?"

Leah unclipped the walkie-talkie from her coat pocket and pushed the button. "Ya, I'm here now." She scanned the drums down the row.

They'd started the fires around nine that morning, aiming to build the smog effect that would create a shield of heat hovering over the treetops. The temperature had dropped below freezing several hours ago, and Leah was already looking forward to tomorrow afternoon when it'd warm up for a few hours and she could get some sleep.

She pushed the talk button on the two-way again. "I had to feed the ones that needed it, and now we're low on lumber at those barrels."

The fires were growing larger, but it'd be quite a night to keep them going. And tomorrow night too. Hopefully, they'd need to keep this up for only two nights.

The strategic placement of the dozens of steel drums was done. The low-lying areas of the orchard had blazing fires going to keep the hoarfrost off the trees so they could continue budding.

"All right," Samuel acknowledged. "I'm in the farthest dip on the west side. It'll be a while before I can get back that way."

"I just filled the wagon with wood. I'll take her a load," Landon chimed in.

"Thanks." She reattached her two-way, smiling at the sound of Landon's voice.

She rubbed her gloved hands together and held them out to the warm drum, feeling a rush of relief as the heat eased her fingers of their numbness. Staring into the soft glow of the flames, she allowed her mind to wander. Long before she'd met Landon, she'd dreamed about leaving the Amish—actually she'd dreamed that for most of her life. But did she really want to separate from the Amish, from her family, and forsake the safety net interwoven among so many relatives? When Kings' Orchard had suffered storm damage, family and church members from across the state had given money and supplies to help them restore the property and purchase this one. Without charging a penny, Jacob and their brother Eli had repaired Amish homes that'd been damaged. Her Daed had provided families with food from the farm—milk, eggs, and homemade yogurts. Every Mamm who was able in the storm-ravaged area had made meals for those whose kitchens had been damaged. No one went hungry or felt isolated or was overwhelmed without the Amish people reaching out, giving all they had to bring comfort.

They didn't do that based on the rules Leah hated so much. They did so because those who kept the Old Ways had favor with all the others who did the same. The Amish were a family.

But if tragedy brought out the best in the Amish, someone leaving the faith brought out the worst in them. Even if she was willing to give up the good parts of living Amish, was she willing to suffer all the angst it'd take to get free?

Landon thought he knew what it'd take for her to get free, but he didn't. The pressure her family and community would apply was similar to the present battle with mother nature, only the harsh, cold treatment from her community wouldn't improve in a few days. Or even a few years.

Still, if she wanted help in leaving, she had the very best—Landon. He wasn't pulling or pushing. But—

Something touched her shoulder, and she gasped. She spun around to see

Landon standing there with a stack of lumber balanced on his right arm and a travel mug in his left hand. He grinned, handing the mug to her. "Didn't mean to scare you, but I gotta admit, it was adorable."

He'd called her *adorable*. She released the breath she'd been holding since he'd touched her. "I need more wood than that. Where's the wagon?"

"Over the ridge where Rhoda's fighting to keep one of the fires going."

She cradled the mug. "Thank you."

"For the cocoa, the wood, or the heart attack?" He turned around and added the logs to the dwindling pile.

"The first two. You'll have to pay for the third one." She sipped the cocoa and let the sensation of sweetness and warmth permeate her. She would miss this—and a thousand things like it—if Landon grew weary of waiting for her.

But she'd seen other Amish leave, and in her experience those ex-Amish spent a decade either embroiled in correction through letters and calls, or they received a cold shoulder—usually both. Eventually, when the families tried to put the differences behind them and open the lines of communication, it was awkward, void of affection, and empty of respect—on both sides.

Did Landon have any idea how much she wavered on the subject? Leaving the Amish for the Englisch world would run a knife through her parents' hearts. It didn't matter what her reason was. Even if she believed it was God's leading, the Amish wouldn't accept that as reasonable thinking. To them, God had placed her in an Amish home, and it was her responsibility to live according to that calling.

Landon knocked some debris from his gloves and coat. "The barrels in this section stoked?"

"I'm standing here doing nothing but warming my fingers, aren't I?"

"Seems so."

"Then they're in good shape."

He walked off, going down the row of apple trees, inspecting the barrels.

"So"—she cupped her hands around the mug of hot chocolate—"my word that all is well isn't good enough?"

He barely glanced at her before motioning he'd be back in a minute.

Her thoughts returned to the struggle it'd be to leave the Amish. Jacob was the only one she'd seen leave and return home without having to go through misery, but he'd simply packed his bags and disappeared. He'd called every so often just to let the family know he was safe. When anyone had tried to convince him what he needed to do, he'd politely gotten off the phone. Then they wouldn't hear from him for months. His parents had quickly learned that if they wanted him to stay in touch, they'd best not push him to come home.

That was Jacob. He'd been very "my way or the highway" with his family, and armed with confidence and strong carpentry skills, he'd made it work for him.

Leah couldn't disappear the way he had. Not only did she lack the skills to make good money, but she had no desire to disappear, leaving her family to long for her.

Was that why more girls than guys stayed Amish? Because their hearts were too tender toward their families? Then, like Jacob, the men often stayed or returned because they'd fallen in love with a woman who was unwilling to forsake her family.

Landon ambled back toward her, a broad smile in place. "The fires are all good in your section, and I don't see any frost accumulating on your trees."

She refused to return his grin. He needed to believe she was plotting against him for scaring her a few minutes ago.

He stretched his hands over the heat.

Leah scowled. "But you just *had* to inspect them regardless of me telling you they were good." Did he get tired of her teasing and being sassy?

"Rhoda said do a visual, and so I did. She's always been like a mother hen over her fruit crops, and if she didn't trust me to do exactly as she asked, I wouldn't be much use to her, would I?"

"Ah." She took another sip of cocoa and decided to move to a different topic. "Do you think Jacob's in Virginia by now?"

"Should be, unless the train was delayed or something."

"I'm proud of him for doing this."

"Yeah, it's cool, I guess."

"You guess? He made mistakes and is owning up to them." Was she not seeing some aspect of what Jacob was doing?

"He helped make the train wreck. It's only right he help clean it up. You sound as if he deserves a trophy."

"It's hard to own up to the bad things we've done. He thought he might go to jail."

"Yeah, I know." He shrugged. "And it's good he's getting it straight. But if you're looking for heroes in this, I think it was pretty cool of Rhoda and Samuel to help him out financially and for Iva to volunteer like she did. I expected Steven to have some strong words for Jacob leaving again while this farm needs him. Did he?"

"Not that I know of."

"See, that's the main thing I respect about the Amish. They help each other out no matter what."

She took a long sip of her cocoa. "As long as one stays Amish."

Landon stepped toward her, removing his gloves. He held out one hand.

She stood there for a moment, not quite certain how to receive this gesture. "I thought you didn't like holding hands."

His lopsided smile made her heart thump. He lowered his arm, jiggling it for a moment, and a booklet slid out of his coat sleeve and into his hand. "Care to take a look at this?"

She took it from him and studied the front of it: *State of Maine Motorist Handbook and Study Guide.* "A driver's manual?" Had she shrieked at him?

"I thought you'd like the idea."

With her index finger she made looping circles near her temple. "Everything keeps churning inside my head. My past. My future. If I leave the Amish, then I give up everything I've ever known and not just the bad but the good too." She removed a glove and flipped through the pages. "But if I stay Amish, will I ever be truly happy? There's no guarantee either way. All I do is waver, and you bring me a book like this?"

He stared at her. "I've been thinking, and it seems to me that whether you stay Amish or not, you should know how to drive. What if there's a real need to drive one day? Maybe something that's an emergency and you can't wait for an ambulance? My truck could be in the driveway, but I might be out in the field somewhere, or I might be the one who needs to be driven to a clinic. Or you could need to call my grandmother and borrow her car, except that plan won't work either because you don't know how to drive. Every healthy adult should know how to drive and have a license. Period."

The war of right and wrong raged within her, and tears stung her eyes. People were wrong about the Amish life being simple. It was so very complicated. Were it not so, she would do everything in her power to hold on to Landon. She'd been so set on leaving the Amish until she'd witnessed how bravely her family had pulled together and faced all the troubles of the past year.

"Leah, am I wrong?"

The manual looked daunting, and she still couldn't imagine asking her mom for her birth certificate so she could get her driver's license. "Not wrong." She tucked the book into her pocket. The idea felt empowering. It also felt... sinful.

Driving aside, would it solve any of her issues about joining the faith if Landon also joined? She didn't know if she even liked that idea. His joining the faith wouldn't lessen her work load or make the rules easier to bear. Nonetheless, she was intensely curious. "Ever thought of becoming Amish?"

Landon almost snorted, as if he was trying to muffle a laugh. "Not even for a moment."

Leah was certain her face was now bright crimson, even in the firelight.

He held his hands over the fire. "I used to dream of helping Rhoda escape the life, except she never wanted to. I understand why she feels that way. It's part of her heart as well as who she is. But it's not the life for me, Leah."

"Because you'd have to give up modern technology?"

"That'd be a sacrifice, but the real issue is I don't agree with the Ordnung. If you do, I respect that—just like I do for Rhoda. But to me it's a list of rules created by men who've decided God doesn't want people to move forward with the times."

"But you've just recently started going to church. So can you be sure what God wants or feels?"

"Nope. But if sin is an issue of the heart, a set of man-made rules isn't going to fix it. Is someone less sinful because they drive a horse and buggy rather than a car?"

"A rig keeps a person closer to home."

"And if sin is in the heart, then the sin is kept closer to home, right?" He chuckled. "Seriously, does washing clothes in a wringer washer and hanging them on the line make the heart more pure than using an electric washing machine and dryer?"

"Women are to be keepers of the home, and our paced ways keep idle hands busy."

"So you, Phoebe, and Rhoda have problems being idle?"

"No, but we're not typical Amish women."

"But you and any Amish woman who might stretch outside the Ordnung boundary have to follow the rule book about how to accomplish tasks in a specific way, even if doing so is a heavy, unnecessary burden on your day. It keeps the Amish beliefs and culture strong, and I get that. It's worth protecting in many, many ways. But you, Rhoda, and Phoebe should be free to handle a day as you see fit. It's between you and God, not between you and the Ordnung. So joining the Amish is not for me."

"Okay, okay." Leah raised her mug in surrender. "I get it. I was only thinking out loud."

"That's fine. I just don't want to lie to you or mislead you. I like to be honest. And believe me, I'll always be honest with you."

The driver's manual in her coat pocket felt like a pile of rocks. "And you think I should learn to drive?"

"I do." He reached into his back pocket and pulled out his wallet. "The day Rhoda's sister was killed, Rhoda was in her fruit garden when she had an insight. In her panic to get to Emma, she fell hard, and when the gunshot rang out, Rhoda went into shock. I was in my truck, going down the road, minding my own business, when I saw her. I peeled her off the concrete, but I knew nothing to do for her other than take her to the closest medical facility." He pulled a card out of his billfold. "Not long after that, I took a course in CPR and first aid. I've not needed it so far, but at least now I have some idea what to do and not do."

She turned the card over again and again. His line of thinking had more than just merit. She now had a valid motive for getting a license. Guilt faded, and she no longer wavered on this one topic. Could he do that with other topics as well? "If I never need to use the license, what harm came of having it? But if an emergency arose and I didn't possess the skill, I couldn't turn back the hands of time."

"Exactly."

"Landon." Leah wasn't sure how she was going to ask her next question.

"Yeah?"

"You have solid reasons why I should get a license. You got any of that for why I shouldn't remain Amish?"

"Actually, I—"

"Hallo." Samuel strode toward them. "Landon, the east dip has a wind cutting through it, so it's used more wood than expected. If you'll drive, I'll unload wood as we go."

"Sure."

As they disappeared over the knoll, Leah was relieved Samuel had interrupted them. Did she really want to know Landon's explanations for why she shouldn't join the faith?

There were things she had to figure out on her own. She pulled the driver's manual out of her pocket and smiled.

And things she needed to learn from sources outside of her people.

TWENTY

Rhoda roused, opening her eyes. It was dark, but the silhouettes surrounding her were of the living room in the farmhouse. The couch under her was soft and inviting, but how'd she get here? She sat upright, trying to read the clock. The digital ones at the Cranfords' were much easier to see.

She squinted, making out the positions of the hands. Five o'clock. The faint memory of coming in around three thirty to warm up teased her brain. Maybe she'd rested her eyes for a moment and fallen asleep.

She breathed in the smells and feel of home with its crooked staircase, oversize hearths, and windows that rattled when the wind howled. Camilla's place was much nicer, but being under this roof reminded her of the old house she'd grown up in. Unlike her home in Morgansville, Pennsylvania, here she was free to be herself—uncomfortable intuitions and all. Samuel saw to that. Jacob would too when he was settled and living here full-time.

Her eyes and body ached, but tending to the orchard was as much a part of her now as it was any of the Kings. The sense of contentment and joy defied logic, especially as they fought against the frost, but she never felt more alive or gratified than when nurturing plants.

She grabbed her overnight bag off a chair and staggered into the bathroom. She flipped on the shower before looking out the tiny window. It was impossible to see much from here, but she caught a glimpse of someone driving a wagon out of the orchard. After a quick shower and some food, she'd relieve Leah.

Before long Rhoda was walking into the kitchen. Samuel sat at the table with his back to the fire and a mug of coffee in hand. A dozen emotions hit her all at once, surprising her. She missed having time with him before anyone else was up. Guilt and fear nipped at her. Apparently Jacob had been more right than she'd realized to want her living with Camilla and Bob. But what about returning here to live?

"Morning." She tried to sound casual. Had she managed it? It'd probably be wise to eat a few bites of food and leave. There was a loaf of breakfast bread on the table. Near it were small plates, each holding separate items: butter, cheese, and fruits.

Samuel glanced up, looking no worse for the wear of working all through the night. "Good morning." His voice sounded hoarse from breathing in the smoke from the wood and oil fires. Did hers?

The plate in front of him was more than half full, so he wasn't done eating. He focused on the contents of his mug.

She sat across from him. Would he forgive her if she said the truth: that she missed talking with him over coffee before sunrise?

His eyes met hers, and she rose and got a mug and a clean plate from the cabinet. "How did the trees fare?" She filled the cup with coffee.

"Good, I think. I saw no signs of frost accumulating, but we won't know for sure until the buds either continue to blossom or wither."

Like relationships, she thought.

When she returned to the table, she focused on the food on her plate. "Did Jacob call?" She knew he'd checked the phone messages before coming inside.

"No." Samuel folded his newspaper and stared at it. "He won't, not with us working around the clock."

"He's a good man." Why had she said that?

"You don't need to justify your feelings to me."

"I wasn't," she snapped, but maybe she was. Or was she trying to remind herself where her loyalties were and why? Desperate to leave the house, she crammed several bites of bread into her mouth and tried to wash it down with coffee that was entirely too hot. With the mass of food swallowed, she wrapped the rest of the items on her plate in a napkin, ready to put it in her apron pocket and go.

Samuel lifted his mug. "It's awkward being in this room without him here, isn't it?"

She took a deep breath. "Very."

She and Samuel had spent months of mornings quietly talking while Jacob was away. What a fool she'd been not to realize how close she'd grown to Samuel during that time.

She shoved the napkin into her apron pocket, not quite as panicked to rush to the door. How did a little direct honesty manage to quiet the storm of nerves in her?

"It's just us, Rhoda. The same me. The same you. I won't cross the line again. Can you trust that?"

Is that what had her spooked, thinking he might say or do something inappropriate? She picked up the mug and held it close to her lips, willing to finish the drink before leaving. "I do trust that."

Samuel briefly touched the back of her hand with his finger, sending shock waves through her. When she looked up, he nodded toward the kitchen door. Phoebe had walked into the kitchen, and she stood there, pale and trembling.

Rhoda went to her. "What's wrong?"

Phoebe's eyes brimmed with tears as she turned her back toward Samuel. "I lost my baby." She embraced Rhoda, sobbing.

TWENTY-ONE

Jacob stared at the gray walls of the conference room. The windowless chamber was void of any decoration, including a clock.

While waiting for the attorney to ask him another question, he let his mind meander. Time. A lot of Amish men removed the bands on their wristwatches and carried the watches in their pockets. He'd never cared to do that. There was no need for it on the farm or at a construction site. He could guess the time and be close enough, but right now he had no clue what the hour was.

Four men and a woman were with him: three lawyers, a paralegal, and a court reporter. Craig had contacted his colleague Tony Gates to represent Jacob. The upside was Jacob wouldn't need his services all that much. Even if Jacob had to return to testify, he wouldn't need a lawyer to accompany him. The downside was the questioning had been going on for more than five hours, and Jacob was paying his lawyer $275 an hour.

His chest ached as the fullness of his wrongdoing hounded him.

"Okay." Tony took a deep breath while looking through his notes. He sounded so bored that Jacob thought he might doze off midsentence. "We know you're getting tired. It won't be much longer."

That had been said several times even before they took a break for lunch. Maybe it was how these men kept from going stir-crazy sitting inside most of the day, hashing and rehashing events they cared nothing about.

Despite the court reporter recording every word, Tony scribbled notes on his own pad.

It was beginning to dawn on Jacob that the more he answered their questions, the more the blame seemed to shift onto his shoulders. If he'd seen what was wrong at the construction site, why had he continued to work for the company? Did he think he had what was needed to fix it?

One of the lawyers slid a paper across to Tony.

Tony nodded and then looked at Jacob. "Should we take a break?"

Compared to everyone fighting the frost at Orchard Bend, Jacob was doing nothing but sitting in this room. Nevertheless, exhaustion weighed heavily on him. "I'm fine." He just wanted to be done.

The day had started with the lawyers bringing in stacks of paperwork and pages of questions, which they'd asked him in quick succession. But as the day wore on, the men seemed to take each of his answers and then ask a different question.

Would his testimony help the families of the two women who'd been killed when the deck collapsed?

He hoped so.

Tony laid the paper on the table and nodded to a lawyer.

The attorney introduced as Patrick focused on Jacob. "How much time passed between when the deck collapsed and when you left town?"

"An hour, maybe a little more."

"What took place between the time the deck fell and when you left?"

Did he have to explain that again? How much shame could one room hold?

"Do you need the question repeated?" Tony asked.

Jacob shook his head and relayed the whole story again. When he learned about the deck, his first instinct was to run. At the time he hadn't really understood why, but it slowly dawned on him. Regardless of having the right motivation, he knew he'd been a part of too many shady dealings for Jones' Construction, and when the deck fell, he'd reacted out of guilt and fear. He'd followed his emotions and checked with Sandra. She'd assured him that, if he stayed, he'd go to jail for crimes he hadn't committed. After talking with her, he believed Blaine had set him up. Now he knew that Sandra had believed that too.

"Did you contact Blaine McAlister before leaving?"

Jacob studied his hands. "I tried, but I couldn't reach him."

"Did you contact Skeet Jones of Jones' Construction?"

"I tried."

"But you believed the men knew what had happened?"

"Yes."

"What made you believe they knew what had taken place?"

"I returned to the office, and no one was there. The safe was wide open and empty. The filing cabinet had been ransacked. I called Blaine's cell phone and discovered it in the trash. So I called Sandra, Blaine's wife, to see if she'd heard from him. She had. He'd come home in a rush, packing and talking quickly. He indicated that he'd set me up to take the fall for ordering substandard parts. His message to her and me was to go into hiding because there would be an investigation that could send a lot of people to jail."

Jacob took a drink from his water bottle. "I didn't know until later that neither the quality of the deck I designed nor the bolts had anything to do with the deck falling. When I found out that the nuts hadn't been attached to the bolts, I realized the fault was negligence by the finishing crew and the inspector."

"If you left within an hour of the deck falling, how do you know that piece of information?"

"About a year later I used a phone with an unlisted number and called one of the men I had worked with. I lied about where I was, claiming to be in California, and I asked about the outcome of the deck falling. He told me what an insurance adjuster had told him, and he said the man wanted to talk to me. He gave me the man's phone number. I assured him I'd call, but I never did."

Actually, now that Jacob thought about it, he remembered feeling almost obsessed to remain in hiding. It'd been immature of him, but after the deck collapse and the company being investigated because of it, he simply returned to his family and hid from the rest of the world, hoping the mistakes of his past would never catch up with him.

One of the attorneys studied another document. "Did you return to Virginia Beach at any point after the deck fell?"

"Two or three days later."

"Why?"

Jacob paused. "It was apparent that Blaine's wife needed to go into hiding, but that had nothing to do with the construction company."

"Why did Sandra McAlister need to go into hiding?"

"She said she'd borrowed money from some loan sharks and couldn't repay it. Blaine disappeared, leaving her with nothing."

According to both Craig's and Tony's instructions before the deposition, Jacob had to answer the questions based solely on what he knew at the time. But the truth was, he never *knew* anything for certain. That's the thing about lies—once inside the storm, even the liars aren't sure what is and isn't true.

The lawyer laid a hospital receipt in front of him. "While in Virginia Beach and helping Sandra McAlister move, you were injured. How did that happen?"

It rattled Jacob to realize just how much these people knew about him. "I had her and her baby girl packed and ready to go when two men showed up. She said they were the loan sharks, wanting the money she owed them. I tried to reason with them. I offered to pay her debt over time, but they wouldn't hear of it. I ended up fighting them while she fled with Casey."

The questions went on and on, and Jacob was feeling increasingly disgusted with himself. He could barely hold his head up. He'd known back then that he should have talked to the police, to the insurance adjuster, to the families of the women who had died.

But he hadn't.

As the meeting came to a close, he remained still while the other lawyers and the court reporter packed up and left.

Tony turned to him. "You okay?"

The same words kept circling inside Jacob over and over. He stared at the table. "I knew those women had died, and I left. I just left. There are no excuses, no reasons that hold up."

"The accident wasn't your fault. We have proof of that. There was nothing you could have done to prevent their deaths."

Jacob knew better. Did the lawyer know it too but just didn't want to say it to Jacob's face? Jacob could have helped put Blaine in jail a year earlier, and that deck never would've been built. Those women would still be alive.

Tony put the rest of the papers into his briefcase and closed it. "Life is murky at best, especially when you're an inexperienced teen. That's all you were when you met Blaine." He headed for the door and motioned for Jacob to follow. "There will be two wrongful death trials, one for each woman. You may be called to testify at both. How much of those trials will be covered in the papers I can't say, but you need to be prepared."

Prepared.

He and Tony walked down the tiled corridors of the huge building.

Each time Rhoda had learned a new piece to the story, she'd taken it in stride. But Jacob hated the idea of returning home with another grievous aspect to explain. He'd tried to tell her everything last October, within a week of moving to Maine, but she'd stopped him, saying she couldn't bear to hear any more. Since that's how she felt, maybe he shouldn't try to bring it up again.

Tony pushed the button to the elevator. "I've been doing this awhile, and you're taking this harder than you should."

"I'll be fine." Jacob stepped into the elevator. Despite his words he didn't feel fine. By coming here he'd done what he needed to do. So why couldn't he breathe?

"You're free, Jacob. You went home for all the wrong reasons. Now you've set everything right, and you can do whatever you want—as long as the courts and I have a way to reach you."

He nodded, but as he stood inside the elevator, he continued to fight a suffocating feeling as the walls seemed to close in on him. The doors opened, and the two men left the elevator and walked through the echoing halls until they stepped onto the sidewalk.

A banging sound reverberated through the air, and Jacob paused, a smile embracing his lips as the word *freedom* rang inside him. He couldn't see anyone, but somewhere nearby construction workers were hammering away—building or remodeling something far more lasting than any work he did when farming.

Could he do some of both?

TWENTY-TWO

Brisk air filled Samuel's lungs as he chucked another piece of wood into the back of the wagon. It'd be dark again in a few hours, and then the temperature would drop quickly. Around lunchtime they'd banked the embers and taken a much-needed break while the sun warmed the earth to thirty-four degrees.

Now they were stoking the embers and adding fuel to the fires again.

"Samuel!"

He looked up to find Rhoda holding a lunchpail.

Speaking of stoking embers and adding fuel to the fire...

"Ya?"

Considering the way he'd pulled her into his arms that day, she probably thought he lusted after her. But it wasn't that at all. That had been a moment of temporary insanity, a moment of weakness after months of being near her night and day.

He was sane now, and he'd accept being ignored or tossed aside as need be, as long as he didn't interfere with her happiness. *That* was not lust. Still, he had more than a fair share of desire for her—desire to marry and have children with her, to cherish her and grow old with her. Instead, he would, by sheer force of will, wrestle desire into silence, leaving only prayers and friendship.

But it would take a while.

"Feels odd not to have at least one dog at my heels." She came to a halt near him.

He knew she'd put them inside to rest. With people working in the field around the clock last night and hauling wood in the wagons, the dogs never stood still. They stayed right beside the workers.

She glanced at the dwindling stack of wood. "Sorry to disrupt your work, but I have news, good and bad. Which do you prefer first?"

He scowled as he grabbed a split log in each hand and tossed them into the wagon. "What I'd prefer is for you not to have any bad news."

"Don't shoot the messenger. I'm just doing my job."

"Job?" He stopped and stared at her. "If bringing bad news is your job, please vacate Kings' Orchard Maine...right after you spend all night helping fight the frost."

"We need a better name for this farm, something more befitting."

"Is that the good news?"

"No, that's a long-overdue observation."

He tossed more wood into the wagon. "Ever heard the phrase 'one thing at a time'? You should try it. I believe it'd keep you from dragging me down that meandering path inside your head."

She studied him, a gentle smile drawing him like a moth to the flame. "This"— she held up the lunchpail—"is the bad news. Camilla had hoped to bring by a pot of lobster stew on her way to somewhere. She said she'd pass right by here." Rhoda shrugged. "Maybe she's just running late, but since we're about to be in the fields for the night, *this* is what's for dinner."

Ideally one didn't stay up around the clock working in the cold without being fed really well, so in that sense it was bad news. "I don't mind even a little. How's Phoebe?"

The sadness in Rhoda's eyes tightened his heart. Should he have asked, trying to ease her grief, or said nothing and helped her not think about it? That seemed to be the age-old question when it came to sorrow, and he didn't know the answer.

Rhoda put her hands in her coat pockets. "It'll take a little time."

"Sure. I told Steven as much. But when you can, assure him that he should stay in with her tonight as much as she needs him."

"I will. Denki." She set his lunch on the back of the wagon. "You have mail from someone in my old hometown." She reached into her pocket and pulled out a letter.

"Ah, the real bad news, eh?" He took it from her, half expecting it to be from her church leaders. He'd caused quite a stir when he'd accused that wretch Rueben Glick of tearing up Rhoda's fruit garden. Samuel had wanted justice for her, but he'd made only a little headway that night. At least many within her district saw her in a better light, and he'd managed to make it clear that Rueben had probably engaged in acts of vandalism against at least one other girl in Rhoda's district.

The letter was a thank-you note from the girl Rueben had harassed. It'd been six months since then. Why had she waited so long? He folded it and put it back into its envelope.

"You don't look as if it was bad news."

He wanted to tease her by dangling the letter just out of her reach. If she tried to grab it, he'd pull it away. The temptation to be too friendly often reared its head when least expected.

Instead, he passed her the letter and sat on the back of the wagon and opened the lunchpail.

"This is a thank-you note." She continued reading. "A really nice one. You probably skimmed too much. I think Iva may have some competition, because this young woman sounds positively smitten."

"Six months after the fact?" Samuel took a bite of a roast beef sandwich.

"Maybe she's just now getting up the courage. She's really shy, and I'm sure it took her quite a while to put Rueben's harassment into perspective before writing you."

He pulled a thermos out of the pail. "That's two women down. Ninety-eight more to hire."

"That's still the plan? We'll have to make a lot of money before we can do that, which leads us to the good news." She pulled a crumpled newspaper section out of her coat pocket. "The cold front should be gone by noon tomorrow."

He kept a straight face. "I looked for that paper hours ago." The desire to call her a thief and hear her laugh was appealing, but he stayed true to his course.

She remained standing, keeping her distance. "I think one of the children must have picked it up. I found it scattered across the kitchen floor."

Oh, how he wanted to tease her that she was blaming the children. "I'm glad you found it and took the time to bring it to me." Samuel poured some coffee into the thermos lid.

She shoved the paper and letter back into her coat. "Do you have the honeybee man lined up to bring out the hives?"

"Since the day we closed on the farm."

"What about—"

A horrific blast vibrated the air around them.

Rhoda spun. "What was *that*?"

Samuel tossed the food and coffee to the ground. Where were the children? Had someone left gasoline or lighters near one of the barrels? "Did it come from the road or the orchard?"

"I'm not sure."

The dogs howled from inside the house.

Samuel headed for the house. "Get a couple of the bridled horses from the barn." When he opened the front door to let out the dogs, he spotted both children playing in the floor. Relief washed over him.

Ziggy and Zara dashed out the door, ran in circles, and then took off down the road.

Rhoda hurried out of the barn, leading both horses. "Orchard?"

"Nee, and Arie and Isaac are inside. It may've been a wreck." He interlaced his fingers and gave her a hand up before pulling himself onto the other horse. "The dogs are heading that way."

Rhoda spurred the horse. Since he was a better horseman, he could have overtaken her, but he stayed behind as the horses galloped down the road. After about a half mile he could see a car in a ditch.

She turned, alarm etched on her face. "It's Camilla! And a utility pole is down." She dug her heels into the horse, slapping the reins against its side.

"Whoa! Rhoda, stop!" There were live wires on Camilla's car. If Rhoda ran to the car, she could be electrocuted. He urged his horse to go faster. "Rhoda! Stop!"

But she didn't seem to hear him.

He maneuvered his horse in front of hers and braced himself for the collision. "Stop!"

She brought her horse to a halt. "What is *wrong* with you?" She slid off her horse and ran toward the car. Samuel jumped down and grabbed her while she was in midstride, picking her up off her feet. He hauled her several feet back from the accident.

"Let go of me!"

Her emotions had the better of her, and he wasn't surprised that she fought so hard to rush to her friend's side.

"For Pete's sake, woman, *stay!*" He held her with both arms. A wildcat would be easier to wrestle with. He had no idea she had such physical strength. "Rhodes, it's too dangerous."

"She needs our help."

"You can't help. Not yet. We'll get help for her!" He grabbed her face. "Look at me!" He shouted it again and again. Finally her eyes moved from the scene of the wreck to him. "That's it." He pointed to his eyes. "Right here. Look right here."

She nodded. Her eyes focused on his.

"Do you have your two-way?"

"A what?"

His words weren't registering. He put his forehead against hers. "Breathe."

She relaxed a bit. "Camilla." Tears welled, and she tried again to head for the car.

He held her firm. "I know. But, Rhoda, those are live wires. We could be injured if we aren't careful, and that will help no one."

As if she were roused by smelling salts, he saw her come to herself.

"Can I let go of you now?"

She took a step back. "I'm sorry. What do you need me to do?"

"Use the two-way. Get someone at the farm to call for help." He pulled himself back up on the horse. He needed the extra height to see into the car without going down into the ditch. "I'm going to stay away from the wires and do my best to talk to Camilla."

He thought about sending Rhoda to Camilla's house to get Bob, but he feared she was too dazed to think about safety and precautions.

As he nudged the horse to move in closer, he saw Camilla trying to open her eyes. He knew nothing about electricity and utility poles other than what he'd read in the newspapers—that going up to a car or getting out of one where there were live wires could result in serious injury or death.

As Camilla became more conscious, her movements increased.

He prayed she would be easier to reason with than Rhoda had been. "Camilla, just stay where you are. Help is on the way."

She screamed and pushed against the car door even as he told her to stay put. He had to do something, but what?

Rhoda.

He spurred the horse and went back to her. "Kumm." He hooked his foot, and she used it like a stirrup. Between that and pulling her by the hand, she was soon situated behind him on the horse. They stayed on the road, well out of range of the wires.

Rhoda grabbed the back of his shirt for balance. "Camilla."

"Get me out of here!" She slammed her body against the door of the car.

"Camilla, it's Rhoda. I'm here with Samuel. Listen to me. You have to stay away from the car door. There are live electrical wires touching the car. You have to stay still. Please. Help is on the way. Until they get here, we'll talk. You can ask anything, and I'll answer. It's your dream come true. Right?"

Camilla brushed her gray hair out of her face and laid her head against the headrest. "Yeah, okay." She rubbed her forehead. "But I can't think."

"What happened? Do you remember?"

"A driver broadsided me, knocked me into this pole, and then just kept right on going."

Samuel turned, needing a glimpse of Rhoda's face. The pain and confusion in her eyes made him ache for her as much as for Camilla, and he realized this was her Achilles heel—others being hurt. As strong as she was in the battles life dished out—church leaders who were against her, hateful people like Rueben, liars who accused her falsely, and even mother nature threatening to ruin her crops—she could get her feet under her quickly and cope. But illness, injury, or the death of her loved ones shook the foundation under her.

Oh, dear God, how much I love this woman.

Her attention was glued to Camilla, but her eyes silently begged for answers as to how someone, anyone, could do such damage to another person and then abandon them.

"Samuel, I'm seeing images." Her voice trembled.

"Of what?"

"Hello?" Camilla called.

"We're right here." Samuel answered. "Rhoda?"

"I'm fine. We'll talk later." She cupped her hands around her mouth. "Watch out for your ears."

He leaned a little to his left, and Rhoda leaned a tad to her right. "Do you have a question for me, Camilla?"

"I want to know…" Camilla angled her mouth toward the half-opened window. "I see things in the Amish community I don't agree with. I want to know if you really want to be Amish or if you're doing so to please your parents or Samuel or your boyfriend."

Samuel could see Rhoda only in his peripheral vision, but he thought she smiled.

"I believe in the Old Ways, and I've never wanted to live any other way. It has its problems—I know that. I'm faithful, not blind. But life has its troubles no matter what beliefs or culture a person embraces."

Camilla relaxed, appearing to think about what Rhoda had said. The horse shuffled sideways, and Samuel tried to steady it.

Rhoda grabbed the back of his shirt again. "I see three people on a sidewalk outside a medical building of some sort—a young man and woman and Camilla. The man is crying. The young woman doesn't look it, but she's pregnant. Arguments are flying between Camilla and the man. The woman is screaming at Camilla to leave them alone." Rhoda paused. "Samuel, she knows. Camilla knows the girl is pregnant. But they go into the building and leave Camilla on the sidewalk, crying."

Samuel tried to shift in order to see Rhoda. He barely glimpsed her before the horse moved and he had to regain control. He had no way of guessing what their next steps concerning these images should be. Maybe he should get her to wait until Jacob was home.

Sirens could be heard in the distance. Camilla's car had all sorts of airbags, and Samuel imagined that, with good medical help, her injuries would heal fairly quickly. But what'd happened here would take him and Rhoda a while to work through emotionally.

Why did so much have to happen whenever Jacob was gone?

TWENTY-THREE

A cold blanket of air closed in with the night. Rhoda drove the wagon between the rows of trees, stopping at every barrel. Her mind and heart remained with Camilla. It'd been terrifying to see her friend in that wreck, trapped by downed wires.

Rhoda shuddered, running her fingers over the old quilt on her lap, which kept her reasonably warm. Phoebe's grandmother had made it, and Rhoda was sure at one time it'd been beautiful, but it was worn and frayed now. She noticed the stitching that held each patchwork piece in place was precise in detail. But even an intricately sewn quilt made in love didn't look all that special unless one cared about its history or took the time to really study the fabric and stitches. Did a new perspective make everything appear different?

She was certainly seeing Camilla differently right now—more vulnerable than the guarded woman who issued warnings like a wise owl. More of a fighter than the abused housewife depicted in the police reports Landon had found on the Internet.

Nothing seemed to be as it had first appeared.

Zara walked beside the wagon, looking up at her every minute. Steven stood in the back of the wagon, pitching wood into the barrels or onto the ground beside them as Rhoda paused at each one.

Her hands still shook a bit, and she couldn't block out the image of Camilla's car in the ditch. But the police, fire department, and ambulance had arrived within twenty minutes.

Once Camilla was in the ambulance, Samuel had escorted Rhoda back to the farm, because they wouldn't allow her to ride in the ambulance, and then he had ridden to Camilla's house to find Bob. Samuel had said if he ended up not returning to the farm right away, he'd call the office and leave a message.

When he'd called, Rhoda had been in the barn, getting a fresh horse. She managed to grab it before the answering machine picked up. Bob had been at home when Samuel arrived, and he was understandably upset, so he asked Samuel to accompany him to the hospital. Samuel didn't say what he was feeling, but she heard it in his voice—people, not the crop, were the top priority—and he couldn't say no to Bob.

That was the last she'd heard from anyone—five hours ago.

Maybe someone had called the office with an update, but no one could spare the time to check, not with the scant night crew of Landon, Leah, Steven, and her.

She glanced into the back of the wagon. It was almost empty. Soon they'd head for the barn to reload—if there was any wood left to fill it. But either way she could check the messages.

"Rhoda?"

She unclipped the two-way to answer Leah. "Ya?"

"What quadrant?"

"Lower east. You?"

"At the barn. There's less than half a cord of wood left. Is your wagon full?"

"Almost empty. But the fires and woodpiles next to them are in good shape for now. We'll have enough to last through the night." She hoped. "Take half of it."

"Okay."

What if they had done all this work only to run out of wood in the last few hours of the cold snap? She clicked her tongue, and the horse moved forward. "You hanging in there?" she called over her shoulder to her brother.

"Ya. I'm fine. Don't worry about me." For all his assurances, Steven sounded exhausted.

They continued on to the last barrel in this quadrant. When she turned the rig toward the barn, Steven crawled over the bench seat and sat beside her.

They rode in silence. Sometimes when she was weary and wanting to be near the house, these eighty acres felt as large as the state of Maine.

Zara started barking and took off running. Steven pointed to a silhouette of a man on horseback topping a hill on the horizon. Samuel was finally home.

Steven held out his hands, offering to take the reins. "He's a good man."

Her shoulders ached, and she gladly put the strips of leather in her brother's control, but she bristled at his statement. "He is, and so is Jacob."

Steven's face was void of any reaction, but she wasn't fooled. He favored Samuel over Jacob.

"I don't care what you or anyone else thinks of Jacob. I know the truth about him, and I love him."

Steven kept his eyes straight ahead. "Don't kid yourself, Rhoda. You do care what we think. You've tried to hide from Daed and Mamm just how out of sorts Jacob is with the Amish ways."

Ire ran through her blood, making her body flush with heat. She jerked the quilt off her legs. "I've never lied to anyone to cover for him. He's the one who said I must never lie for him, and his past is being wiped clean by what he's doing right now."

"Never—"

"Hey." Samuel waved as he rode toward them. "Leah said you two were out here."

Rhoda was glad Samuel had arrived in time to stop Steven from finishing his sentence. Moreover, she longed for news. "How's Camilla?"

Even as the woman's name crossed Rhoda's lips, she saw patchwork images—Camilla begging her son, her purse overflowing with money, her son turning his back on her. Rhoda knew the money was symbolic, not literal, but what did it mean? What was that medical building they were standing in front of? And why couldn't anything simply look like what it was?

Steven brought the rig to a stop just as Samuel halted beside them.

Samuel fidgeted with a large brown bag in his hand. "She's good and improving, but they're going to keep her overnight. Aside from the shock she experienced, she has first- and second-degree burns from the lobster stew she was bringing us. She sent Bob home to get some sleep, so he dropped me off." He slid off his horse, still clutching the bag. "I went into the house before coming out here. Phoebe was sitting in the kitchen, just staring at the fire." He held the reins to his horse out to Steven. "I think you should go inside for a bit."

Steven climbed out of the wagon. Once his feet were on the ground, he looked up at her. "To finish what I wanted to say. You didn't lie to anyone? How about to yourself?"

A dozen retorts came to mind, but she bit her tongue. Besides, in what way did he think she'd lied to herself? But Steven was exhausted, concerned about his wife, and grieving their loss. Otherwise, he would've kept his opinion to himself.

Samuel climbed onto the bench beside her. "What was that about?"

"A brother under stress, saying things he doesn't mean."

"Really? I'm a brother. I have two of them. I've never known any of us to behave that way."

She picked up the reins. "Speaking of liars."

He smiled. "Did you ever eat?"

"No. I wasn't hungry."

"Hungry or not, you're stopping to eat." He held up the brown bag.

Despite her stomach rumbling with emptiness, his commands irked her. "I hate it when you get bossy. You know that, right?"

"I do. Now set the brake. We're pausing to snack." He put the bag between his feet.

She stifled a laugh. "Why do you do that?"

"What? Dare to say what needs to be said?" He glanced up, a smile in place. "Because you need someone who'll do it." He opened the bag, looking into it. "You want to get angry with me? Do so. But just so we're clear, I'm no bossier than you."

"Ya, but when I'm doing it, I'm not annoying."

He froze for a moment, looking perplexed that she'd say such a thing. Apparently he hadn't realized she was teasing. A moment later amusement danced through his eyes.

"Uh-huh." He pulled out several small plastic containers. "Bob stopped by a store, and I bought some slices of cake. Do you prefer carrot cake, red velvet, chocolate, double fudge, or yellow cake with chocolate frosting?"

The slices were huge—large enough to serve three or four people. Her stomach rumbled. "Carrot cake, please."

"I would've guessed something with chocolate." He held it and a fork out to her. "So how are you?"

"Exhausted and irritable." She took the items. "You?"

He chuckled, seeming different from before. That thought caught her off guard. Different? How? It'd take some pondering to know those answers, and she wasn't going to do that. Other than their getting along and keeping their relationship from veering off course, it didn't matter what differences she saw in him.

Samuel opened a container for one of the other cake slices. "I'm feeling the same. After the temperature warms up and we get some rest, I'm betting everyone will be arguing or tempted to complain over anything and everything—at least for a few days." He dug his fork into the double fudge cake.

She stared at the dark sky. The stars were so bright it looked as if she could touch them if she only reached up into the sky. "How long would it take to get to the closest star?"

Samuel propped his foot on the footrest. "The sun is the closest, about ninety-three million miles away, if I remember correctly. I once read that if you traveled a hundred miles per hour, it'd take more than a hundred years to reach it. Of course, that same article said that even with current spaceship and space-suit technology, you'd be ashes while still something like three million miles away from it."

She studied the sky's brilliance. Its beauty was unmatched at night. During the day the orchard was a close rival, especially at picking time, but night-time views outdid the daytime sky regardless of the season. "Seems so odd they fade to nothing during the day."

"They don't fade at all. They're there, just as bright." He stared at the expanse. "It doesn't seem like it though, does it?"

She took a bite of cake, and her mouth watered as she enjoyed the cream cheese frosting. "Do you know the constellations?"

"A few. But as the earth rotates, the constellations show up in different parts of the sky. And then there are times we can't see some of the stars in those constellations. So even if you're looking at one you know, it might not appear as such."

"Even the heavens look different than they actually are." A chill of excitement ran through her. "If you only saw me here like this, you'd think I was on a picnic or something—not taking a moment to rest because I'm worn-out and hungry."

"Interesting thinking." He grabbed the quilt off the seat and tossed it over her lap. "Where are you going with it?"

She took another bite of cake. "I'm not sure."

He chuckled. "Okay."

But she found comfort in the thought. Maybe because she was trying to connect the dots the way people do with the constellations, by using the snippets she'd seen with Camilla and her son and by trying to free herself of visions of Emma. She knew all the dots weren't visible, and maybe they never would be—not to her. "What am I going to do with what I saw today about Camilla and her son?"

"There are only a couple of choices, aren't there? Hold on to it or share it with Camilla. But why would you receive it if you were to hold on to it?"

He was right, and she felt silly for asking. As she thought about their time at the accident scene, she recalled fighting with Samuel while trying to get to Camilla. "I was rough on you this afternoon."

"I'm fine. You have a lot of strength hidden behind those girly clothes. Did I hurt you?"

"Nee." She dipped the fork in some icing and licked it off.

From the corner of her eye, she saw a silhouette shift. She refused to look. Maybe it was shadows from the flames in the barrels, but she imagined it was Emma. "I have a weird question for you."

"Does that mean I need to have a weird answer?"

She dipped up another forkful of cake. "Why doesn't it bother you that I see Emma?"

Samuel shrugged. "Not sure. We hear about murders and such, but I can't imagine having to survive it happening to a family member. Especially for someone like you."

Just what did that mean? "Like me?"

He glanced her way. "You feel *so* deeply, Rhoda."

"Oh." It was true, and maybe much of the reason she'd spent most of her life hiding in her fruit patch, tending her acre of vines. Those thorns and prickles only went skin deep, and it was so peaceful inside that picket fence.

He pulled out a carton of milk from the bag and passed it to her. "When my *Daadi* Sam died, I'd walk through the orchard at night talking to him... or rather to myself and imagining it was him. I think needing to do that in order to cope probably changed my perspective about people and mourning. Grief is every bit as powerful as love. And that's saying something, isn't it?"

She nodded. "You were a teen when your grandfather died?"

"Sixteen, and it was really difficult. Maybe it shouldn't have been. But I never once imagined he might die at sixty-two. He was healthy and fit. My greatest consolation is he wanted me to run the orchard, and I needed something to keep me occupied. But that first year, whenever the day was quiet, in my mind's eye I'd see his hand push up from the ground and grab mine."

"Only the first year?"

"Ya, I stepped in a yellow jacket's nest and needed to be taken to the doctor, and I told him what I kept imagining...you know, in case maybe I was nuts."

She chuckled. "I know that feeling all too well."

"He said, 'Maybe he's not reaching up to grab you. Maybe you are the one afraid to let go of him.'" Samuel didn't say anything for a really long time. "That doctor was right. I knew it the moment he said it. So I aimed to find peace with having to let go of Daadi Sam. It took a while, but when the image came to me, I just mumbled to myself, 'It's okay to let him go. He's fine. I'm fine. It's okay.'"

Her soul seemed to vibrate, and when she closed her eyes, she felt as free as the winds soaring through the orchard. She could find peace with Emma being gone, and somehow she'd uncover how to let her go.

Samuel drew a heavy breath. "I never told anybody that before."

She'd needed to hear it, and she sensed that he'd needed to tell it. "Denki." The word came out as a whisper.

She could tell that he felt about his grandfather the way she did about her sister. "When we talked at Camilla's week before last, I told you I hoped you had answers about Emma, but you didn't mention anything about your Daadi Sam."

His brows furrowed. "I didn't think about it then, and I didn't bring it up tonight to be helpful. We were just talking, and the conversation meandered that way. Was it helpful?"

"Definitely." It seemed odd that he'd managed to stumble onto help for her time and again simply by thinking and sharing his thoughts. "It never dawned on me that I might be the one trying to hang on to Emma. I see myself as more of a runner."

"A runner?"

"Ya, I started running after I had my first premonition when I was four or five. I told Steven a few months back that it was like he and Daed and everyone else watched, pleading with me to go faster. I think that panicked feeling of running is part of the reason I understand Jacob. We both run, just from different things. And I know we both want to stop."

"No reason you can't. Seems like this new settlement is the perfect place for you and Jacob. Fresh start. Your brother is the spiritual head. In the past he may have spurred you to outrun who God made you to be, but I know he can understand you better now."

"I doubt Steven's ever had to run from parts of who he is."

"You might be surprised. I imagine most people run from something like that at one point or another."

She couldn't imagine Samuel running from anything. "Even you?"

He dug into his cake without answering.

She poked his arm with her elbow. "After all I've just told you about me, you're not going to answer?"

His eyes met hers. "You should know the answer to that without asking."

As crisp and clear as the night air, she knew. He ran from the desire to pursue her. He ran from all he felt for her.

She shouldn't be here. Shouldn't have wanted time alone to talk with him. Shouldn't be gazing at the stars. Enjoying desserts. Discussing matters of the heart and longing to know what was on his mind.

TWENTY-FOUR

Jacob grabbed his overnight bag as the train pulled into the depot at Old Orchard Beach. Since he'd been in a Virginia Beach motel, he had gone to the beach on Friday night and walked it for hours.

The sand and surf used to be the love of his life, the one thing that stirred him when nothing else did. He hadn't been able to take joy in it since the construction company debacle. Now that some measure of respect had been restored to him, he'd enjoyed feeling the sand under his feet and watching the rolling waves while recalling his many times of scuba diving and deep-sea fishing.

As he'd ambled along the water's edge, more hope had filled him. The world of construction and the magic of the ocean seemed to have opened their arms to him again. Was it possible he wasn't done with both of them as he'd thought? The idea was somewhat appealing, and maybe in a few years, when the orchard wasn't as labor intensive, he could enjoy seasons of both construction and the ocean.

But right now he was more than ready to get home to Rhoda. He longed to start a life with her. Just the thought of it made him smile, but he suppressed the desire. Since he was in his Amish clothes, he figured he stuck out enough without grinning like a possum. As soon as he got home, he'd tell Steven he was ready to begin the instruction period so he could join the faith. Rhoda's words of love echoed inside him, giving him confidence in their future. They could marry this fall, just as soon as the harvest and canning season were over. Would she prefer to marry before or after Thanksgiving?

The *clackity-clack* of the train slowed until the huge machine came to a smooth stop. Three other people were also waiting to get off. Maybe taking a train to the shore on a Sunday morning wasn't a prime time for beachgoers. He waited his turn and then stepped onto a small platform enclosed with a rail. To his right was a short set of steps that led to the long platform running alongside the tracks.

Iva was a ways down the platform, a camera masking her face. She wore Englisch clothes—a casual dress and a fitted jacket. Her hair was pulled back in a loose ponytail, and he noticed her light brown hair had a touch of blond in it.

He eased up behind her. "Excuse me, but Amish don't approve of such things."

She turned, camera in place as the shutter seemed to click dozens of times per second.

Jacob backed up, but she moved in closer, snapping images.

He held up his hand, blocking the lens. "I surrender. Stop already."

She lowered the camera and gestured across the road. "Welcome to Old Orchard Beach, Maine."

"Been here long?"

"Not even an hour yet." She pulled her jacket tighter. "Hard to believe it was freezing until lunchtime yesterday. It's still chillier than I expected."

"There's always a breeze coming off the ocean. How are Sandra and Casey?"

"Good. Happy, I think. We found a really cute place. It's tiny, but it's light and airy, with a playground nearby."

"I can't tell you how much I appreciate your help." But he was ready to spend every bit of the day's free time with Rhoda. He gestured away from the tracks. "Any chance you're ready to mosey homeward?"

"Really?" She searched his eyes, clearly trying to decide if he was teasing.

They went up a set of concrete stairs. "I've been traveling since this time yesterday, and I'm anxious to see Rhoda. I know the last few days have been tough on the farm."

"Well, sure, but the frost is over. I wanted to get some pictures of the ocean, lots of them, and of the amusement park." She held up the camera. "Since arriving, I've been waiting right here, making sure I was in sight when you got off the train."

He said nothing, and disappointment flickered across her face. "Okay." She pulled the keys out of her jacket pocket. "You ready, then?"

Guilt nibbled at him. He'd asked a huge favor of her and had yet to ask what he could do in return. Surely after she'd spent three and a half days away from the farm to help him, he could take a little time to let her enjoy an afternoon at the beach. He glanced around. "Looks like an interesting place. Let's walk around a bit."

"You sure?" She clutched Landon's truck keys in her palm.

"Yeah. Who knows, maybe I can tell Rhoda about it, and she'll want to come see for herself." It was apparent that both of them were in the Englisch mode—their speech patterns fitting in with those they'd been spending time around. Had she left the Amish at one point as he had? She might have, since she had a driver's license and a camera, but not necessarily.

"It takes only two hours to get here by car." She followed an elderly man with her camera, taking shots of him as he pushed a stroller. "I've learned just enough about this little vacation spot to show you the best parts. There's a pier that is sort of an outdoor shopping mall, loaded with restaurants and souvenir shops. The food smells delicious. Then there's a carnival area almost on the beach. It's called Palace Playland, and among other things it has a Ferris wheel and carousel. Ever ridden either?"

"Nope. They never looked interesting. How about you?"

"Never been on one, and they look extremely interesting. The carousel has a rooster." She dipped her head before looking up at him. "Please. I've been very good with the money Rhoda gave me."

"You ride. I'll watch."

"I can't go on the Ferris wheel by myself. I'd die of fright. But you don't have to ride the carousel, although it has a bunny and an ostrich. You'd look cute riding either one."

"Cute?" He scratched his face, feeling the stubble of not having shaved since yesterday morning. "Cute?" That word just seemed wrong. "Why do I suddenly feel as if I'm two and running around in my footy pajamas?"

She grinned. "It'd be such a treat to snap a picture of you riding on a blue sea horse."

"My goal is to be nice, but just how many times do I have to ride this thing?"

"Ten should do it."

He laughed. "No. I'll do one. Creature of your choice, but just one, and we'll ride the Ferris wheel. But first we eat."

"And walk on the beach, no shoes."

"Okay, but no more than a mile."

"I can agree to that, but a mile down the beach ends up being two by the time we're back to the starting point. Right?"

How could he say no? "True."

"Then we have a deal. I'm famished."

"Lead the way to the food."

She paused a dozen times to snap some pictures, but soon enough they were on the pier, searching for the right restaurant. He wanted a steak, but he'd settle for a hamburger to save money. After they came to the end of the restaurant choices, they looped around and went into Hooligan's, which appeared to be a family spot. When he looked at his life compared to his family's, he never felt Amish enough. But when he looked at it compared to the average Sunday beachgoer, he felt too Amish.

Once seated, Jacob looked over the menu. "So how do you like working at the farm?"

The conversation rolled along comfortably while they waited for their food and then ate. Talking with her was like bobbing along in a boat on the ocean. He didn't have to do anything for the conversation to drift from one spot to another. By the end of the meal, he knew a lot about her.

He poked a few crumbs on the table, fidgeting. "You mentioned your community in Indiana and how tough times are there. I know the economic downturn has been rough even on the Amish who don't rely on selling goods to tourists, but what happened in your district?"

"Years ago our men slowly gave up trying to make a living by following the Old Ways. Bit by bit they entered the Englisch work force. About half the men in my Daed's generation went to work at a factory that built recreational vehicles. Nearly all their sons followed in their footsteps. It seems that in doing so we gave up the ability to ride out a downturn the way the Amish usually do."

Jacob tore tiny bits of paper off the straw he hadn't used. "I was still away when the downturn began, but I'd call home, and my Mamm would fill me in on what was happening. My parents had two incomes: the orchard and a small dairy farm. My Daed sells organic milk to an Englisch guy who turns it into yogurt and stuff. Even the demand for organic milk dropped drastically, and you know what the orchard situation has been. My Daed's passionate about supporting mission projects and giving within the Amish community wherever there is a need, but for a while every penny earned was needed to keep the family fed and clothed."

She folded her arms on the table and leaned in. "You'll explain it to me one day? All of it?"

"I guess. If you care to hear about it."

"I do. In my home if you want to know anything about the men's world, you have to wear pants."

"You need me to loan you a pair?"

She laughed. "I'm serious. What happened that my community was trapped between the worst of both worlds—Englisch and Amish?"

"The worst of both worlds?"

"We did without modern conveniences, like all Old Order Amish, and once we got caught in the recession, we did without money, like the Englisch world."

"That is the worst of both, isn't it?"

"I have a brother who calls our group the Englisch Amish." She shrugged, making a face. "He thinks it's funny, but the reality of living that way was we were no better off during the downturn than our less self-sufficient neighbors."

"Before you were born, the men had to change how they made a living in order to survive. Maybe you're being a little tough on them about that. Before I was born, my uncle never accepted a construction job that kept him from returning home at night. But by the time I worked with him, we traveled wherever the best jobs were, staying for weeks at a time. Some of the men's wives went also, to do the cooking and laundry, keeping down the cost of working out of state. It was a good, economical way to do things."

She raised an eyebrow. "More than just saving money, I'm sure the wives on those trips eased the other wives' concerns about what their menfolk were up to while they were away."

The subject of husbands and wives felt strangely intimate, and Jacob wanted to change the subject. "So, Iva, what do you think of Samuel?" He turned his glass around, fidgeting. Was that too obvious?

"He's nice. I couldn't ask for better people to live with."

"I'm glad you feel that way. But I meant, well, do you feel anything for him?"

"If you're trying to nudge him toward someone, he's not ready."

Jacob's heart skipped a beat. Did she know about Samuel and Rhoda's... incident? "What do you mean?"

"His grief is deeper than Leon's by a lot. That's what I mean."

"The man your dad wanted you to marry?"

"I know Leon loves me...or loved me before I disappeared, but his grief for the wife he lost two years ago is so thick it steals all the air from the room. I'm not interested in being someone's oxygen machine so he feels as if he can breathe again. What about me? I need to breathe too."

He took a long sip of his water. She could see that in Samuel? Jacob hadn't seen it. Had Rhoda? "How can you be so sure?"

"I just am. Once someone who's drowning in grief has courted you, it's easy to recognize that kind of pain when you see it again. Leah said he had a girlfriend in Pennsylvania."

"Yeah, but that was a long time ago, and he's the one who broke up with her."

"Why?"

"I'm not sure, other than he lost interest in..." As Jacob added up all he knew, it dawned on him that Samuel wasn't just a little infatuated with Rhoda. He hadn't just been lonely. His brother *loved* her—apparently since before they left Pennsylvania.

Jacob wanted to grab Iva's arm and drag her to Landon's truck. But he'd promised they'd go on some rides, and he would honor that. Then they'd drive for a couple of hours before finally being at the farm.

But he wanted to be there now!

If Rhoda was aware of how his brother felt, she was hiding it from Jacob. Would she do that?

Surely not. Then again, by her own admittance the two were close.

His heart cried out, a slow screaming pain that wasn't going to end, not if his worst fears were true.

Regardless of believing, of knowing that Rhoda was faithful to him and loved him, one thought pounded inside him above all the others. Was she in love with Samuel?

TWENTY-FIVE

Leah walked along the shores of Unity Pond. What a lovely Sunday afternoon. Landon hurled a tennis ball, making Ziggy and Zara run full force in a heated race to retrieve it. She giggled at the dogs' competitive nature, and Landon smiled at her. It was still cold, but the freezing temperatures had passed. The weather forecasts indicated no more crop-damaging cold snaps for the rest of the month. A light wind played with the bright sunshine on the water, and the afternoon rays kept them warm inside their coats.

"It's beautiful out here." Leah turned, taking in the scenery. Blue water wavered and shimmied as a variety of evergreens stood proudly in patches.

"I thought you might like it." He turned back to Ziggy and pulled the ball out of the dog's playfully growling mouth. "After these last few days, I knew you could use an afternoon away from the orchard."

Leah held tight to the driver's manual in her pocket, too embarrassed to pull it out and ask if he'd study it with her. What if doing so made her look like an idiot to him? "It's a little early to tell, but Samuel thinks we'll lose less than ten percent."

"I heard." He wrestled the ball from Zara's mouth this time, a rare win for the meeker dog. "Anything else bothering you?"

Her heart jumped. Could he read her that easily?

He tossed the ball. "The girl I know never holds back. She's too sassy and talkative."

She released a sigh and pulled the manual out of her pocket. "It's like reading German, and like German, I should be better at it than I am."

"Is that all?" He smiled. "After all your questions the other night, I thought you were going to say you'd decided to stay Amish."

"What? You should know better."

"Should I?" He took the manual from her. "I seem to know precious little when it comes to figuring you out."

She thought about it and nodded. "You are rather lost, aren't you?"

"All the time. You asked my opinion, but later you didn't seem to want it."

"For a clueless man, you pick up on a lot of clues."

"Ah, so I'm right?"

She nodded. "I'm not ready to have my opinion swayed by anyone else's reasoning. You know that."

"I do, but I wasn't going to give *my* opinion."

"You weren't?" Her heart beat faster with excitement. "Whose opinions were you going to give me?"

"No one's. I was going to suggest better questions to ponder."

Did she need *more* questions pounding around inside her brain?

Landon gestured. "Hey, look. A moose."

Across the glimmering water on a hillside, a large animal approached the pond. It lowered its massive head and began to drink.

Leah's worry faded into excitement for a minute, and she almost squealed. She'd never seen a moose before, and as silly as it seemed, it was fascinating to know that some peculiar creatures actually existed outside of her books. Should a moose be considered odd?

She squinted and tried to imagine the creature next to a horse. "How much do you suppose he weighs?"

"Dunno, but I think they get pretty big." He leaned down and grabbed the dogs by their collars before they noticed the moose.

"You don't suppose we could put the dogs in your granny's car and try to pet him, do you?" Leah started down one of the trails that led around the pond.

"Definitely not. We shouldn't even try to get close. They're wild animals." Landon stood, holding the dogs by the collar. "You're not going to make me chase you to get you to come back this way, are you?"

She paused. "I suppose the answer should be no."

"You think? I read somewhere that there are more moose attacks per year than bear, lion, and tiger attacks combined, most likely because people—like *you*—forget they're wild animals."

"Oh." She watched as the creature finished drinking and trotted back into the woodland.

Landon laughed. "These dogs never took their eyes off the ball."

"We'd better hide all the balls when they're supposed to be watching the orchard for deer."

He chuckled. "I agree." He patted Zara. "It's nice to see little Zara come out of her shell a bit. She's always so timid when there's no ball involved." Landon threw the ball again, this time with a much slower pair of dogs chasing after it.

"Landon..." She circled her shoe in the dirt. Now that she knew he had questions he thought she should be asking herself, she had to know what they were. "Can we talk about what you were going to say the other night?"

"Sure, if you want to know."

"I think I do."

"Seems to me you're asking yourself all the wrong questions: Is the Ordnung right? Is it wrong? Can I make myself leave the Amish? Will I be happier if I stay or if I go? I think you should ask things like, what do I really want to do with my life? Do I want to be a wife and mom and full-time homemaker? Do I want an education? Do I want to learn music? Usually parents open up all those possibilities to children while raising them. Yours didn't. But when you know yourself, you'll know how you want to live. There's nothing wrong with having a limited education if that's who you are. And there's nothing wrong with attending college—if that's who you are."

She wanted to hug him. He'd nailed what was holding her back—knowing herself. The questions shouldn't be about whether she could make herself leave. All her ponderings had been on the negative. The real answer would be found in the positive: What did she really want out of life?

"I know one thing I want for sure."

"Shoot."

"I want us to be friends for the rest of our lives."

Landon's smile was weak at best. "Okay. It might be a little tough to steer to that kind of relationship, but if we don't give up, we can do it."

He was such a strange bird, so open and honest with her. She used to believe all Englisch teens and young people were the coolest, but she also believed they were selfish sinners who didn't understand anything about God, family, and friendship the way the Amish did.

What an arrogant girl she'd been, even while looking down on herself because of her lack of education and her family being farmers. And even while drinking and sleeping with Michael, she'd thought she was more pure than the other girls who were doing the same thing.

Strange, really. And embarrassing.

It struck her that she'd been a hypocrite, rationalizing why she was better than the very people she was acting like.

But why was she thinking about that now?

Then she knew. If she was going to figure out what she wanted from life, she had to understand how and why she thought as she did.

The more she understood herself, the more she'd know what she really wanted from life.

Iva turned on the blinker and steered Landon's truck onto the road toward home. They were almost back at the farm, and she felt rather pleased with herself—and even more relieved. "Whew. We're back safe and sound."

"Did you doubt we'd arrive okay?" Jacob stared out the window. He'd seemed distracted ever since their conversation at the restaurant.

"I had my moments...or hours or days of doubt, yes." She stopped at a four-way sign. "In a couple of years of driving a car, I'd never covered one-fourth the distance of the last four days."

"Lots of guys get their license, but you're the first Amish girl I've known to get one. Did you own a vehicle?"

"I did."

"Impressive. Did you pay for it yourself?"

"Yeah. From the time I graduated at twelve until I was seventeen, I scrubbed a lot of floors and toilets and did way too much baby-sitting for Englisch neighbors. I'd hoped to drive to all sorts of places and take pictures—not far but farther than a rig could go. Then after I paid for it and insurance, I didn't have enough money for gas to go much of anywhere. Ain't that the way?"

He glanced at her. "Sometimes it is."

Iva wasn't sure why she was trying to keep him engaged in conversation, but she hoped it was helping or, at the least, he didn't mind. "It wasn't much of a car. Nothing like this truck. So I needed to stay fairly close to home anyway. It was a hand-me-down from a long line of Amish who'd owned it before each one joined the faith."

"I've seen that happen many times. Is that why you gave it up?"

"No. Look at me." She gestured at her Englisch clothes. "I haven't joined the faith yet. If I had, I wouldn't be driving now."

"Makes sense. What made you give up driving?"

"My car came up missing. Do you know how hard it is to drive a vehicle that isn't there?"

"Missing?" The distant look faded from his green eyes, and she had his full attention.

She tapped the steering wheel with her thumbs. "My dad needed the cash, and when I was at a baby-sitting job, he sold my car."

"Because he didn't like you having a car, or because he needed the money that badly?"

"Yes."

His smile seemed to say he approved of her and understood where she was coming from. She liked that. Most men didn't realize what it was like to grow up in a patriarchal society where a daughter's opinion often counted only slightly more than a dog's. At least that's how it had worked in her household.

Jacob rolled down his window a tad.

She turned off the heat. "My mom was hoping I'd come here and find work for at least some of my family."

"It's possible we could hire a few men in a couple of years, but we're not there yet. We'll hire pickers for the harvest, but if they've never done this kind of work, they probably wouldn't move fast enough to be worth their pay."

She pulled into the driveway. "I doubt any kind of work for Kings' Orchard is right for them anyway."

"How so?"

She eased toward Landon's usual parking spot. "They'd need to do as Rhoda instructed. I imagine they'd quit the first day and lodge a complaint with the church leaders."

"Or they'd adjust. Samuel knew that she was skilled and that Kings' Orchard needed her skills, but he struggled to work with her at first. I was the go-between. If I hadn't been, those two would've gone their separate ways long before the tornado came through the orchard. My Daed hated the idea of partnering with a woman. He about choked to death when Samuel first mentioned the idea."

Once in the right spot, she turned off the engine. "And you?"

"I think businesses, Amish *and* Englisch, are overlooking amazing resources if they can't see that women approach business problems so differently from men. And when they're combined on the same team, it creates a powerhouse where everyone wins."

She removed the keys from the ignition.

He opened the truck door. "You're a good driver, and apparently stepping out into the unknown is one of your skills."

He paused, searching the different areas of the farm. The dogs weren't in sight and weren't barking. Jacob strode toward the house. Iva followed, appreciating his sentiments. After spending a little time around the King family, she felt like a new person—one who could dare to dream and believe it'd be okay to pursue parts of those dreams.

Jacob entered the kitchen. "Hey."

Steven sat at the table, coloring on a book with his son. "Hallo. Welcome back, you two."

Of all the people on this farm, Steven was the hardest to read. He looked perturbed with Jacob, but was he?

Jacob looked through the window that faced the orchard. "Where is everybody?"

Steven took a crayon from his son. "Phoebe is resting with Arie. Leah's out with Landon because she's in her *rumschpringe* and has that right. My sister is at Camilla's, because that's where she lives."

There it was—a hint of accusation wrapped inside an honest answer.

Steven set the crayon down. "And Samuel is at Camilla's because Bob came by about an hour ago and asked him to join them there."

Jacob frowned. "Why?"

"Camilla was injured in a car accident on Friday, and Samuel and Rhoda were the ones to call for help. I think Camilla wanted to see both of them to say thank you."

When Jacob's eyes met Iva's, she saw frustration and maybe distress.

Iva jingled the keys. "I need to get the truck back to Landon. Would you like for me to drop you off over there?"

"That'd be nice. Thanks."

Steven studied her. "Perhaps if everything has been handled in the Englisch world for now, you'd like to change first and address your hair."

"Oh." She looked down at her outfit. It was an A-line dress with tiny flowers, and the short sleeves were covered with a jacket. It seemed quite modest to her, but apparently Steven found it unacceptable. Her hair was pulled into a ponytail, which she believed kept her from appearing Amish while helping Sandra move. "Right away."

She scurried up the stairs, and in less than two minutes, she was in an Amish dress. Since the apron needed straight pins to put it in place, she simply slid a coat over her dress, hoping Steven wouldn't notice. While winding her hair into an Amish bun, she hurried down the stairs, her prayer Kapp between her lips.

When she didn't spot Jacob, she went outside. He was leaning against the truck. Despite his laid-back posture, she noticed the irritated glint in his eyes.

"Sorry." She put on her prayer Kapp, hoping it'd stay in place until she had time to pin it.

"You're fine." He climbed into the truck.

She turned the key. "I tried to hurry."

He said nothing.

She tried to think of something to say. "Oh, I forgot to tell you that I worked out a plan with Sandra so you two can keep in touch. She'll write to the farm but not put her name or address on the envelope. Since I pick up the mail, I'll get rid of the envelope before passing you the letter. Then you won't know where she is…until you've finished testifying. We got her a new phone so you can't reach her that way, but I can call her and relay whatever you need. It's a little convoluted, but it won't matter after the trials."

"Thanks, Iva. I appreciate it." His tone sounded empty. "What are the chances of some misfortune happening every time I go out of town?"

"Life's busy. Always something going on. So I'd say it depends on how often and for how long you're gone."

He propped his elbow on the truck door and sighed, staring into the distance. "I have to get Rhodes away from here."

"Away from the farm?"

He blinked, shaking his head. "I didn't mean to say that out loud."

"I won't say anything, but I bet Rhoda would have an opinion. Isn't she like half of the heart of the orchard?"

"Half." He mumbled, rubbing his forehead.

Iva slowed at an intersection. "Which way?"

"Left. When we come to the next intersection, you can let me out, and I'll walk from there. If you go right after about two miles, you'll know where you are and can easily find your way to Landon's."

"You sure? I don't mind taking you all the way to the Cranfords'."

"There are a lot of twists and turns after that, and I'm afraid you'd get mixed up trying to get from there to Landon's. It'll be hard for him to take you back to the farm if you can't get to his place."

"True." She suppressed a yawn. "If you took Rhoda away, wouldn't you miss the farm like she would?"

"I don't think so. I never really wanted to spend my days working in an orchard. I was fourteen when I moved to Lancaster to apprentice as a carpenter with my uncle. My dream was to start my own business one day. That desire is part of why I left to work for other construction companies. I wanted to learn all there was. That passion consumed me. But then I hit that troubled spot and had to return home. It wasn't easy, but I've made my peace with it. Then Rhoda stepped onto the farm, and life became more than I knew was possible."

"So if you were without family obligations, what would you do?"

He released a whispery scoff. "Something I was too broken to do before meeting Rhoda—carpentry work." He sighed.

Seeing how Jacob loved Rhoda only made Iva want to find someone who would love her in the same way. "Couldn't you start a carpentry business here?"

"Maybe."

"But that'd defeat your desire to move elsewhere with Rhoda." Who could blame him? Rhoda and Samuel were constantly together, and she could only guess that's what had him so upset right now.

"Something like that. Thanks to my brilliant plans, the Kings now own two orchards, one here and one in Pennsylvania. There are only three King sons, and I'm the one who convinced Samuel and Rhoda to establish this one. How can I abandon that?"

Her interest peaked. "You have another brother?"

Jacob turned, staring at her.

"Don't get quiet on me now." She grinned. "Is he committed to someone or drowning in grief for a lost love?"

"Not that I know of. He's nineteen."

She'd be twenty-two in another two months. With the intersection coming up, she pulled to the side of the road. "Hmm. I'd be considered an older woman, but I could live with that if he could." She laughed, teasing. "No! I've got it. Why don't you swap places with him? You and Rhoda go there. He comes here. Forget the canning business for the Maine orchard. I want to meet a King who's not committed to or grieving over someone."

Jacob studied her. "You know"—he opened the truck door—"that's not a completely bad idea. We can't afford to forget the canning business, but does that mean Rhoda has to live here the other nine months of the year? Maybe in a few years, Leah could head up this canning operation." He got out, looking in at her. "Thanks, Iva. For everything."

"You be sure to tell Rhoda and Samuel I'm a vital part of this business." She pointed at him. "Do not let them send me back to Indiana."

"I won't."

While she watched Jacob walk down the road, Iva wondered if that third King brother was anything like Samuel and Jacob—capable of caring deeply and believing women were as valuable as men.

If so, she'd certainly like to meet him.

TWENTY-SIX

Snippets of images hounded Rhoda as friendly chitchat went around the room. From her place on the couch next to Samuel, she tried to stay tuned in, but it seemed impossible.

In her mind's eye Rhoda imagined Camilla as a young mom.

Tell them.

This time the phrase *tell them* was her own voice, simply nudging her to speak up. When she'd first heard the words, it'd been terrifying. The voice had been very strange—a young man's voice one moment, a child's the next. It'd happened during Rhoda's first night at the farm. Only Leah, Phoebe, and the children were with her. She awoke between three and four in the morning.

Jacob had been with Sandra. Landon was still driving up to the farm and pulling a trailer. Samuel was with him. Steven was on a train with the livestock.

The stress of the move had been unbearable, and she'd thought her mind was playing tricks on her.

Samuel cleared his throat. "Rhoda."

She blinked, turning on the love seat to face him.

He angled his head for a moment and chuckled. "I think she's speechless."

But she knew he was covering for her, aware she'd heard nothing.

"Your offer to build Rhoda a canning kitchen on the farm is extraordinary, but…" He let the sentence dangle, waiting on her.

"Oh." She couldn't believe she hadn't heard that. "No. We couldn't let you do that. You're wonderful friends, but that is too much. Way, way too much."

Bob sat in a ladder-back chair next to Camilla's recliner and held her hand.

They'd put a love seat on the other side of her, up close, and had insisted Rhoda and Samuel share it.

Camilla frowned, looking more frustrated than hurt. "You're not listening, are you? Where is your mind tonight—with that beau of yours?"

"Easy, Camilla. They've had a rough few nights too." Bob picked up a glass of water and passed it to his wife.

Rhoda straightened. "No, I'm not thinking about Jacob at all." Should she tell Camilla where her thoughts were?

Bob took some papers out of a drawer. "Our money is making nothing right now. It's just sitting in a bank." He passed the papers to Samuel. "Those are plats of your land, and I've marked several areas where a kitchen could be built, spots where you could easily get a building permit. You'd have to avoid being too close to the farmhouse, the creek, and the road. Other than that, there are several good sites on the fifteen acres that aren't being used for the orchard, house, barn, driveways, or greenhouses."

Samuel unfolded a two-foot-by-three-foot piece of paper. "How is it you have this layout of our property?"

"Camilla and I have been discussing this since Rhoda received the news that the farmhouse can't serve as a canning kitchen. Rhoda hasn't found anything close by that can be rented or renovated to meet your needs. Camilla did some checking, and she didn't find anything either. A few weeks back I was at the courthouse to renew my car tags, so I went by the tax assessor's office and got someone to help me pull the plat for your property."

Samuel studied it.

Rhoda placed her hand in the middle of the plat, breaking Samuel's view. "It's very good of them, isn't it?"

Samuel nodded. "Very."

Rhoda turned to Camilla. "But we can't."

Camilla handed her glass back to Bob. "Is it because the Amish can't strike a business deal with us?"

Samuel shook his head. "No. We can in some cases. Since Steven knows the situation and he's our church leader, that could help a lot."

Rhoda wanted to pinch Samuel, but she settled for giving him a stern look. "I don't agree with this and would appreciate you backing me up, not them."

The serious lines on his face said she was asking for an argument in front of Bob and Camilla. What position could he possibly take that she'd agree with? He probably thought that Camilla needed to make this offer out of gratitude and that Kings' Orchard needed a boost if God chose to give it one. Those points were not enough to accept an unwarranted gift.

Rhoda folded her hands in her lap. "We appreciate the offer."

"Perhaps"—Samuel leaned in, whispering—"our answer needs to be 'We'll think about it.'"

"No. I don't need any time, but thank you."

Camilla closed her eyes, shaking her head. "If this suggestion is allowable for the Amish, and if Bob invests in small businesses whenever he sees fit, why not?"

"I'm living with you rent free. You invite me to eat with you regularly. I use your kitchen to experiment with recipes. You get up with me in the morning, and we share a meal and coffee. You are very generous to me. But *this* is too much. Besides…" Rhoda wrestled with whether to mention Camilla did have family. She was almost sure of it. But was her friend up to hearing it?

"Go on."

Rhoda moved to the edge of the couch. "Let's talk later. You need to rest."

"I don't need rest. I need you to be less stubborn." Camilla peered around. "Samuel, is she always like this?"

"You have no idea." He grinned, clearly teasing. Rhoda found nothing amusing. Perhaps she needed rest more than Camilla, but mostly she wanted some support from Samuel, not a fight.

Camilla laughed. "I might understand a little. The first time I woke up in that car, I heard you two yelling at each other. I probably wouldn't have recognized who it was had it not been for the day you came by to flag the trees. I used to think you and your brother were at fault, but now I'm not so sure."

Camilla's words stung. Maybe Rhoda did need to compromise more, regardless of what she personally wanted. She'd work on that, but Camilla's offer was not the place to start.

Bob adjusted the fleece blanket that had slipped off of Camilla. "Samuel, according to the courthouse records, the property is in your name."

"Yes, it is. But that was done for a lot of reasons that had to do with getting a loan. Rhoda, her brother, their Daed, and Jacob also invested in the land."

"Nonetheless, legally you have the final say."

"True."

Rhoda's blood began to warm. "Samuel King," she mumbled through gritted teeth.

Camilla glanced at Bob, a slight smile of victory on her lips. "Since we've narrowed it down that the roadblock is Rhoda, who is just being stubborn, I say the issue is settled." Camilla pointed at the plat. "Of the places Bob marked, choose your favorite."

Anger burned through Rhoda, causing her face to prickle. "Camilla, you said I should keep my kitchen separate, perhaps even in my name, and now you'd go around me because the land is in Samuel's name?" Rhoda took the plat from Samuel and folded it. "And you, Samuel. Didn't you give me your word before we left Pennsylvania that you'd not go behind my back or around me ever again?"

"You're right here." Samuel gestured at the room. "And I haven't agreed to *do* anything. We're talking...or at least trying to."

Rhoda took a breath. "My answer is no, but thank you."

Camilla held out her hand, and Rhoda took it. "Child, why?"

The sincerity in Camilla's voice erased much of Rhoda's anger. "I've explained why."

"But there's another reason. There has to be, because saying no is against everything you've been searching for. It's the answer you need. So tell me the real reason."

Rhoda shook her head. "We'll talk later...when you're better."

"Talk about what?"

"Not now." Rhoda patted her hand. "Just rest."

"This is about Jojo, isn't it?" Camilla asked.

Rhoda stood and moved to the window. "I believe you have a grand-daughter."

"Rhoda, you're not only stubborn; you're like a hound with a bone." Camilla sighed. "You *think* you know. Trust me, all that's going on is that you've picked up on pieces of information you've heard or read or seen in the newspapers or overheard people say. My son was a kid himself when he died. I don't have a grandchild."

Rhoda's mouth was so dry she couldn't swallow. She prayed for the right words. "I see snippets at times, as if God is trying to get a message to you. And I know it sounds crazy, but I think you're wrong."

"I don't believe in God. Never have."

Rhoda had wondered about that. "Still…I saw what I saw."

"If God exists, I'd have a few things to say to him. Zachary became religious, and about six months later he was dead. You care to try to explain that?"

"He does exist, and we can't begin to fathom what He's like. How could we? People struggle to understand one another, and we're from the same century, the same country, and we experience many of the same things from attending school to falling in love. And yet really understanding another human being is almost impossible."

Samuel tapped the folded plat on his knee. "There's a verse that basically says on this earth all things are in subjection under His feet, but for now we don't see all things under Him." Samuel fidgeted with the plat. "To me, what's being said is we live on a fallen planet, and we don't yet see it redeemed from all evil."

Camilla stared at Samuel, looking lost in thought before her face twisted in pain. "My first husband left me for a woman who could bear him children. That's when I began believing I had no value at all. So I started living with whomever I wanted. At forty-two years old, I came up pregnant. I was terrified, but I thought it was my chance at the American dream—a family. My child's father was successful at business, but other than that he wasn't much. Since I believed I was worthless, I signed a prenup that gave me nothing if we divorced. I was just grateful he agreed to marry me." She searched Bob's face.

He rested his hand on her head and nodded. "He was the problem, Camilla. Not you. Nobody can make up for what's missing in a person's heart."

She plucked at the fabric on the arm of the recliner. "My son was a tender-hearted boy. So precious. And I loved him with all my heart. For months at a time his dad would be decent. He'd play ball with him and come to his recitals and tennis matches. But then he'd go on a binge, drinking and beating me. My son begged me to leave him. He didn't understand. We were far from rich, but his dad was a good provider, and I...I thought I'd be useless on my own. I was nearing retirement age. Who was going to hire me? But if I stayed, I could give my son everything he needed—music and tennis lessons, summer camps, and the best schools. When my husband was sober, he'd give sacrificially. If I'd left and he'd paid only child support, we would've lived in poverty. I wanted Zachary to have his choice of colleges, but he never got that far. He left home at sixteen, and he hated me for putting him through the emotional turmoil of a loving, hateful dad. He said I'd ruined his life because I cared more about security than peace." Camilla stared at the wall in front of her. "Funny, but I finally found the courage to leave his dad after that."

Rhoda moved back to the love seat. "In my mind I saw you in front of a medical building, arguing with Zachary and Jojo. I don't understand what I saw."

All color drained from Camilla's face. "I understand it. I was there."

"Then you believe me about having a grandchild?"

Camilla swiped at a tear. "It was an abortion clinic."

Hurt for Camilla outweighed everything else, but Rhoda felt foolish not to have put it all together. No wonder Camilla was so certain she didn't have a grandchild.

Camilla's eyes brimmed with tears. "I stayed in my car the whole time they were inside that building, and they were in there for more than two hours. Jojo left the clinic in control, but when she saw me in my car, she burst into tears. My son came to me, and he said I'd made everything harder for Jojo. He told me to leave them alone, and even though I cried every day, I did as he asked. I owed him that much.

"About six months later he contacted me. I walked on eggshells, hoping for a chance to reconnect with him. We'd meet somewhere neutral for coffee or lunch, and we kept the conversations as light and breezy as possible, but we couldn't talk about our reality or it'd shatter us. I asked about Jojo, and he'd said that topic was off-limits. I supposed they weren't together anymore. At one point he asked for us to see a family counselor. We did twice, and I thought healing was taking place, but before the third visit came around, he was killed in a car wreck—by a trucker who fell asleep at the wheel." The pain reflected in her eyes was unbearable.

Bob stood beside her, a hand on her shoulder as he held the glass for her. "Is it possible Jojo changed her mind?"

She sipped from the straw. "No. She left that clinic completely broken."

Bob set the drink on a side table. "Rhoda?"

She shrugged. "I wish I could say for sure. Sometimes I see a piece of something and I assume the wrong thing, but isn't it worth investigating?"

"They weren't married, and I don't even know the girl's last name." Camilla ran her unbandaged hand through her hair, as if trying to pull a memory from her brain. "Whenever Zachary would say her name, I'd think Jojo Jade."

Rhoda paced the floor, needing to release some of her pent-up nerves. "Dumont. Look for Joella Dumont."

"I told you they were underage, and I didn't sign a paper."

"Would his dad?"

Camilla's eyes bugged out. "What? Zachary disowned him...but if that boy wanted to marry her bad enough, and if he caught his dad in the right mood, he could've talked him into anything."

Rhoda's chest ached. "The day I came through the woods following your music, I heard a little girl's voice. She called you Grandmamma."

Camilla gasped. "When Zachary was little, he always said he wanted a grandmamma. My parents were dead, so we agreed that when he had children, they could call me that."

Rhoda had to sit.

Camilla lay back, breathing deep and weeping. "I might have a grandchild. But if this is true, how can I find her?"

Bob scratched his chin. "Zachary told you he was living in Maine, and you said his car tags indicated the same thing. So maybe that's where the child was born. We'll start looking at records, but it'll take a while since we're not sure when the child would've been born."

Chills and excitement skidded through Rhoda in waves. "After he told you to leave them alone, when did he contact you again?"

"It was four years ago, but I don't really remember the month." Camilla thought. "Wait, it was right after Thanksgiving. I remember because when the phone rang, I was carving the leftover turkey to make a potpie."

Rhoda rubbed her arms, trying to dispel the chill bumps. "I think he either had held his daughter or it was close to her birth. His sense of hope and joy were strong, and he needed to connect with his mom. And when the time was right, after more counseling, he would've told you about your granddaughter."

Bob held his wife's hand. "There's a records office in Augusta. We can go there and look through the birth records. We'll verify her birth date and then put ads in the paper looking for Jojo. We'll hire investigators if need be."

"What if Jojo doesn't want me in her life?"

Rhoda's head pounded from the energy pumping through her. "One issue at a time, okay?"

Camilla stared, wide eyed. "Of course. Sorry."

Rhoda felt like clothes on a line during a storm.

Samuel leaned in. "I've never been more proud of you." His soothing voice made her relax a bit. She looked him in the eyes, and he nodded. "And that's really saying something."

His words made her eyes sting with tears, and she took a deep breath, relaxing. She'd done it. She'd finally managed to share what she needed to.

Someone knocked at the front door, but Camilla and Bob were whispering and teary eyed.

Samuel stood. "I'll get it."

A few moments later Rhoda heard the front door open and then… Was that arguing? She slipped out of the living room and went to the foyer.

Jacob. Her spontaneous smile waned as she heard his cutting words.

"So why is it, *brother,* that whenever I return, you're with Rhoda, even when she's not at the farm?"

Rhoda's chest constricted. That awful sense of powerlessness returned. She was caught between a rock and a hard place. If she defended Samuel being here, she'd make Jacob feel as if he'd been stabbed in the back. If she allowed Jacob to stew in his anger against Samuel, she was guilty of coming between the brothers.

She decided to respond as if she hadn't heard anything. "Jacob." She went to him and embraced him. The warmth of the hug wasn't what she'd hoped for, but she didn't let go. Her disappointment in his harshness with Samuel faded, and she rested her head on his chest. "You're home."

"I am." He kissed the top of her head. "Is Camilla okay?"

"Minor injuries." Rhoda backed away and cupped his face with her hands. "I'm so glad you're home."

"Jacob, right?" Bob moved forward, his hand extended.

"Yeah."

"Come on in. My wife and I are trying to talk Rhoda into something. I think we have Samuel convinced. How do you feel about Rhoda's canning kitchen being built on your property?"

Jacob rested his hands on Rhoda's shoulders as they went into the living room. "I think there's no money to do that right now."

Jacob took a place on the love seat beside her, watching as Samuel brought in a chair from the kitchen. There was a couch on the far side of the room, but Bob had set up this area to surround Camilla so they could easily chat.

Bob explained about the accident, and Rhoda cringed when he told about Samuel and her sharing a horse so they could make eye contact with Camilla and keep her calm.

Rhoda interlaced her fingers with Jacob's as Bob then explained their desire to invest in the business by making it possible for them to build the canning kitchen.

Bob passed him the plat. "Samuel seems to think it's a fine idea."

Jacob released her hand and studied the plat. "I'm sure my brother likes the plan. It'd keep *everyone* so close." He looked at Samuel. "Right?"

Samuel's jaw clenched, but he said nothing.

"Well,"—Camilla laid her head back, closing her eyes—"much has happened in the last twenty-four hours. We can't sort it all out tonight. You need to think on our offer, and Bob and I will think about my granddaughter." Camilla smiled, eyes still closed. "Thanks to Rhoda."

Jacob frowned and held out the plat to Bob. "Why's she thanking Rhoda for a grandchild?"

Bob took the plat. "You don't know?"

Rhoda's head began to pound. "We haven't talked about it."

Despite noticeably bristling, Jacob managed a smile. "I've been gone too much, but I'm putting that behind us as fast as I can."

Was his absence all that kept them from talking about serious matters?

Jacob held her hand. "It sounds as if Rhoda and I need to talk before I'll know what to think." He turned to her. "How did the battle with the frost go?"

Rhoda looped her arm through his. "Really great, we think."

He brushed her cheek with the back of his fingers. "You look exhausted."

"Between that and Camilla's mishap, and…other things I'll tell you later." Like Phoebe losing the baby and Rhoda's insight concerning Jojo.

"Then we should talk." Jacob smiled.

"I look forward to that." She squeezed his hand. "Tomorrow when you pick me up to take me to the farm?"

Disappointment flashed through his eyes, but he nodded and stood.

"I'd love to tonight." Rhoda rose. "But I'm exhausted. Is your rig here?"

"Iva dropped me off."

Bob pulled some keys from his pocket. "I drove Samuel here. Come on. I'll give you men a lift back to the farm, and the womenfolk can crawl into bed early."

Rhoda walked with Jacob to the porch while Bob and Samuel went on to the car.

Jacob gazed into her eyes. "It'll be different for us from here on. I may have a few more responsibilities to fulfill, but because of the immunity, I'm free, Rhoda. You're the only one who could've gotten me to do carpentry work again. You're the only reason I did what had to be done so I could get cleared. And you're the only one for me." He leaned in, kissing her on the lips. "I'll be here an hour earlier than usual so we can talk, and we won't stop making time to talk for the rest of our lives."

Every word was filled with a promise, and he meant them. She knew he did. "I look forward to a fresh start in the morning." And she did, but she was apprehensive too. His words would be soft-spoken and kind, even interlaced with humor and understanding, but he'd ask hard questions, ones she wouldn't have an answer for, like how did she and Samuel seem to be inseparable when he was away?

Circumstances just seemed to work out that way, but Jacob had a right to feel frustrated.

And yet, in some ways he didn't.

All of that aside, she was hopeful. He saw what they needed, and he was committed to her in ways that had been impossible before now.

TWENTY-SEVEN

The sun had yet to rise as Jacob waited in the buggy outside the Cranfords' house. It was too early to tap on their door, and Rhoda was usually waiting for him on the porch when he arrived. He didn't see any lights on.

Now what?

He supposed he'd wait. She'd certainly done plenty of that for him.

It had been impossible to sleep last night. Without realizing it, Iva had made crystal clear that there was a romantic relationship of some kind between Samuel and Rhoda. Well, *crystal clear* might be the wrong words. His thoughts about Rhoda were almost as muddied as ever, but he knew his brother was in love.

Was it Samuel's fault? Was it Jacob's? Maybe the responsibility belonged to both of them to some degree. But accountability wasn't the most important part. The only thing that really mattered was where Jacob and Rhoda landed in the end.

She didn't need to live on the farm and be near Samuel. Jacob was confident of that. The question was how to convince Rhoda.

If he could, he'd whisk her away from Maine. Maybe Iva's playful idea wasn't altogether silly. Rhoda loved tending fruit and canning. Jacob had a newfound urge to try his hand at carpentry again. He thought he was finally free to pursue that—not just physically but also emotionally. The Pennsylvania orchard had a summer kitchen that she loved. It had been damaged by the tornado, but it could be repaired. Of course they had moved all the equipment to Maine, and it was now in storage in the barn. But that could be replaced. Anything could be replaced—except Rhoda.

As the sun rose, spreading bright pink and orange hues across the sky, he continued to stare at the house. Where was she?

His mind continued to churn with frustrations and half-baked solutions. Finally the front door opened, and Rhoda stepped outside.

He hopped out of the carriage and hurried to open her door.

"Sorry." She slid her arms into her sweater while walking toward him. "I overslept."

"Guder Marye." He bowed.

She laughed softly before placing her warm cheek against his cold face. "I'm so glad you're home."

"Me too." He wasn't going to lose this woman. If he had to abandon the family business and disown his brother in order to keep her, he'd do it. "Anyone who's battled mother nature and won, or at least mostly won, deserves to sleep in."

She kissed him on the cheek and then wiped the same spot, her eyes admiring him. "This is our new beginning."

"Absolutely."

She climbed into the buggy. Clearly, she was pleased to see him last night and today. That helped. A lot. It was a far cry from the last time he'd returned, when he found out Samuel had kissed her only moments earlier, and it was a world better than what he'd feared most of yesterday.

He went back around the vehicle and grabbed the reins. As he pulled onto the main road, one question hounded him: How would she feel about the idea of moving to Pennsylvania? She could still do what she loved to do—tend to fruit crops and can. And Jacob would get what he wanted—distance between Samuel and her.

Of course, he couldn't yet afford to buy land or a house there. The Pennsylvania orchard wouldn't produce enough work or income to support him, Rhoda, and Eli full-time, not for years yet. But he and Rhoda could live on the King farm. She and Eli could work the orchard, and he could...

A desire that had been niggling its way free for days, maybe months, finally overtook him. Passion and excitement ignited.

Construction work!

He could work for his uncle, doing the vocation he'd once loved. From his first weeks of knowing Rhoda, she'd helped him learn to love it again. He could hire a driver to take him to and from Lancaster every day.

Now *that* wasn't a bad idea at all.

"I really am sorry for being so late." She stretched, yawning. "But, oh, how good that bed felt this morning."

"Forgiven. You've certainly had to wait on me plenty. But that time is over. You know that, right?"

"I do."

Despite hugging him moments ago and her encouraging words, her voice sounded hollow, similar to when he used to call her while he was away. He'd spend the day looking forward to talking to her, but once on the phone, he felt less connected, not more.

He came to a yield sign and then headed away from the farm. "It was dark when I got to the farm last night and when I left this morning. How do the buds look?"

"Healthy." She tightened her sweater. "Didn't you ask that last night?"

"I did." But right now he was aiming for something peaceful to talk about, and since the only thing coming to his mind were daydreams of their imminent return to Pennsylvania, he couldn't think of much to say. "How's your family back home?"

She blinked. "Fine." She sounded a bit perplexed. "You've never asked about them before."

Jacob stifled a sigh and shrugged. Why was she right next to him and yet seemed so far away? The answer, obviously, was Samuel.

Jacob wasn't sure what irked him most—the fact that he had been the one to cajole her into moving to Maine or that she was so tied to the orchard he couldn't imagine her leaving it for months.

When Samuel had wavered on whether Rhoda and he could work together, Jacob had helped smooth the way, thinking it'd give him good reasons to be near her and it'd give him time to get to know her. Now he wished he'd let Samuel and Rhoda go their separate ways during any one of the arguments that'd threatened to end their partnership.

But no...he just *had* to be the peacekeeper.

"How did the deposition go?"

"Good, I suppose. It's hard to dissect months of mistakes while lawyers are asking so many questions."

"Ya. I can imagine."

He reached for her hand. "Why didn't you tell me about Camilla having a grandchild?"

She squeezed his fingers reassuringly. "It wasn't intentional. You and I have dealt with a lot this past year. And when we're together, we don't talk about those kinds of things."

"So what do we talk about?"

She smiled, her sincerity evident. "You tell me jokes and make me laugh. You harass me, trying to put melted marshmallow in my hair or pulling on my coattails while I'm working. We've mostly talked about Sandra and the troubles you walked into."

"That's it?" Wasn't there more between them than childish playfulness and Jacob's burdens?

"We're us. Who else do we need to be? You see me better than I see myself, and you helped me find laughter again." She held his hand with both of hers. "I accepted your many secrets, and we've traveled that bumpy road together. You made me look at the facts concerning Emma's death—that even though I knew what was going to happen, I couldn't have gotten there in time."

He'd have preferred for her to recall more touching things and end her explanation with a proclamation of love. "When did you first get a hunch about Camilla having a grandchild?"

"My first night on the farm."

"Ah." He tried to sound nonchalant. "When did Samuel know?"

Her face flushed. "I...I'm not sure."

"Not sure? What does that mean?" He sounded like a jealous boyfriend again. He hated that. If his humor drew her to him, would his suspicions push her away?

"I wanted to talk to him that night, but he said I had you for that. Then I mentioned it again at some point because it was hounding me, and you were staying with Sandra." She played with the edges of her sweater. "Jacob, he's a good brother. He worked hard and avoided me like I was the plague most of the time you were gone. I didn't realize it for a long time, but I grew angry that you weren't here and Samuel wasn't available. He'd disappear to the farthest parts of the orchard. When the pressure got so bad because of my legal issues, Samuel feared I was going to have a nervous breakdown. Then he stopped hiding from me because I needed some support. Would you want any less?"

She had a way of making him look at things differently.

"No, he did the right thing." Jacob could see that his brother had tried to stay loyal to him, and he wanted to feel that was enough. Biting back his jealousy, he lifted her hand and kissed it. "I understand." He swallowed hard. "But is it possible you and Samuel are too close?"

She didn't flinch as she turned her gaze out the window. An uncomfortable silence filled the carriage, but he resisted the desire to prod her.

She finally nodded. "That thought crossed my mind while you were in Virginia."

Hurt engulfed him, and indignation against Samuel burned. Jacob fought the temptation to withdraw into himself and say nothing.

He lowered the visor on the front windshield, blocking the sun. "But"—he cleared his throat, trying to find his voice—"you still want to marry me, right?"

"Jacob,"—disbelief radiated in her eyes—"are *you* having second thoughts?"

"What? No. Of course not."

"Then why would you ask me that?"

"I feel insecure about us. Can you blame me?"

She sighed. "I'm doing all I know to prevent that. What else can I do?"

He had the answer. It was as clear as the cloudless spring day ahead of them. They needed to get away from Samuel as soon as possible. But Jacob feared if he suggested that right now, it would be too much of a shock to her

and possibly challenge her desire to marry him. And he knew they needed
nothing else to undermine them at the moment.

Nothing.

He shrugged, and she looked out the window.

Thoughts of walking on the beach by himself mere days ago came to him,
and it seemed the lostness between Rhoda and him right now was as vast as the
breadth and depth of the ocean he'd once enjoyed.

For the life of him, he couldn't see a way to get her to leave Maine for
months to come. He'd love to. But even if he could get permission to marry her
outside of the wedding season, they couldn't do so until he went through instruction and joined the faith. That'd take the rest of the summer. Besides, she
wouldn't leave Kings' Orchard in a bind, and she'd need months to train Leah
and Iva to handle the canning business without her—*if* she was willing to leave
the work in their hands. Landon knew a lot about Rhoda's side of the business.
He'd been with her for years, and Jacob was sure he'd stay here, near Leah.
That was good.

But for now all Jacob could do was stay close to Rhoda, be the man she'd
fallen in love with, and go through the steps to join the faith.

TWENTY-EIGHT

Sunlight dispersed through the greenhouse like a soft glow from a halo as Rhoda watered the herbs. Her thoughts were as numerous as the drops of water spraying from the hose. The battle with the frost had been over for almost a week, and by all outward signs, it appeared they'd won. So why did she feel so defeated?

She ran her fingers across the petals of the scarlet bergamot and the soft, leafy gray greens of sage. Almost two months ago the police had returned these containers with mostly dead plants, but she'd nursed them back to health—or planted new ones. Could she be as successful in cultivating her relationship with Jacob?

Landon opened the door, the backpack with his computer on his shoulder. "There you are."

"I thought you were staying home today to update the website."

"I was, but a couple of things about the site came up that I need to talk to you about before I approach Samuel with them in a few days...or weeks, whenever he finds the time."

"I doubt he'll like the topic."

"It's not his favorite, but it's not yours either. I think it's a necessary evil in order to increase the number of wholesale buyers for your goods." He set his backpack on a table away from any moisture. "Since Samuel hasn't really looked at your website, I don't want to spring something on him that might freak him out. So I wanted to get your approval first." He took a seat on the dry workbench next to his equipment. "I've been hunting for you. Where's your two-way?"

"I left it at Camilla's this morning."

"Why do I get the feeling you did that on purpose?"

She released the nozzle, shutting off the water. Indeed, she had knowingly walked out without it. Leave it to Landon to realize that. Of course, on his side, he had years of knowing her. But if she could be easily reached, Phoebe would want her to come in for lunch. Samuel would have business questions, and with Jacob back she didn't want to be around him. Steven would use it to ask where she was, and then he'd look at her as if he knew what was best for her more than she did. Someone always wanted something, and today she had nothing to give, not right now anyway. And Jacob, well, he wasn't far, and since he seemed to know where she was all the time, he could find her whenever he wished.

She didn't want to explain her behavior to Landon, though. Hopefully, she could redirect his questions. "What's up?"

"Don't want to answer me, eh?"

She flicked the hose his way, making the spray of water hit just short of him.

"Hey!" He grabbed his backpack and put it behind him.

She released the nozzle. "Could you get to the point?"

"Keep the water away and I will."

While he got out his computer and set it up, she turned off the water and hung the nozzle on a nail, then grabbed a scrap of a dry towel from its hook.

He pulled his phone from his pocket, touched the screen several times, and set it beside his computer. "I'd like to create a montage with music and a voice-over. It'll need to be uploaded to YouTube, but then I can put it on your site."

She dried her hands. "Despite teaching me a few computery things over the years, you have to know I understood almost nothing of what you just said."

"I figured." He tapped on his keyboard, opening a web page. "Here, look at this."

She moved in closer to see the monitor.

"This is YouTube. It's an Internet site where video clips can be uploaded, like this one." He clicked on an arrow covering a picture of some type, and it began playing.

She watched as an Englisch man in an orchard started talking. "How'd you get an Internet connection out here?"

"It's called a Personal Hotspot, and the connection is coming through my iPhone. And this"—he clicked on an icon in a sidebar—"is a video I'd like to put on your website. This is only on my computer. I haven't uploaded it yet."

Colorful images of the orchard floated across the screen.

He clicked again, only this time the video became as large as his laptop screen. "Iva took the photos, and I played with them until they come across like a movie."

She wound the towel this way and that, fidgeting. "This is from pictures?"

"Yep. All I needed was a little time with them and a program called Final Cut Pro."

A few of the snapshots showed distant images of them tending the orchard—Samuel, Jacob, Leah, Steven, Landon, and Rhoda. Tastefully done, giving a feel for the work without showing or blurring their faces. "Iva's really good, isn't she?"

"She definitely has a good eye for photography. When I asked her about it, she said free lessons came with the camera, and she went to every one she could. Anyway, I'd like to add some background music to it with either written words or a voice-over to tell a bit about the orchard, unless that's a problem."

"Create it. Then see what Samuel thinks. Since it's been done this carefully, I imagine he'll be fine with it."

"Okay." He closed the laptop and slid it into its case. "I'd like to say that's all I need to know, but it's not."

She tucked the towel into the bib of her apron. "What's next?"

"It's a mixture of personal and business." He fidgeted with his computer bag, zipping and unzipping one of the compartments. "There's a lot riding on the success of this orchard, and I never doubted that you and the Kings would know what to do to restore these trees, but lately it seems like your green thumb and determination may not be enough."

"No, there are always weather issues and pests to contend with, and we can only do so much to battle those."

He looked up from the computer bag in his lap, disbelief in his eyes. "You really think that's what I'm talking about?"

Now that he called her on it and made her realize she was being dismissive, no, that's not what she thought he meant. Something was eating at him, and, want to or not, she was about to find out what it was.

"Is everything between you and Jacob going to be okay?"

It had taken a lot for Landon to confront her like this. So much so she actually felt sorry for him. When she went to him to discuss anything, he didn't mind sharing his opinion, but he wasn't one to probe into her relationships.

She leaned her back against the work station, inches from her friend, staring at the dirt floor. "No, everything isn't right. But it will be. It'll take some time, but my will is set on restoring our relationship just as much as it is on protecting the orchard from all dangers, like the frost."

When Landon didn't respond, she turned to look at him.

He intertwined his fingertips and circled one thumb around the other. "You're in love with him?"

"Yes. Absolutely. And it's in poor taste that you'd even question me on that."

"Ah, come on, Rhodes. You said you set your will toward mending the relationship, and you compared it to revitalizing the orchard, which is taking massive efforts from everyone."

"That's not what I meant, and you know it." She went to her bergamot, finding a moment of pleasure in the brilliant red flowers. "Like a garden, relationships have times when they need extra tending." She inhaled the citrusy, earthy aroma of the plant. "These are far more than just pretty. Their greatest strength is their medicinal effects. A poultice with this can heal skin infections and wounds. Jacob and I are finding ways to apply natural healing to our relationship. That's all."

"What happened between you and Samuel that set off the worst in Jacob?"

She touched her lips, remembering the power of those few moments. "It doesn't matter."

"Are you kidding me? Of course it matters. I've kept my mouth shut for too long. But between Jacob and Samuel and the business, I want to make sure you're watching out for yourself." He crossed his arms. "So what happened?"

"We kissed." She didn't have to tell him to keep it between them. She knew he would.

Landon lowered his head, shaking it. "Rhodes."

"It didn't mean any—"

"Do not finish that sentence." He pointed at her. "I don't want to hear it or be forced to figure out whether you're lying." He paused before rolling his eyes. "What were you thinking to get so attached to Samuel?"

Couldn't Landon see? It had happened so naturally, so organically, she hadn't realized it'd taken root until she was in his arms. "You're angry with me."

"No." He elongated the word, sounding quite perturbed. "But I'm aggravated about the position you've put yourself in. For the first time in your life, you have the chance to be really happy, a kind of joy that can build from year to year, as it should." He got off the table and put his hands on her shoulders. "Look, I want whatever you want. You believe that right?"

She nodded. "Ya." It was his strong suit—to long for his friends to get their heart's desire.

He removed his ball cap and raked his hand through his hair. "So what do you want?"

"A life with Jacob."

He sighed and put on his cap. "Then you'd better pull your act together."

His words felt like a slap across her face. "What does that mean?"

He blinked. "You don't see it, do you? Your eyes light up whenever Samuel comes into view. He can be a speck on a distant hill, and what's evident on your face isn't good, not for you and Jacob. When Samuel says anything, whether in the office, field, or at the kitchen table, you're intense, wanting to hear his opinion. You may not agree with him, but when he speaks, it carries weight."

Her skin rippled with pinpricks as embarrassment rushed through her. "Don't be ridiculous. I like Samuel a lot. But that's all you're seeing. We simply let a fleeting emotion rule our actions."

There, she'd finally confessed. Unfortunately, in doing so she could see why she'd defended Samuel so strongly to Jacob. And why Jacob felt slighted by what must've sounded like a half-hearted apology. From the moment Samuel had pulled her close, she'd wanted to kiss him as much as he had her. But that only meant they were two lonely, single people who were attracted to each other and had been forced into close quarters for too long, right?

She swallowed hard. That was right, wasn't it? "I haven't been fair to Jacob."

Landon angled his head, staring at her. "Well, there's good news—when Jacob is around, you're better at controlling your reactions to Samuel. You barely let yourself look his way. But if you intend to keep Jacob *and* give Samuel the signals of a woman who's already taken, I suggest you deal with what's between you and Samuel before Jacob catches a *real* glimpse of it. If you don't, all your work ethic and green-thumb skills won't be able to fix the damage."

Deal with it how? Maybe she should've talked to Landon long before now. "I…I have no idea what that means."

"Understand what you feel for Samuel and own up to it. Once you've faced it, file it. Then you're free to use all the space inside you for Jacob. You had to file things away when Emma died, didn't you?"

"The only thing I was successful at concerning Emma was owning up to how I felt. I was guilty, and I didn't know how to file that. It took up all the room in my heart and my every thought for years."

"I remember, but this is different. You didn't have a choice with Emma, and that kind of pain and shock takes years. With Samuel, this is your decision."

"Okay. I see what you mean." Out of the corner of her eye, she saw a hazy image of her sister. Rhoda turned.

Emma.

Her sister stood there, hands folded, a warm smile on her lips. Then she faded away. Rhoda hadn't seen her in weeks. Why now?

"Rhodes?" Landon touched her shoulder.

She pulled back from her thoughts, ready to change the subject. "How are you and Leah?"

She would still prefer for Leah to join the faith. Loyalty was the key to the most godly, obedient lives. Wasn't it? "You're still going out?"

"Yeah. But she's young and trying to figure out which way is up. That's even harder inside an Amish world that says there is only one way up—through the Ordnung."

"You sound like you're ready for whatever she decides."

"She may not know for years yet, but I'll stick by my motto: hope for the best, be braced for the worst."

"You finally know what you want out of life." Rhoda remembered how adrift he'd been about life when she'd first met him. But even then his actions had matched who he was—relaxed as his boat bobbed on the ocean.

"Yep. Apparently you do too. So don't sabotage yourself, okay?"

Ready for time alone, she picked up the nozzle. "You should take your computer and go before—"

"Landon?" Phoebe called through the two-way.

"Yeah?"

"Do you know where Rhoda is?"

Landon raised his eyebrows, asking what he needed to do.

She took the two-way. "In the third greenhouse. Why?"

"Camilla's here. She's asked to see you and Samuel. She'd like to see you alone, so she's waiting for you at her car."

Did she have news about her granddaughter? "Coming."

If Camilla had good information, wouldn't she want to talk in the house?

Nervousness hounded Rhoda as she rushed toward the driveway. If she'd gotten their hopes up for nothing, she'd struggle for years to find peace with herself.

TWENTY-NINE

Samuel had been in the office when Bob pulled up. Now they were standing near the Cranfords' car, talking while waiting for Rhoda. Samuel was sure Jacob would appear out of thin air soon. He'd barely let Rhoda out of his sight since returning home last Sunday.

Camilla held a rolled paper in one hand while gazing toward the orchard. "Is she far?"

"No." He touched the two-way attached to his suspenders. "She was in a greenhouse. Would you care to come into the house or the office and sit?"

"No. I just need to see both of you. We'll only be here a minute. I need to get off my feet soon."

Rhoda had shared her hunches with them five days ago, but Samuel couldn't tell if they had good or distressing news.

He removed his straw hat. "I'm surprised to see you up and about this soon, Camilla."

Bob shoved his hands into his pockets. "She's worn out. But there was no keeping her in that bed another day."

"Hello!" Rhoda waved, hurrying toward them.

Camilla unrolled the paper. "Look! We went to the records office in Augusta this morning."

As soon as Rhoda could, she eased the paper from Camilla. Once Rhoda read it, she beamed at Samuel before she moved to stand beside him. It only took a glance to see it was a copy of a birth certificate!

Rhoda looked up at him, so relieved. "Sophia Grace Dumont."

Samuel was speechless. He'd believed in Rhoda and the gift God gave her, and yet as he stared at the proof, he couldn't wrap his mind around the enormity of it.

Rhoda gently embraced Camilla. "You have a granddaughter!"

Camilla laughed. "I do! I really do!"

"Congratulations." Samuel shook Bob's hand. She wasn't Bob's granddaughter, but the man seemed thrilled at the discovery that Camilla was a grandmother.

Rhoda gave the paper back to Camilla. "So, Grandmamma, what's the next step?"

"We hire an investigator and then wait. But, Rhoda, we can't thank you enough."

Rhoda's cheeks turned red. "Please don't say that. I mean, you're welcome and all, but I'm nothing in all this. Left up to me, I'd have known nothing, and when I did know a little something, I botched it up beyond recognition. If God had His way, I think I would've known how to share this information seven months ago."

"Well, be that as it may," Bob said, "we've talked and talked, and we believe Rhoda is wrong to turn down our offer." He leaned against his car.

Rhoda glanced at Samuel, probably hoping for reinforcements. "We discussed this on Sunday night, and as exciting as your news about Sophia is, it doesn't change how I feel about your offer to invest in this business."

"I'm not giving up that easily." Bob chuckled. "This business of yours is a worthy investment, and we need time with you two so we can discuss why you should allow us to invest. How can it not be a wise move? Rhoda's sixth sense can direct your business moves."

"It's not like that." Rhoda motioned to Camilla. "I don't possess an ability like she has with music. I don't have a skill like a nurse or something. At times information comes, and most often when it does, it's about strangers and something that's weighing on their hearts. I've never had a clue about business, not that I remember."

Bob folded his arms. "Nevertheless, you need our capital to build a canning kitchen."

Rhoda shook her head, her lips pursed. "We can figure it out."

"What is the problem with letting us invest in you? I take it you two have talked about it since Sunday, right?"

Samuel wished they had. "No."

"Why not?" Bob asked.

In truth, it was probably because of Jacob. He stood sentry between Samuel and Rhoda at all times, and Rhoda let him. Some days Samuel wasn't sure how the three of them would manage to run the business together. Would Jacob get better after he and Rhoda married? Or worse?

"Rhoda." Camilla ran her fingers along the edge of the birth certificate. "Can you at least help us understand why you're so against it?"

Rhoda fidgeted with a string to her prayer Kapp. "I'm not sure I can. In many ways I'm just now coming to grips with my gift of knowing things, but I can't allow myself to be compensated for telling you something God shared with me to share with you. I have no peace within me that it would be okay to accept your money—not as a gift, a loan, or an investment." Rhoda gestured toward the birth certificate. "But I'm glad you're on your way to finding Sophia."

"You're being stubborn." Camilla raised her eyebrows. "We wanted to build your canning kitchen before you told us anything about Sophia."

Samuel studied Rhoda. If he accepted Bob's investment, he would probably disrupt Rhoda's newfound confidence in allowing God's gift of insight to reveal itself at will. He kicked at a piece of broken concrete on the driveway. King's Orchard Maine was desperate for a kitchen before the harvest. *He* was desperate for one, but he turned to Bob. "We can't accept your offer. I'm sorry."

Bob sighed. "Well, I have a backup plan, and we took something into our own hands today." He reached into the car and pulled out a checkbook. "You'll need to go to the bank with us to put your John Hancock on the signature cards. If you won't let us invest, let us loan you some money so you can get started."

Rhoda shook her head. "That's very kind, but—"

Bob held the checkbook out to Samuel. "It's a loan. That makes a difference, right?"

Samuel swallowed hard and shook his head. He wouldn't take any money from the Cranfords, not without Rhoda's approval. He'd expect the same of her. They were partners.

"Well, shoot." Bob slapped the checkbook against his palm. "At least come over and let's talk about some other solutions. We know this area, and we know the Realtors, and I'm quite clever when it comes to finances and business."

Camilla nudged Rhoda. "Come on, we have reason to celebrate, and we don't want to spend the evening alone."

Samuel rubbed a knot out of his shoulder. "Sure, we'll come over tonight. Right, Rhoda?"

She jolted, her eyes large with surprise at his response. He realized too late that today was Friday—a courting night for her and Jacob.

"You can go, and I'll see them later tonight." Rhoda crossed her arms. "I've talked to a few Realtors, and they're mailing me some brochures. It's not as if we're completely stalled on the topic."

Samuel held up a finger to Camilla and Bob. "Could you excuse us for just a moment?" He motioned for Rhoda to follow him toward the barn. When they were a safe distance away from the Cranfords, he stopped. "You're being rude. They're excited about Sophia, and they want time with *you*. I'm tired of racking my brain on my own about the canning kitchen. You're never around to discuss it, and you've turned them down as investors and rejected borrowing money from them."

"So you're blaming me?"

"No. I understand your thinking, but I think you can give up one date night with Jacob to help celebrate and brainstorm with Bob and Camilla."

"Why can't we do this another night?"

"Because it's Friday. I know how the weekends work. You and Jacob have plans for the next three nights. The Cranfords have amazing news *today*, and you should be excited for your part in their discovery."

"But Jacob...won't like being left here. Couldn't he come too and help us sort through the different ideas?"

Samuel wanted to snap, *Get real, Rhoda. He doesn't care* anything *about finding solutions for this farm.* But he drew a deep breath. "The Cranfords didn't invite him. They will if you ask them, but they want to enjoy their good news with you and me. Can't you do that for them?"

Her shoulders slumped. "Ya, but—"

"Tell me the rest of it later. Kumm." He strode back toward the Cranfords. "Sorry about that. There were other plans for tonight that we needed to talk about, but we've decided we'd rather accept your invitation if it's still open."

"Then it's settled," Bob said. "And, Samuel, maybe while you're there, we could talk more about your beliefs. You and Rhoda have a faith in a supernatural God, but you two seem so levelheaded, like people we could have intelligent conversations with. So I'd like to hear what you believe."

Rhoda's eyes met Samuel's, and clearly she found Bob's wording amusing. But they both liked the Cranfords—despite the couple being so very different from anyone they'd ever known and saying what they thought when it suited them.

Bob held up a hand, laughing. "Let me be clear. It's not that we're interested in converting or whatever you religious people call it. But after having the proof in our hands that Camilla has a granddaughter, we need to hear what you believe and why—just out of curiosity as we try to make sense of this craziness concerning Rhoda's *knowing.*"

It sounded to Samuel as if this might be an opening for planting some good seed. Was Bob searching for what else might be true that he didn't believe in?

Other than living by example, Samuel had never had the privilege of planting seeds of faith in someone's life. The Amish weren't evangelical in the least. In Pennsylvania he could get into trouble with the church leaders for opening the Bible to nonbelievers. God was to do the leading, not man, and the men God elevated as church leaders were to do the sharing within the Amish community. But if Bob was curious, shouldn't Samuel explain what he knew?

"It's settled then. We'd better go." Bob went around the car and opened Camilla's door. "She should rest for a bit. Do you want me to pick you up in about three hours?"

"No, we'll drive the rig."

Rhoda made a face at him, silently asking what he was doing.

"See you then." Bob climbed into the driver's side, and Camilla waved as they pulled out of the driveway.

"Why are we going by carriage?"

"Because we need to think and talk. You're the one who begged me to do whatever it took to keep this farm afloat until the harvest, and I sold acreage to keep this place going. We have to have a kitchen, Rhoda, and maybe if you'd stop tiptoeing around Jacob, you could quit being so indecisive and make some intelligent decisions, the kind of hard decisions you made when you were running your own business."

She massaged her forehead. "You should've let Bob pick us up. Other than that, you have some reasonable points. But—"

At that moment Jacob rounded the side of the house, walking toward them. "Hey, what's up?"

Surely Jacob could understand the importance of their figuring out how to build a canning kitchen for the orchard—in a way Rhoda could agree with. If not, then he'd either have to get angry with Samuel about it or get over it.

Or both. Samuel wasn't sure he cared which way Jacob went with it.

As Jacob approached, he held out his hand for Rhoda. "What was that all about?"

"Samuel and I need to go to the Cranfords' tonight. But to make up for you and me missing our night out together, Samuel's giving us the whole day off tomorrow." She looked to Samuel. "Isn't that right?"

Even though Samuel's plans with Rhoda tonight centered solely on business, his upcoming time with her now seemed tainted. He knew it was wrong, but more than ever before he wanted to fight Jacob for Rhoda's hand in marriage. "Sure."

Jacob didn't look thrilled as he silently stared at Samuel.

Rhoda looked at Jacob. "Iva brought back more money than expected, and I haven't been to the beach since I was a little girl. What if Landon gives us a lift to the train depot in Bangor tomorrow and we ride the rails to Orchard Beach?"

Jacob's surprise turned into a grin. "Now this is what I call a deal." He wrapped his arm around her shoulders and turned her toward the house, whispering something in her ear.

Samuel sighed in disgust. How were the three of them going to navigate a lifetime together?

THIRTY

Golden sunlight played on miles and miles of rippling water as waves crashed and frothy water rolled back and forth on the beach. Stunning swaths of pink and orange sky hovered over the ocean along the horizon.

Sunset.

The sea gulls and surf played a kind of music for them.

Cool sand squished beneath Rhoda's bare feet as she walked hand in hand beside Jacob. She grasped his arm with her other hand. "This has been a perfect day."

Jacob smiled peacefully as he studied the horizon where the water met the sky. "It has. It's sort of sad we have to let it go." He paused, standing close to the edge of the ocean, and remnants of retreating waves occasionally ran up against his feet. His green eyes reflected his pleasure. "We're good at minivacations."

She smiled. "We are."

The two of them had played Frisbee and then joined a beach volleyball game with a group of strangers, causing their side to win three times before time for Jacob and her to leave. She'd forgotten how good he was at making her laugh—all people really.

They'd gone on a few rides and had even boarded a whale-watching boat that went out twenty miles or more from shore. She'd found it a bit scary, but he had loved every second. Actually, she wasn't sure *love* covered how he felt. *Exhilarated, renewed,* and *mesmerized* weren't quite strong enough either.

Out at sea they had only a single brief sighting of a whale's back. But the two of them seemed to catch glimpses of each other. For that she was grateful.

He tugged on her hand, trying to get her to dip her toes into the cold water. "Kumm. Get your feet wet. We have to leave soon."

She shook her head. "I'm fine right here."

He frowned playfully. "You don't need to be afraid of water this shallow."

"But it's painfully cold."

"This from a woman who worked in open fields during a Maine winter." He shook his head, an endearing grin on his face.

She arched her shoulders. "I'm going to pay for all those games of volleyball."

Jacob moved behind her and rubbed them. The breadth of the ocean stretched out as far as they could see. "Rhoda,"—he wrapped his arms around her, whispering in her ear—"we should come here more often."

She nodded. They needed times like this. Since Landon had taken them to the train station that morning, Jacob had relaxed and become himself again, almost as if Samuel had been erased from his memory.

She, however, wasn't that free of him, perhaps because of the conversation she'd had with Landon the day before. His words rang true. She needed to deal with what was between her and Samuel, to look at what she felt and why. And she liked the idea of filing away every rogue and unwanted thought of Samuel and using all that space for Jacob.

He was everything any woman, including Rhoda, would want—kind, gentle, intelligent, humorous. So what was it about his gruffer, more challenging brother that drew her even a little?

Gentle waves crashed one after the other. Despite their variations they were so predictable and a constant source of enjoyment. She wanted Jacob and her to be like that for each other—having a rhythmic sameness that was spellbinding.

"Rhoda?" Jacob sang softly in her ear before he propped his elbows on her shoulders.

She turned a bit, just enough to see him for a moment. "Ya?"

He chuckled. "Have I already told you too many tales about my deep-sea fishing and scuba diving?"

Suddenly she realized she'd been daydreaming of who she wanted Jacob and her to be rather than focusing on their relationship right now. She turned, grabbed his collar, and pulled him into a kiss. She would live fully in every moment with him. Listen carefully. And love deeply.

Absolutely.

Positively.

And she'd do so as steadfastly as the ocean beat against the shore.

Leah patted the horse's neck, talking to it softly while aligning the animal between the shafts of the carriage. She hadn't been off in nearly three weeks, not since the Sunday after the frost came through. And she'd worked double time two Saturdays ago when Jacob and Rhoda went to the beach. She was edgy and irritable and needed a break. She'd done enough chores today, and she was taking off early regardless of what else was on anyone's to-do list. End of story.

Her nerves were taut as she planned to drive on unfamiliar roads. Even though she could talk a good game of being brave and use sarcasm like a weapon, a lot of things, even normal things like driving a rig, taxed her.

The drizzling rain continued to slow, promising a glorious afternoon for a ride. Samuel walked into the barn, wet spots speckling his light blue shirt except where his broad-brimmed straw hat had protected it. He held the mail in his hand, opening an envelope.

He looked up. "Hey, finally going out in the carriage?"

"No. I just thought I'd do this for the fun of it."

Samuel grinned. "If one asks a stupid question, one should expect a smart-aleck response." He unfolded the letter and began reading it while Leah continued harnessing the horse to the rig.

It'd been three weeks since the frost, and the orchard looked to be in very good health. The trees were in full blossom. With pleasant temperatures and the good rains they were getting, everyone was hopeful concerning the crop. In another week or so, the blossoms would fall, and then they'd have to wait about five weeks to catch a glimpse of fruitlets. At that point they'd have a good idea how much the orchard would yield this year.

Samuel held the letter out to her. "Look." He sounded pleased.

She skimmed it, reading about each person in the Miller family. "They sound very interested in moving here."

"Large family with three young, single men. If they visit and like it enough to move here, it could be exactly what we need."

"I guess."

Samuel frowned. "Give me that." He snatched the letter from her, laughing. "If I'd known you weren't going to be excited about it, I'd have kept it to myself."

His lighthearted response didn't keep guilt from swooshing through her. He was trying so hard to make this new settlement viable, and he had no one to really talk to. Steven spent all his free time with his family or with Jacob, helping him through the instruction. And Jacob was no longer the brother to Samuel he used to be. For her part Iva wasn't much interested in anything but photography, meals, and organization. And Leah, well, she felt like a hypocrite discussing how to make the settlement stronger when all she did was ponder whether to leave it.

Leah grabbed another leather strap. "Sorry."

Samuel smiled and read the letter again.

Families wanting to move to Orchard Bend was a big deal. Huge, in fact. They had to believe they could make a living here, probably through farming whatever acreage they could purchase, and they had to have enough money to make the transition. They also had to be members in good standing within their own communities for their bishops to support their moving. Steven, as the spiritual head here, would have to get to know them and agree to accept them into the fold.

Still, their desire to move here indicated this new Amish district in Maine had a good reputation among other Amish communities. If they didn't, no man would consider uprooting his family from the safety net of the familiar and their multitude of relatives to enter the unknown.

Apparently, Rhoda and this new settlement hadn't received a black eye because of her legal difficulties. In fact, these people seemed to admire the strength they'd seen through the news outlets.

Leah buckled the last straps together. "Rhoda will be thrilled about the news. Find her and—"

"Nah." Sadness shadowed his face for a moment. Or maybe heartache. "She's too busy." He patted the horse's neck. "So where are you off to?"

She should've known better than to tell him to find Rhoda. "It's a test drive mostly." Since Landon had given her the driver's manual more than three weeks ago, she'd memorized most of it, and she wanted to look at the roads with that information in mind. "But I'll eventually make my way to Landon's and surprise him."

"Ah." Samuel looked as if he'd tried to smile but hadn't quite made it. "The Millers and their three single sons will visit soon. Keep that in mind, okay?"

"Sure. Maybe I'll find one of them as intriguing as you find Iva."

Samuel all but flinched, and Leah wished she'd thought before she spoke.

"What else arrived in the mail?" she asked, hoping to undo her more callous remarks.

"Information from a Realtor about houses that could be converted into a kitchen."

"Any prospects?"

"None that I saw. They're either too far or too expensive or too run-down to have ready by August. Unless we find something basically free that requires mostly hard work, there's not a lot we can do until I receive the check for the acreage. And we can't finalize that sale until the survey is complete. That surveying company seems to move like an injured turtle."

"Can't Rhoda agree to borrow the money from the Cranfords until then?"

"Does everyone in the house know about that?"

"I think so. I overheard Jacob telling Steven before they shut the door for his instruction time. Speaking of, I didn't know the Amish would allow instruction to take place outside of Sunday church services, did you?"

"With Steven being the only minister, he can't preach Sunday service and teach Jacob his lessons at the same time." Samuel turned. "I'm going to leave what the Realtor sent on the desk, and if you see Rhoda, let her know the information is there. Maybe she'll see potential in something I didn't."

"But even if she found something that fit what you said—low cost and lots of work—its quality and size would probably get us through only one canning season, so that wouldn't be ideal, would it?"

"Nothing in this settlement has been ideal."

That was an understatement, but Leah kept her sarcasm and irritability to herself as she climbed into the buggy. "You didn't answer my question. Why can't we accept the Cranfords' loan just to tide us over until you get the money from the land?"

He shrugged. "This business is a partnership. I won't circumvent Rhoda to do what I think is best. Besides, we've all seen what her intuition can accomplish."

"Ya, from what I've overheard, I'm alive because of it." As were her two younger sisters, who, except for Rhoda's warning, would've been asleep upstairs when the tornado removed most of the second story of their home.

"So we respect what we know is true and sit tight."

It seemed odd how much he'd changed since meeting Rhoda. A man once fully persuaded to operate within the male rights of a patriarchal society had learned to yield to a woman as an equal. That was such a huge development it defied all Amish logic.

Leah threaded the reins into the carriage. "I can't imagine where you'll have this farm and settlement in five years." She smiled, hoping he believed that as fully as she did. "Bye." She waved and drove out of the barn and across the driveway. *"Geh begreiflich."* She gently tugged on the reins, urging the horse to go easy as he entered the road.

The reins felt odd in Leah's hands. It'd been quite a while since she'd driven a buggy. The roads were wet, and she breathed deeply, taking in the aromas of spring and wet asphalt as the sun peeked through the clouds. Since it was the end of the month, she wondered if June would continue this kind of weather. She hoped so.

She drove for more than an hour before guiding the horse toward Landon's place. An old boarded-up house hidden behind overgrown hedges caught her eye, and, curious, she pulled onto the dirt path that led to it. The building was white clapboard with peeling paint. The door had an outside padlock, apparently a fairly new one compared to the rest of the place.

The sight of it gave her chills of excitement. But why? It intrigued her, yet she didn't recall ever noticing it before. Hmm. It was about the size of the summer kitchen back home. Could Jacob turn it into a canning kitchen?

With her heart thumping wildly, Leah backed up the rig and got onto the road. Before long she was pulling into Erlene's driveway.

Wouldn't Landon be surprised that she'd driven here? She tethered the horse to a nearby spruce tree, went to the door, and knocked.

Erlene opened it with a cordless phone to her ear. She smiled. "This is a nice surprise."

Leah nodded, unsure whether to speak since Erlene was on the phone.

"I'm on hold." Erlene motioned for her to enter. "I don't mean to be rude by answering the door this way, but I knew Landon wasn't going to budge from the game he's watching. I'm talking with my sister about knee surgery she apparently needs. While we were working through what I could do to help out, her son beeped in on call waiting." She closed the door behind Leah. "Landon." She elongated his name. "Leah's here."

"Hey." Landon's voice echoed from somewhere inside. "Come on in."

Erlene gestured. "He's in the living room." She tilted her ear toward the phone. "Yeah, I'm still here. I've been thinking. What if we make this easier on everyone by my coming down to help out while you're recuperating?"

Unwilling to eavesdrop, Leah waved to her and hurried into the living room.

Landon's full focus was on the television. His ball cap was crooked, his face unshaven, and his T-shirt wrinkled. Funny, he didn't come to work unshaven or in wrinkled clothes.

"Hi." He smiled but barely glanced at her before moving his laptop off the spot beside him. "Have a seat. I'm watching the Red Sox trying to score against the Indians."

She sat. A quick glance assured her the Red Sox were a baseball team. Unlike most sports, baseball was one she knew something about. She'd played it a lot during recess at school. But what was the appeal of watching people he didn't know?

Landon set his laptop on the end table beside him. "I'm hoping Will Middlebrooks will hit another grand slam like he did a few weeks back."

Will who? "Is he a friend of yours?"

"No." Landon chuckled. "I haven't met any of them, but I'm well versed in their stats and where they hail from and who's likely to be traded next season."

Hail from? What did that mean? Her earlier hope faded. Not only did he seem unimpressed that she'd gotten to Erlene's on her own, but he also didn't seem to care that she was even here. She sat back, waiting for him to snap out of it. When he didn't, she decided to speak up. "Don't you think it's odd that I'm here?"

Landon glanced away from the television. "Oh, I should, shouldn't I? How did you get here?"

"I drove the rig."

"Really? That's—" The television blared as the crowd roared. Landon motioned at the television. "What the heck was that? Come on, ump! Pay attention!"

It seemed so strange. He talked to a box and ignored a real human, one who was supposed to mean something to him. Apparently she meant a lot more to him when the television wasn't on.

"You do know they can't hear you, right?"

"And clearly the umpire can't see either," Landon complained.

Leah wondered what Landon was going to say before he'd interrupted himself to yell at a box. This was supposed to be a happy visit, a chance for him to quiz her on the manual and for her to tell him all she'd learned. But right now the only thing that mattered was between him and the television.

Would he find it even a little impressive that she'd nearly memorized the driver's manual?

Landon leaned over, holding out the bowl of popcorn to her. "Something wrong?"

She'd never expected to feel so ignored and out of place while sitting next to Landon. Is this what her life with him would be like?

She shook her head and grabbed a handful of popcorn. "I just stopped by for a minute."

"Only a minute?" Landon frowned. "That's weird."

"I was just practicing how to get a rig on the Maine roads." She ate some popcorn. "If I don't see Erlene on my way out, tell her bye for me and that I'll see her another time."

When he didn't answer, she left. This is what she used to feel like all the time with Michael and even her family—unwanted and nothing special.

Before she got halfway to the horse, she heard the front door open.

"Leah." Landon hurried after her. "Is the game that boring, or do you really need to go?"

She was sure the truth was written all over her face: embarrassment and agitation. So she didn't turn around.

He caught her by the arm. "Hey. What's going on?"

"Nothing. Just go watch your stupid game." She pulled free and hurried onward.

"Whoa, Leah." He stepped in front of her. "Does me watching a ball game warrant all this?"

"No." She paused. "Maybe."

"Okay, what's going on?"

She rolled her eyes. "I came here all excited because I drove the rig on some unfamiliar roads, because I'd studied the stupid driver's manual, because I saw a place that might make a good canning kitchen." She raised her hands and waggled them. "Woohoo for Leah! Isn't she amazing?" She rolled her eyes. "But I don't know or understand half of what interests you, and I didn't expect to be ignored because of something on television."

"Oh." He relaxed, an understanding smile stealing her heart. "We're in for some rocky roads if those few minutes already make you feel like a baseball widow."

A what? "Just go back to your game."

"You're right. I should've shut off the game when you came in."

"Too late for that now!"

"Leah, I wasn't thinking."

"I'll never know how to hold your interest like that."

He smiled. "You could brush up on the Sox players and stats."

"You think it'd be that easy? I don't. And I have no interest in learning it."

"Leah, breathe already. I'm kidding. None of this is a big deal. So you don't know about professional baseball. A lot of couples don't share an interest in the same hobbies. Most of the novels you love hold my interest for about two paragraphs. You can read while I watch baseball. We don't have to like the same things or be good at the same things to connect."

"Sometimes the idea of remaining Amish is comforting."

"Of course it is. But what's that got to do with anything happening here?"

She shrugged. "At least there's not a world of subjects I'm clueless about. And being ignored for a lifeless box is strange."

"We've had a lot of fun watching that lifeless box. You can't suddenly hate it because something was on that you didn't like."

"It made me feel stupid."

"So? Deal with it. And don't dump it on me as if it's my fault you don't know about the Sox, okay? People feel dozens of emotions in a day or even an hour, but they will change and fade. We can't let fleeting feelings change and fade who we are. We have to be stronger than that, or we won't last."

He made sense. Leah took a breath, wishing she hadn't let her emotions get the better of her. "I should go." She untied the horse from the spruce and turned to face him. "You're missing the game."

"Come on, Leah. You're being silly about the whole thing."

The annoying thing was, she knew that. She knew her behavior was immature. But it didn't erase that she wished she hadn't come. She just wanted to go home.

Landon stared down at her, stepping so very close.

She backed up, bumping into the side of the rig. She wanted to kiss him so badly.

The way he looked at her she knew he wanted to kiss her too. She should resist. It would only confuse the decisions she needed to make about her future, the ones between her and God. "I guess I could learn to manage better when negative feelings hit."

He placed his hands on the carriage, around her head, his eyes soaking her in. "Yeah, that's a good goal." His voice sounded distant.

With her heart thumping, she tried to swallow. "I...I should go."

He leaned in close, his lips mere inches from hers. Leah's heart pounded, begging for a kiss.

But he paused, lowered his arms, and took a step back. "Sorry."

Unable to respond, she peeled herself from the side of the rig, opened the door, and climbed in.

"You sure you can't stay?" Landon nodded toward the house. "Granny's probably off the phone by now."

In that moment she saw more of Landon than she ever had. For every ounce of immaturity she had, he had a dose of maturity, and she loved him for it.

Loved him.

She did love him. "Not this time."

He was entirely too kind for someone like her—a plain Jane month of May, with a thunderstorm one hour and sunshine and birdsong the next. But she wouldn't always be like this. She had some things to figure out, things between her and God, her and her family, her and Landon.

Landon propped his foot on the buggy step. "You drive safe."

"You sound like a parent."

He wrinkled his face. "That uncool? Man, no wonder you're taking your horse and going home."

She giggled. "I'll tell Rhoda about the abandoned building I saw."

"Is it the white clapboard about a mile from here?"

"Probably." She liked the idea of talking about something more normal before leaving. "Windows boarded up and barely visible for all the overgrowth?"

"Yeah, that actually belongs to Granny. She used to run a little grocery store and gas station before the station in town ran her out of business. If you'd gone around the side, you'd have seen the old gas pumps. The Kings could have it practically free of charge, but I've already told all that to Rhoda and Jacob. But it has three strikes against it. It's too far from the orchard. It doesn't have any plumbing or a reasonable way to get water to it. And getting it up to code for a license would cost way too much."

"That's a shame. I really liked that little building."

"You want to go poke around in it? It has years of interesting stuff inside, like an old attic. And I have the key."

"But your ball game."

"I'm recording it."

"Going through that building sounds like fun."

"You want to drive us? I'll tell Granny or leave a note. I don't know why I didn't think of us going there sooner. You'll love looking through all that old stuff." But instead of leaving, he stayed right there, staring at her.

Leah felt a little uneasy as he watched her. "Something wrong?"

His eyes didn't move from her, and he smiled. She could see it in his eyes. He liked who she was, stumbles and immaturity and all.

THIRTY-ONE

Jacob startled awake as the dogs barked. He crawled out of bed, pulled his pants over his boxers, and went to the bedroom window. While putting one arm through a suspender, he saw Rhoda getting out of the passenger's side of Bob's car. Jacob couldn't help but smile at the sight of her, even at this ridiculous hour. But what was she doing up and coming here now?

Rhoda waved to Bob and strolled toward the barn. She wrapped her arms around herself and paused, staring at the night sky. Jacob doubted she'd be here this early unless something was bothering her.

They had taken a train to Old Orchard Beach two weeks ago. As great as their time had been—and it had been amazing—something between them wasn't all it should be. Was it because he needed to tell her how he felt about them living in Maine? Not doing so meant he was keeping secrets again, and that ate at him.

Or maybe he wasn't the only one withholding his thoughts and emotions. She was complex. He admired that. Truly. And she was worth every minute of trying to figure her out, but who would've thought a young woman who'd spent her life in the quietness of a fruit garden and canning kitchen could have as many facets as a carnival's house of mirrors?

Her attention moved to the house, and slowly she found him. He raised his hand, and she smiled before blowing him a kiss.

He indicated he'd be down in a minute, and then he grabbed clean clothes and headed to the bathroom to get ready for the day.

The sun and surf of the beach had been a start to everything they needed—time alone and away from this farm. He could still hear her laughter as the wind played Frisbee along with them. He'd chortled at her squeals of delight while she clutched his arm as the Ferris wheel went round and round. But most of all, he could feel her love as they strolled hand in hand along the beach, talking while watching the sunlight play on the top of the water.

Their relationship had soaked up that day like growing crops drank in the rain.

It had helped Jacob to take a relaxing breath, but it didn't change the fact that his brother was in love with her too. Jacob had no doubt about that. If Rhoda was aware, she hadn't even hinted at it. They avoided any discussion of Samuel, but the matter lay between them like a sleeping guard dog.

He was soon out the front door and heading into the office. "There she is."

She grinned and tapped her cheek with her index finger. He kissed right where she'd pointed, inhaling the aroma of what she most reminded him of—sunshine and freedom.

"Denki." She smiled, kissed the ends of her fingers, and placed them over his lips.

"Guder Marye, my sweet Rhodes." He sat on the edge of the desk.

"My sweet Rhodes—what a nice thing to say. Makes it sound as if my name is Rose."

"I thought so."

"The dogs wake you?"

"Ya."

"Sorry about that."

"I'd rather be awake with you than asleep without you."

She chuckled. "I still think you must practice saying all the right things."

"So what has you up so early?"

She pulled a folder out of a drawer and opened it. "It would be nightfall again before I could cover all of that. But in a nutshell, concern about Camilla's granddaughter and the need for a canning kitchen."

"Still no word from the investigator?"

"He tracked Jojo and her daughter to a trailer where they once lived, but they'd been evicted, and there was no forwarding address."

"I'm sorry. It'll turn around soon. You'll see."

She passed him fliers on a run-down house for sale.

"Rhodes, this is pretty bad, and it's twenty miles from here."

"It's also affordable. It's the closest one I've seen so far. We have to find something we can get a license for and have operational by harvest." She pushed her chair back. "I'm open for suggestions."

He shrugged. "No peace about Bob and Camilla's offer to invest or to loan the money?"

"None."

"Then I don't have any suggestions, but this house isn't a solution." He held up the fliers. "Look at these pictures. If that's what it looks like here, I'd rather not look at it for real."

"But you're a skilled carpenter. I've seen your work."

"I appreciate your confidence in me, but this doesn't need a skilled carpenter. It needs a magician. According to this, the water pipes are no longer up to code, which means they all have to be replaced. I'm no plumber. The new owners may need to plow it under and start fresh."

She took the fliers and tossed them into the trash can. "I need some air."

"Perfectly understandable when one's office is in a barn." He grabbed a blanket and followed her. Maybe after she walked awhile, she'd be ready to find a spot and watch the sunrise.

He took her hand, and they walked deeper and deeper into the fields.

"Isn't it magnificent, even in the dark?" She gestured across the fields. "The trees are in better health than anyone could've hoped for."

"And the cause for us to spend weeks thinning them." He wanted her to have a successful canning season. He needed them to get away from Samuel, and she needed a bountiful harvest to can. Between Rueben and the tornado, she'd had two peaceful times of harvest stolen from her over the last year.

Rhoda brushed stray hairs from her face as they climbed the highest hill on the farm. "I don't know what to do about the canning kitchen, but I feel paralyzed, as if imprisoned until an intuition guides me. But will it? And I can't sleep, because it's my fault Jojo and Sophia are still missing. I really don't like this side of me—the one that gets paralyzed, the one that sees some tiny part of something, hesitates for too long about what to do, and then makes a mess of everything."

"Whoa. Whoa. That's my friend you're picking on. Stop looking at the glass as half-empty. Why do you think it's your fault that the investigator hasn't yet found Jojo and Sophia? If it weren't for you, no one would even be looking for them. Also, understand that the stresses of this farm are enough to erode anyone's confidence and peace." *Except maybe Samuel's.* His brother thrived on the challenge.

Once they were at the top of the hill, she stood still. "I love this place."

"You love tending fruit-bearing crops." Jacob spread the blanket. "This orchard, with twice the acreage of the Pennsylvania orchard, is too much work for the ways of Amish farms."

Rhoda all but gaped at him. He'd intended to wait to have this conversation, although he wasn't sure exactly what he was waiting for. Maybe reassurance that she would understand. Maybe knowing that they were strong enough to be this honest. But apparently he'd held his tongue on this for as long as he could. At least they'd had a couple of good weeks since the beach. Hopefully she was ready to hear some of how he felt.

He sat, and she did the same. When they were settled, she made a circling motion with her finger, telling him to keep going.

"Look, when I suggested Kings' Orchard move here, I had no idea that the extra acreage and the condition of the orchard would require so much overwhelming work. But it drains us all the time. Not just me or you or everyone else, but especially *us,* as a couple."

"What are you saying?" She stared at him.

He hoped he knew, but most of all he hoped she was ready to hear him. "Doesn't it feel as if this farm is more than any of us bargained for?"

She shook her head. "Half the stress of these past seven months has nothing to do with farming."

"I know. A lot was personal stuff. But don't you want more days like we had at the beach? More mornings like this"—he gestured across the land—"where we watch the sunrise together, preferably sipping coffee and without a three-day work list that needs to be accomplished in a scant twelve hours?"

He propped his foot on the blanket and rested his arm on his knee. "Rhodes, I think maybe I was wrong to suggest we buy this place. You were devastated after Rueben destroyed your fruit garden. Then the tornado stole your next dream. Samuel needed a new hope to latch on to after the tornado had practically destroyed his orchard. And Kings' Orchard needed income while the Pennsylvania orchard was reestablished."

Disbelief radiated from her features. "So we're feeling pressure from all the troubles that've made farming hard this year, and the need for a canning kitchen is bearing down on us, and for those reasons you're sorry we came here?"

"No, not exactly like that." What he was sorry about was that his brother was in love with her. Right now he needed to know how to ease into the idea of getting her away from Samuel.

While he thought about what to say, the black sky turned a royal blue as daytime approached. Blossoms swept from the trees, gliding and twirling on the breeze as they fell, much like leaves in late fall. He drew a deep breath. "You and I are in a different place now than when we met. I'm able to pursue carpentry. You've earned respect concerning your hunches or insights or whatever they are. We're both free to rethink what we want."

Her eyes searched his. "You don't want to farm?"

Jacob tried to measure his words carefully. "It was never in my heart to do it. I returned to it because I had no choice. But the desire to return to full-time carpentry is growing." He plucked a white-and-pink petal from an apple blossom off the blanket. "Surely once we're married and have children, you'll enjoy tending to something much, much smaller, right? Like what you had before Rueben destroyed it."

"When I think of having a family, I picture being here, juggling scheduling and baby needs and farming as naturally as we adjust to the change of every season."

He stifled a sigh and circled the back of her hand with his finger. "A better plan might be for us to figure out a way to live where paydays aren't connected to a harvest and you would be free to enjoy a fruit garden, not strapped with year-round work." He hated to say the next part, but it had to be said. "And I think the best way to do that is to move away from here."

"Move?" She pulled away from him, gesturing with both arms. "This orchard *needs* me."

"It does. But you don't have to live here year round to consult and keep a hand in the operation. There are Amish families desperate for work. Iva's family comes to mind. Either way, Samuel can hire some good men, and we'd be free to do more."

Her stare was unnerving. "You don't want either of us to be involved with the orchard full-time?"

Anxiety rippled through him. "My thoughts are a lot to take in, I know. But after this orchard is healthy, you could do most of it by phone and only be here during canning season. We could return to Pennsylvania. You'd be closer to your folks, and you could have an acre or more of the King farm to plant a fruit patch. A couple of seasons from now, you could run the summer kitchen for Eli. That orchard will be producing a pretty good supply of apples by then. Or you could do both. But let Eli hire farmhands if need be and get the weight of all the farming off your shoulders. I could do carpentry work for my uncle and build up a clientele until I could start my own business. We'll travel here by train as needed. That way you could oversee the success of all the canning operations without the farm owning our lives."

She stood and folded her arms, facing away from him, and a cold chill ran down his spine. "How long have you felt this way?"

"It started out as a few scattered seeds I barely realized were there."

"When, Jacob?" She didn't even glance at him, and her voice was void of surprise.

"Maybe from the time I first talked to a lawyer and he believed I could get immunity in exchange for my testimony."

She turned, eyes wide. "That was months ago, and you haven't mentioned a word until now."

"It's just an idea."

"A pretty well-thought-out one." She stretched out her arms toward the orchard. "I love it here." Rows and rows of trees spread out before them. Everywhere they looked, they saw healthy green foliage and smelled the sweet scent of apple blossoms.

He stood and plucked a blossom from a tree. "It's all pretty amazing, but that's because of the amount of work everyone's put into it. All you and I have had are a few hours of courtship here and there and a single trip to the beach. Don't you want more? If we were able to employ the right people, you and I could move back to Pennsylvania, which could give both of us what we want—me working as a carpenter and you cultivating a fruit garden again."

She stared at him, clearly bewildered and apparently speechless.

"Rhodes, say something."

"You…you want to move *back*? I cared about that orchard, but it belongs to your family. The land and trees seem branded like cattle. At best, I was a guest there, but in the eyes of your Daed, I was an intruder. Here, this orchard has as much of me as it does any member of the King family."

"It has you and Samuel in it."

All traces of confusion melted from her face. "Is *that* what this is about?"

He was knee-deep now, and he couldn't change the subject. He pointed up at a tree. "Soon we'll see clusters of fruitlets on the trees. It's like you and Samuel are apples on a tree, sharing the same cluster, but I fell to the ground months ago. I'm rotting while you and he grow stronger each day."

There, he'd said the truth. He wanted to return to carpentry full-time, and he felt it was important for them that she not have so many work responsibilities on her shoulders. But his real issue with this farm was Samuel.

She looked out over the valley of the orchard. The sun had risen, and the light glimmered on the dew. She finally nodded.

That was it? Nothing more than a nod of her head? His heart pounded with anger. With hurt. With emotions he didn't understand.

On the other hand, she wasn't upset or walking away. She was listening and considering his viewpoint.

He dusted his palms together. It was rather depressing to discuss marriage in such businesslike terms.

He shielded his eyes from the sun, wishing he'd worn his hat. "I'll make a good living doing what I love. We can raise a family and be happy."

Her eyes reflected a disappointment he wasn't prepared for. She sat and looked up at him. "You'll go off to work before dawn each day and return after dark, six days a week in good weather. Farmers are at home, where their children are."

He sat next to her. "But it's a regular paycheck. No ruined crops after months of hard labor. And I'll have extra days off here and there in the winter to make up for it."

She picked up a blossom from the grass. "Is moving away from here the only way you can feel secure concerning Samuel and me?"

He shifted, putting his hand on the blanket behind her. "Listen." He didn't like what he was about to propose, but he couldn't tolerate being the bad guy. She had to know in her heart that leaving here was the right thing to do. "I'll continue going through instruction, and you think about what I've said. If you decide we should make our home and raise our children here in Orchard Bend, then that's what we'll do."

"And carpentry?"

"I can probably find construction work here as well as anywhere." He couldn't imagine going off to work each day, leaving her around Samuel. Surely, after she'd thought about all he'd said, she'd see what they'd need to do to protect their relationship.

"You mean that, Jacob?"

"I trust your judgment."

She leaned against his shoulder. "Denki."

Jacob kissed her head. Had he just turned their future over to someone who cared for his brother more than she knew?

THIRTY-TWO

Samuel rocked back in a kitchen chair, staring at Landon's laptop.

Iva and Phoebe were stirring around, starting dinner. Samuel and Landon couldn't go to the barn office because Jacob was there with Steven, the door closed as Jacob continued going through instruction. Leah was upstairs reading to the little ones, and Samuel imagined Rhoda was in the orchard, tending her beloved trees.

It was the first of June, and they still had no canning kitchen or even plans for one.

He tried to concentrate on what was in front of him because Landon needed answers. But so much was going on inside him that he couldn't focus.

"I've given the whole site an update." With a slide of his finger on a metal pad, Landon moved the electronic arrow around the page, pointing out things. "I changed the location and product line. I've upgraded the ordering system and installed a new contact page."

Samuel was okay with this Internet stuff as long as Landon ran it for them. If they barely looked at it throughout the year, it wouldn't be considered a problem among most Amish. Advertising had been allowed for decades, but in the past the Amish paid for magazine or newspaper people to list their advertisements. Now ads were done on the Internet. Not a ton of difference in the Amish involvement—they still paid someone to put the information where Englisch people would see it. Some of the more conservative communities shunned this type of marketing, but Steven had a peace about it, so that settled it for Kings' Orchard Maine.

"Follow the cursor." Landon made the arrow jiggle. "When I click on this"—he pressed the metal pad—"a form pops up, and this is how people can

place their orders. But if they click on Contact Us, they can e-mail us directly...
or rather e-mail me directly. Several people and businesses have asked to be sent
regular updates. Do you want to accommodate that?"

"Sounds time consuming."

"Depends on how often we send out updates. We could do it four times a
year, once for every seasonal change. Iva could take photos of the orchard, and
we could use a few to show the beauty of the orchard in each season of the year.
We could also share a day in the life of an Amish orchardist or tell what you are
or will be doing for the orchard during a particular season."

Samuel pondered the idea. "Sounds fine. Let's begin with an update for
each season. If anyone enjoys doing it, we can send more out each year."

Life inside this tiny Amish settlement was buzzing—like the multitude of
honeybee hives the beekeeper had set up throughout the orchard. But when it
came to making a decision about the canning kitchen, Rhoda seemed as dor-
mant as a tree in winter. Even so, Samuel trusted she would either make a decision or step aside and let him do it.

But time was drawing short, and Kings' Orchard needed answers.

Jacob strode into the kitchen, the way only his younger brother could
when he felt right with the world—with confidence and zest.

Steven entered and went straight to his wife, whispering. He then held up
a letter. "Another Amish family has contacted us. They'd like to visit and check
us out and give us time to get to know them. It's a man with nine children—
ages eleven to twenty-three." He grinned. "There must be at least one set of
twins in that group."

"The more the merrier." Samuel chuckled.

Jacob moved to the end of the table near Landon, straddled a chair, and
peered at the laptop for a moment before looking up. "What's for dinner?"

Iva tapped the spatula on the side of a pan. "Amish six layer."

Steven pulled up a stool at the corner of the table so he could see the screen
too.

Jacob rubbed his stomach. "Just six layers? What if I want more?"

"Then I'll heap two portions onto your plate."

He frowned. "What if I don't want twelve?"

Iva stirred the browning hamburger meat. "What if I want to swing this spatula at Samuel's head?"

The room broke into laughter.

"Me?" Samuel feigned being shocked. "What'd I do?"

Iva shook the spatula at him, grinning, before returning her attention to the iron skillet.

"So what's up?" Jacob turned the laptop so he could see it better.

Samuel gave Landon time to show Jacob around the site.

"Samuel, I've been wanting to show you this part." Landon clicked on something, and a video began playing. "Iva took the pictures, and I turned them into a short video."

Soft music played as Landon's voice explained the history of Kings' Orchard's move to Maine and the type of work it took to care for the trees.

"This is really good." Jacob turned to Iva. "Have you seen it?"

She shook her head, and Phoebe and she moved in closer. Landon restarted the video.

Iva rested her hands on the chair behind Samuel. "It makes working in the grove look much more charming than it actually is."

Jacob scratched the back of his head. "That wouldn't take a lot."

This was the brother Samuel remembered from their teenage years—a guy who didn't want to be tied down to an orchard.

When the video finished, Iva returned to the stove and Phoebe to the sink.

Landon clicked on another link. "This is where a fair amount of the traffic has been coming from. It's a series of articles written by Diana Fisher, the blogger Rhoda met at the mulching seminar last October. She writes for two different blogs: Maine Organic Apple Orchards and US Organic Apple Orchards. She linked each article to Rhoda's website. When Rhoda was in the news, people ran Internet searches on her to see what they could find. What they found were pieces by Diana that led to Rhoda's site."

Samuel picked up a pen and pointed at the screen. "So if our business is referred to in the articles by one name—Kings' Orchard Maine—but the site goes by Rhoda's former business of Rhode Side Stands, how are people finding Kings' Orchard?"

"Two ways. There are direct links to Rhoda's website from Diana's articles, and I bought other domain names—like Kings' Orchard Maine, Amish Orchard, and Rhoda Byler—that people might use when searching online. I redirected those sites to this one."

Jacob clasped Landon's shoulder. "You're brilliant."

"I know, right?" Landon clicked on another tab. "But all this marketing about canned products is only going to do us some good if we actually have the goods to sell."

Samuel tapped his pen on the notepad. "We'll have them. I know that for absolute certain. The only thing we don't know is the when, where, and how of the canning kitchen."

Jacob folded his arms on the top rung of the ladder-back. "What happens if Rhoda is completely off-base about not accepting the Cranfords' offer?"

Iva set a tray with four glasses of lemonade on the table. "What offer?"

While Jacob explained it and Rhoda's reservations, Samuel outlined a to-do list for the month. By the first of July the fruitlets would be visible, and they'd need to spend every waking hour for weeks thinning them. They wouldn't be able to get any other orchard work done during that time, so these few weeks leading up to that had to be spent wisely.

But in truth this list was like everything else Samuel did—a stab at distracting his heart from any thoughts of Rhoda Byler.

Phoebe passed out napkins with an unpeeled orange in each one.

Iva wiped her hands on her apron. "I don't get it. So Rhoda shared a hunch with Bob and Camilla. Now she feels obligated to turn down an offer they were going to make before she shared what she knew? Could Rhoda make this any more complicated?"

"Probably." Steven peeled the rind off an orange slice. "Don't tempt her. But she comes by her feelings on the matter honestly. If you'd witnessed her gifting and everyone's reaction to her while she was growing up, you'd understand why she struggles."

"And," Phoebe added, "she has a really tender conscience—too tender for anybody's good. So she'll stick to what she thinks is right regardless of what it costs her."

Phoebe's last sentence struck Samuel hard. Was there any chance that's what kept Rhoda and him apart—her overzealous sense of loyalty toward Jacob, the business, and the King family? Samuel cared about all those things. Too much so, he imagined. But if Rhoda would go with him, he'd walk away from them, and although he'd be sorry for the pain it would cause everyone, he'd gratefully pay the price to be with her.

Jacob's eyes moved to Samuel's and stayed there, and Samuel knew his brother was also bothered by what Phoebe had said.

Steven looked to Iva. "Now?"

Iva's face reflected stress, but she nodded.

Phoebe put her arm around Iva's shoulders. "It'll be okay. You'll see."

"What's going on?" Jacob asked.

Iva reached into the hidden pocket of her apron and pulled out a small stack of letters. "These arrived today. I'm receiving several each week from my community. They want me to come back, because they think that I'm in sin and that I've abandoned my parents when they need me most."

Samuel couldn't believe this. "But your Mamm sent you."

Iva nodded. "My Daed hasn't let me talk to her lately, and I imagine he's not telling anyone she had a hand in sending me here. I'm certainly not willing to spread that information to anyone writing to me. It could get her into a lot of trouble."

Steven tapped the table with the tips of his fingers. "I've spoken to her Daed several times. He's got the backing of the church leaders, and the pressure from her district is building day by day. If need be, they'll pull in other church leaders to stand against me."

"She's twenty-one." Landon closed his laptop. "Doesn't she get a say?"

"Her age actually works against her right now. Her Daed has voiced concerns that she's in rebellion because she should have joined the faith by now and hasn't. He also feels it's wrong for her to live out from under his authority when she's not married."

Landon looked from one person to another, disbelief evident on his face. "But, Steven, don't you have any authority in this?"

"No. I'm young, and I've not yet been properly chosen, according to Amish traditions. All I can do is try to persuade her Daed to view the situation differently. Even if she was ready to be baptized into the church, and by doing so she'd be under my authority, we can't do that. She has to be in good standing with her former district, or those ministers won't allow her to join elsewhere."

"That's archaic and absolutist." Landon slid his laptop into his backpack.

"It's what?" Phoebe asked.

"Sorry." Landon offered a humble-looking smile. "Leah hates when I do that. *Archaic* means 'old-fashioned,' and *absolutist* means 'having absolute authority.'"

Phoebe made a face. "Then why didn't you say so?"

"I blame my mother. She had a thing for vocabulary, and my earliest memories of her are the games we'd play as she taught me what she called 'big words for a big boy.'" He laughed. "So here I am a 'big boy,' and sometimes I forget and use words without thinking."

"Ah." Phoebe wrinkled her nose. "Next time I need a ten-dollar word, I'll know where to go—your mother."

The light chuckle eased some of the tension in the room from Steven's news, but it lifted none of the weight from them.

"Here's the thing, Landon." Steven interlaced his fingers. "You may not see it as it should be in this house, but we, as Amish, believe the head of a home is meant to love as Christ loved the church but also to have the authority to lead everyone in it. The same is true of church leaders over their flock. I agree with those things, but Iva isn't in sin."

Landon brushed his fingers across the smooth surface of his laptop. "Since she's not a minor, they can't make her go back. She has rights."

"That stance only has merit if she's willing to rebel against her family and the church by using the US laws to her benefit. Amish don't believe in using government laws to gain freedom from church authority. If she returns home, they can't make her marry, so that's good, although they will pressure her. But if I can't change her Daed's mind and we try to keep her here anyway, we'll come across as rebellious too. Handled wrong, this will cause a scandal among the Amish that could undermine this settlement and pit one state of Amish against another, and anyone considering moving here will back out."

Samuel had been clueless that all this was going on. "What's at the heart of the problem, Iva? Do they miss you that much? Or do they fear you're up here living a life of sin? Or what?"

"Money." She whispered the word, embarrassment etched on her face. "They're struggling to hold on to their house, and the man they want me to marry is wealthy."

Landon looked disgusted. "It's disconcerting, uh, upsetting that selfish men can be found in every walk of life, including the Amish."

Samuel clenched his jaw. "Then let's begin by sending as much of her back pay as we can scrape together. Then we need to find her a position and title that will make it very clear to her district that she's an important part of this district."

"Which she is, Samuel." Jacob's defensive tone made Samuel bristle.

"Of course." Samuel nodded. "I wasn't saying otherwise. I simply meant we need to make that clear to the people who don't live here. Saying she helps with meals and mail isn't going to cut it. One would have to be here to see how much that and everything else she does means to us as a new settlement, a new business, and a new church."

"And as part of the family," Jacob snapped.

If Jacob wanted to keep challenging Samuel at every turn, Samuel was up for the fight. "Her Daed does not care that we feel she's part of this family. Actually, his knowing that would only make the situation worse since she already has a family who wants her to come home."

Phoebe patted Iva's back. "We'll find a solution. I'm sure of it."

Steven ate the last bite of his orange. "Would it help clear Rhoda's head about the kitchen if I went to the orchard now to shake her up a bit? We could all three go—Jacob, Samuel, and me. She has to snap out of holding us up on the canning kitchen."

Jacob shook his head. "I don't think the three of us confronting her will work. She knows how Samuel and I feel. But she's your sister. So you go ahead."

"Afraid of a girl, are you?" Iva teased.

Uncertainty marked Jacob's face. "I like to keep my girlfriend happy and calm and peaceful, in life as a whole and with me in particular. I've given her more than enough grief in our time together, and I won't add to it because her brother wants to rattle her into a decision."

Samuel was glad to hear Jacob be so honest with himself and others. More than anything else, Samuel wanted Rhoda to be happy. Since the power of her contentment was in Jacob's hands, all Samuel could do was pray and hope his brother cared enough to put her ahead of himself.

"But"—Jacob focused on Iva—"I agree with Phoebe that we'll find ways to satisfy your Daed. You can trust that. Okay?"

Iva smiled, taking in each of them individually. "Denki."

After nods from those in the room, they each seemed to return to their thoughts. Samuel's musings landed directly on Rhoda. Again. Was she in love with Jacob? He couldn't say she looked overly happy or peaceful of late. But that could be due to the damage Samuel had caused between them, or maybe it was from some damage Jacob had caused on his own.

"Samuel,"—Steven pushed back from the table—"will you go with me to push Rhoda on this kitchen matter?"

Samuel jolted from his thoughts. "If I thought that was the right thing to do, I'd be fine with confronting her with you. She wouldn't hesitate to do the same to me if she believed it would help the business. But this situation is different, and all of us are going to leave her alone about it."

"But she's holding the business hostage, and I need to do something about it." Steven stood.

Samuel eyed him, wondering if they were about to have their first argument. "No, you don't. This isn't a matter between siblings or between a church leader and a member of his flock. And even though she's both of those to you, I want her to be left alone with regard to the Cranfords' loaning us any money." He eased a chair out with his foot. "Take a seat and then take a deep breath."

Steven just stood there and glared at him.

Samuel tapped the notepad. "Let's talk about what we can do."

"Hey." Landon reached across the table and tapped on Samuel's notepad. "I've just had a wild notion about the canning kitchen, and if it worked, Iva could be given a specific title in the business *and* wages for her work."

Samuel was glad for the change of topic, and he hoped Landon's plan was a good one. "By all means share it."

"Actually, I need to call Granny first. Just give me a minute." Landon walked out of the room.

Samuel went back to his list, talking to the others about what they needed to accomplish between now and July, when the fruitlets would be thinned. As the meeting continued, he made out a tentative schedule.

Landon returned to the kitchen, grinning. "Granny's excited about the idea."

Samuel looked at him. "What is it?"

"Granny is going to Florida in August for an extended stay because her sister is having knee surgery. So what if we renovate *her* kitchen and use that? She'd need to vacate the house sooner than she'd planned, but she said she doesn't mind. Her kitchen has great bones for what Rhoda needs, so it shouldn't take a lot of money and probably not more than a week or so to get it ready. I know her place is much farther away than you wanted, especially for a permanent kitchen, but it could work for the first harvest. We'll need to build a huge trailer that we can hitch to my truck, and I'll drive the apples there as needed."

Samuel's heart turned a flip. "Erlene *likes* this idea?"

"She said she did. She was going to Florida anyway. This just moves up her departure. We'll have time to renovate the kitchen and get a license."

Steven threw his napkin and rinds into the trash. "I don't understand. I thought we couldn't get a license if the canning kitchen is in someone's house."

Samuel tossed the pen onto the pad of paper. "The issue is the kitchen can't be used to feed a family throughout the day *while* being used to can goods. It's probably the safety codes as well as health codes."

Steven nodded. "Then Landon's idea is the best we've come up with yet. Surely Rhoda will agree to it."

"Possibly." Samuel pushed the talk button. "Rhoda…"

After several seconds she answered, "Not now, please."

He stared at the two-way. She didn't sound like herself. But to his ear she hadn't sounded like herself for the last few days. He pushed the talk button again. "We have an idea about the kitchen. Can we talk to you about it? Where are you?"

"Changing codling moth traps. Whatever you need to say, it'll keep." She was probably covered with molasses and didn't appreciate having to handle the two-way at that moment.

"Where are you?"

"Bye." A definite click came through, and he knew she'd turned off her walkie-talkie.

Samuel looked at Jacob. "I think I should've let you contact her."

Jacob closed his eyes and raised his brows for a moment before shrugging. "Probably. But I didn't think about that. It's too late now."

Phoebe set a mixing bowl on the table. "Now there's a woman who wants some time alone."

A sheepish look crossed Jacob's face. "We can find her easily enough, but should we?"

Samuel knew that living and working as they did on this farm was very different from what drew Rhoda as a young girl to spend hours alone inside her one-acre fruit garden. For all her passion and determination, Rhoda longed for the peaceful, quieter side of cultivating fruits. The solitude and serenity were a gift to her, one that seemed to be a balm to her soul long before she retreated to the garden after her sister was murdered.

Samuel trusted that with a little more time, another year at most, he— they—could give her the periods of solitude she longed for. But now was not that time. After months of uncertainty, Landon had put a solid option on the table.

Samuel got up. "I want to talk to her about this idea. Now. Steven's going too. Jacob, are you coming?"

Jacob tilted his head for a moment, apparently deciding how this possible invasion of Rhoda's space might go.

"It might help her." Samuel pushed his chair in. "At the least she'll appreciate having you and your more gentle approach on her side."

Jacob nodded. "You're probably right."

Landon closed his laptop. "Does anyone mind if I step upstairs to see Leah?"

"Take these"—Phoebe passed him a little basket with oranges and napkins—"and tell her dinner's running a little late but should be ready within the hour. Will you stay?"

"Maybe." Landon rubbed his stomach. "I'd like to,"—he held up his cell phone—"but I may need to go. Would it be okay if I let you know in a bit?"

"Sure." Phoebe turned to Jacob and passed him an orange. "As far as I know, Rhoda hasn't had a bite since breakfast."

Samuel clipped the two-way on his suspenders. "Let's bridle some horses."

THIRTY-THREE

Rhoda pushed the four-wheel wooden handcart toward the next tree. She couldn't take a full breath. The feeling of suffocation had barely eased in four days, ever since Jacob had made his hopes—his requirements for marital happiness—known to her.

When Samuel demanded something despite her wishes, at least he was up-front about it from the start, and he didn't mind if she argued back. But Jacob didn't believe in raising his voice or arguing. His way was to slowly reveal what he wanted and then gently apply pressure until she gave in. That gentle pressure currently felt like a bushel of apples on her chest, all forty-two-plus pounds of it.

But she loved him.

So what was the problem? She unhooked a codling moth trap from its branch and returned to the handcart. The plastic container once held a large amount of vinegar for pickling vegetables from the garden, but a wide mouth had been cut in it so that it was now a homemade codling moth trap.

Maybe Jacob was right. If their relationship was to become as strong and healthy as they wanted it to be, as it had been before he was gone and out of touch with her for months at a time, they needed to move away.

Tears threatened, and the weight on her chest made breathing difficult, but she doubted that she needed to see a doctor. She poured the gooey mixture that was filled with moths into the trash can strapped to the cart.

If she lived elsewhere, married to Jacob and having his children, she wouldn't need to do as Landon said and understand what was between Samuel and her. It would eventually evaporate. It'd be replaced, just as this orchard had replaced the one in Pennsylvania. She rarely even thought of the original Kings'

Orchard or her fruit garden she'd grown up tending. People moved on and started anew.

"Rhodes?"

Jacob's voice jolted her. She turned to see Steven, Samuel, and Jacob peering down at her from horseback. How had she not heard them approaching?

Jacob slid down and held out an orange. "Hungry?"

Not one of them was on a saddled horse. She peered around him, trying to give Samuel a warning look. She should've known that shutting off the two-way wouldn't mean she'd be left alone.

Her chest tightened again, and breathing became even more difficult. "How did you find me?"

Jacob gave a slight nod toward the ground. "I listened."

She glanced down and noticed the dogs were panting. Clearly Ziggy and Zara had raced toward them, barking, and she hadn't heard that either.

Jacob tossed her the orange.

She grasped it, trying not to squeeze the life out of it. "Next time I'll tether the dogs to the cart and duct tape their snouts."

Jacob covered his mouth and barked, a muted, pitiful sound, then patted the dogs. "Mommy didn't mean it, guys."

She knelt and rubbed the dogs' ears. "I would never do that to Ziggy and Zara. But I might"—she glanced at Samuel—"to you."

Samuel dismounted. "Then gag me and put me in the doghouse, but I needed to talk to you, and you turned off the two-way."

Ready to ignore all three of them, she tossed the orange back to Jacob and turned to her handcart, wishing they would go away. She plucked a ragged square of an old sheet out of its box and wiped out the plastic container, removing even more dead moths. She hadn't yet decided the best way to dispose of the trap mixture she'd poured into the trash can, but it couldn't be dumped anywhere near the orchard or it would attract ants. And they'd infest the trees.

Without looking up from her work, she nodded toward the row of trees. "Since you're here, would you mind going down the row on this side? Get the traps from the trees, pour the old mixture into the trash can, and use the scraps to wipe down the sides, getting out as many moths as possible. Okay?"

Jacob bent, meeting her eyes. "Hi."

She swallowed, wishing her breathing were easier. "Hi, Jacob." She caressed his cheek.

"If all the niceties are done…" Samuel dropped the reins, clearly trusting the horse to stay put.

"Is there a problem, Samuel?" Maybe sarcasm would get him to back off. If she had answers about the kitchen, she would have shared them.

"Lots of them." He removed his hat. "But Landon came up with a plan about a canning kitchen that may settle one."

She doubted he'd come up with one she hadn't already thought of and ruled out as ridiculous. She finished wiping out the canister and tossed the gooey rag into a bin before she poured fresh molasses into the container.

"What is it?" When she glanced up, Emma was standing in the midst of the three men. She hadn't seen Emma since talking with Landon about Samuel in the greenhouse three weeks ago.

It became even harder to breathe.

"Rhodes?" Jacob took her by the shoulders. "You okay?"

She didn't dare pull away from him. It'd hurt him, and it would end up taking more time and effort than it was worth. Instead, she stood on tiptoe and kissed him on the cheek. "Of course." But she'd managed only a whisper. Why couldn't she catch her breath?

Jacob brushed a wisp of hair from her face. Love—vast and powerful—radiated from him. He kept no secrets about that.

Samuel smacked his hat against his leg. "Landon said his granny had plans to go to Florida in August to help her sister. But she'll leave a few weeks earlier and maybe stay a little longer so we can renovate her kitchen into a canning kitchen. I think we should consider it."

"That's the plan—to displace an elderly woman, take over her home, and make a profit?"

"Are you even listening? She's leaving this summer and will leave a little early in order to help us."

"Good heavens. She's an elderly woman! If it's not emotionally and physically exhausting enough to leave home to be a nursemaid to an ailing relative, we—people she's known for less than a year—are going to ask her to leave weeks earlier and come home weeks later than she needs to. Are you serious?"

"Could you possibly manage to hear me out?" Samuel yanked his hat onto his head. "Or is that asking too much?"

"I did hear you, and I am being reasonable. She's way too nice to say no. I'm not sure she could turn Landon down about anything even if her life depended on it. We're not accepting her offer."

"The least we can do is talk to her. If we pick up on any hesitation, any discomfort from her about changing her plans, then we politely and gratefully turn her down, but not before."

"Samuel King, if—"

"You know,"—Jacob stepped back—"I think I should be helpful and do some work." He winked at her and turned to Samuel. "You be nice." He walked off, going toward the next tree to gather a trap. Steven went with him.

Why would Jacob come all this way and simply walk off, leaving her here to argue with Samuel, and why did she have so many feelings for Samuel when he was the most stubborn man she'd ever known?

Ignoring Samuel, she poured molasses and water into the container.

"Rhoda, you're not even willing to have a conversation. What's going on with you?"

His softer tone tapped into a dam of emotions, and tears threatened again. The truth? She'd rather argue with Samuel and be a part of the life on this farm than live anywhere else. But would staying here be fair to her relationship with Jacob?

Samuel snapped his fingers. "Hallo? If you can't be open minded about Landon's plan, then admit it, and let someone else decide for you."

"Who's going to decide? Steven? He has no clue what an orchard this size would need to get through one canning season, let alone years of it. Not yet, he doesn't." Thankfully, her frustration gave her a lungful of air. She poured yeast into the concoction and stirred. "Are you going to decide, Samuel? Or Jacob?" Her voice echoed off the hills, but at least she could breathe freely again. "Neither of you can see this issue clearly enough to have an answer. Your visions are blurred, each wanting different things from me." She glanced at Jacob's retreating back before taking the trap to the tree.

Samuel followed her. "Seems more like Jacob and I want the same thing."

Her heart quickened. He'd spoken softly, almost through gritted teeth, but had he realized what he'd said?

She looked into his eyes, and for a moment she saw—felt—the torrent of love that raged within him. But the terrifying part was that she returned some of those feelings. Did hers match his?

He backed away. "I...I meant businesswise."

Steven and Jacob continued down the row of trees, gathering traps. Did Jacob come out here to make sure he stood between Samuel and her? If so, he was clueless what was happening some fifty feet from him.

Jacob's trust in her had been renewed. Part of her wished it hadn't been, wished he was right by her side.

Trembling, she attached the homemade trap to its hanger, emotions beating against her as if she were a rock at the bottom of Niagara Falls.

Jacob was right. There was too much between Samuel and her. She turned to go back to the handcart.

Samuel grabbed her arm. At his touch Rhoda heard bells ringing. Some vague idea formed in her head. She looked from him to his hand.

He released her. "I'm sorry." He fidgeted with his hat. "I...I shouldn't have." He walked toward his horse. "You and Landon talk to Erlene and *then* make a decision."

Choose... Emma stood between Jacob and Samuel, although the men were quite a distance apart.

"Samuel." Rhoda had barely managed a whisper, but she had so many questions she needed to ask him. He could make mud clear for her when he wanted to.

Why did Emma most often show up when he did? She even appeared when Landon was talking to Rhoda about Samuel.

Samuel strode back to her.

"Why you?"

"What do you mean?"

"Remember the second or third night we were on this farm? Jacob was not yet here, and we didn't know where he was, and I'd followed the sounds of an instrument and voices out to here. You found me staring into the woods and talking to myself."

"Ya."

"When I looked your way, I saw Emma behind you. I was disappointed she hadn't stayed in Pennsylvania."

"It's not her."

"We've established that, and the more I listen to my heart, the less Emma shows up. Except...with you. When I see you walking into the barn or across the orchard, she's with you. Why?"

His earlier irritation seemed to evaporate. "Maybe because you told me she connected to your grief of losing her, so in that sense I understand something about you that no one else does."

It sounded reasonable enough.

Samuel's eyes reflected an apology, probably for fussing at her a few minutes ago. "Or when you see me, you're reminded of her and all the times her image annoyed you. Maybe that's it. I annoy you. She annoys you." A faint smile graced his lips. "*There's* the connection."

But that wasn't it.

While he stood there, she prayed, and awareness of what lurked in her heart gushed into her consciousness. She looked from Jacob to Samuel. As Jacob moved farther away, she wanted to cry out to God to help her. But as she stayed rooted in place, she realized her feelings for Samuel weren't new. They'd been an unseen vine thriving on its own for a very long time—like brambles in wild.

But how had she not known her feelings for what they really were before now?

Choose... Emma's voice was strong.

Her sister moved effortlessly to stand behind Samuel.

A commanding desire for a lifetime with Samuel filled Rhoda. Tortured her. A thirst for who Samuel and she could be made her knees go weak.

Emma smiled at her. *"It's time…"*

And finally Rhoda understood what her heart had known even before she met Samuel. That *he* was the one.

But it was too late. When she'd met Samuel, he had a girlfriend. Rhoda had dealt with her disappointment and let Jacob into her heart.

"Samuel,"—she stared into his brown eyes—"I'm so sorry."

He studied her, saying nothing.

But visions of Emma made sense now. When alive, Emma knew Rhoda, knew her hopes and dreams—all of them. When Emma died, Rhoda buried most of her heart with her sister. Rhoda went through life doing all she could to steer it where she thought it should go, refusing to listen to her own tender soul. So her subconscious conjured up Emma, the one who'd known and owned her heart for so long. Emma showing up was the only way Rhoda would pause even for a moment to try to hear.

Her sister faded into nothing. Rhoda didn't need her anymore, and she wasn't likely to see Emma again. Rhoda had finally heard what she'd been trying to say. But of everything Rhoda had experienced in life, this was the scariest—loving Samuel, the brother of a man who adored her.

All the pieces finally fit. In his own way, and unlike anyone else, Samuel had helped her put them together like a puzzle. *He* understood her. For all his determination to grab the bull by the horns and lead life where he wanted it to go, Samuel had the patience to be a truly great friend to her. A leader. A helper. A protector.

A husband.

The word *choose* came to mind again. What choice was there? Rhoda wanted to scream, "I have chosen!"

Samuel continued to study Rhoda, waiting patiently for her to wrestle with herself. Did Jacob even know this side of her, the one that had to fight to know herself?

She backed away. "What am I supposed to do?" Tears stung her eyes.

His silent stare was unnerving, and she imagined he understood far more than she wanted him to.

"He's your brother, and I will *not* come between you. I will *not* injure the

King family, the one God gave to your parents and they so carefully nurtured."
She swallowed and wiped a lone tear. If she had any control at all, that would
be the last tear she would shed in front of Samuel. "Jacob loves me. He worked
his way free from his past for *me*! He's going through instruction to marry me.
Do you understand?" She grabbed his arm, trembling. "I would rather die than
hurt him."

Samuel remained unmoving. He looked to his brother and then to her,
and he nodded. "I understand. I have since the day I realized I loved you." He
swiped a hand across his watery eyes. "But—"

She fisted her hands. "I've made a mess of people's lives since I was young.
You want me to unleash that on your family?" Why was she saying more? He'd
already agreed with her.

"But, Rhoda, if he's not the one for you, then you're not the one for him.
But only you can decide that."

She couldn't stop her tears. "I have chosen, Samuel. I did so while you were
courting Catherine."

He closed his eyes. Seconds passed, maybe a full minute, before he finally
nodded. He turned and walked to his horse.

Like watching the video clip about the orchard on Landon's laptop, she
saw what had to be done about the kitchen.

"Wait." She peered across the blank space between the orchard and the
woods. Beyond where she could see, she knew there was a perfect place for a
kitchen. She heard the bells again. It was a timer going off. She could feel the
heat from the stove. A shrill whistle pierced the air—a pressure cooker no
doubt. "A kitchen. I know where we need to build it—on this property."

"Now?" He gestured toward heaven, rolling his eyes. "After all this time,
now you're talking about the same basic plan as Bob and Camilla have been
proposing?"

"It's as much of a surprise to me as it is to you. But we've been waiting for
me to *know,* and now I do. And all you want to do is stand here and argue
about it?" She motioned for Samuel to give her a hand onto the horse. He
linked his fingers together and hoisted her up. "Kumm."

She trotted north toward the road, but they were a long way from it. "Jacob! Kumm."

Samuel got on a horse, carrying the reins to the third horse to his brother. Steven seemed a bit lost, but she wasn't worried. If he wanted to follow them, he'd walk. What had to be said needed to be in the presence of only the three of them—Samuel, Jacob, and herself.

She rode, her heart pounding with excitement. They went past the orchard and kept going to an area of the farm she'd never explored.

Her mind raced with snapshots of wagons filled with apples that were being unloaded at the door of the kitchen—just like last harvest before the tornado. She could see the canning kitchen, larger and laid out better than the summer kitchen in Pennsylvania.

"Whoa." She pulled on the reins. "Here. It's perfect—flat, not too close to the creek or the orchard. A driveway could be put in that leads to the road." She got off the horse.

Samuel and Jacob did the same.

"A home could be built less than a half mile from this spot."

"A house?" Samuel's brows furrowed deeper. "Ya, I guess it could… eventually."

Emotions choked her. She and Jacob couldn't stay here in Maine. It didn't matter that she loved this farm. Property could be replaced. A bond between brothers couldn't.

Added to that, she did love Jacob. What they had seemed flawed in the light of all that had been hiding in her heart for Samuel. But that's what commitment and loyalty were about—a love that went deeper than any emotional or temporal desires.

But Jacob and she could stay here through the first harvest. She'd train Leah or Iva. Or maybe the answer was to make Landon a partner. He could oversee the canning. Landon, Leah, and Iva combined would be a team she could train to replace her. Landon knew far more about the business and the recipes than he realized. If he was interested, what he lacked in know-how, he could learn in a matter of months.

Each harvest Rhoda and Jacob could return for a few weeks. They'd stay long enough to oversee the operation, make sure it was running smoothly, and confirm that the product deserved the Byler and King label.

"It's a good plan." Samuel studied the lay of the land. "We can do it. Is it a problem accepting a loan from Bob and Camilla until we get the money from the Pennsylvania land?"

Rhoda felt a nudge inside her. "You should do as *you* see fit, Samuel."

Jacob walked a section, heel to toe, and she knew calculations were zipping through his brain. "We'll need to give the county a set of architectural plans to get a building permit. And we'll have to allow time for county or state inspectors to approve certain phases, like before and after pouring concrete for the footers and the foundation. Then we can go to the next phase."

Rhoda swallowed. By all outward appearance, Jacob seemed fine with her plan. The only way she knew he wanted off this farm is because he'd told her. She shook free of that thought and blocked the sun from her eyes, studying the tree line. They might need to move a bit closer to the road. They needed the canning kitchen as far from the orchard as possible. The aromas of the kitchen would attract insects, and then they'd find the orchard.

"Bob said the head of every department at the county courthouse is a friend, and he believes we can have the building permits in record time." He'd barely mentioned that and other things one morning as she was leaving for the farm, and she hadn't really understood what he'd been saying. How was it so very clear to her now?

"Gut. Sounds gut." Samuel's voice carried the rumble of a heartbroken man holding on to hope for the future. "Even so, I don't suspect it'll be operational during the first weeks of the harvest. Maybe we can find a cellar so the apples will keep."

"We won't need to." As ideas poured into her, Rhoda could hardly look at either man. Had her outburst to Samuel only minutes ago caused her to betray both of them?

She shooed a gnat away from her face. "We'll invite your family and mine and the Amish families that want to visit, and we'll have an old-fashioned barn raising—only it'll be a kitchen raising. A harvest kitchen."

"Harvest kitchen?" Samuel looked around, bewildered at all she was covering.

"It's not a summer kitchen, and I don't like the name canning kitchen either. You know what else, Samuel? You should name this place Orchard Bend Farms. That way, if you have married daughters or granddaughters who wish to carry on the canning business, they won't have to refer to it as Kings' Orchard if they don't carry the King name."

"Grandchildren," Samuel mumbled. "Is she seeing me so old that I'm retired before we've even poured the footers for the harvest kitchen?"

Jacob moved next to her. "Ya, but apparently only you are going gray or bald. I wasn't mentioned in that little scenario."

She slid her hand into Jacob's. "We won't be here after this first harvest." She closed her eyes, fighting tears. "He wants to be a carpenter in his uncle's business until he can afford to start his own."

She wasn't sure what reaction she'd expected from Jacob, but not a muscle twitched. There was not even a hint of his signature smile. Had she just confessed to him how she felt about Samuel?

Samuel's demeanor showed his grief, but her intuition told her that his sorrow was more for her loss of this dream than anything else. She knew guilt pounded him for what he'd done to her future by that kiss, but it wasn't him. It was both of them. Maybe all three of them.

She smiled at Samuel. "It's a good plan. The only one that will really work."

He nodded. "It is."

She tugged on Jacob's hand. "All three of us need to be together when we tell the others."

THIRTY-FOUR

Aromas mingled from the dishes on the kitchen table. Leah had found them enticing only moments ago, but now they turned her stomach. She couldn't budge as Jacob finished explaining Rhoda and his new plan.

Orchard Bend Farms. She knew they would be referred to as the Orchard Bend Amish. Leah swallowed hard. They were losing half of who they were while gaining only a name.

Jacob's smile was reassuring, but his hands trembled a bit when he took a drink of water. "I know this sounds as if it changes everything, but actually it'll only be a new division of labor, and it'll help Iva's situation because Steven will be able to use our leaving as an argument that this business needs her. Landon will manage supplies and shipping on a daily basis—spices, sugar, jars, shipping boxes, labels, and such. Leah will manage the product itself, making each batch of apple butter, jelly, jam, applesauce, pie filling, salsa, cider, and everything else according to the recipes. And Iva will handle the canning and cooling and packing. So the whole operation should run smoothly."

Phoebe studied Rhoda. "This is what you want?"

Rhoda clasped both of Jacob's hands. "It is. A wife's place is with her husband, no?"

Phoebe turned to Steven, looking bewildered, and then faced Rhoda again. "I never dreamed you'd turn over to anyone your grandmother's recipes and your business of selling canned goods. You've been doing this since before I knew you."

Jacob put his arm around Rhoda's shoulders. "And she'll keep doing it to some degree."

The room fell silent, and finally Steven shifted in his chair. "Let's pray."

When the silent prayer was over, Leah still couldn't move, even as bowls of food were passed in front of her.

"Here you go." Jacob plopped a serving of Amish six layer on her plate. "Dinner you didn't have to cook. Isn't that always your favorite?"

Leah stared at the steam rising from the food. Rhoda was leaving? Not only was the news shocking, but it made Leah's heart ache to think of losing Rhoda. Jacob too, but Leah had adjusted to his going away a long, long time ago. How old had she been when he moved to Lancaster to apprentice with their uncle? Eight or nine? He came home some, certainly on holidays and birthdays, until he left to live among the Englisch when she was around thirteen.

Truth was, she'd spent more time with Rhoda since waking up half-drunk in her fruit garden than she ever had with Jacob. Rhoda was the first person to really believe in her. Well, Jacob did, but he was never around to battle for her the way Rhoda had. She'd argued with Samuel until he saw that he didn't value his sisters as he did his brothers. Samuel then stood against their Daed for Leah's sake.

Leah's stomach hurt as concerns for what else this meant kept coming at her. What would this do to her chance to break free? Jacob was excited to have his freedom back, but in the process it appeared he'd chained Leah to the business, to being Amish. She couldn't just walk away, not if she *had* to help fill Rhoda's shoes. Jacob knew Leah wasn't sure if she was staying.

And if Landon wasn't just an assistant to Rhoda but was an integral part of running the business, he couldn't help Leah leave the Amish. Despite the trouble it would cause for a spell, he still might have been able to keep his position as Rhoda's assistant, as a simple farmhand, but the Amish ways wouldn't let him stay as a managing partner if he did anything subversive against the Amish. With Rhoda gone, what would it do to the business if Landon had to leave? Or if Leah left?

Jacob had to know that. He was ruining everything. Then another truth dawned on her, and concern for Rhoda weighed heavy.

"This is wrong, Jacob." Her voice wavered. "You're taking her from all of us because your sense of wanderlust has hit again. This won't be the last time. Did you tell her that?"

Jacob set his fork and knife on his plate. "Leah."

"No." She tossed her napkin over the pile of food on her plate. "You won't stay in Lancaster. That's Uncle Mervin's territory. You'll only stay until you're reputation is established and you have some money."

Rhoda seemed surprised by what Leah had said, but it faded quickly, and Rhoda leaned in. "Leah, I'm marrying your brother, and we're leaving to make a different life for ourselves. Maybe it's shocking news, but if you dig a little deeper, you'll discover it's good news, ya?"

Leah looked to Landon. Was she building a case against Jacob because her emotions were so raw, like the nonsense she'd pulled with Landon when he'd ignored her while watching a ball game?

Is this how freedom worked? For one man to have it, he had to take it from someone else? That's how it seemed. Jacob had taken every choice from her and from Landon. Maybe she was overreacting to Jacob and Rhoda's news. How things felt and how they really were could be quite different. Leah steadied her breathing until she had more control over her panic, and then she walked around the table to Rhoda. "Congratulations."

Rhoda stood and held her tight. "Denki."

Jacob waited by her side. "I know this is hard, but it's a good thing, Leah. For all of us."

Leah hoped so. Oh, how she hoped so. When she released him, she saw a unity in the two, something built on compromise and yet beautifully romantic. Was it real, or was Leah letting years of romance novels fill her head? "If it's okay, I'll eat a little later."

As soon as the others nodded, Leah left. She hurried out the front door, into the barn, and up the ladder to the haymow. Its familiarity brought comfort, reminding her of the one she'd hid in for hours at a time, reading, while she was growing up. But she didn't have shelves of books up here, in part because she had a bedroom of her own, but mostly because life was so very different here. She didn't need to hide during her off time. She had freedom and respect. Samuel had seen to that.

How must he feel about this news? She imagined he had a set of chains that Jacob had clasped on him too.

"Leah?" Landon stood on the ladder, waiting. "Can I come up?"

She sat on a hay bale and stared out the open door. "You know what this means, right?"

He sat down next to her. "I know." He propped his arms on his thighs. "The business stood a real chance of stabilizing over the next year. Now it could be five, at least. Nobody knows the canning side like Rhoda."

"After this I'll need to be here for Samuel, trying to help him like Rhoda has. I won't be a smidgen as good, but I can't abandon him."

Landon interlaced his fingers and sighed. "You're a good sister."

His words sent a chill through her. "You'll be here too, right?"

He angled his head, staring at her, a hint of confusion flickering through his eyes. "Rhoda is trusting me to do that, so yes." He nudged her with his elbow. "Unless *you* plan on running me off."

His words held out comfort to her, but she couldn't quite grab hold of it. "If you're anchored in this job as a partner, holding a position with my brother, we can't be the freewheeling underlings who could break away without causing the business to fold. Samuel can't do it all."

Landon's wry smile radiated patience. "So today, without any doubts, you're dreaming of breaking free?"

"Don't make fun of me. I know I constantly waver about what I'm going to do, but I want the right to choose, the right to follow as God leads."

"Then it seems He's leading you to wait, whether Rhoda stays or leaves."

"What makes you say that?"

"There's a saying that I think is true: if in doubt, don't. And, Leah King, you constantly doubt what you're going to do. You've just been given good reasons to stay put. Samuel needs that, and the truth is, we need it."

"We?" She screeched the word at him, but when she did, she knew what he meant. She needed a few years before deciding anything. That terrified her too. Would he wait? Would they still care about each other years from now?

He held out his hand to her.

The gesture caught her off guard. "You got another learner's manual up your sleeve?"

With his other hand, he shook the short sleeve of his T-shirt. "Nope."

He wanted her to take his hand, and she wasn't quite certain how to receive this gesture of affection. "I thought you didn't like holding hands."

He shrugged. "Sometimes when dating a young woman and everything seems confusing and frustrating, the only thing a man can do is hold her hand and wait."

She slid her hand into his. "When Jacob calls my folks with the plan to build the harvest kitchen, they'll come. I can't let them find out that we're dating or that I'm attending a church in town."

He tucked her arm inside his, holding her hand. "Then don't."

Leah quieted her nerves and looked out at the acres of vibrant trees, and all she could think of was that Landon Olson was holding her hand.

THIRTY-FIVE

Iva walked down the paved road toward the area where she should soon find the building site of the harvest kitchen. The late June weather was absolutely delicious. Midseventies. A light breeze.

She paused, pulled the viewfinder to her eye, and snapped a few pictures of the first mourning dove she'd seen since arriving in Maine. It stayed on the ground, alert and silent as she eased closer and then knelt. She continued to get shots even as it flew away. She lowered the camera until its weight was fully on the strap around her neck. Once she'd returned to the road, she patted her apron pocket, verifying Sandra's letter was still safe.

After numerous meanderings from the road to take pictures, she finally rounded a slight bend, and the building site was before her. She blinked several times.

Was that it?

What lay before her was considered good progress?

It'd been three weeks! No wonder Jacob had told her she hadn't missed much since the groundbreaking. She was busier than a new Mamm with triplets now that Jacob spent his days building instead of working in the orchard.

Oh, he was going to hear about this. She smiled, imagining his reaction to being teased.

The good news was that Steven had spent tireless hours on the phone with her Daed. She'd never seen a more kindhearted, patient man than Steven, and he'd finally won her Daed's approval. Because the thriving business needed her, Iva could stay here—as long as she sent half her salary home to help with the family's needs. Iva didn't care about the money. Her Daed could have all of it, but Steven said she needed to keep her portion.

Steven Byler, champion of women, especially his own wife. His daughter, Arie, was a very blessed little girl. How different would Iva's life be if her Daed valued her that same way?

Jacob pushed a shovel blade into a pile of gravel in a wheelbarrow and tossed it onto what appeared to be nothing but ground. She zoomed in on him until she could see the sweat glistening on his forearms and soaking through his pale blue shirt. She might have to delete these, but she couldn't resist taking them.

With the scope of the camera, she could see a concrete border around a cleared square of dirt with plastic over it. A pile of half-broken boards lay to one side, and a large heap of gravel was beside it.

So this was the early stage of construction? With the naked eye it wasn't much to look at, but through her camera lens—fascinating. She made her way up the gravel lane, taking dozens of shots. Since she hadn't uploaded any images to Landon's computer in a while, she could only hope her memory card didn't get full. It would hold about seven hundred images, but when one didn't own a computer or have easy access to a photo center, that wasn't a lot of space.

She zoomed in on a stack of lumber. This building site would be a great place for taking photos next week. That's when Rhoda's and Jacob's families would arrive, along with his uncle's construction crew. She could already feel the thrill of taking pictures of their work—in the early morning light, as a summertime thunderstorm approached, as the moon rose over the apple trees. She'd have to be discreet and avoid getting their faces, but she'd learned long ago how to capture the heart of an event without crossing a line.

Oh, this is what life was meant to be—fresh, exuberating visions to be captured by a camera.

Gravel crunched under her feet as she walked down the long driveway, snapping more pictures. Jacob didn't look up. Could he not hear her over his shoveling?

Two pipes stood erect inside the border. She focused on them—nasty looking, really. One was probably four inches in diameter, caked in dirt and mud, with some type of cap on top. How did something so hideous become a part of a place that would be filled with delicious aromas and spices?

The plan for her to work in this kitchen with Leah and Landon was daunting at best. But it also meant freedom, and even though months of long, hot days in a kitchen wasn't her dream job, it was exciting to be a part of a new business.

She lifted the camera, taking more shots. Her feet smacked into something hard, and she fell forward. "My camera!"

A blur surrounded her, but a pair of strong hands eased her fall right before her face struck the ground. Her knees screamed in pain, as did an elbow.

"Iva?" Jacob righted her to a sitting position. *"Bischt du allrecht?"*

Her hands shook as she inspected her camera. "I'm fine." When she couldn't find a scratch on the camera, she looked up. "Denki." She'd landed inside his concrete border onto what eventually would be the floor.

"You're bleeding." He pointed at her elbow.

"I'll heal. You saved the important part."

"Your camera?" He held out his hand.

She grabbed his hand, her knees yelling at her as she rose to her feet. Hopefully the faux sincerity she was about to inflect would bring a smile to him. "Oh, no. I meant the dirt-and-gravel floor."

He laughed. "What?"

Pleased with herself, she knocked the dirt off her apron. "May I sit on this border?"

"Border?" His laughter returned before motioning for her to sit. "It's a footer. You'll hear it referred to as the foundation when the crews arrive."

"Footer is a gut word for it. I ran my footer into it, and it knocked me off my feeter."

"And onto your kneezers."

She sat. "Oh, a letter came for you today." She dug it out of her pocket and held it up.

"Envelope removed, I see. Have I mentioned lately that I appreciate what you're doing to help us?"

Late at night, just before she would drift off to sleep, thoughts niggled their way free of the place she hid them during waking hours. She hadn't helped move Sandra just because she wanted to prove she was worth keeping as a hired worker. If Jacob believed in this cause with Sandra, Iva believed it too.

She turned off her camera to save the battery. At least the solar panels outside Rhoda's greenhouses were hooked to a small converter, which gave her a way to recharge it.

"I was concerned for a little bit that maybe I was doing something wrong by helping to hide Sandra."

He lowered the pages of the letter. "I didn't realize that, although I guess I should have considered it. Do we need to talk about it?"

She shook her head. "If you think it's wise and necessary, I trust that."

His face didn't yield to a smile, but his green eyes reflected appreciation before he went back to reading the letter from Sandra. "She sounds surprisingly peaceful and maybe even happy."

"You'd like where she is. I think she does too."

"Look." He held up a piece of white paper with colored scribbles. "Casey drew me a picture. Sandra wrote that Casey says she loves me and misses me every second of every day."

His faint smile warmed Iva's heart.

"I can't wait until all this cloak-and-dagger stuff is behind me." He folded the letter and shoved it into his pocket. "Denki."

"Anytime." She began reviewing the images on her camera just to be sure it hadn't taken an unnoticed hit. "So if I pose a question extremely politely, do you mind answering it?"

"Can't imagine why I would." Jacob picked up his shovel and moved back to his pile of gravel.

"You've been working out here for three weeks, from right after breakfast until dark, ya?"

"Ya." He dug the shovel into the wheelbarrow of gravel.

"Rhoda, Leah, or Phoebe brings food to you."

"Ya."

She kept scrolling through her images. Some were really good. "So why is this tiny bit of work all you've gotten done?"

Gravel thudded near her, some of it hitting her shoes.

She jumped up. "What'd you do that for?"

"That was a politely worded question?" He chuckled.

"Compared to 'What in the world have you been doing all these days while I've been taking over your jobs on the farm?' Ya, it was."

"I see your point. But you don't understand construction. We had to decide on plans and have them approved by the county before we could get the permits to build. Then the ground had to be leveled." He moved around, pointing as he spoke. "I set the pipe, dug the footers by hand, and installed the form boards and steel. Mixed and poured the concrete. And while that cures, I've set the ground covering, and now I'm adding a layer of gravel."

As he talked and showed her around, she was surprised he'd gotten as far as he had. "That's it?"

He raised an eyebrow. "Listen, Iva Lambright, I know your Achilles heel. It's wrapped around your little neck, and if you want to keep it safe, I'd apologize if I were you."

"This is what a man looks like right before he smashes the prized possession of a homeless waif." She took a picture of him. "Come any closer, and I'll say it's one of you as you reached to smash my camera."

He shook his head and began shoveling again. "You should go home and have those cuts tended to."

"And if I wasn't injured, would you say what you really mean? You should go home."

He didn't glance her way, but his smile was undeniable. "Something like that. As far as progress on this job goes, you'll see a lot once the families get here. It won't take us more than a few days to dry the place in. For you learners that means framing the exterior and interior walls, decking the roof, adding the subflooring and windows, and hanging the exterior doors. Then comes the finishing work, but the families won't stay for that."

"How long will that take?"

"By myself, it would be six months, maybe eight. But my uncle owns a construction company, and in exchange for me coming to work for him after the harvest, he's going to send some crews in shifts, as needed, until it's complete. Hopefully, before the harvest begins."

"Crews?"

"Most carpenters have particular skills, so they move faster and do a better job in those areas. One crew will put up the Sheetrock, and another will finish it. Another does siding, cabinets, flooring, trim work—"

"Got it. So what's your best area?"

"Lead carpenter. That's quality control. Squaring buildings. Laying out walls. If in the end something is wrong with any part of the job, it's my fault. I'm supposed to make sure the job is done right. But in this case, to ensure that we're building according to code and the law, I'll work under a licensed contractor, who'll show up every day to inspect and instruct."

Even though he'd seemed content enough to farm this land, it was unusual to see this side of Jacob, with a gleam in his eye as he talked. "You love this type of work."

"I used to. The joy has been pouring back in of late. The mess with Sandra's husband and the construction company I worked for caused me to hate it. I couldn't pick up a hammer for years. The thought of it made me sick."

"Sandra told me about a deck collapsing and two women dying. It broke my heart for those women's families."

"Sandra told you?" He seemed taken aback.

"While I was helping her move, ya. I'm sorry. I wasn't supposed to know?"

After a moment of silence, he finally sighed. "For a while I thought it was my fault. I'd designed the deck and even helped build it. But then I was called off that site and onto another one a day before we were done."

"Jacob." Her hoarse whisper caught his attention, and he quit working. "How awful for you."

"Not like it was for the families of those women."

"But for someone as sincere as you, it must have half killed you on the inside."

His eyes met hers, a rarity for him—although it was typical when he was looking at Rhoda. "It was a nightmare." He took off his hat. "Without even knowing about my past, Rhoda helped me move beyond it."

"How?"

He wiped his brow with his shirt sleeve. "I don't know. There's a powerful presence about her that I need, just as there is humor in me that she needs."

"Interesting." Focusing the lens toward the wooded area, she zoomed in on one spot. "I'd sharpen that wit if I were you."

"Why's that?"

Iva spotted what looked to be a belted kingfisher. Was that possible? She eased in that direction, but it flew off before she could get a decent shot.

"Iva?"

"Ya."

When it landed a few feet farther out, she zoomed in on it.

"Why do you say I need to sharpen my wit?"

"Because, from what I can piece together, Rhoda is leaving everything she loves for you." She snapped a dozen images, still not sure if it was a belted kingfisher. It flew away, and she lowered her camera and scrolled through the images. "Isn't she?"

When he said nothing, she looked at him. His hat lay at his feet, and his stricken face stunned her.

She turned off her camera and went to him. "Did I say something wrong?" Her Daed was forever telling her that she didn't think before she spoke. But what had she said wrong? Surely he knew how Rhoda felt. Or was love that blind?

"No. You're fine." He grabbed his hat and put it on before he scooped up another shovelful of gravel.

But if it was fine, why did she feel as if she'd just ripped tape from his eyes?

THIRTY-SIX

Rhoda put fresh sheets on Jacob's bed while Phoebe dusted his furniture. July's warmth and mild humidity floated through the open window, as did the sound of black flies and the chirps of a nearby family of cardinals. A scent of honeysuckle clung to the air.

She tucked the edges of the sheet under the mattress. This would become her parents' bedroom when they arrived. Landon had gone to the train station to get them, her brother John and sister-in-law, and their five children. Even though Landon had borrowed a van that seated ten people, he said that between people and luggage, he didn't have room for anyone else to go with him to the station.

Jacob's family would arrive tomorrow.

Two emotions warred within her—joy that her family would arrive soon and grief that in the blink of an eye it would be time for Jacob and her to pack their bags and leave this farm, to return for only a week or so each harvest.

She moved to his window and looked out. She could see the barn, the driveway, and some of the front yard from here. The view from her bedroom window—or rather what was now Iva's room—was much nicer. But once Samuel and Jacob's family arrived, Iva and Leah would bunk with Rhoda at the Cranfords' house.

Phoebe shook a pillow, beating it strongly before plunking it on the bed. "I don't know how we're going to feed and house this many people for a week."

Samuel rounded the back of the barn and went inside the closest door. A dozen emotions, from longing to grief, ripped at Rhoda.

She grabbed the bedspread and moved away from the window. No sense in dwelling on Samuel.

"Steven said the last supply truck arrived at the building site early today. That should be all the supplies the men will need to construct the harvest kitchen."

Rhoda couldn't swallow. She could hardly breathe. "That's gut." She tossed the cover onto the bed.

Phoebe tugged on the bedspread and slid her hand across it, straightening the last wrinkles. "Ya. With plenty of supplies and food, those men will fly through getting the place dried in."

Rhoda's head pounded. "Ya."

"Before we have communion this Sunday and Steven becomes an official preacher for the Orchard Bend Amish, we'll see that harvest kitchen dried in and ready for the finishers to begin." Studying Rhoda, Phoebe worked the kinks out of her back. "Do you need me to keep making silly chitchat, or are you going to do us both a favor and really talk?"

Rhoda took the dust mop by the handle and ran it over the floor again. "Chitchat, please."

"Could you answer one question?"

"Nee, but denki for asking." Rhoda picked up pieces of dirt from the rug. "Do we need to drag this out to the line and beat it again?"

Phoebe took hold of the mop handle. "Rhoda, please."

Rhoda relinquished the dust mop and moved to the edge of the bed. "What do you want me to say?"

Phoebe closed the door before sitting next to her. "How about the truth concerning what's going on?"

Rhoda couldn't explain, not even to Phoebe or Camilla.

Phoebe put her hand over Rhoda's. "If you were feeling apprehensive or disappointed about needing to move again, I could find encouragement to share. A man who holds your heart and you want a family with is worth any move. But I think whatever is going on is much, much deeper than packing your bags again."

Rhoda willed herself to keep her mouth shut. "I love Jacob. I do. But…"

"Ah, so your brother is right." Phoebe chuckled and put her arm around Rhoda's shoulders. "He'll never let me live this down."

Rhoda fidgeted with the strings to her prayer Kapp. "I don't understand. Jacob and I began our courtship just head over heels for each other. He's so good at saying the right things, and he used to make me laugh so easily. Phoebe, he's so in love. And…I love him too, but…what's wrong with me?"

"Maybe it's not you or him." Phoebe leaned her head against Rhoda's. "It was unbelievably hard when I lost the baby. We were so excited to be expecting again. The little one was conceived in love, and I take good care of myself. Steven is a really good husband and Daed. None of that was enough. The doctor believes the baby wasn't healthy enough to cling to life." Phoebe paused, clearly aiming to get control of her emotions. "Not every relationship, even when started in true love, is strong and healthy enough to last as we believe it should. As we long for it to."

Phoebe's comparison was beautiful, and it pierced Rhoda's heart to see the truth of it.

Someone tapped at the door.

"Kumm." Phoebe stood.

Iva stepped in, holding out a handful of wildflowers from Phoebe's garden—purple asters, orange lilies, and white daisies. "I was wondering if you'd like these put in a vase for this room." The girl's feet were bare, and she had on a white cotton scarf in place of her prayer Kapp, not uncommon when cleaning house. Her tan skin had a healthy glow. *She* was thriving inside this home. Rhoda felt like a vine withering in a sunbaked drought.

Sweet, sweet Iva. Rhoda's first concerns about her had been wrong. She was a treasure, not a troublemaker.

Rhoda stood and straightened the bed. "My folks will love them, Iva. Denki."

"Gut. I thought so." Iva closed the door, and Rhoda heard her scamper away.

"Rhoda." Phoebe picked up the dusting rag and swiped it across the top of the window. "We can heal from our losses, but if you marry Jacob for the wrong reasons, you'll damage both of your lives."

She was sorry for Phoebe and Steven's loss, and she didn't mean to think light of it, but the fact was they would have more children. If Rhoda let Jacob go, it'd rip his heart out, and she'd end up without anyone. Samuel should know he could never build a lasting relationship with someone who'd once planned to marry his brother. Every time Samuel would try to hold her hand or spread a blanket on a hillside for a picnic or take her for a buggy ride, he'd remember that she did those same things with his brother. And each time it'd put more distance between them until he stopped trying.

She knew that. Maybe Samuel did too. But she and Jacob could build a strong family, filled with faith and happiness. She knew they could.

"It's ridiculous to care for anyone besides Jacob," Rhoda whispered. "And I'm not giving in to any temptation that tries to lure me from him."

Phoebe dusted the tops of the doorframes. "An engagement or even talking of marriage is a commitment, but it's not a vow made before God. It's a hope of making that vow, but if it's no longer a hope, if it's only uncomfortable determination, is God or man asking you to follow through and take the vow?"

"You're not hearing me." Rhoda wiped grime out of the windowsill. "I choose Jacob. What's more, I love him, and you need to back me up, not fling the barn doors open, encouraging all heathen animals and foolish women to escape."

"That's a strange thing to say." Phoebe tucked the rag and cleaners into a bucket. "I'm not so sure a woman should be kept in a barn with the animals. And a woman would be even more foolish if she didn't escape when clearly she should. My concern is one day you'll look back at this time and think, why didn't I listen to my heart?"

Rhoda tossed her stuff into the bucket. "I am listening to my heart."

"Maybe. Your heart aches for Jacob, and you're clearly hearing that, but maybe what you're listening to most of all is your sense of duty."

Rhoda heard the words *and guilt* as clearly as if Phoebe had said them. But it wasn't guilt. Well, it wasn't only duty and guilt. She loved Jacob.

It was a different kind of love than she had for Samuel. Jacob enjoyed her company and loved to make her laugh. But Samuel understood more of her— from her passion for nurturing to her stubbornness that couldn't let go when facing defeat to the bleakest, loneliest parts of who she was.

Rhoda gave a throw pillow one last fluffing. "Jacob feels as if I'm the support under his feet."

"What about you, Rhoda?" Phoebe opened the door. "Can you imagine if the bottom dropped out from under you?"

Once Rhoda was on the landing, Iva seemed to come out of nowhere.

She held the vase of flowers. "That was so horrific, and I feel so awful for Jacob."

"For Jacob?" Rhoda glanced at Phoebe. Just how much had Iva overheard?

"Of course. I mean, what happened to those women and their families was awful, but Jacob's guilt was just as bad." Iva took the cleaning items from Phoebe and passed Rhoda the vase. "Is cleaning my room next?"

"Iva,"—Rhoda rubbed a soft petal of a daisy between her fingers—"what do you mean?"

"Ach, did I misunderstand what you were saying? I thought you were talking about Jacob designing and working on that deck that fell, the one where those two women died."

Died? As if someone were holding her under water, Rhoda couldn't catch her breath.

Why didn't she know anything about this part of Jacob's troubles? No wonder he'd hated carpentry with a passion when she'd first met him. He'd told her about the deck collapsing and many, many other things that she still didn't have straight inside her head, but he'd never mentioned anyone dying.

Finally she could draw air into her lungs. "He felt responsible." She was fishing for answers, but it seemed Iva had learned a good bit more than Rhoda had, maybe from her time with Jacob after moving Sandra.

Was Jacob ever going to tell Rhoda everything?

Iva flopped a dust cloth over her shoulder. "Of course he felt responsible. How could he not? The poor man. And when I think of all the time he spent feeling guilty before he learned that it wasn't his fault, it hurts even me. Sandra said he left town immediately afterward, but if you ask me, he's just now leaving the grief of it behind him."

Phoebe passed Iva the dust mop. "Why don't you start cleaning in your room?"

Rhoda took the vase to the nightstand in Jacob's room.

Phoebe closed the door. "I'm sure it's not as bad as it—"

Rhoda's hands shook. "He just left?" *That's what someone did to Camilla.* Maybe running her off the road had been an accident. Maybe the deck falling hadn't been Jacob's fault. But to just leave?

Whether he was there or not, shouldn't he have gone to the hospital when he learned of the incident and given answers for why a newly built deck fell? To express sorrow to the families for their loss as a man who'd worked for the construction company that built the deck?

That kind of heartfelt response brought healing to those involved in an accident.

She felt sick, not just for herself, but for Jacob. A familiar question circled inside her brain: Did she know him at all? "I'm going to find him. We have to talk before our families—"

A horn blew, and even though the dogs were bedded in the barn office to keep them away from the visitors, she heard them howling. She went to the window. Landon pulled into the driveway with a carload of her loved ones. She closed her eyes, searching for strength.

Phoebe put her hand on her shoulder. "It'll have to wait. Kumm." They left the room again.

Leah came out of Phoebe and Steven's suite with Arie on her hip. "Did I hear a horn?"

"Ya." Phoebe took Arie.

Isaac stomped down the stairs, yelling for his grandparents the whole way.

Rhoda took a deep breath, steadying her pulse as she followed Phoebe down the stairs. After putting off her parents' visit until Jacob's secrets were no longer lurking in corners, she would still have to face her family while trying to cover her thoughts and feelings about him. Could she hide her disappointment and hurt from her family…and from Jacob until a more appropriate time?

Her Daed spotted her the moment she stepped onto the porch. He grinned. "Rhoda!" He opened his arms wide, and she flew into them.

Her tears dampened his neck as she clung to him. Then she hugged her

Mamm, their tears mingling when their cheeks touched. At least for now she could cry with her parents believing they were tears of joy.

Her brother John had a baby carrier in each hand, and his wife, Lydia, had a little one on her hip and two by her skirts. She glanced to Phoebe who was hugging Rhoda's Mamm. Would it sting even more to see John and Lydia with so many children? Would John and Lydia think having only two children would be a nice break at times?

Did the grass on the other side of the fence always look greener?

THIRTY-SEVEN

Jacob waited in the rig in the dark of the early morning, watching the Cranfords' home for signs that his three passengers—Rhoda, Iva, and Leah—would come out soon. Scores of birds chirped in anticipation of daylight. It should be a time of rejoicing. His life was in order. He'd returned to his first love, carpentry. And Rhoda was planning to go away with him in the late fall.

But discontent with him seemed to weigh on her.

Rhoda's family had been here for almost two days. His family had arrived yesterday, along with the three families who were weighing a move to these parts, all on the Fourth of July. And it had been quite an evening of fellowship and construction talk. Unseen fireworks had boomed in the distance as the families discussed a dozen things at once. The new Amish families, two with single men around Leah's age, were staying elsewhere while checking out possible homes to buy. Thankfully, the men would help work on the kitchen while they were here.

Today would be the first full workday since everyone had arrived, although the men had organized the supplies and created a plan yesterday. Jacob's uncle Mervin had arrived yesterday too, along with his work crew, most of them related to the King family.

It was an exciting time, and yet…

The front door opened, and soon Rhoda, Iva, and Leah climbed into the carriage.

"Guder Marye." Jacob gave each a nod as they took a seat. Iva and Leah got in the row behind him.

Rhoda sat next to him. "Guder Marye." She barely made eye contact before closing the door and saying nothing else.

He clicked his tongue and tapped the reins against the horse's back. The rig left the driveway and bounced along in silence as the horse's hoofs hit the asphalt at a steady pace.

Despite the silence, Jacob could no longer deny the loudness radiating from Rhoda. They hadn't been able to get a minute alone since her family had arrived. When he caught a few seconds with her, even though others were in the room or nearby, he detected frustration and felt distance toward him.

Did she know that even a hint of hardness and coldness cut him to the core? He remembered when Sandra had acted that way toward Blaine. It had about been the man's undoing, only Blaine had earned it. Jacob hadn't.

He pulled onto the cracked concrete of the driveway. Unlike when he'd left here earlier, lanterns were now lit inside the home. The house was brimming with people, and when the first rays of light dawned, they would spill out into the orchard to admire it. As soon as breakfast was over, they would start raising the harvest kitchen.

Jacob stopped the rig just outside the barn. He strode to the other side, but Rhoda was already out, holding the door while Iva and Leah maneuvered from the back of the box to the ground. As the three women headed for the house, Jacob caught Rhoda by the arm. She looked up. Her brilliant blue eyes had an edge of dullness for him, but she said nothing.

Leah glanced back at them, and Jacob motioned. "We'll be there in a minute." He waited until they were inside before turning to her. "What's going on with you?"

"This isn't the time. We'll talk when everyone goes home."

"That's five days from now. And you're clearly upset about something."

"I'm fine."

"Rhodes, don't say the opposite of what you mean. Not to me."

"Why not? You keep things from me all the time."

"What are you talking about?"

The black sky eased into navy blue. Voices rode through the windows of the home. The aroma of coffee and bacon filled the air.

Rhoda gestured for him to follow, and they walked toward the other side of the rig.

Even though they'd begun their relationship with every conversation being stimulating and exciting, he hadn't expected it to be that way all the time. But now it seemed they seldom got to enjoy that part of who they were together. When was the last time he'd made her laugh?

He knew the solution. They needed to be away from here. Then they'd do more than finish healing. They'd become one again. They'd share joy and laughter and even tears without any brick walls of disappointment crashing down on them for reasons he didn't understand. Maybe they should leave as soon as the harvest began. Could he hire some of the visiting young women to assist Leah and Iva? Even if he could, would Rhoda leave that soon?

She turned. "I thought I knew everything."

He smiled. "Most women tend to think they know everything."

Disbelief flickered through her eyes. "Really? Humor? Now? Two women died! You didn't consider it important for me to know that?"

Her sharp, shrill accusation jabbed him like a knife, and Jacob's heart sank. Would he ever get out of this hole? He rested the palm of his hand against the back of his neck. "It sounds worse than it is."

"Is that even possible?"

Her bitter disillusionment with him stung beyond words. "I should have stayed. I know that." He kept his voice low, hoping it'd calm her. No wonder she hadn't wanted to mention this. Her soul was on fire against him. "But I wasn't there when it happened. Ambulances had arrived by the time I heard about it. There was nothing I could do by stepping forward but cause trouble for Sandra and me. You can't imagine how completely sorry I am for how I handled that. And I've paid a high price for my mistakes."

"Why am I always the last to know? I try so hard to see you, but even after all we've been through, all I get are glimpses."

She tried hard to see him? Did she think it was easy for him to see her? "Rhodes, listen—"

"Just tell me one thing: Why can't I hear about these things before you're backed into a corner?"

Had Samuel told her? "Speaking of, how did you hear of it?"

"Iva. She told me without realizing I didn't already know about it."

"Sandra told Iva. Not me. And I did try to tell you once. Remember? It was back in October, not long after we moved here, and I started to share about the whole awful mess. Just as I was getting to this part, you said you didn't want to hear any more. You were gone all the next day to be alone and think and pray, and when you returned, you said you knew I'd walked into that mess because I wanted to help, and you had peace that you didn't have to figure it out or understand it. You felt the whole situation was between me and God."

Her stare reflected disappointment, but he was certain she was reaching within herself to take responsibility for her part. She nodded. "You're right. I'd forgotten…"

"Rhodes." Jacob reached to touch her face, and when he did, tears poured from her eyes.

"Who are we, Jacob? I keep looking at who we used to be, and I can't find us."

He pulled her close and kissed her forehead. "But we found ourselves again, only two months ago. Remember? We went to the beach and rediscovered the best of who we are."

"I'm not looking for something magical that happens as seldom as a day at the beach."

She didn't see what he meant, maybe because she saw little value in getaways. He hoped to change that once they were on their own.

He wrapped his arms around her. "It's been a hard year in so many ways, and much of it is my fault. We just need a fresh start. That's all. Once we leave here, you'll feel the weight of all this fall from your shoulders."

She eased from him, wiping tears from her face.

He ached for the disappointment and hurt she felt. "Maybe we should try to leave before the end of the harvest. I'll have finished instruction by mid-September. We could get married then."

"Jacob, no." Her husky voice carried as much grief as he could tolerate.

"You know we need it, Rhodes."

"What I know is that I've agreed to all the concessions I'm going to. When are you going to stop punishing me for what happened?"

"Rhodes, nothing I want for us is a punishment. It'll be freedom. You'll see. And we can settle elsewhere in time to do some fall planting for a fruit garden."

"But where would we live?"

"With my parents."

"Your parents?" She sounded horrified.

"Just for a little while. I'll find us something better or build us a little place if we can afford it."

"Your Daed falls about a hair short of hating me."

Jacob knew how his Daed felt, but he hadn't been aware she knew it—certainly not to this depth. "What would make you think that?"

A whispery scoff escaped from her. "Oh, that's right. You don't know that was made common knowledge to all the Amish communities across Pennsylvania. You weren't there the night I had to sit before the church leaders. You're never *there*. And then when you return, we don't talk about what happened while you were in hiding. It's not fun enough for your tastes."

Her anger hit him full force, and he couldn't find a single word to share with her.

"Say something, Jacob! Please, fight back."

Is this how she viewed him, or was this just anger they needed to work through?

She held up her hands. "I need to help get breakfast on the table."

He stepped in front of her, blocking her. "I'm in a battle for you, for us. I've known that since the day I stepped into the barn and realized a flame burned between you and Samuel. But I'm not a fighter, Rhodes. Not like what you're throwing at me. That's Samuel you're thinking of."

She lowered her head, taking several deep breaths. "Okay," she whispered, "I'm sorry." When she looked up, he didn't see an apology as much as a surrender. "But I can't live with your folks. I know the bedroom in the summer kitchen is a tiny pantry and the place has only a half bath, but maybe it would work until you can find or build better."

Was this how they'd continue to approach getting married, like a bargaining table between developers and construction workers, hashing out what the other could or couldn't agree to?

When Jacob wanted to find her, he listened, and he could hear her joy even when she was silent. He closed his eyes for a moment, and all he heard was her weeping. What had he done? Or was it her? Or Samuel?

"Please, Rhodes, for us."

"Rhoda?" Leah called.

Jacob stepped from behind the rig, seeing Samuel about halfway between the barn and the house, heading for the front door. Had he started this way and overheard Rhoda and him?

Anger reared its ugly head. Jacob's relationship with Rhoda should be more private. But it seemed to be an open book for Samuel. Jacob's patience with living here couldn't wear much thinner.

He focused on his sister. "She'll be right there." He eased his finger under Rhoda's chin and looked into the sadness reflected in her eyes. His heart broke. Were they going to make it out of here together? With uncertainty eroding his hope, he now understood why neither of them had said a word to their parents about their plans to marry or to move away from the farm after the harvest. According to Amish tradition, no one except the bride- or groom-to-be would mention their intention to marry or the plans they were making. So none of their visitors knew.

Did their wedding plans feel more like sad news than happy to Rhoda? He feared so.

And he knew what he had to tell her. "I love you, Rhodes." He brought her fingers to his lips and kissed them. "With all that is in me. You know everything now. I believe in us, who we can be, how happy our life will be. Do you still believe in us?"

Fresh tears welled in her eyes even as she nodded. "I do. But you seem to think Landon, Leah, and Iva can jump into the middle of this canning business and run it the same as if I were here."

"No, sweet Rhodes. I know better. But money is all their mistakes and bobbles will cost. *We*, you and me, are much more important. That's what I think, what I know."

She pursed her lips and straightened her apron. "Okay." Her whisper sounded as if she was too sad to speak any louder.

Jacob was still reeling from her anger, but when they left here, they'd put hurt and disappointment behind them. He looked forward to their building a life that would be as pleasurable as anything he'd ever built. He wasn't sure when they'd get to leave, but he knew Rhoda would stay true to her word, and she'd find a good time to break free.

He needed to get the harvest kitchen built and help her get it in good running order. After that, they couldn't leave here soon enough for him.

THIRTY-EIGHT

Leah drove a wagon of food to the construction site. After easing as close to the long, makeshift tables as possible, she set the brake and hopped down.

Noise echoed—men shouting instructions, laughing, hammering. A line of young boys stood at an entry to the harvest kitchen, tapping nails into the frame. She'd seen Jacob put them there hours ago, assuring them they were helping the building to stay upright. What he'd done is gotten them out of the way while making them feel good about themselves. Of course they didn't stay there the whole time. Some would run off to play while others hammered, and then they'd reverse roles.

She'd never seen Jacob like this—a confident leader and exuberant in his work. Carpentry suited him, and she could understand better why Rhoda was willing to sacrifice her desires for his.

"Leah's here." Her aunt motioned.

Several women scurried to the wagon and began unloading the food. For days the women had hustled about, tending to babies and toddlers while keeping the men fed.

Leah hopped down and grabbed the box that held the flatware and a roll of paper towels. She spotted Landon at the foot of a ladder about to carry a load of shingles to the roof. Her heart skipped a beat. That man was so attractive.

He'd worked every bit as hard as any man here and had used his truck to make dozens of trips to the stores as needed. It was a shame neither of them could be accepted like this if she left the Amish and he helped her. But one couldn't be considered a trustworthy supporter of a group if they were proven disloyal.

But she didn't need to think about any of that, not for a couple of years yet.

There was no telling what God could work out in their favor between now and then—if He wanted to.

She set the box on a worktable, grabbed the paper towels, and began wrapping the flatware in the oversize napkins so she could set them at each place. Her Mamm was at the far end of the six-foot table, dispensing cups of cold water from a ceramic crock. Despite how Mamm was doling out water, the Amish believed in family-style mealtimes, and that's what the women were getting on the table. Buffet style was rarely appreciated.

For this meal, like all the others, the men would eat in shifts—her Daed and brothers, Rhoda's Daed and brothers, Leah's preacher uncle and his construction crew, her bishop from home, several male cousins, and the men from the two visiting Amish families.

What a week it'd been—five days, actually. After lunch one group of men would install the last windows while another crew put on the last shingles.

It looked like a building. An unfinished, rough-hewed shell of a building. It didn't have siding or Sheetrock or linoleum or interior doors or bathroom fixtures or...

"You cause quite a commotion when you arrive."

She'd only known the man for a few days, but she recognized the deep voice. She glanced behind her. Crist Schrock, at six feet three inches, towered over her.

"Admit it, woman." He grinned while removing his tool belt.

"I'll do no such thing." Leah shooed him. "Be gone with you before you end up eating pasta casseroles and applesauce with your fingers."

Her Mamm walked over and handed Crist a glass of cold water, and soon the two were talking feverishly about something.

The Millers and Schrocks were an interesting lot. Boisterous and funny while working. Wouldn't they add a welcome flavor to this district if they decided to move here?

Crist liked to cut up and laugh. If he caused all eyes to turn to him, he'd deflect it by casting his humor onto someone else. But all the people who'd come this week were hardworking folks filled with hope for this settlement. If the Millers and Schrocks moved here, Leah could certainly put Crist's energy to good use. But each of the new families would run a separate business from Orchard Bend Farms.

Crist and two of his brothers had already said that if their parents moved here, they'd be willing to pick up extra hours and pay by helping with the orchard as needed. She doubted they'd make good pickers. That took specific skills best found in those who'd grown up picking. So they'd hire migrant workers and their Pennsylvania Amish relatives who had years of picking experience behind them.

When her Mamm saw other men heading for the water crock, she hurried to fill glasses for them. Leah's Daed ambled toward her Mamm.

Crist turned back to her. "I think I've talked your Mamm into fixing ice cream tonight."

"Probably so." Leah plunked another folded napkin on the table. "I thought I had the gift of gab, but it seems I'm wrong."

He straightened up, looking pleased. "Like I always say, I can talk my own ears off."

Leah paused her work. "And you consider that a compliment?"

Crist laughed. "You don't?"

She suppressed a smile and resumed wrapping flatware.

Leah's aunt walked to the table with a tray of cookies. Crist backed away. Her aunt spoke, set the tray on the table, and took a huge stack of prepared flatware.

Crist took one of Phoebe's chocolate-chip cookies from the tray. "Is it true, Leah, that you'd rather work in the orchard than cook or do laundry?"

Leah laughed. "I'd rather do none of the above. Who told you that?"

"Your Daed. He seems very proud of his eldest daughter."

"Really? No one told me that."

"I'm no one?"

She chuckled, shaking her head. He was bold and had a dry sense of humor when in a crowd. But by himself, he had a quiet, subdued nature.

She only knew that quieter side of him because, after Landon had gone home and the Amish were visiting among themselves, she'd slipped off to the porch swing to wait for Jacob to take her and the others back to the Cranfords'.

Crist had joined her where it was quiet and restful. He'd said little, but when he talked, it was revealing and thoughtful. He liked nature and baseball. He'd lost his dog a few months back, one he'd had since he was little, so he took a shine to Zara and Ziggy. And if it was up to him and if they moved to Maine, the Amish there would be the first Amish to build a meetinghouse. He saw no reason for families to expend all the extra energy getting ready to have church in their homes and feed everyone a meal before they left. A permanent meetinghouse could provide everything they needed.

She had to admit that would be nice.

But after several nights of joining her on the swing, that's all she knew. He knew even less about her. By that time of day, she was spent. Besides, she was seeing Landon. If Crist did move here, would he feel cheated when he learned she was taken? Or angry that she was attracted to an Englisch man?

"Landon!" Jacob stood on the roof, motioning.

Leah turned to see Landon getting a drink of water only a few feet from her.

Jacob held up a box of nails. "These aren't roofing nails. The supply company sent a box of the wrong kind. Can you go to the hardware store before we run out?"

"Sure." Landon pulled his keys out. "Now?"

"Eat first. I'll check the rest of the supplies."

"Sure thing."

Leah gestured toward the cookies "Hey, Landon. Care for a sweet before lunch?"

He smiled. "Don't mind if I do."

She wished they had a moment of privacy to talk, but that wasn't going to happen for a few days yet. "You've done a little of everything this week. I've seen you put up walls, install roofing, plumbing, decking, windows—"

"Don't forget," Crist mumbled around a bite of his cookie, "he's also run every errand too."

Landon wiped condensation from the cup in his hand. "It's been interesting. I wasn't aware that the Amish knew how to put in electrical wires. Were you?"

"Me?" Leah asked.

He nodded.

"Ya, I knew, but that's because of Jacob. Well, and maybe also due to my uncle. All newer Amish houses and businesses have to be wired for electricity to meet the building code even though we don't connect it to the outside."

Crist grabbed another cookie. "Seems like a waste of time to me, but regulations must be kept."

Landon lifted his glass toward her. "I think the non-Amish may have the goals all wrong. Who needs years of expensive education when you can learn while working?"

Was he just sharing or trying to tell her she should remain Amish? Or…

"Are you thinking of becoming Amish, Landon?" She laughed, keeping her tone light, but she needed to see his reaction.

"What? Leah, you know better. I couldn't do it, but I can see why so many young people raised Amish hang on to that way of life. Don't something like eighty percent stay?"

Crist nodded. "That's what've I heard, although my grandfather says that only a few decades ago it was ninety percent." He was twenty and not yet a member of the church. He'd told her that too, but had he gone out into the world for a while like so many young men these days?

Crist finished his drink and set the cup on the table. "I'd better get back at it. Will I see you again tonight—same time, same place?"

Leah froze. What could she say? Her Daed, Mamm, and Landon were all right there, watching her. "Maybe."

"Maybe?" Crist made a fist and thrust it to his chest, mimicking being stabbed. "This is what I get for trying to be the first in what's sure to be a very long line of men." He laughed and walked off.

Leah glanced at Landon, knowing she could say little in front of her folks. He seemed reluctant as he meandered off, but he couldn't stay there as if his goal was to talk to her. Leah set aside her flatware and put small stacks of cookies between paper towels. She then began distributing them to the workers. It wouldn't ruin their appetite. They were burning a gazillion calories an hour. She slowly made her way toward Landon and finally was close enough to put the paper towel and cookies in his hand. They were amid several groups standing around and talking, so hopefully their talking didn't stand out to anyone.

"How ya doin'?" He kept his voice low.

"Good." Her eyes met his. "But ready for a break from company."

"I'll start taking shifts of people back to the train station early Monday."

"I hate to see them go, and yet... It's odd to feel two opposing things at once, isn't it?"

Landon tore off a piece of cookie and popped it into his mouth. "Actually, I think it's normal and you're just now figuring that out."

Leah believed that. "I'll be back. Don't go anywhere." She moved onward, looking as natural as possible while passing out cookies. When her hands were empty, she grabbed a pitcher of water and began filling people's cups.

"You're back." Landon held out his empty cup.

"I'm sorry for what Crist said. It's not how it sounds."

"I get the situation you're in." He looked in his cup as if it had a foreign item. Then he tossed the last bit of water onto the grass. "Look, we can't control the spot we're in. But it did make me wonder if the idea of remaining Amish is becoming more comfortable."

Leah took the cup from him, staring into it. "No." She raised her eyes to his.

"Good." He swiped his hand across his lips, wiping off invisible crumbs. "Could you do me a favor?"

"Anything." She poured fresh water into his cup.

"If it does become what you want, for whatever reason, will you let me be the first to know? Let's not pretend otherwise, like Jacob, Rhoda, and Samuel have. Okay?"

She understood why Landon thought like that. It was her fault, really, always feeling pulled one way and then another. But they had a plan now, one that felt right—to work next to each other while helping Samuel for a few years to come.

"Leah?" Her Daed waved. "Do you have a two-way to reach Samuel?"

Her brother was working the orchard by himself, thinning fruitlets, while everyone else worked construction or supplied food.

"Ya. Coming." Leah motioned. "I give you my word, but in case you didn't know, you already have my heart."

Landon smiled as he turned away from her. "About time, don't you think?"

"I do." She brushed her hand against his and ducked away to do her Daed's bidding.

THIRTY-NINE

Samuel walked through the orchard and toward the woods. His heart was so heavy he found it difficult to move normally. He'd damaged his relationship with Jacob for all time, and at one point he'd about brought the business to the brink of ruin, but the part that tore him to shreds was how much destruction he'd done to Rhoda's life.

Unforgiveable, really.

All because of a moment of weakness.

The farm was quiet now except for the lone sound of Jacob's work at the harvest kitchen. He'd thought the roofing work was finished days ago, but he didn't know much about construction, especially compared to his brother. The last of the family and construction crews had left a couple of hours ago.

Samuel's muscles ached from the days of thinning fruitlets—hours spent on a ladder with his hands stretched out and his body twisted as he removed any fruitlets that touched another. Apples touching while maturing meant both would rot at the point of contact.

Thinning fruitlets made sense. It had to be done, and Jacob couldn't tolerate him being around, not that Samuel blamed him, so he'd spent the week staying busy in the orchard, pruning the abundance caused by Rhoda's green thumb.

But if every aching muscle and bone in his body were combined and lodged in his heart, it wouldn't compare to the pain there.

He stepped into the edge of the woods, not sure what his destination was. He wanted to find a way to let go of even a little of his grief. The hardest part in all of this was how sad Rhoda seemed.

Jacob believed getting her off this farm was the answer. Samuel prayed he was right.

There was a lot left to do on the kitchen, but the building was on track to be completed at least a week before the harvest began. Siding would arrive tomorrow, flooring the next day, followed by interior doors, cabinets, sinks, a commode, shelving, and whatever else it'd take to finish the job.

Rhoda was sitting high on a rock that jutted out from the ground, staring in the opposite direction from where Samuel was. He turned, easing away from her and cringing as leaves and twigs broke under his feet.

"Samuel King."

He was caught, and as much as he wanted to talk to her, he didn't want to be the cause for any trouble. "Sorry."

She motioned for him.

He closed the gap between them, but she was several feet higher than he when he came to a halt at the foot of the rock. "I had no intention of stumbling upon you."

She pulled her bent legs up to her chest, her dress flowing to her feet. "That could be our motto." She smiled a sad smile. "No?"

He swallowed hard. "I'm sorry, Rhoda. You have no idea how sorry."

"I know. All of us are. But it wasn't your fault. The kiss was a side effect of what was happening between us, not the cause of all that followed."

Rustling noises filled the air around them. She peered behind him, but when he turned, he didn't see anything. Probably a rabbit or a deer. Those creatures made a lot of noise when walking over the ground covering in the woods.

She propped her chin on her knees. "It's sort of funny how hindsight is so clear."

He had dozens of thoughts swirling inside his brain, but he couldn't imagine anything intelligent to say. "You don't look as if much of anything is funny right now."

A gentle wind played with the strings of her prayer Kapp, and Rhoda brushed them behind her back. "I had a carriage at one time. Well, it was my Daed's, but I was driving it when the wheels of a passing car flung what had to be a tiny stone at the windshield. It barely left a mark. I inspected it, and it seemed to be only an insignificant chip. As time wore on, I noticed a small crack. Then another. And another. All starting at that tiny chip and spreading out and widening until it covered so much of the windshield it was impossible to ignore and difficult to see through. One morning when I went to the rig, glass seemed to be everywhere except where it was supposed to be."

What sort of man allowed himself to chip anyone's window, especially his closest friend's as well as his brother's? "I'm sorry for being the chip."

Her wry, peaceful smile caught him off guard. "Did the tiny stone decide to hurl itself against the window?"

"We're not lifeless pieces of debris. We have choices. We make decisions."

"That we do. But sometimes life jerks the choices from us—like when a tornado comes through. And when it's over, all we can do is cope, accept, and figure out what to do next."

Samuel couldn't believe she had compassion and grace for him. He didn't deserve it. "It's good of you to try to help me feel better. I wish I knew something I could do or say to help you. If I could go back, I'd keep my feelings in hiding."

"Would that be enough?" She shook her head. "I think not. It all would have simply played out differently, and we'd still be right here, mired in heartache. But it'll get better, for all of us. Jacob's right. We can't all stay on this farm. After I'm gone, I'll talk to Landon and Leah regularly, making sure they know what needs to be done and how. I'll write out all I can about what I know and send it in letters."

"We'll take good care of the orchard, Rhoda." Samuel propped his foot on the rock. "There are parts to our story that I know God was clearly orchestrating. Leah stumbling into your fruit garden, causing us to meet. You and me relating through our keen interest in growing fruit. Rueben giving you cause to join Kings' Orchard, and you saving my family from dying in that tornado."

The wood popped and crackled again, only louder this time. She glanced behind him, but when her focus returned, he didn't bother looking.

"I didn't save Jacob."

"It was a rainy day. The Kings always slept in an hour or two on rainy days.

Daadi Sam, my grandfather, began that tradition when his children were young. He said if you want your family to pray for rain regularly, you reward them when it does rain."

She chuckled. "Smart man."

"If you hadn't been there and Jacob hadn't been smitten with you, he'd have been in his bed with all the other Kings when the wind ripped off the second floor."

"You sound like me, Samuel. We're looking for every silver lining. It helps to view things that way."

He jammed his hands into his pockets. "Did you know that I found you so irritating those first few weeks and months that I went to Leah for answers. She gave me a girly book to read—*Pride and Prejudice*. It helped. Some."

"You read that, for me...to be able to get along with me better? Even while still seeing Catherine?"

"What can I say? You got under my skin, and Kings' Orchard needed your expertise."

"Good grief." Jacob's voice rang out.

Samuel wheeled around.

Jacob's hands were stuffed in his pockets. He rolled his eyes. "You both get under my skin." He ambled toward them before stopping to lean against a tree. "When I saw Samuel heading for the woods not long after Rhoda, I started this way." He motioned with his thumb, pointing behind him. "You'd be amazed what you can see from the roof of the harvest kitchen. And what I thought I'd say when I arrived was, if I lose Rhoda to the likes of you, when I leave, I'll take as much of her heart with me as possible."

Samuel's thoughts, his guilt, his concern he'd again made things worse for Rhoda made his head swim.

Jacob walked past Samuel and took a seat on the rock. But unlike Rhoda, who'd climbed to the high point of the rock, he kept his feet on the ground and stayed more than a foot below her. "But you two have really deep, confusing conversations that, by the way, are in need of a few jokes."

Rhoda seemed unusually calm or perhaps too weary to react.

Jacob's eyes met Rhoda's. "Odd as it is, I can't help but see life differently when I eavesdrop on you two talking. And this much is very clear to me: you need to be here, on this farm, for far more than a few weeks during canning season. You need to be here for every season." He grasped his suspenders. "I'm not cut out to stay put. Leah's probably right. After I repay Uncle Mervin for the crews he'll send the next few weeks to complete the harvest kitchen, I'll get an itch and want to move to another Amish community. Then a little later, another one, going wherever the best construction jobs are." He rubbed his chest. "Man, this hurts. I'm telling you, love stinks." He held out his hand for Rhoda's. "That little spiel I just gave about wanting freedom to move and you wanting roots—although we know it's only a small piece of the truth, it's what we're going to tell others."

Rhoda had tears now, and Samuel's heart ached for her.

Jacob squeezed her hand. "It has to be this way. We tried, Rhodes. We really did." His voice cracked, and it was several minutes before he spoke again. "You don't actually need me here to finish the kitchen. Uncle Mervin can send a master carpenter, and his men can take a few extra days to do my part." Jacob cleared his throat. "Because I gotta get away from here."

Rhoda covered her face with one hand, sobbing, but she nodded.

"My sweet Rhodes." Jacob got off the rock and helped her down before he pulled her into a hug. "She's incredibly stubborn." Jacob wiped at his eyes. "Good luck with that. I think I'll go look for someone a little less interested in work and a lot more prone to think I'm the best thing since the apple was no longer a forbidden fruit."

As Jacob walked off, Samuel expected Rhoda to run after him, confessing her love. But she leaned against the rock, staying right there, her face covered with one hand.

"Jacob." Samuel strode toward him, unsure what he'd say when he got there.

Jacob clasped his shoulder. "She loves you. I know that, but I doubt she will fall into your arms any time soon." He studied her. "Serves you right. I could be married and have two children before she lets go of her guilt and her sense of propriety." He smiled. "If that's not true, it certainly helps me feel better thinking it is. And when you get angry, go easy, okay? She's just a young woman doing her best, and she's more fragile than you think."

Jacob saw her as delicate as a flowery herb while Samuel saw her as strong as the newly built harvest kitchen. He realized that both were true.

Samuel struggled to find his voice. "You're the best of the King brothers."

"In the words of Landon, *I know, right?*" He kicked at a patch of decaying leaves. "But you two were meant to be. All of us were blessed as God moved us around to get you two where you had to be and to keep you connected until love bloomed. She needs someone who doesn't mind arguing with her. And for the pain I'm experiencing from the breakup"—he tapped his chest—"I'm free to pick up my tool belt, pack my bags, and go build houses. I'll soon be free to be in Sandra and Casey's lives. I needed Rhoda to motivate me to face my past…and now my future."

Jacob was no longer one to run or hide from the truth. He'd learned to face it, deal with the fallout, and move on.

Samuel put his hand on Jacob's shoulder, hesitant to embrace him, but he wanted to. Jacob took the lead and hugged him. Each of them was sniffing when they parted.

Samuel stood in the shady woods, too shocked to absorb what was happening. It might take days. Maybe weeks.

"When, Jacob?" Rhoda trudged through the woods toward them, still wiping at tears.

"Within the hour."

She nodded. "Can we go to the house together?"

"I've never said no to you yet."

She and Jacob started walking. She turned. "Kumm."

Samuel followed.

Her heart was as heavy as his. He could see it in her movements, but maybe she needed to stay active right now.

Would she stay in motion, moving away from him for years to come?

However long it took to find healing, he'd be grateful that the three of them would navigate through the time without losing themselves or each other—although he doubted if they would see Jacob much, not for a few years.

The three walked in silence.

In heartbreak.

In forgiveness.

In unity.

FORTY

Iva stood on the driveway near Landon's truck, surrounded by the Kings and Bylers. She couldn't believe what was happening. Jacob was leaving? Rhoda was staying?

Did they realize what this meant? Kings' Orchard wouldn't need her. When her Daed caught wind of this, would he insist she return home?

Jacob had promised to help her, and he had. But his leaving undid all that had been set right. Unfortunately for her, Jacob was clearly too upset to think about her future or the promises he'd made.

Leah hugged her brother. "When will we see you again?"

"I'm not disappearing. I'll be in Lancaster, near Uncle Mervin. At least for a year or so. And I'll be home for Christmas. If you get to Harvest Mills for the holiday, I'll see you then."

Leah nodded. "I feel bad for the selfish things I said."

Iva could hear Leah's guilt for challenging Jacob when he told everyone Rhoda and he would be leaving Orchard Bend.

Jacob squeezed her tight. "Don't you ever feel guilty for speaking the truth. Not ever." He released her and turned to Iva. "Samuel will have my address. You can forward Sandra's letters, and after the trials are over, you can let me know where she is."

Iva swallowed hard. She'd like a hug too. But she didn't budge from her spot. "I will."

He looked sad, but she thought she detected a little relief, similar to what she'd seen in his eyes after he'd given his deposition.

Steven shook his hand. "Keep up with your instruction classes."

"Ya." Jacob turned and hugged Phoebe. "Take care of those little ones."

Iva wanted to scream, *What about me? Does anyone realize what this is doing to me?*

Steven caught Iva's eye, and he nodded, an assuring nod. He then put his arm around Phoebe and whispered something to her. She turned to Iva too, giving a reassuring wink.

At least Steven remembered what was at stake for her, and he was now a church leader. But he wasn't willing to go outside the Amish ways like Jacob was.

Could Steven keep her Daed from pulling her home?

Rhoda felt detached from her body. Her life seemed disconnected from reality. Was this really happening?

Despite the heartache and disbelief, she also sensed an unusual peace circling within. She watched as Jacob climbed into the passenger's seat of Landon's truck. He propped his arm in the open window and held up his hand, waving a final good-bye only to her.

Her heart shattered. Jacob then turned and never looked back as the truck drove off, quickly disappearing over a hill.

It was done.

There was no turning back.

She stood there, feeling lost and traumatized. The group slowly dispersed, all except Samuel. He stood several feet away, looking as wounded as Jacob and she.

Rhoda took a deep breath and dried her tears. There was a room in the house for her again, but she couldn't sleep in what had been Jacob's room. Grief was exhausting, and she longed to crawl into bed until late tomorrow. And for now, her bed was at Camilla's.

She wished she had a divine clue to share with Camilla. "I'm going home."

Samuel nodded. As she passed him, she paused, facing him. She had no words, and apparently he didn't either. They just stood there. Numb. In shared agony.

How could a person feel both at once?

He rubbed the back of his neck, his eyes misty. "All I can think to say are things I've said too many times already: I'm sorry, and are you okay?"

She didn't know how to answer him, so she didn't. She'd heard Jacob tell Samuel that they were meant to be together. Did Jacob really believe that, or was he trying to believe it in order to release her?

Peace stirred within her again, like a refreshing breeze before a gentle rain. As she stood there, a thought came to her—an insight. "Samuel, I believe I've been thinking about Jojo and Sophia all wrong."

He seemed relieved to discuss anything other than Jacob's leaving. There was only so much that could be said. She wished that were true when it came to thoughts and feelings.

He studied her. "How so?"

She and Samuel were here, together. Able to talk. Able to be themselves. She would miss Jacob for a long time, but she was truly grateful to have Samuel fully in her life again.

Rhoda shrugged. "When I know something, I tend to think of it in the negative. Like last winter when I knew the police would find my fingerprints on those bags of marijuana. I thought God was warning me to brace myself, but He was trying to encourage me."

"I remember."

Of course he did. He'd been here with her—every step of the way.

She took a cleansing breath, the first in a very long time. "The investigator is looking through women's shelters for Jojo and Sophia Dumont, right?"

"That's my understanding."

"The problem is he's doing so based on what I told him. But everything I shared was my perception based on Sophia's point of view. Samuel, she's a child. When a little girl says she is about to lose her home, what would you think?"

"That things are going from bad to worse."

"But what if they aren't? What if she was simply frightened by the changes?"

Tenderness for her reflected on his face, not from a quick friendship of two who barely knew each other, but from a man who knew her as deeply as she did him. "So why were they evicted from the trailer?"

"I don't know. That's not important. What is…" Chills ran over her skin. "Music." She walked toward the edge of the orchard. "That's why I heard music."

Samuel strode beside her. "What is why?"

On Rhoda's first night here, she'd heard music. It ran through her mind even now, and another God clue came to her. "The little girl is a Dumont. She was so adamant about it. But why?" The answer came as quickly as the question. "Because her mother was changing their last name, and Sophia didn't like it. She was frightened, and the name change wasn't because of marriage."

"That's why the investigator can't find them. But why would Jojo change their name?"

Rhoda closed her eyes. "I don't know. But Sophia is gifted in music. Everything Jojo has done has been to protect her daughter."

"I'm glad it's clear in your mind, because I'm confused."

She couldn't help but smile. "It's not clear. Not at all. Something dangerous is out there, just out of sight. But we can help find Jojo and Sophia. You and me."

"That I'm not confused about." He stared into her eyes. "*We* can do anything God sets before us."

They stood side by side, looking out over the orchard. The breeze played with the leaves, but as the air glided by, she heard voices—Samuel's and hers radiating with pure joy.

The orchard seemed to be a metaphor for their lives—a place of seasons, a place of deep roots that had to be nourished, a place that yielded bounties and sometimes very little. This orchard connected Samuel and her.

For a moment she saw the two of them, years from now, standing in this same spot. Love and all its goodness filled them. But she also saw ominous clouds on the horizon, ones with the names of people she loved and with names she couldn't make out. Even so, she felt God's strength assuring her that He would guide them.

She folded her arms, watching the orchard. "Ya, I agree. *We* can do anything God sets before us."

Apple Crisp

*This is an old family recipe provided
by Aunt Marion Woodsmall.*

8 tart apples, peeled and sliced (Courtland, Macintosh,
    or your choice)
$1/2$ cup orange juice
1 cup sugar, divided in half
$1/2$ teaspoon cinnamon
$3/4$ cup all-purpose flour
$1/4$ teaspoon salt
6 tablespoons margarine or butter

Place the sliced apples in an 8" x 8" ungreased pan. Pour
the orange juice over the apples. Mix $1/2$ cup sugar and the
cinnamon together, and sprinkle over apples. Work the remaining $1/2$ cup sugar, flour, salt, and margarine or butter
together using your fingers or a pastry cutter. Mixture should
be crumbly, pea size or smaller. Spread over the apples and
pat smooth. Bake at 375° for 40–45 minutes until crust is crisp
and brown and apples are tender. Serve with milk or cream.
Enjoy this very old recipe.

Old-Fashioned Apple Cake

*A family recipe shared by Imogene Moody,
the mom of Carla Moody Weatherly, a longtime friend*

2 cups granulated sugar
1 cup oil
4 eggs
$1/4$ cup orange juice
2 teaspoons vanilla
3 cups all-purpose flour
3 teaspoons baking powder
$1/2$ teaspoon salt
1 cup chopped pecans

Filling:
3 teaspoons cinnamon
4 teaspoons sugar
2 cups apples, peeled and thinly sliced (Courtland,
   Macintosh, or your choice)

Combine sugar, oil, eggs, orange juice, and vanilla. Beat together for ten minutes.

Mix the flour, baking powder, and salt together, and add them to the wet mixture. Fold in pecans.

Mix cinnamon and sugar and set aside.

Pour $1/3$ of the batter into a greased Bundt or tube pan. Spread 1 cup of the apples on top of the batter. Sprinkle with 3 teaspoons of the cinnamon-sugar mixture. Add $1/3$ of the batter. Spread 1 cup of the apples over that batter, and add remainder of cinnamon and sugar. Cover with remaining batter.

Bake at 325° for $1^{1}/_{2}$ hours.

This cake is best if baked 1 or 2 days in advance.

Main Characters in *For Every Season*

Rhoda Byler—A young Amish woman who is skilled in horticulture and struggles to suppress the God-given insights she receives. Before her fruit garden was destroyed, her canning products were carried by stores in several states under the label Rhode Side Stands.

Samuel King—The eldest of three sons. Loyal and determined, he's been responsible for the success of Kings' Orchard since he was a young teen.

Jacob King—The middle King brother. Irrepressible and accepting, he began courting Rhoda a few months before the opening of *The Winnowing Season*. He struggles with repercussions from mistakes he made while living outside the Amish community.

Leah King—At eighteen, the eldest King daughter and the only one who moved to Maine with her brothers Samuel and Jacob to establish a new orchard.

Landon Olson—A single, non-Amish man who has worked as Rhoda's assistant and driver for several years. He's a loyal friend of Rhoda's and has reluctantly, with many reservations, fallen in love with Leah.

Erlene Olson—Landon's grandmother, called "Granny," who has lived in Maine all of Landon's life. For years she sent Landon realty magazines about Maine property for sale.

Steven Byler—Rhoda's brother who moves to Maine to help found the new Amish community.

Phoebe Byler—Steven's wife.

Isaac Byler—Steven and Phoebe's five-year-old son.

Arie Byler—Steven and Phoebe's three-year-old daughter.

Emma Byler—Rhoda's younger sister, who was murdered three years ago.

Iva Lambright—A twenty-one-year-old Amish girl from Indiana.

Minnie—Iva's married sister who remains in Indiana.

Craig Ryer—Jacob's lawyer from Massachusetts.

Eli King—The youngest of the King brothers. He stayed on the farm in Pennsylvania.

Benjamin King—The father of Samuel, Jacob, Eli, Leah, and their two younger sisters, Katie and Betsy. He runs the family's dairy farm.

Mervin King—Benjamin's brother. He's an Old Order Amish preacher in Lancaster, and he owns a construction company.

Karl Byler—Rhoda and Steven's father.

Schrocks—A large Amish family who is considering joining the new settlement in Maine.

Crist Schrock—One of the single Schrock men who is considering the move to Maine.

Millers—A large family with three young, single men who are considering joining the new settlement in Maine.

Catherine Troyer—Samuel's former girlfriend and Arlan's sister.

Rueben Glick—The young man who destroyed Rhoda's fruit garden in book one, *A Season for Tending*.

Nicole Knight—In *The Winnowing Season* a young Englisch woman who helped Samuel install solar panels, and they became friends.

Glossary

ach—oh, alas

alleweil—now

Daadi—grandfather

Daed—dad or father (pronounced "dat")

denki—thank you

Englisch—a non-Amish person

gut—good

hallo—hello

Kapp—a prayer covering or cap

kumm—come

Mamm—mom or mother

Mammi—grandmother

nee—no

Ordnung—means "order," and it was once the written and unwritten rules the Amish live by. The Ordnung is now often considered the unwritten rules.

Pennsylvania Dutch—Pennsylvania German. *Dutch* in this phrase has nothing to do with the Netherlands. The original word was *Deutsch*, which means "German." The Amish speak some High German (used in church services) and Pennsylvania German (Pennsylvania Dutch), and after a certain age, they are taught English.

rumschpringe—running around. The true purpose of the rumschpringe is threefold: to give freedom for an Amish young person to find an Amish mate; to give extra freedoms during the young adult years so each person can decide whether to join the faith; to provide a bridge between childhood and adulthood.

singe—sing

ya—yes

Pennsylvania Dutch phrases used in *For Every Season*

Bischt du allrecht?—Are you all right?

des iss—this is

Duh Du will helfe?—Do you want help?

Geh begreiflich.—Go easy.

Guder Marye.—Good morning.

mich kumm raus—me come out

un du—and you

Witt geh?—Do you want to go?

---

* Glossary taken from Eugene S. Stine, *Pennsylvania German Dictionary* (Birdsboro, PA: Pennsylvania German Society, 1996), and the usage confirmed by an instructor of the Pennsylvania Dutch language.